PENGUIN BOOKS

NATION OF FOOLS

Balraj Khanna was born in the Punjab, India, in 1940. He was educated at Punjab University, Chandigargh, then moved to England for further studies, but instead took up painting. He has lived in England and France since 1965. One of India's leading contemporary painters, Khanna has often been compared to Paul Klee. His paintings have been exhibited in London, Paris, New York, New Delhi and many other cities and his work is represented in over fifteen public collections. Balraj Khanna now lives in London. *Nation of Fools* is his first novel.

D1509605

Balraj Khanna

NATION OF FOOLS

OR

Scenes from Indian Life

Penguin Books

To the memory of my mother,
and to Bibish

Penguin Books Ltd, Harmondsworth, Middlesex, England
Viking Penguin Inc., 40 West 23rd Street, New York, New York 10010, U.S.A.
Penguin Books Australia Ltd, Ringwood, Victoria, Australia
Penguin Books Canada Ltd, 2801 John Street, Markham, Ontario, Canada L3R 1B4
Penguin Books (N.Z.) Ltd, 182–190 Wairau Road, Auckland 10, New Zealand

First published by Michael Joseph Ltd 1984
Published in Penguin Books 1985

Made and printed in Great Britain by
Richard Clay (The Chaucer Press) Ltd,
Bungay, Suffolk
Typeset in Bembo

ONE

Paro wasn't a beauty, nor was she an ugly duckling. In her mid-thirties, she had the oval and somewhat coarse face of a Punjabi jatni, a woman peasant of the Punjab. She had almond-shaped eyes, milk-white teeth and round lips which, on certain days when her husband, Khatri, was coming home, were stained orange-red with the bark of the walnut tree.

On such days she washed her hair and had it oiled with mustard oil by Lallu's mother, Banto, who lived next door. The two women sat on the verandah floor, one behind the other. Banto sat behind Paro and oiled, massaged and combed her hair until it glistened. Normally Paro wore the kamiz shirt and salvar leggings — the normal Punjabi wear — but on such days she wore a sari that showed six inches of her belly. On such days her sixteen-year-old son, Omi, liked her more.

'Tell you what I saw the other day, Ma,' Omi said one such after-noon in the early winter as Banto did his mother's hair.

'What?' Paro said.

'Two monkeys, sitting just like that. They were picking lice from each other's hair and . . .'

Paro picked up her jutti and hurled it at her son.

'. . . They were eating it. By the look of it they seemed to be enjoying it.'

Paro aimed her second shoe at Omi.

'True, Ma. Why not try it?'

A friend of Omi's called from the street and he went out, smiling.

'Don't come back too late. Your father is coming,' Paro said after him.

3

'As if I don't know,' Omi shouted back, putting an arm around his friend, Bhajju.

Paro slapped her forehead and looked up at the sky.

'What did I do in my past life, God?' Paro said.

'Nothing wrong with your Omi,' Banto said.

'Nothing wrong with this matric-failing son of mine?'

A lorry came to a halt outside to an enthusiastic welcome by Dabbu, their street dog. Dabbu, loved by Omi and detested by Paro, barked and barked.

'There,' Banto said, preparing to leave. 'Your man is a bit early today, no?'

They heard Khatri murmur his thanks to the lorry driver and Banto hurried away.

'Like father like son. Come and go when they please,' Paro said.

Usually Khatri came later, in the evening, in time for dinner. But today he had got a free ride on a south-bound lorry.

Born in Peshawar in the North West Frontier, Khatri lacked the proportions other frontier men were noted for. Yet he had something noticeable about him — his peshawari turban, its starched end bit sticking out in shaan dignity of the frontier. The rest was less noticeable. Five foot and about as many inches, small eyes, small mouth, small teeth and a sharp sword-moustache. Khatri wore a longish kurta shirt over a loose sutthan and carried his woollen waistcoat on his shoulder — it was a warm afternoon. He looked at his wife and smiled as he guessed what she was about to say.

'Why aren't you wearing your wasscut?' Paro said by way of greeting.

'Where is the boy?'

'Eating the air of the Camp with his loafer friends. Where else?'

'Needs a good repair job done on him. A good shoe-beating,' Khatri said, pointing to his Peshawari chappall sandals. 'And why are you done up like that? Got a friend, a yaar-shaar coming?'

Paro moved from the verandah to the inside of the house. As she did so she glanced at him over her shoulder, her chin raised. Khatri thought she still looked like a young girl.

'I say, got a yaar-shaar somewhere?'

4

'How *they* talk? Forty and still an anari novice.' Paro, like all Hindu women, often addressed her husband in the third person and in the plural.

The anari novice rubbed his hands. He removed his turban and hung it on a wooden peg in the verandah wall and rubbed his hands again. Paro, like a dutiful Hindu wife, bent down to remove his sandals. Khatri slapped her on her bottom as she stood up.

'Anari novice, are we then? Forty and still anari, eh?' He slapped her bottom again. This time he let his hand remain on that delicious roundness.

'Ram, Ram, Ram!' Paro muttered and touched her ear lobes in consternation. 'Ram, Ram, Ram! What will the neighbours say?'

The hand resting on that soft rotundity became the conveyor of a current that went straight into his sutthan, causing a delicious uprising there. Khatri cleared his throat, gave a good rub and moved closer. He was right behind her, touching her.

'Hai, hai, hai, my mother! Badmash wicked man. Only been here two minutes and look at *them* . . .'

Khatri was a house on fire, desperate to get out of himself.

'Shut up and shut the door, Parvati, woman.'

'What will Banto say?'

'As if she doesn't know. I bet that husband-eater is watching.'

'And what about your son?'

As if by magic, Omi appeared, followed by Dabbu. Khatri was not amused.

'Reading-writing well, boy?'

'Yes, Father,' Omi said, bowing down to touch his father's feet.

'Must pass your matric this year.'

'Of course, bilkul, Father.'

'That's what you said last year.'

'Last year was different, Father.'

'Every year is different, boy. If you fail again, I will break your left leg. Understand? Now go and do your reading-writing in your room.'

Khatri washed his hands and face and sat down to read the *Milap*, the Urdu daily. Paro went about her business in the kitchen. When the food was ready, Khatri shouted for Omi.

'Oi, come and get your supper. Take it to your room and eat it there quietly.'

Paro had cooked karela, one of Khatri's favourite vegetables.

'Wah wah, wah wah!' Khatri said and sat down on the kitchen floor. He insisted that Paro ate with him. But Paro demurred. The husband must eat first — she was a Hindu wife.

'No, Begum. You eat with us today. We eat together or I eat you.'

With a shy smile, Paro succumbed and sat down next to him, their knees touching. This not being enough, Khatri pulled her nearer and pushed his knee under hers.

'What will people say? What will Banto say?' Paro said.

'Shoot her with a bullet. I am double hungry, big double hungry . . .'

Paro knew the double hunger.

'. . . Eat then. On the double.'

'Ram, Ram Ram . . .!' Paro complained, but she complied.

'. . . What sort of place is this Panchkoola that does this to *them*?'

Panchkoola was a bus stand in the middle of nowhere. It was a large clearing by a cross-roads surrounded by lush trees. Behind it ran the vast seasonal river, the Jhajjar. In front of it — seven miles away — lay Chandigarh, the great new capital of the Punjab. On its right towered the Kasauli mountain and the Himalayas beyond; on its left was the rest of the world, including Camp Baldev Nagar, twenty-odd miles south.

The world, on its way to Chandigarh, stopped here for a rest, giving rise to many flourishing sweet shops and dhaba food stalls. There were other shops and stalls which sold everything including locally made terracotta images of Goddess Chandi of the famous temple nearby. The new capital was named after her.

Separated by a few hundred yards of nameless bush and shrub, of the thorny kikar tree, whose branches Indians chew to clean teeth, and the rubbery cactus, akk, which sheds drops of white milk when you break a stem, was the old village of Panchkoola itself. Its mudlets and huts and mud walls looked on to the great Jhajjar which remained divided into streams and trickles until the rains came.

6

When the rain came, the river roared with mud water and the few lanes of Panchkoola became coated with a few inches of the potters' slip. Children slid and fell and cried and laughed. The bulbul bird in the lush trees sang during the day. At night, frogs croaked noisily to drown the incessant orchestration of a million nameless insects. Cockroaches and beetles appeared from nowhere. Flies and mosquitoes multiplied and, to the delight of the children, there came, from nowhere, a harmless insect the size of a housefly with a coat of brilliant scarlet velvet — a wonder of nature. The children called it veer vohti and collected it by the dozen and carried it around on their hands, arms and faces.

The bus stop in the rains became a puddle. Buses came to a halt here, splashing mud all around. No bulbul sang here, but frogs croaked and insects shrieked at night. No veer vohti came to the buses, but flies and mosquitoes did, in hordes. Business went on as usual, rain or day, summer or winter. And though money was being made, the place was wilderness, as became clear every evening at dusk, once the last bus had gone. Night howled at the empty shops and dhabas where men sat huddled in silence in the dim light of lal tan, their kerosene lanterns. They chewed paan (betel nut) or pulled at the hookah, talking of the good old pre-Partition days. For they were all displaced persons, refugees of Partition, impoverished and destroyed by it. They had come here from the neighbouring towns in the Punjab once the construction of the new capital was under way. They had come here to scratch a living. In the event some, like Shadi Lal Khatri, were doing more, if only slightly more. He owned the largest sweet shop there.

But for all its prosperity Panchkoola was fit only for charras, desperate men. No women or families lived here, it wasn't a place for them — it was wilderness. Like the others, Khatri went home whenever he could, usually once a week.

It was an unhappy arrangement. But it would come to an end one day (and this was his dream which made this separation bearable and dulled the pain of Partition): one day he, Shadi Lal Khatri, ex of Peshawar and now of Camp Baldev Nagar, would own a proper place of red bricks — not like this wood and corrugated-iron dump, nor like that shapeless mud house in the Camp — in 'our new capital'. Khatri liked to call Chandigarh 'our new capital'. By doing so he felt he had acquired a stake in it.

And in Chandigarh he would educate his son like a gentleman's son.

But Khatri did not like to think too much about his dream. It would offend Goddess Chandi. Instead, with a lump in his heart, he would look in the direction of her temple three miles upstream, take a little bow and simply remind her of it. Often, when feeling like this, he would think of home and miss the physical presence of his wife. If someone was going south, he would send word home: to expect him. Towards the end of the day he would call Seva Singh, a gentle Sikh of advancing years and the senior of his two servants, and leave him in charge of the shop for the night. Khatri was always double hungry and a house on fire when he got home, Paro's orange lips and naked belly adding fuel to the fire.

'So this is what Panchkoola is like, full of desperate charras, eh? Look what it has done to you . . .!'

Khatri had taken her hand to the middle of his sutthan which was sticking out as if it had a wooden peg in it.

'. . . Shame on you. At your age?'

'Don't move your hand nor your tongue. Just eat on the double.'

Paro obliged and kept her hand around the draped wooden peg.

'I bet Banto is watching our light.'

'That husband-eater. Her Banarsi should fix her more often. She needs it. She's always got that man-eating look.'

'Maybe they got a bet on our light. Banto says half hour, Banarsi says one hour.'

'Up, up, then, Begum. I want your Banto to win.'

Khatri led and Paro followed, holding the peg in the sutthan.

'Isn't it getting longer and longer?' Khatri said.

'Longer and longer and longer. You could have laid it across the Jhajjar as a bridge. It would have solved all our problems, our bridge.'

The bridge . . .

The Punjab had its new capital and it was growing in size. So was the motor traffic to it. The motor traffic had to ford the usually shallow river Jhajjar near Panchkoola which in the rainy season was often dangerous. But the Government was playing a trick on Panchkoola. It was building a bridge across the river a few miles down. This bridge would make it unnecessary for the motor traffic to ford the river. Not only that, it would lop several miles off the journey. That would be the end of Panchkoola bus stand — khalas and khattam shudh, the end.

'A matter of our karma,' the Panchkoolans said and resigned themselves to their fate. But Khatri did not agree with them. He shook his head.

'Maybe it is our karma. But surely there is an upai, a way out, as there is one to every problem,' Khatri thought and he kept on thinking of an upai.

One afternoon a renowned swami, Gokul Baba, stopped at Panchkoola. Panchkoola came to a standstill. All business stopped and people thronged at his feet. Khatri, also at Gokul Baba's feet, begged him to be his guest for the night. After some pleading, the toothless swami agreed to stay. When the two of them were finally left alone, Khatri sat at the holy man's feet again and talked with him till midnight.

Next morning Khatri wore a new look on his face. The swami left for his ashram near Kalka a few miles up north. In his wake arrived Bhola Ram, an old friend and a lorry driver. Bhola Ram lived in Manimajra, a nearby town. Khatri handed him his usual cup of tea and took him to the back room of his shop. There he talked to him in whispers for a good half hour, both nodding gravely from time to time.

'I knew it, Lala ji. I knew you weren't just sitting on your backside, wearing out your sutthan like those two over there . . . Wah wah, wah wah . . .' Bhola Ram said.

'Those two' were Aneja and Juneja, Khatri's chief business rivals. They were also from Camp Baldev Nagar but they were not on speaking terms with him.

'And you've got to do what you've got to do, Bhola Ram,' Khatri said.

'Right away, Lala ji,' Bhola Ram said and went.

Twenty minutes later Bhola Ram was back, with Aneja on his left and Juneja on his right. Hands were shaken warmly and all old enmities forgotten. A long conference took place in Khatri's back room, followed by a lot of visits by the four to the old and the new Panchkoolas. That evening, after the last bus had gone, a meeting was held in the square attended by everybody, including the village panchayat council and its patwari headman. The Panchkoola Traders Union was born.

They had a letter-head printed. Another meeting was called. A letter was sent to the Minister of Transport in the capital. It was a protest against the bridge.

No answer came.

They called another meeting and sent a stronger letter. Still no answer came. As the date of the opening of the bridge drew nearer, Khatri took an afternoon off to visit Gokul Baba in Kalka. On his return he called Aneja and Juneja to his shop and dispatched yet another letter. When even that letter remained unanswered, they called a general meeting and took a strong decision.

'A march on the capital. If that doesn't work, hunger strike.'

Supported by the people from the neighbouring villages they arrived one day in Chandigarh. They were a few hundred strong. Escorted by a few idle-looking policemen they marched through the street shouting slogans and went and sat outside the Minister's office. '*Your Bridge, Our Ruin,*' they chanted and beat their breasts. '*Down With The Minister.*' More policemen arrived and they were ordered to call it a day. They refused. The police stiffened up and brandished their steel-tipped lathi batons. Scuffles broke out. A few bricks were thrown, a few heads were split. The demonstration had become ugly. Anything could happen now — arrests, even a lathi charge.

But what did happen completely changed the mood of the demonstration. The Minister sent word that he would see the leaders. Everybody shut up. Khatri, Aneja and Juneja went, accompanied by the patwari headman of old Panchkoola.

The Minister was a huge man, an absolute pehalwan wrestler type. He looked like his own bodyguard or that of his PA, who was half his size. He wore the Congress leaders' uniform — spotless white homespun khadi kurta and pyjama, Nehru coat and Gandhi cap.

The adversaries looked at each other. It was an ill-paired match.

Four pairs of hands went up in namaskar greetings of great respect and four heads bowed down to the Minister. The Minister

10

looked at them for a long time. Then, without a warning, he pounced on them.

'You want me to pull the bridge down . . .?' the Minister said in the gentlest imaginable voice. It was so sweet that it was birdlike.

The four leaders were mesmerized by the softness of his voice and the simplicity of its message. They hadn't come prepared for it. Not a word came to any one of them. The Minister looked at them for another minute or two.

'. . . I'll have the bridge blown up. No problem. A few sticks of dynamite and . . .'

The Minister sounded as if he meant every word of it. It was amazing.

'Sir . . .' Khatri ventured to open his mouth at last.

'Yes?'

'. . . Sir, we have a much less drastic request to make,' Khatri said, looking at his feet.

'Pray tell us. That's what I am here for, to listen to you.'

'Keep the Punjab Road Ways route as it is, via Panchkoola, for twelve months. That will give us, the traders of Panchkoola, time to establish ourselves elsewhere . . .' Khatri stopped. He got the nasty feeling that the Minister was about to lose his temper.

'Is that all?' the Minister said as gently as before.

'. . . And we ask you to assist those of us who wish to start afresh in our new capital, because your bridge is our ruin.'

Khatri was right. The Minister went mad. The sparrow roared.

'Mad, mad, mad. You are raving mad. No wonder India doesn't make progress. No wonder foreigners ruled us for hundreds of years. Because we are a nation of fools. Just look at yourselves — thorns in the flesh of the country's progress! Do you know what Pandit Nehru would say to you, and he is a great man? He would say — Lala ji, go drown yourself in the Jhajjar. He would probably say the same to me for sitting here listening to your blackmail. Just look at us Indians. Independent Indians.'

The Minister stood up. The interview was over. He took a step towards the door and Khatri realised it was now or never. He did a thing he had never done before. He removed his peshawari turban and placed it on the floor, in front of the Minister. The Minister shrank back.

'What is the meaning of this?' the Minister said.

11

It was a trick and everybody knew its meaning.

'We've been ruined once before, in '47. But then it was a foreign ruler and an age-old enemy. To be ruined a second time in seven years by our own Government which had promised us milk and honey Ram Raj and not another British Raj . . .!' Words failed Khatri. He shook his head at the Government cruelty. '. . . Help us, Sir.'

'Help us, Sir,' Aneja, Juneja and the patwari said.

Three more turbans were laid next to Khatri's. The trick was complete.

'But you are like the monkeys of the children's story. I won't be tricked by you. Do you realise how many hundred thousands it will cost the Government to drive the buses through Panchkoola for a year . . .?' The Minister gave them a frightening figure. '. . . The world will laugh at me — still fording the Jhajjar in spite of the bridge . . .'

A long discussion followed and a compromise was reached. Six months and the assurance of help in the capital. The General Election was close and the Minister did not want to enter it with the blood of a community, however small, on his hands.

'You are mad, Lala ji. All of you. Now pick up your monkey turbans and go.'

When the four leaders came outside there was a deafening new slogan. *'Long Live The Transport Minister.'*

Khatri wanted to go home that night, but he didn't. He had some hard thinking to do.

Camp Baldev Nagar was a mud settlement which started life as a refugee camp after Partition in 1947. It was situated between the two Ambalas — the Cantonment and the City — by the railway bridge which had a camel's hump in its middle. Here the famous Grand Trunk Road joined the old Simla and the now new Chandigarh Road.

Every evening the Camp was shrouded in smoke which had the smell and the taste of cowdung. Every evening an even stronger odour was blown in from the camel-bridge side. There an uncultivated tract of land was used by the inhabitants of the Camp as the common latrine. Most people did not have this facility at home.

But even those who did still preferred to *go out*, as they called this exercise; it was so much nicer in the open air. Ladies went in groups, gentlemen individually, all carrying a brass gadva of water.

Between the *going out* area and the houses was the market. It was a couple of hundred yards long with a single row of shops made of mud. Facing the shops were scores of rehri stalls on wheels. The location of the market was perhaps not ideal — on evenings when the wind blew hard it seemed even less so — but nobody really minded. The smell was there like the trees or the grass and that was that. Besides, there were so many other smells — frying garlic, frying onion, frying spices . . .

Evenings were the best time of the day. School boys and the unemployed young men of the Camp (all young men there were unemployed) hung around in knots at paan shops and the food stalls. There was not much they could afford, but that was not important. What was important was to be there. Paro used to say that unless her son spent the evening loafing there, he wouldn't digest his supper. Only when Khatri was home would Omi digest his food in the company of his books.

But today Khatri was in Panchkoola, doing some hard thinking. So after supper, Omi, his father's height and still growing, wearing his usual khaki shorts, a white shirt and a grey sleeveless sweater, ambled along leisurely to the market. The majlis assembly of his cronies had gathered at Bhaia's paan shop at the far end. Among them were Bhajju, Bali, Des, Punnu and Harpal Singh — all classmates.

'Omiiiii . . .' Harpal, a Sikh boy, shouted from across the market.

It sounded urgent. Omi ran and was at the paan shop in seconds.

'A special silver paan for the son of the hero of Panchkoola,' Harpal said with a flourish, throwing an anna piece at Bhaia.

This was unusual generosity. Omi was nonplussed. But he did not like his father being mentioned like that.

'A very special paan for the only son of the hero of Panchkoola.'

'Watch your tongue, Harpal, son of an untouchable bhangi.' Blood rushed to Omi's head.

'True, yaar. Absolute truth. Ask anyone. Your old man a pukka hero sahib now.'

Like his father, Omi was frontier born. His temper flared.

13

Action preceded thought and his right fist lashed out, knocking the turban off the Sikh boy's head.

'Your head striking twelve o'clock or something?' Omi said.

Omi shouldn't have knocked off Harpal's turban, the Sikh's izzat self-respect, nor should he have insulted him. The Sikhs are the Irish of India. Most of the jokes in the country are about them. Most of the time, the habitually good-natured Sikhs laugh at these with the others. But they don't take kindly to the mention of 'twelve o'clock', for, according to the joke-makers, there is a legend about it. Something happens to a Sikh at twelve noon when the sun shines directly above, making him lose his head. It also makes him likely to lose his temper which is no less lethal than the frontier temper. That was why both the Sikhs and the frontier men were enlisted as martial races by the British and made to fight their wars for them in their thousands. They won a few VCs, but lost many a thousand martial bodies.

A market is always interesting, a fight makes it even more so. This one suddenly became very interesting as the two boys rolled in the dust. Everybody rushed to see the tamasha fun as these two, who were the best of friends a minute ago, tried to take each other's life. The paan wallah, a UP man, jumped off his seat and prevented that.

'True, Omi babu. Your father is a big man now. He defeated the Minister in the capital,' Bhaia said in Hindi, separating them.

The story came out and Omi felt ashamed of himself. He looked at Harpal. Harpal seethed with anger. His shirt was in shreds and so was Omi's. Omi went up to him and embraced him. But Harpal wouldn't have it. He turned his head away.

'Come on, Harpal,' the market begged.

Harpal succumbed. The two boys embraced each other and a roar of applause went up. Omi turned on his heels and dashed off home.

'Ma, Ma . . . Father has done it. Our days of misery in this dump are over . . .'

'Hai, hai, hai. Hai, my mother. Who beat you up?' Paro said.

'Say goodbye to this dump, Ma.' Omi grabbed hold of his mother and started to hop about bhangra-dance fashion.

'Your face. Your shirt. What will you wear to school tomorrow?'

'Goodbye Camp . . . Goodbye school . . .' Omi danced the bhangra.

But schools are difficult to say goodbye to.

The morning brought tingling of bicycle bells. Bhajju, Bali, Des, Punnu, Harpal and the others had come to call Omi to go to school.

'Tell them, Ma. Tell them I am through with that horse shit school.'

'Out of this house . . . or . . .' Paro appeared with the washing bat.

Anglo Sanskrit High School was a mile away, past the railway line that went to Chandigarh, past the Grand Trunk Road on which once marched great invading armies from the Khyber Pass to the battle-fields at Panipat and to Delhi and beyond. It was a ten-minute ride.

'New name for school — HS High School. Guess what HS stands for?' Omi said, on the way to school.

'Harpal Singh High School,' Bali said.

'Horse Shit High School,' Omi said.

Harpal took offence. 'Much shit in your arse, no, Omi son? I am going to get it out and bury you in it.'

Harpal rammed his bike into Omi's. Other bikes collided with theirs and a pile-up occurred. It was only because of the confusion caused by it that another fight was averted. Omi hadn't thought that HS could mean anything else.

'Great mistake, Harpal. Beg great apology. Honest, yaar,' Omi said.

'One more mistake, great or small, Omi son, and . . .'

'Pukka promise. Unbreakable promise.'

At school everybody knew of Omi's father's triumph. It was in *The Tribune*, *Milap* and *Hind Samachar*, the English, Urdu and Hindi dailies.

'Big man now, our Omi son,' everybody said.

'Who is the lucky bastard, then?' Tirath Ram, Omi's form master, said during roll-call.

The class laughed. Omi went red in the face.

'Every dog has his day,' Tirath Ram added.

'Maybe you will have yours one day,' Omi mumbled.

The class roared with laughter.

'What did you say?'

'Nothing.'

15

'What did he say?' Tirath Ram asked Harpal.

'Didn't hear him, Sir,' Harpal said.

'Son of a bitch . . .' Tirath Ram said and dismissed the matter.

Omi knew Tirath Ram didn't like him. Teachers don't like boys who double up a year — they are cheekier and a bad influence. They are simply bad eggs. But he didn't like anyone anyway, even the good eggs. His standing threat was that he would make a bhurji, scrambled eggs, of anyone who stepped out of line. He also made chutney, hot chutney, of those he disliked intensely. Omi was lucky. No chutney was made of him that day.

Khatri was doing some hard thinking. He got an idea.

'You got brains all right, Lala ji,' Bhola Ram said. 'But . . .'

Khatri knew what that meant: Khatri needed support and secrecy, and here in Panchkoola you couldn't even belch without the whole place knowing. Who could he turn to for support? 'Those two?' He meant Aneja and Juneja.

'Sometimes your enemy is your best friend. Nothing like trying, Lala ji.'

'And Hari Das?' Khatri said. Hari Das, an old man bent with age and the burden of life, owned a little shop in Panchkoola.

'Hari is no problem. Hari is my problem,' Bhola Ram said.

The problem was 'those two'. Khatri thought and thought until he was sick of thinking. When dusk fell he gave Seva Singh a five-rupee note and sent him to buy a quarter of Red Fairy, the ruby-red country whisky. He drank it with soda and savouries from his own shop and he still didn't feel he had mustered enough courage to take his rivals into his confidence.

'Bad idea anyway to do things with Red Fairy inside you. I will catch the bastards in the morning.'

The Panchkoolans went every morning to the Jhajjar for their daily ablutions. The river was vast and full of rocky niches and cavities. Boulders of all sizes littered the sandy bed. Water was plentiful and clear.

People *went out* behind a bush or a boulder, broke a kikar twig to clean their teeth and on their way back dipped themselves in the cool, fresh river water. They cupped their hands to the rising sun and muttered the gayatri mantra.

Khatri, while out for his constitutional next morning, *chanced* upon Aneja. They shook hands warmly and decided to have a stroll together.

'Something happened, Shadi Lal?' Aneja asked.

'Something may happen, something good — for all of us — if . . .' Khatri leaned over and whispered his idea.

'You got brains, Khatri old cock.' Aneja hugged him in the morning sun. 'Must hand you that.'

'I am a simple fellow like you.'

'Crafty old cock.' Aneja laughed.

'But what about Juneja?'

'Juneja is no problem. Juneja is my problem.'

'But, but, but . . . But what about the world? What about it?'

'To hell with the world. We are the leaders of the Union, or aren't we? We defeated the Minister. Right? You *go out* and come back as fast as you can.'

On his return Khatri found Aneja, Juneja and Bhola Ram sipping his tea. He took them to the back room of his shop. There they conferred for an hour, weighing the pros and cons of Khatri's daring scheme. They drank more tea and broke one of his sweets, the famous Khatri laddu, into their mouths. When they left Aneja scratched the middle of his sutthan.

'Brains . . . Got to hand you that,' Aneja whispered, jerking his head.

Bhola Ram kept his word. He persuaded Hari Das to sell his shop secretly to Khatri. Aneja and Juneja did similar deals with the owners of two little shops. Now the three of them would be able to claim not one but two shops each in the capital. But Khatri still worried and he felt ashamed of himself.

'Why is man never content? God gives me enough. And yet.'

The question was, who would mind Hari Das' shop? The answer was that shops couldn't be left to servants to run even when they could be trusted with a heap of gold. Who then? Somebody close to the family, of the family.

'But certainly not that owl's son, Bhajjan. Bilkul not.' Bhajjan was Paro's 'dearer-than-life' sister Vidya's husband. Khatri had employed him once and was cheated out of 'hundreds of rupees' according to his calculations, though Bhajjan only worked for him

17

for three months. 'He deceived me once, he will deceive again, that snake.'

Khatri chased away a kirli house lizard from the calendar with Nehru's picture. One never harmed or killed this creature: it brought bad luck. One only chased it away.

Who then?

Omi.

No.

'I want my boy to become a gentleman, not an illiterate halwai sweet-wallah like me.'

Khatri worried.

'But the boy doesn't actually have to work in the shop, Lala ji,' Bhola Ram said. 'He will only be there for appearance's sake. What you can do is hire a private tutor for him.'

That was an idea. Omi's exam was just round the corner, in a mere three months. A few more months and they would be in Chandigarh and life would be different. Omi would go to College.

That night, Khatri went home. Paro neither wore a sari nor were her lips stained orange.

'What happened to your yaar-shaar, then?' Khatri said, slapping her on her bottom.

'How *they* talk?'

Khatri hung his turban on the wooden peg in the verandah wall and had a wash. He slapped her bottom again as she undid his chappall sandals.

'The boy will prepare for his exam under my very nose in Panchkoola . . .'

'And leave me to Dabbu here?'

'. . . I will come home every other night. How about that?' Khatri rubbed her buttocks and winked. 'The boy will come back in a couple of months for his exam. Then it will be our new capital. Once there, things will be different. Happily different . . .'

Paro was not keen on his scheme. Nor did it impress her to be told of his meeting with the Minister.

'Only talk comes out of khadi dhoti and Gandhi topi. How can you be such an anari novice? Have you forgotten what they said to us in Peshawar, both Nehru and Frontier Gandhi? Life is not important to them. Important is only their leadery. Besides, we are not unhappy where we are.' Paro was quite unmoved by the lure of Chandigarh.

'In this dump?' Khatri was about to lose his frontier temper. But he knew his wife and knew that she not only had the face of a Punjabi jatni, but also her strong head.

'Home suddenly become dump, eh? We've become a rubbish heap now?'

'No wonder India doesn't make any progress. We simply don't want progress. We are happy where we are — on a dung hill or in the gutter.'

'Where have *they* learnt this fancy talk? Doesn't impress me. We are not unhappy where we are.'

Paro had a point. All her friends were in the Camp. And Chandigarh was too fanciful a place by all accounts — fashionable and full of rich people who had such nakhra superior airs.

'We will have a proper red-brick house there, send the boy to College.'

'Not if he goes on failing exams every year. You should see how much reading-writing he does? Home from school, thump goes the satchel on the floor and out bolts your son to loaf and brawl in the market.'

'The son of a bitch will have to behave differently in Panchkoola if he doesn't want his skin peeled off. In our new capital everyone will have to behave differently — it is not like this dump, you know?'

'I know. It is Vilayat. England.'

The mother and father argued, but Omi was jubilant.

'Not the end of your school work, understand? I don't want you to end up a halwai like me. I want you educated, go to College, become a gentleman. Understand?'

Omi understood. He nodded his head. But there was something he did not understand, this sudden change in his fortune. What he had done in recent weeks, what good deed, to get out of HS High School just like that?

'A matter of karma,' Omi thought. It must be. What else could it be?

19

'And don't get too excited. I'll send for you when things are ready. In the meantime do your reading-writing here. Now go to your room and work.'

But Omi was too excited for that. He turned the pages of his books for a couple of hours and decided to retire for the night. He could not sleep. He tossed and turned in his bed and heard the woman next door sing a lullaby to her baby. When she stopped he heard the sleeping baby breathe noisily; the wall was paper thin. Then he heard the long wailing whistle of the Bombay Express which passed the Camp at midnight. The engine driver, Kailash, lived in the Camp. Whenever he drove the train, he made that interminably long whistle. It sounded like someone somewhere in the darkness groaning in deep pain. People said it was Kailash crying for his new bride, killed in Pakistan during Partition. Others said worse things happened to her — Muslim men kidnapped her.

In the morning it was his friends' bicycle bells that woke him up.

'Posti, opium-eater,' the boys said and drove off.

The question was what that dog Tirath Ram would say.

Tirath Ram was delighted. He was always delighted whenever a bad egg arrived late. It meant chutneys and bhurjees and omelettes.

'What lies are you going to piddle today for your lateness, Omi?' Tirath Ram said.

'I overslept, Sir.' Omi decided to tell the truth for a change.

'What do you Khatris eat for dinner? Opium?'

'Father came home unexpectedly last night and we talked late.'

'What did you talk of?'

'Of plans for my future.'

'Ah, plans for your future. How interesting!' Tirath Ram turned to address the rest of the class of some forty boys. 'Why don't your parents ever make plans for your future, you bastards?' He returned to Omi. 'Well, well, well. But what plans?'

Bali answered for Omi.

'His father buying him a shop, Sir.'

'Lucky son of a bitch. You'll sell us things at a fair price, won't you? No cheating with old customers, Lala ji.'

'Lala ji', a term used for a shopkeeper, became the word of the

20

day. It went with Omi wherever he went. But he didn't really care. He felt like a mere visitor to the school now. He was furious, though, with that dog, Tirath Ram. He had only one lesson with him, a geography lesson, the last period today, and then he wouldn't see him for a whole week except for the morning roll-call.

Tirath Ram was late. The classroom buzzed with the general noise of forty tongues. At the back of the room where Omi sat next to Harpal, something of great interest was taking place. Punnu, a one-legged boy and another two-time matric-sitter, was entertaining the back benchers. He had a hugh erection — his penis was so enormous that it was generally referred to as his second leg. He was entertaining his friends with his somewhat original method of masturbating. He had a large test tube which just fitted his penis. He was jerking it up and down rhythmically, saying, 'Hai, hai, hai . . .' sonorously. The boys clapped in unison and waited for the test tube to go suddenly milky.

Two things happened simultaneously. A little pebble came flying from somewhere and landed on the test tube, shattering it and lacerating the foreskin. Punnu cried out in pain and at the sight of his blood. The hand-clapping stopped and an unnatural hush fell over the room. Just then Tirath Ram walked into the classroom.

'What's going on here?' he said, going straight to the trouble spot.

'Nothing, Sir.' Punnu said innocently.

'Your white pyjama. It's all red.'

'Red ink, Sir.'

'I don't see any red ink on your desk.'

'Omi's, Sir. Ask him.'

'And the broken glass?'

'Test tube, Sir. It broke.'

The red stain on the white pyjama was getting larger and larger. Tirath Ram shook his head and scratched the middle of his dhotti.

'Amazing. Absolutely bloody amazing,' Tirath Ram said, slapping his forehead in disgust.

'Amazing what, Sir?' Punnu said.

'You better go to the first-aid room . . .'

The boys laughed. The first-aid room was a closet in the library and the librarian was a woman. Understandably Punnu didn't want to go there.

'What for, Sir?'

'. . . or you'll bleed to death. Sharma, take the fool there.' Tirath Ram sent Punnu with the class monitor. He slapped his forehead again and looked at the class. His eyes fell on Omi.

'Let us do some geography. Tell us, Lala ji, tell us about Vladivostok. Question number one, where is Vladivostok?'

Vladivostok, Vladivostok, Vladivostok. Where is it? Where has it gone? It had been on the very tip of his tongue only a minute ago.

'He doesn't have to know it now, Sir,' Bali said.

'He will be sitting in his own shop soon soon soon, Sir,' Des said.

'Rich man now, Sir. Don't need geography now, Sir,' another boy said.

'Maybe. Maybe Lala ji will be making jalebi tomorrow. Even barfi, pera and chum chum sweets. That's tomorrow. Today geography. Question number two. Vladivostok — is it a mountain, jungle, desert, lake, river, city, volcano or what? Stand up and answer, Mr Om Parkash Khatri.'

Omi stood up.

'Come on, take a guess,' Tirath Ram said.

Omi took a guess.

'A volcano.'

There were sniggers. Omi knew he had made a mistake.

'A volcano, eh? Which continent is it in? Asia, Africa, America, Australia, Europe? Take another guess.'

Omi took another guess.

'Australia.'

'Australia, hain? Sure it is not under your father's arse?'

'Watch it, Master.'

Omi did not say Master ji, and this was insult. Tirath Ram's nostrils flared.

'I asked you a simple question and this is how you answer — disrespectfully. I asked what was Vladivostok and you said it was a volcano. Fair enough. Then I asked where it was — in Asia, Africa, America, Australia, Europe or under your father's arse . . .?'

'Under your mother's cunt. That's where it is, Master.'

Omi, the fool. What had he done? Tirath Ram's face, until then healthy and smiling, suddenly took an unhealthy and menacing

22

turn. Omi's end had come. The class waited in pin-drop silence for Tirath Ram to advance, catch the vermin by the hair and make the hottest chutney of the fool.

Tirath Ram knew what to do. He took a step towards Omi. Omi did not know what to do. He just picked up a pair of compasses from the open geometry box on his desk.

'Touch me and I will give you a taste of this,' Omi said, not believing the turn of events.

This was unheard-of. The boys longed for action. Tirath Ram's hands itched to grasp the son of a bitch by his hair and make a total bhurji of his face.

'Drop that thing or I'll call the police.'

'Call the Governor if you like. You insulted my father and now you want to beat me.'

'Only make a simple bhurji and chutney of you. In one simple go.'

'Try.'

'You'll be expelled for this, you two-time matric-sitter . . .'

'Sir, he is leaving school anyway, Sir,' somebody reminded Tirath Ram.

'. . . May snakes bite you. May dogs pee on your corpse.'

'On yours too.'

Tirath Ram whispered something to a boy. The boy dashed out.

'Omi, he is calling the police,' Bali said.

'Put it down, you fool. You'll go to jail otherwise,' Harpal said.

'It will be the end of your shop,' Des said.

'Give it to me and make a run for it,' Bhajju whispered.

Omi had half a mind to do so. But he stayed. Suddenly the tall and burly figure of Girdhari Lal, the headmaster, appeared at the classroom door.

'Class stand,' Tirath Ram said.

The class stood up.

'Class sit,' Girdhari Lal said.

The class sat down, including the culprit.

'What is the matter, Master ji?' Girdhari Lal asked Tirath Ram.

'Stand up, Omi,' Tirath Ram shouted.

Omi stood up. He still held the compasses in his hand.

'He has gone mad, Sir. He was threatening to take my life with that.'

23

'Give the compasses to Master ji, Omi Parkash.'

Omi shook his head.

'GIVE IT TO US. AT ONCE,' Girdhari Lal whispered and just took the compasses away.

'You going to make chutney of me, Sir,' Omi panicked, pushing back the tears.

'Best chutney ever. You've asked for it. You have become a rakshas monster. Master ji, PP for the boy at the end of this period,' the headmaster said and left. He took with him the instrument of the uncommitted murder.

PP was Public Punishment, reserved for the gravest of school crimes. It took place once or twice a year and it took place in front of the whole school. Caning by the headmaster was not only painful but, worse still, the greatest imaginable humiliation. Omi hadn't expected to make his exit from HS High School like this.

When the bell went, the school, mad with excitement, flocked to the hockey pitch where the spectacle was to take place. The teachers stood facing the thousand boys sitting in the field. Tirath Ram stood at the end of the teachers' row. Amid the noise of a thousand tongues he suddenly felt alarmed. Where was Omi? Tirath Ram had brought the boy out here by the hand, stood him in front of him, but where was he now?

Tirath Ram ran to the cycle shed. He saw Omi cycling towards the school gate on the left, past many rows of parked bicycles. He ran and placed himself between the gate and the approaching Omi. Omi was trapped.

'Now, where will you go, you son of a bitch?' Tirath Ram shouted.

Omi came fast. Cycling for his life, he took a lunge at Tirath Ram, upsetting his balance. He completed the job with a kick and broke free.

'Go lay your mother, Tirath Ram dog,' he shouted his last message to HS High School.

That night, Omi arranged a lift with a truck going north the next morning.

'I am going to Father tomorrow,' he said to his mother and told her why. 'If I go to school tomorrow they will peel my skin off.'

'What did I do in my past life?' Paro started to cry.

24

At sunrise Omi was on his way. He shivered as the lorry raced through the cold morning air from the blue Kasauli mountain.

'Left your mother to dogs?' Khatri said.

Omi gave a full account of yesterday's events.

'Tirath Ram insulted you, Father. I simply couldn't take it. After all.'

Khatri ground his jaws as he always did whenever he was thinking, and scratched the middle of his sutthan.

'Then Mother suggested I came here.'

There was no way Khatri could verify any of it.

'Absolute truth, Father. Otherwise, would I do a thing like that?'

Khatri held his son's eyes in his. Omi found looking into his father's eyes very uncomfortable. He bent down to do up a perfectly done-up shoelace.

'Alright. Get your things off the lorry and take a plate of something and a cup of tea to the driver,' Khatri said.

Khatri was in the process of acquiring Hari Das' shop. It was a quick transaction. In the presence of Bhola Ram and another witness, Khatri had read out the deed to Hari who, being unable to write, then applied his thumb impression as his signature above the back-dated line. That done, Khatri counted out a wad of notes, wetting his finger now and then. Hari counted them again, licking his counting finger now and then. Later, but separately, Hari pressed a couple of notes in Bhola Ram's hand and Khatri handed him a handsome basket full of his famous sweets.

'For kid-kiddies,' Khatri said.

'Lala ji!' Bhola Ram protested as he placed the parcel next to his seat.

Omi realised that his father had just bought him his shop. He looked around and instantly fell in love with Panchkoola. He loved its tall and lush trees, the wide river Jhajjar and the blue Kasauli mountain. A water mill coo-cooed endlessly from behind the trees and he loved that too.

'This is life, Omi son. Your new life,' he said to himself, in disbelief at being so free so suddenly.

But this feeling of elation evaporated just as suddenly when he was ushered into his shop. Flour, pulses, ghee, oil, sugar, gurstone-sugar, salt, spices and shrivelling vegetables were its only wares. Why hadn't his father told him that it wasn't a sweet shop? Why hadn't his mother?

'I am not going to sit here for months until we go to the capital. I am not going to sell this rotten stuff out of these rotten canisters on those oily shelves from this black hole of Panchkoola? I am not. I am going back.'

But Omi knew what that meant.

'My karma.'

Omi was trapped.

'My fucking karma.'

Bawa, Khatri's second servant, a rustic lad of Omi's age and height, brought him a cup of tea. But Omi was too cross to drink it. He sulked and sat cross-legged like his father, shaking his right knee and leg like his father, and watched the world go to Chandigarh. A couple of buses arrived, raising clouds of dust. Young boys from the shops, like Bawa, assailed them with brass trays laden with laddu, pera, jalebi and other sweets. Doors were flung open and out came men, women and children, eager for a stroll and a look around. Omi noticed that people from the plains — from Delhi, Ambala and Patiala — had dark and dusty faces. People from the mountains, who came in small matchbox-sized buses from Simla side, had clear and healthy faces. Their women were fair and had rosy cheeks.

When more than two buses arrived at the same time, Panchkoola became a place of much raunak, hustle bustle. Business and noise increased, resulting in a flurry of activity. Suddenly everybody started to shout in order to be heard. People from the buses moved around the shops buying knick-knacks, stopping to eat a puri or a spiced cutlet or to drink a cup of tea. Those who stayed inside the buses usually had food and fruit brought to them.

Then suddenly the buses blew their horns. People scrambled back into them. More horn blowing, more clouds of dust and all that was left was a sudden emptiness.

Omi watched this tamasha fun and sulked. In less than an hour he was fed up with his new life. He cursed himself for his behaviour yesterday. He felt quite sick about it.

'You should think sometimes. Especially before you open your mouth.'

26

All his own fault. But it was too late now. He had burned all his bridges.

'Dabbu is much better off than you, back in the Camp.' Omi missed the dog.

Another hour and he couldn't stand it any longer. He walked over to his father's shop which was doing brisk business. People were eating and drinking and chatting happily.

'Father, I have wonderful idea . . .'

'Have you?' Khatri knew that all his son's ideas were usually wonderful.

'. . . Wonderful and simple. Why not let Seva run the other shop? Then I could be of help in our own.'

'You talk foolish like your mother.'

'But, Father . . .'

'No but-shut. Go read your books while you wait for customers.' Khatri was curt.

'. . . Customers don't come there.'

'Go wait for them.' That was the final order. Any more talk and Khatri would get angry. 'That's how they come, customers.' Khatri dismissed his son.

Back in his shop Omi gave a kick to his school satchel, the khaki army haversack.

'You asked for it, Omi son. You asked for a shop and you got one now.'

He kicked the empty galla, the tin cash-box, and sent it rattling against other tin canisters in the shop.

'This arsehole of a shop. Proprietor, OP Khatri, second time matric-sitter.'

He retrieved the galla and sat down crossly.

'How does Father expect me to pass all these months here? By killing flies? Obviously.'

He tried to catch a fly that seemed to insist on sitting on his nose, but missed it. At lunch he got up and walked back to his father's shop in the hope of getting a nice meal, if nothing else.

'Left the shop to dogs?' Khatri snapped. 'Run back quick quick or I break your leg.'

'But Father . . .' Omi tapped his belly.

Bawa brought lunch to Omi's shop. The lunch was poor. Its only item of interest was a handful of bundi, little pearl-shaped

27

drops of barley flour fried in ghee and then dipped in syrup. Omi ate that first and wiped the plate clean with a morsel of chappati bread. He wondered why Seva had not spread the bread with butter or ghee.

'My first day here after all. He could have done that. Must ask him.'

As Seva Singh sat cooking for him that night, Omi asked him.

'Seva Singh, you got something against butter or ghee?'

Seva understood. He smiled and, as a treat — for Omi's first day here — made him butter parathas instead of the dry chappati Khatri preferred for his digestion.

'Another one?' Seva Singh asked after the third one.

If his father had been there Omi would have said no. Two butter parathas for a young boy were quite enough, four were simply too much. Bad for the boy and bad for the mind, as his mother would have said.

'That's why you failed last year. When it comes to eating there is no difference between you and an average hog. Same about thinking.' His mother's words echoed in his ears.

But she was in the Camp and his father had gone to Manimajra. Omi said he would have another one.

'Seva Singh, why has Father gone to Manimajra?'

'Lala ji has gone there to see Gulati sahib, driver Bhola's nephew. A very important man, Omi bau.'

'What does he do?'

'He makes miracles, Gulati sahib does.'

Omi did not understand.

'He works in the Government in the capital . . .'

Omi still did not understand.

'. . . Now that you have two shops you need two permits to buy things like flour, suji, sugar, oil and the like at controlled prices.'

'But mine is not a sweet shop, mine is an ordinary shop.'

'That's exactly why Lala ji has gone to Gulati. Only he can get you the shops and the permit. He has much pull in the capital.'

'Is Gulati a friend of Father's?'

'Gulati is anyone's friend,' Seva Singh said, shaking his head.

'I see. So that's why Father had Bawa carry that basket of sweets.' Omi looked worried saying that.

'Don't worry, Omi bau. Lala ji knows what he is doing. He can handle people like Gulati.'

'But what do we need provisions for? Mine is not a sweet shop.'

'Ah, but these provisions will be used later. In the capital. Understand, Omi bau?'

Omi said he did although he didn't.

Smoke from the kitchen filled Omi's nostrils. Still skimming under the surface of sleep, he heard his mother crying out, 'Wake up. The boys will be here any minute and you'll still be rubbing your eyes like a baby.'

'Up, up, you opium-eater.' It was Khatri calling him.

Outside, through the door, through the curtain of smoke rising from the shop fires being prepared for the day, Omi pictured the mud wall of Banto's house back in the Camp. The hand-pump was squeaking rhythmically under her hand.

'Up, up, you posti. Whatever did you eat last night?' His father's voice. Omi recognised it at last. He wished he was at home. '*Go out* to the reeds by the river,' Khatri said.

Omi rubbed his eyes and went to the river. In the reeds he selected two squarish stones and arranged them carefully before squatting on them. He hummed a tune and waited. But nothing came. He got bored and came back to his father's shop.

'Now go and bath under the pump,' Khatri said.

Bawa worked the pump as Omi sat under it wearing a kuchaa, his homemade underwear with fading blue and white stripes. In the chill morning air the water, coming up from the bowels of the earth and smelling of grease and leather from the pump valve, warmed him.

'Now come and get your breakfast,' Khatri said when Omi was dressed.

Khatri was handing cups of steaming tea to a group of men who had just got off a bus from Ambala. They were congratulating him on his victory over the Minister. Omi felt proud of his father.

'No joke beating a Minister like that. Needs brains,' one man said, shaking his head with awe. 'Some have it, some don't.'

'I am not the son of an ordinary man,' Omi thought.

'Seva Singh, give him a glass of milk and something to eat,' Khatri said, noticing Omi.

29

'I thought your son was at school in Ambala City,' the tea drinker said. He poured tea from the cup into the saucer and blew at it before drinking it. 'Nice big boy, nice big boy. Reading-writing well? What is you name, son?'

Omi told him, taking his glass of milk which Seva Singh had measured out for him from the vast iron karrai wok in which milk was simmering slowly over a low coal fire. In a few hours a crust of malai cream would be formed on the surface. Omi loved malai.

'Nice big boy. Just right for the army. Let him sit for the army exam, Lala ji.'

'What army exam? Can't pass even his matric. Second year running.'

'Boys pass and fail. Don't worry. He'll be alright. He looks alright and intelligent.'

Omi thought he liked the man.

'Oi, take your breakfast along to your shop and wait for the customers,' Khatri said to his son. 'And don't leave until I send for you. Understand?'

It was nine o'clock. The Camp boys would be cycling to school, the sods. Omi felt sorry for them and glad for himself. But when he arrived at his shop he felt like crying.

'Why did Father take this arsehole of a shop?'

Omi had his first customer, a Rajasthani woman labourer with a child at her breast. She was young but she looked old. She was very thin and her child was even thinner. She wore a colourful sari, spoke Hindi and wanted some rice and some dal lentils.

Proudly Omi poured rice on the scales and took a great deal of care to weigh it right.

'You weighing gold, babu ji?' the woman said, raising her eyes to look at Omi.

Omi felt ashamed of himself. The reproach was justified; Omi had been rather over-enthusiastic with the scales. He let the rice outweigh the two-pound weight. The woman's eyes lit up. Omi did the same with the dal.

'One rupee, ten annas,' Omi said.

But the woman did not have any money.

'Pay you as soon as I get work, babu ji,' she said.

Omi was in a fix. The question was, should he extend credit to a total stranger? The answer was straightforward. But the child started to howl and the woman pleaded with her enormous Rajasthani eyes. Besides, the rice and the dal were duly packed in brown paper bags in her hands.

'Alright,' Omi said and wrote down her name and the amount in one of his exercise books.

'May God make you pass your exam,' the woman said with a smiling face.

Omi had more customers, more Rajasthani women stonecutters with children clinging to them. They all had large pleading eyes and they were all out of work. They all said the same thing.

'May God make you pass your exam, babu ji.'

Khatri dropped in to see how things were going. He looked pleased. He had seen all that coming and going at Omi's shop.

'How much have you taken, boy?'

'Taken what, Father?'

Khatri's nostrils flared. He didn't even bother to look at the empty galla and whacked Omi on the head.

'Son of a dog. Think you are the son of the Maharajah of Patiala, giving free alms?'

Khatri whacked him again and gave him a lecture about the ills of giving credit to people, especially poor people.

'It spoils them. They become lazy.'

'But Father, they had no money.'

'Is it my fault?'

'They have no work.'

'Then they should look for it. Your policy from now on — cash today, credit tomorrow. Understand?' Khatri whacked him on the head again.

A little later, Bawa brought a wooden notice board. *Cash Today, Credit Tomorrow*, it said in bold letters. There was an appropriate reminder underneath in small letters: *tomorrow never comes*. Bawa nailed it to the door.

'Lala ji wants you, Omi bau. You go and I will mind the shop.'

'What now?' Omi wondered, walking slowly to his father's shop. He found him in the company of a tall young man.

'This is the boy. Teach him well, Ashok bau. His main drawback is sleeping too much.'

What had his father arranged?

'If he doesn't listen to you, twist his ears — he has a wind tunnel

31

between them. What he hears through one ear he lets out through the other. From now on he is in your hands, Ashok bau. Oi, are you listening? This is Mr Ashok, BA, LLB. Brother-in-law of my close friend, Gulati sahib. He will be coaching you for your exams. Understand?'

Omi took a good look at Ashok, appearing to be duly impressed by his qualifications.

'What subjects does he need coaching in?' Ashok asked.

'Oi, answer yourself.'

'Maths, English and Science,' Omi said.

'It is sixty rupees then, Lala ji, as we agreed last night.'

'You said sixty for all five. You must make it less for three. Say fifty.'

Ashok thought for a moment.

'Then you will have to send him to Manimajra. If I come here it will be . . .'

'Alright, alright. He will from tomorrow. It won't hurt him to cycle up there. Only a couple of miles. But teach him here today as you are here.'

Omi and Ashok sat in the sun at the back of the shop, out of sight of the hustle and bustle. Bawa minded Omi's shop. At lunch, two hours later, Ashok rose.

'Teaching is hard work. Did you know that Om Parkash?' Ashok said, smiling.

Omi did not know what Ashok meant, but he was glad to see the back of him — he was desperate to *go out*. He told Bawa to stay on another few minutes. But while he was out, Khatri yelled for Bawa. Bawa had left the Delhi *de luxe* unattended.

'Where in hell are you? Let me lay my hands on you.'

Bawa didn't want that to happen. He abandoned Omi's shop and ran back to Khatri's.

'I was waiting for Omi bau to return, Lala ji,' Bawa said.

'Return from where?'

'He's *gone out*, Lala ji.'

'But he has been *out* once today. I sent him *out* myself.'

When Omi returned from the river Khatri called him.

'Diarrhoea or something, Oi? Been in the sweets behind my back last night?'

'Constipation.'

'Same thing. Sweets. Take care. If I catch you stealing sweets I will beat you into the shape of a peacock's arse. Understand?'

'But I was not eating sweets, Father. I am constipated because of the change of air and water.'

Seva Singh, listening, knew the real reason. He smiled to himself.

'Air and water. I know. Don't let me catch you mouthing the sweets, or . . .' Omi was hurt by this public display of his father's temper.

'Only my second day here,' Omi said to himself. He had not been anywhere near the sweets, but he decided not to let an opportunity go by.

'After all, what is the use of being the son of a halwai if you can't even taste the stuff.'

'I am going home tonight. If I find one grain of bundi missing tomorrow I will peel your skin. Understand?' Khatri showed him now. He pulled apart two imaginary pieces of paper glued together.

Khatri started going home every other night.

'How are you doing, boy?' Khatri asked his son after the first week of lessons.

'Fine, Father. Ashok ji is absolute first class well-read and well-written.'

'That so? Let's see, then. Go bring your books, boy.'

Khatri asked a few questions. Omi managed to answer most of them. Khatri was a little surprised but also pleased — he was getting his money's worth. He let the boy off.

Omi, having come out of the questioning with his skin intact, felt triumphant. For weeks his bike saddle had been in need of repair — a few springs and additional stuffing. He had to pedal standing up, with the crossbar between his legs. He had asked his father every day but, not having to cycle himself, Khatri did not know where it hurt.

'Another day, boy, another day,' Khatri had said each time Omi asked for money.

Feeling that it was now or never, Omi took the matter in his hands.

'Money, Father, for the saddle. It hurts.'

'Take it from me tomorrow, boy.'

It was absolutely now or never.

'The longer I leave it the worse it will get. Then it will have to be a new saddle altogether, and that will be very expensive as you know, Father.'

'Alright. You are your mother's son. Never spare me for money.' Khatri dipped a hand in his galla and gave him a two-rupee note. 'I want the change back. Understand?'

Omi had his saddle repaired in Manimajra, where there were several bicycle shops. He shopped around and had it done where it cost the least, fourteen annas, less than even a rupee. He hid the other rupee. He would spend it one day in the capital. When Khatri asked how much it cost, Omi quickly produced the change from the rupee he had used. Khatri knew there was something behind this ready show of honesty.

'Not keeping anything behind, boy?'

Omi pulled out the corners of his pockets.

'Honest, Father. Absolutely bilkul.'

But Khatri chanced upon the hidden rupee a few days later. He was clearing the table in the back room of the shop where Omi kept his books. Omi's geometry set fell to the floor. Picking it up and replacing the spilled contents in the box Khatri saw it.

'Son of a dog,' Khatri laughed. 'Lied to me. Wait till he gets home.'

Omi's tuition started at two and finished at four. He was usually back half an hour later. But today it was past six and still there was no sign of him. Khatri worried.

'Bawa, go borrow Aneja's bike and go and see what he is up to. Go quick and fast.'

Bawa went and was back as soon as he could, half an hour later.

'Ashok's family say Omi bau left usual time,' he said, breathlessly.

Khatri was sure something had happened to his son.

'How many times have I not told that son of a bitch to drive carefully. Hundreds of times. But does he listen?' Khatri said loudly and looked towards the distant temple of Goddess Chandi, pleading with her.

Another half hour passed. Khatri feared the worst and decided to go himself to look. But just as he put his peshawari turban on his head, Omi appeared through the darkness, singing a film song. With a sigh of relief, Khatri felt his nostrils flare with anger.

'Where the hell were you?' Khatri gave him a slap with the back of his hand. 'Where the hell were you? Speak or I'll give you another.' Khatri gave him another slap.

'I was at a Sangh meeting.'

'Sangh. Sangh. I was worried to death and this bastard, this son of an owl, was at Sangh. Who gave you permission to go there? Was your father dead that you couldn't ask him?'

Khatri slapped and kicked his son.

After tuition, when Ashok had suggested going to this meeting, Omi knew that his father would object. Sangh, a youth organisation, was affiliated to the right-wing Jan Sangh party which opposed the Gandhian Congress party. Khatri was a Congress man. Omi knew this well, but Ashok, a staunch Sanghi, said that Dev Raj Sharma was speaking and that he was very good. Anyway, Omi intended to go there only for a while. Dev Raj Sharma proved to be a very good speaker and time passed quickly as he spoke of 'our past glory', 'our future glory' and 'our great destiny'.

Seva Singh had to intervene.

'Forgive him, Lala ji. He is only a child. He will learn.'

'A child! Eats like a horse, takes two years to pass an exam. Child! Boys get married at his age. Son of an owl.'

That night Khatri ate very little. Seva Singh knew he was sorry for beating the boy. 'Never mind, Lala ji,' Seva said. 'It doesn't do any harm for a boy to get a little slap now and then. He will have forgotten it by tomorrow.'

But Omi hadn't forgotten it. He had gone to bed without eating his supper and sobbed till he could cry no more. When he woke up next morning the only thing he wanted to do was to pack up his trunk and take the first bus back to the Camp, school or no school. But his father's eye was on him whatever he did.

'Come on, Om,' Khatri called him. He called him Om on rare occasions, when he was mellow. 'Had your breakfast?'

Omi maintained a sullen silence.

'Seva Singh, give Om his milk and whatever else he wants.'

The father was sorry for his son and the servant took it upon himself to show it to the son. He gave Omi a generous handful of barfi, the famed creation of Khatri — a milk and pistachio affair. He also gave him gajerela (carrot halva), Omi's favourite sweet, and made him his own speciality, a butter paratha.

'If only you had said you would be late returning . . .' Khatri said. '. . . Do you want to go there again, Om?'

Sangh meetings were held daily. Boys and young men were given physical training and made to participate in patriotic discussion such as, *If Pakistan Invades* . . .

Omi nodded.

'Alright, but don't stay too late. Back before it gets dark. Understand.' Khatri did not mention the rupee.

Omi's life in Panchkoola changed the day that Satish, Aneja's son, got off the Ambala bus. Satish, also a matric-sitter, had been called from the Camp for the same reason as Omi — to sit in a second shop. Soon the contents of their shops dried up and they often slipped out to spend hours on the river, fishing and bringing down birds with catapults.

Satish seemed to have some peculiar talent with his line. He seemed to have an understanding with the fish and the water. The fish not only bit at his bait, it actually got hooked. This seldom happened to Omi.

In the mornings when he *went out*, Omi took his line along. Sitting securely on his stones he would fling his line out, holding the six-foot rod in his hands. If there was a bite he would jerk the hook out of the water and the atta, the bait, would be gone.

'The bitch of a fish. I will catch you one day. I am my father's son,' Omi would say. He would replenish the bait, giving it a smooth finishing touch by wetting it with his own pee. Satish had told him that human pee was irresistible to fish.

'A fish goes mad at the taste of it,' Satish often said.

Omi never caught one. But he never gave up trying. He was his father's son. One day there was a strong bite followed by a powerful pull. It upset Omi's balance. He was almost dislodged from the stones. Something was caught. A big fish? Half in and half out of his shorts, he shot up and pulled the line out.

'A snake' he yelled.

It was a wriggly, thirty-inch eel. Omi had never seen one before. It wriggled and wriggled and snapped its tail. Omi was frightened. He held it on the line and bashed it on the pebble-strewn bank. The hook cut through its ugly mouth and the thing jumped and writhed and gasped. But it did not wriggle away like a snake. Then Omi saw the fins.

'Some fishy kind of snake.'

He crushed its head with a rock. It lay in front of him — a slimy length of black rope with fins and whiskers, glistening in the morning sun. It looked angry and ferocious. It still wriggled, but it didn't have much life left in it.

Omi washed himself. Then he put the hook back into the eel's ugly mouth and ran back to Panchkoola with it dangling in the air. He looked for Satish and saw him at the hand-pump with Seva Singh.

'My first catch and it had to be a river snake,' Omi said.

'It's an eel. It tastes delicious,' Satish said.

'Go wash your face, Satish. I am not a snake eater.'

'It is not a snake. It is a fish that looks like a snake.'

'It is a snake that looks like a fish.'

'And it tastes delicious.'

'True, Seva Singh?'

'True, Omi bau. I'll cook it for you when Lala ji is away. You come too, Satish bau. It is big enough for three.'

Khatri was going to the capital on important business with Gulati. He saw his son showing off his catch proudly around the shops.

'You taken to snake-charming now? Do your reading-writing while I am gone, or else.'

As Khatri boarded his bus, Seva hoisted a saucepan onto the fire for the eel. Satish came over as soon as he began to smell roasting garlic, tamarind and other spices.

'Wah wah, wah wah– Aré Seva Singh, you are quite an ustad-guru-master type. One wouldn't say that looking at you,' Satish said, licking his fingers. 'Wah wah, wah wah!'

At tuition Omi told the story of the eel to Ashok.

'Ashok ji, it looks like a snake but people eat it like fish. Who is God joking with — the eel, fish or man?'

'It is like God making a horse different from a mule and a mule different from a donkey. One is intelligent, one is stubborn and one is stupid. Same family, though.'

'So why eat the eel and not the snake.'

'They do in some countries. Japan. In some countries they eat

37

worse things. In France they eat snails and frogs and what-not.'

'But the French are European, no? I thought they would be civilised.'

'They only look it, the Europeans.'

Back home Omi told Seva and Bawa that the Japanese ate snakes.

'I saw a man eat a snake in my own village. A live one too, Omi bau,' Seva said.

Omi thought Seva Singh had struck his twelve o'clock.

'Where is your village then, Seva Singh? Near Tokyo?'

'You think I've gone nuts? You think I've struck my twelve o'clock? But Seva is a true servant of the Guru. Seva never tells a lie. And I am here to tell you that I saw a man eat a live snake.'

'A dead snake maybe, but a living snake . . .?'

'Listen, Omi bau, listen. This juggler comes to our village. He swallows swords, pushes needles through his cheeks and makes his servant vanish in a basket. But we've seen all that. What we haven't seen is this snake trick.'

'Eating a snake, live or dead, is no trick. It is madness,' Bawa said.

Seva Singh, the senior servant, gave Bawa, the junior servant, a back-handed slap. 'You think I have gone bonkers and struck my twelve o'clock? Shut up and listen. Listen, Omi bau. Juggler does more tricks and then asks — anyone got a snake? The village laughs — we kill snakes, not keep them. "I do," juggler says.'

'Was he also a Sikh?' Bawa interrupted again.

Seva Singh gave him another back-handed slap and went on with the story.

'Juggler dips a hand in a basket and brings out a live snake. He holds it by its head. The snake curves and coils around his arm. "See its head?" juggler says and shows us its fangs. Women and children begin to scream and get up to go. "Sit you down, sit you down, sisters. Nothing to worry. Dangerous snake, this. But worry not and fear not. We are going to destroy it. Tricky thing, this, destroying of snakes. They come back to life when you leave them thinking them to be dead. They come and find you and bite you and fill your body with their venom. Your body goes blue, the veins burst, your eyes pop out and you die a horrible death. But mothers and sisters, with meharbani kindness, sit you down and don't be afraid — this snake has reached its very last day. No joke, no kidding, no lies.

Absolute truth and I go to show you what I mean.''

'Saying this, the magician bites off the snake's head and spits it on the ground. Women and children shriek in terror. The beheaded snake wriggles so violently in the air that we are afraid it is going to get out of his hand, fall on the ground, join up with the head as snakes are known to do, and attack. It is a horrible sight, Omi bau, horrible. No twelve o'clock, absolute truth. Magician chews up the rest of the snake, bit by bit. He finishes the act by drinking down a glass of water and issuing a loud belch. Absolute truth. What do you say to that, Omi bau?'

Omi said nothing, but thought it was bakwas and nonsense. The smile on Bawa's face told him that Bawa thought the same but wouldn't offer an opinion for fear of receiving another back-handed slap. Later, while studying with Satish, Omi sought his opinion. Satish was quite forthcoming.

'Typical Sikh talk, pure Khalsa stuff. They believe in anything. That's why they make best soldiers. Ask the British. Englishman says — Khalsa, left turn, German enemy in front. Fire. Khalsa fires. Khalsa never asks silly questions like who is a German? Too much trouble. Englishman had said he was enemy. Enough for Khalsa. Simple as that.'

It had become a habit with Omi and Satish to *go out* together in the morning. They sat a few yards apart, each behind his own bush or boulder, and flung their fishing lines in the water. Omi never caught a fish, nor another eel, but Satish often did.

'It is my pee. Obviously. And the fish love it. Simple as that,' Satish explained.

'Try fishing in the sea, yaar. You might land a mermaid. I read in a book that their pussy is best in the world.'

One morning Satish told him how, when he had been staying here during the Christmas holidays, the Rajasthani women stone-cutters used to come here to wash clothes and bathe. Satish used to watch them from behind the bushes.

'Were they naked?' Omi asked.

'Stark naked.'

'And you could see everything?'

'Everything.'

'Lucky bastard. Why don't they come any more?'

'They do, but not here. The work has moved further up the river, near the temple, Chandigarh Mandir. On Sunday afternoon they come to bathe.'

'Shall we try next Sunday and see if we can see something?' Omi got excited.

'Very risky, I am telling you.'

But Omi wasn't worried about that.

'Tell me if you could see everything. *Things*, I mean.'

'As much as you can see of a naked woman standing.'

That was quite enough.

'Well, then. This Sunday. Settled?'

'Alright, if you don't mind looking like a peacock's arse, for that's what you'll look like if their men catch you.'

'We'll take care. We are not fools.'

Omi couldn't wait for Sunday to arrive. But when Sunday did come his father wanted him to go to Gulati's in Manimajra. Gulati was holding a havan for the name-giving ceremony for his baby son. The Khatris were invited. When Bhola Ram came to pick them up, Omi tried to hide.

'Omiiiii . . .' Khatri screamed above the noise of the bus stand. Omi knew what would happen if he did not show up. Quietly he climbed into the lorry.

Manimajra was a maze of dirty lanes with open drains running through them. Khatri gave Omi a white hankie when they alighted at the mouth of Gulati's street.

'Cover your head with this, boy,' he said. 'And leave your shoes outside with the others.'

A good half of the street on both sides of Gulati's door was occupied by shoes of various sizes and kinds. Gulati's door wore a fringe of mango leaves with a red-painted sign of the swastika. Inside, the verandah was packed with people squatting on the floor. The Pundit sat in the middle, feeding a fire of twigs with spoonfuls of ghee and handfuls of samagri — a holy substance — and chanting mantras. Next to the Pundit sat Gulati, a man younger than his father. Next to him sat his wife. She held the infant boy in her arms. His head was clean-shaven in accordance with the ritual. He bawled from time to time. Each time the Pundit sang out the last bit of a mantra the whole verandah, man, woman and child, echoed it in unison. The little boy bawled.

40

Somebody made room for Khatri and he sat down. Omi looked around for a place. He tried to reach Ashok on the other side but there were too many people and he sat down halfway, afraid that he was making a nuisance of himself. Crossly he watched what was going on, wondering if Satish had gone to the river on his own.

The holy fire crackled as the Pundit fed it with ghee at the end of each mantra. Golden flames shot up out of it, followed by smoke and smell of the holy samagri. The crowd echoed the tail words of each mantra.

'And it will go on and on,' Omi thought sulkily, his mind still on the banks of the river and the naked women. 'And this bastard Pundit.' Omi was angry with the Pundit. 'The longer he makes it the more money he will get.'

Suddenly, Omi became aware that he was sitting next to Ashok's fifteen-year-old sister, Guddy, and that their thighs were touching. She sat upright, looking straight at the holy fire, mumbling the last bit of each mantra.

A fire swept through Omi's body and he edged closer to her. He feared that she would move away. But Guddy did not stir. She sat as before, looking straight at the flames. 'Perhaps she doesn't even know that it is me, Omi, sitting next to her.'

But Guddy was too still, sitting too upright. And now she was not echoing the mantras. She was just staring vacantly ahead of her.

With the length of his burning thigh Omi could feel the whole of hers. With the tip of his burning right elbow he could feel the soft bulge of her young breast. He moved his elbow a little and she slid her arm backwards a little. The whole of her breast came under his touch. He was ablaze with the longing to touch it.

'What if she slaps me in the face? Ashok will probably break my jaw and Father both my legs.'

Folding his arms on his chest, he extended his left hand from under the right arm, and waited for the slap he knew he deserved. But Guddy remained still, breathing heavily. In a moment, he feared, everyone would hear her. As his finger caressed the curvature of her breast she edged closer. Delicious flames leapt up from his groin. Omi became total pulp. He could have died.

The last spoonfuls of ghee and samagri were being fed to the holy fire. The last of the mantras were being sung. The child's name was given. People were standing up. Guddy stood up abruptly and stood back a little with her arms joined on her mango-shaped breasts, waiting for the Pundit to say the last line. The Pundit gave out the holy tulsi water. People shuffled, Guddy vanished. His body still aflame, Omi didn't know what to do, which way to go — backward or forward. Then he saw Ashok looking at him.

'He saw me doing it.' Omi shivered.

Ashok was talking to his father.

'He is telling Father all about it.'

His father and Ashok beckoned him to them. Omi staggered forward.

'He will not only pass, he may even get a good division,' Ashok was saying. 'You alright, Om Parkash? Why so pale?'

'Om isn't without brains. He just doesn't like work. Only sleep,' Khatri was saying. The usual story. What relief!

A number of Sangh boys were helping with the food for guests. Puris, channa chick peas in bowls made of banyan leaves stitched together, lumps of cauliflower bhajee next to a heap of karra halva in brass trays. They were serving the guests who were now scattered in the house and the street. They ran to and fro briskly, looking very busy. Out in the street and away from the invited guests stood the beggars, the untouchables and the stray dogs of Manimajra. They were waiting patiently for the feast to be over to get their natural right — the leftovers.

Omi felt he should give a hand. He went to the kitchen where the ladies were preparing the trays. There his eyes met those of Guddy. She was pouring out channa from a giant cauldron with a long ladle. She shied away.

Omi had seen Guddy every day since he started going to her house for lessons with Ashok. She was always around, busy with some chore or other, but she never said a word to him. She was not supposed to. They were not supposed to have anything in common, not even cordiality. A young girl was someone else's daughter or sister, to become someone's else's wife one day. You had nothing to do with her. It was understood.

When the guests were fed, the family and helpers sat down to eat. Guddy sat with the ladies, Omi with the men and boys. From time to time their eyes met.

'If it was England or America I would walk across and sit with her. Be with her.' Omi had read that in those countries boys and girls could talk to each other, even eat together. 'Here, all you can do is press a girl's tits in a crowd and tell her with stolen glances that you love her. India. Independent India.'

A lame dog came in from the street and Omi gave him his banyan-leaf bowl of channa. The grateful dog lapped it up in no time while everybody gave Omi a dirty look.

'You gone crazy or what, giving dog best food?' a Sangh boy said.

Khatri also gave him a quizzical look. But Omi had other worries.

'What now? Our affair. Where do we go from here?'

Omi was dying to tell Satish. But he was afraid.

'Can he keep it in his stomach, keep it to himself?'

If he didn't, it would be all over Panchkoola and Manimajra. That would be broken jaws and broken legs.

But Omi couldn't help it. Next morning when they were *out* together, Omi shouted from his bush.

'Tell us then. Did you go to see the naked women yesterday?'

'Didn't. Wouldn't. Not by myself. Too far. If only you didn't have to go to that havan.'

'It was the greatest havan you ever saw. Open your arse and listen . . .'

Omi told him what happened. He did not reveal Guddy's name.

'And she is pretty,' Omi said.

'Pretty or not, that's not the thing. The thing is you got a girl, a real girl with tits and all. Understand?' Satish said.

But the question was, what was Omi to do now? A beginning must have a continuation.

'Write her a letter asking her to meet you somewhere,' Satish said.

'You mad, Satish? What if the letter is caught?'

'Risk you got to take, Omi son. Or wait till Gulati has another son and another havan. More chances of your being caught handling her titties than passing on a chittie, I think.'

But Omi wasn't sure. That day he had his best shirt and shorts ironed by Bawa. He oiled his hair and combed it ten times before setting out for his lesson.

'Concentrate more on your books and less on your looks, Om Parkash. In the examination hall no one is going to look at your face,' Ashok said.

Guddy was not to be seen all afternoon.

'Where is she?' Omi wondered. 'She is not showing up deliberately, to make me want her more. Perhaps she regrets what happened yesterday. Perhaps she doesn't want to seem too willing. Yes, that must be it. She is shy. What if I asked Ashok where she was?'

Ashok would have smashed all the teeth in his mouth.

'Where are your thoughts today, Om Parkash?' Ashok asked during the lesson.

Omi's thoughts were with every sound in the street, thinking it was Guddy. But Guddy didn't come. It was a very reluctant Omi who accompanied Ashok to the Sangh. But the moment the saffron-coloured flag was taken down for the night, Omi hopped on his bike and shot off without saying goodbye to Ashok. He went back to Ashok's house. He had left a book there on purpose, hoping to get a glimpse of Guddy when he went back for it. And he saw her. She opened the door to him and gave him the book. Her face was all eyes and her eyes were all smiles. Omi felt foolish, but happy, happy beyond belief.

But talking with the wind on his way home, he suddenly felt miserable. He should have taken Satish's advice and had a letter ready. One thing, though. Omi must not make a habit of leaving books behind.

'Ashok will find out and smash all your teeth and hand them to you as a wedding present.'

A peacock flew across the road and Omi smiled. He didn't want to look like its arse.

He arrived at Panchkoola, singing like a bulbul.

'You go done-up like that for tuition by a master or by a randi whore?' Khatri said.

'Father!'

'I am going home tonight. Is this what you want me to tell your mother?'

Double hungry again that night, Khatri slapped Paro where he liked it best.

'Begum Paro, your son is catching the modern air. Has become a pukka banka of Lucknow, a real dandy.'

44

'Whose son is he, then? Like father like son. Randy dandies, no?'

'That so? You think Banto got a bet with Banarsi on our light? I want her to win.'

Khatri was busy. The permit had come.

Early one evening Bhola Ram parked quietly behind Khatri's shop and delivered an important passenger — Gulati. Gulati waved a brown paper envelope at Khatri. Khatri called Seva. 'Not Red Fairy today, but Solan Number One,' he whispered to Seva, giving him two ten-rupee notes for the expensive Vilayati English whisky. The British had started making it during their Raj at Solan in the Simla Hills. Affluent Indians drank it now.

Before going to the liquor shop which was tucked away behind the bus stand, Seva spread a clean dhurrie on the floor of the back room and produced three long sausage-shaped pillows. The three men sat down on the dhurries and reclined on the pillows like nawabs. Khatri rubbed his hands, Bhola Ram scratched the middle of his sutthan (his balls, to be precise) and Gulati unbuckled his belt, to relax.

'Well, well, well. You are a badshah king now, Lala ji,' Gulati said.

'Only a poor halwai, Gulati Sahib. All your meharbani kindness.'

Bhol discreetly went for a pee and Khatri pressed a wad of notes in Gulati's palm.

'Lala ji!' Gulati protested, putting the notes in his pocket.

The permit was soon followed by the supplies — huge sacks of sugar, suji, flour and canisters of ghee and oil. Khatri had had these sent discreetly home to the Camp where they were carefully stored away to be used in Chandigarh. Khatri was happy. He was also happy because life had suddenly become hectic: the Elections were approaching. Canvassers in jeeps, lorries and tongas stopped by to refresh themselves. Election banners criss-crossed Panchkoola square. Painted on cloth, the oxen of Congress, the Lamp of Jan Sangh, the Tiger of the Independents, the Hammer and Sickle of the Communists flapped and ruffled in the cold wind coming from the Kasauli mountain. In the first rain their colours started to run. In the sun they all started to fade.

Winter set in. It was cold. People wore coats or shawls or thick cotton khes, also used as bedding. One day two men, wearing Congress achkan coats, came and replaced the fading Congress banners with newly painted ones and Panchkoola learnt that Nehru himself was to pass through there on his way to Chandigarh.

This piece of information did something to the Panchkoolans. Everybody started wearing white khadi homespun. Khatri, too, ordered a khadi kurta and pyjama for himself and his son. But Omi was a Sanghi. He shook his head.

'You wear this on the day Pandit ji comes, or . . .' Khatri said.

'Father's politics are Father's,' Omi said to himself. 'Why put me into this khadi rubbish? I would look a fool. What if my Guddy saw me in it?'

Nehru was not officially expected to stop here. But the Panchkoolans were determined. 'Only for a darshan sight of him,' they said to the police inspector who had posted a policeman every hundred yards along the road.

'Pandit ji is a great man. He has no time to waste in this wilderness. What for? To look at you fools? He has a hundred thousand intelligent people waiting in the capital,' the inspector said.

Nobody took any notice of the inspector. Everybody turned out in white khadi on that historic morning. And everybody carried garlands of marigold and chameli.

Nehru was scheduled to pass through at eleven. The people from Panchkoola, and from villages for miles around, had thronged in since well before then. Eleven struck and a hush fell. Half-past eleven, but still there was no sign of Nehru. At twelve a dot appeared where the road, the trees and the sky met.

'Pandit ji, Pandit ji,' the crowd hissed and the inspector looked worried.

But it was a police jeep. It flitted past. No motor cycles, no cars followed.

'Must have taken the bridge,' some people said and returned to work. Others remained.

At one o'clock a roar went up from among the children.

'Chacha Nehru, Uncle Nehru . . . Chacha Nehru, Uncle Nehru . . .'

Pandemonium.

The Panchkoolans had managed to halt Nehru's cavalcade in spite of the police inspector. Nehru got out of his car and came and stood among the bewildered Panchkoolans. He patted scruffy village children on their cheeks and gave them the garlands he was being heaped with. Satish, although a grown-up boy, was also patted on the cheek and given a garland. This burned the inside of Omi who had got bored and gone away. Somehow he wriggled his way through the crowd and went and stood in front of Nehru. Nehru patted him on his cheek and said something inaudible which Omi missed. Nehru patted him on his other cheek and handed him a garland. Next minute it was all over. The fair face of Nehru was gone. The cavalcade was on its way in clouds of dust. Omi, his garland around neck, came back to his father's shop.

'What did Pandit ji say to you, oi?' Khatri asked.

Omi tried to think what a great man like Nehru would say to a fool like him.

'He said to me, "How are you?" ' Omi said.

Khatri slapped his own forehead in disgust with a sad face. He knew his son was lying. He took the garland from Omi's neck and hung it reverentially on the nail supporting the calendar with Nehru's picture. Then he blew out a sigh.

Khatri was a Congress man. He had grown up with Congress. It was not just politics. It was something more. It was a way of life. It meant a new India. It meant Independence, which India had not had for a thousand years. It meant Ram Raj, the Hindu ideal of freedom, equality and plenty. It meant men like Gandhi and Nehru, above all, Gandhi. How Khatri had wept when he had heard the news of Gandhi's murder! Little Omi had come running across the dusty Camp street shouting, 'Gandhi is dead, Gandhi is dead', having heard it from someone. How everybody had wept! People flocked to wherever there was a radio set, hardly half a dozen in the whole of the Camp. They sat huddled together, listening to the non-stop account of the event. Mahatma Gandhi was dead. Assassinated with three bullets. Men wept, women wept, children wept, the sky and the earth wept. Man understands death, but that death was difficult to understand. Like Partition, it was the fault of the times, an outcome of the evil genius of the sub-continent.

Khatri sighed again as he thought of Partition. It was an evil thing. But it had happened. Whoever's fault it was, the material and other consequences to people on both sides had taken place. It was past and over. Now it was a painful memory of a very painful upheaval of history. Now the future was the thing.

'Our new capital and the building of this son of mine's life.'

Khatri was going to Chandigarh and Omi wanted to be taken along.

'And who will do your lessons? I am not paying for them for nothing.'

'I'll go on Sunday instead, Father.'

Khatri thought for a moment. He had been promising the boy for weeks that he would take him to see our new capital.

'Alright then. Change into your woollen patloon. I don't want my son to look like Bawa in the capital.'

Omi ran to the back room of the shop. Leaving his pyjamas in a heap of two circles on the floor, to be picked up by Seva, he slipped into his grey worsted trousers. He examined himself in the mirror and wished he possessed a tie. The only time he had worn one was for last year's school-leaving 'farewell' photograph of his class. He had borrowed it from Lallu's collegiate brother. All the boys wore a tie for that photograph. Some wore one even though they wore pyjamas at the bottom. Your legs didn't show in the photograph.

'Are you ready?' Khatri shouted. The bus was leaving in a few minutes.

'Shall I ask Satish if he wants to come?'

Satish was only too willing. Aneja gave him a rupee, saying, 'Don't spend it all.'

The boys wanted to take Omi's bike with them, to get around more easily. Khatri said yes and the boys hoisted it up onto the roof of the bus.

'Come on, then, boys,' Khatri shouted.

Omi wanted to take a pee, but the bus was ready. He decided to wait: it was only seven miles. The bus stopped briefly at Manimajra. The bus stop faced Guddy's school. Omi peeped out to see if he could spot her. He was disappointed.

'What do you expect of her — to be waiting at the gate because Lord Laat sahib is passing by? Who do you think you are — Nawab Latti Khan?' Omi said to himself, wondering if he could slip off for a second to take a pee behind the bushes. It had become urgent. 'Only five miles to go now. I'll wait.'

At the next stop, Power House, the situation became desperate.

'I'll only be a minute,' he said to his father and got off. He was still doing it on a bush when the bus started.

'Stop, stop, stop,' Khatri shouted. 'My boy is outside.'

Startled, Omi ran towards the bus, getting the last bit of his water on his trousers. It showed conspicuously on the grey. The bus stopped and the conductor held the door open for him and pulled him inside. The conductor was well known to Khatri.

'God save us. What would happen to our timetable if all the fifty-four passengers started peeing every four miles?' he said, laughing.

The whole bus laughed. Omi wished he was dead.

'Chutia sala, sister's cunt,' he called the conductor in his throat.

At Manimajra, Omi had wished that Guddy had taken the same bus; they might have met in Chandigarh. 'What if she had?' Omi now asked himself and tried not to think about anything any more. Life was not worth living. It had too many ups and downs, mostly downs. Look at this kirla lizard of a bus conductor. People like him should be shot.

They got off the bus in front of the cinema in Sector 22. Khatri gave Omi a rupee.

'Don't spend it all. And be here by six. The last bus is at half-past-six,' Khatri said. He hailed a cycle rickshaw and told the man, 'Secretariat.'

Omi looked around and blew out a deep breath.

'Are we still in India, are we?' Omi said, at his first sight of Chandigarh. The roads were wide and spotlessly clean. The buildings, pink and white and cream and grey, were strange but beautiful. They had straight lines, grilled façades or square pigeonholes stuck to the front. Omi was baffled a little but impressed a lot.

'Best and beautiful, this is,' he said.

'Wait till you see the rest. They got an Englishman to design all this,' Satish said. 'His name was Corbusa or something, a pukka Angrez.'

'Fucking intelligent they are, Englishmen. Just look at all this,' Omi said.

'Where shall we go now? Shall we have something to eat to start with? Sight-seeing is best on a full tummy.'

'My tummy is full. Had lunch before leaving.'

'Let's have something special. A dhosa.'

49

'What's that? Where do you get it?' Omi had good reason to ask this, for there weren't any food stalls or rehris or dhabas anywhere.

'There. Across the square. Read that sign — Annapurna.'

Satish took him to the large but cheap restaurant, Annapurna. Omi locked the bike outside and walked behind Satish into the busy world of dhosa-eaters. He couldn't walk straight. He thought everybody was looking at the village idiot.

'Walk like a man, you fool. No one is looking at you,' Satish nudged him.

The dhosa was like a folded chappati, but crisp and full of vegetables and coconut sauce. 'Like it? Speciality of Madras,' Satish said in a hushed voice.

Omi did not know whether he liked it or not, but he was impressed. Madras, like Bombay, spelled unapproachable glamour.

'I say, did you notice they are showing *Nagin* at the cinema?' Satish said.

Nagin was the all-time box-office record-breaker.

'Greatest film ever made. Vijayanti Mala, yaar. Fantastic tits. You got to see.'

'But we've come here to see the capital, its famous buildings, Satish.'

'You are going to spend the rest of your life here, aren't you? Well, then. But you won't get another chance to see *Nagin* and Vijayanti Mala in it. Those tits. Ummm . . .' Satish held something round and imaginary in his hands and kissed the stale air of Annapurna.

'What about my father? What if he finds out? What will we tell him?'

'He won't find out. The show finishes at five-thirty. We will be at the bus stop before he returns. And when he asks what we saw we can say we saw the High Court, the Secretariat, the Assembly, the Lake, the Governor's Palace . . .'

'What if he asks what they look like? You don't know my father.'

'Say the Secretariat looks like a huge American hotel, the water of the lake is too muddy and the High Court looks like the grandstand of a racecourse.'

'I am no good at lying to my father. Somehow he always finds out.'

'But why should he even suspect you of lying today? Hurry up if you want to get the tickets. You are going to see *Nagin*, you know. Did you see the crowd at the cinema? These dhosa-eating men, too. Everybody is going for those tits.'

There was a big crowd at the ticket office in the front of the cinema. But that was for the expensive seats — one rupee five annas and two rupees ten annas. They were going to the side of the cinema where the ticket office sold tickets for the cheap seats at ten annas. At the ticket office the all-male crowd was crushing, its mood unpredictable. Every now and then there were ripples suggesting a fight somewhere. It was hopeless standing there.

'Shall we go sight-seeing then?' Omi said. He was intimidated by the rough crowd.

'Wait, we'll get tickets alright.'

'But how, yaar?'

'On the black market.' Satish winked.

'I haven't got enough money.'

'No problem, I have. Pay me the difference another time.'

A man passed whispering, 'tickets, tickets,' close to their ears.

'How much?' Satish whispered back.

'One five,' the man said through his teeth.

'One rupee,' Satish said.

'You must be joking, babu ji,' the man said and walked away.

'What now?' Omi said. He felt uncomfortable by all that whispering. It had an air of illegality about it.

'Don't worry,' Satish said.

Another man passed whispering, 'tickets, tickets.'

'How much for two?' Satish asked in a whisper.

'Three rupees.'

'You must be joking,' Satish said.

'In five minutes it will be two rupees a ticket, babu ji.'

The two boys looked at each other.

'No,' Satish said.

The man walked away.

'Let's go sight-seeing, yaar,' Omi said.

'Trouble with you is you give up too easily. Wait here a minute,' Satish said and left him. A few minutes later he was back. He flashed two tickets at Omi.

'How much did you pay?'

51

'Two eight for the two.'

'But that's double the price.'

'This is not your Camp, Omi son. This is Chandigarh.'

The interior of the cinema was even more impressive than the exterior. Soft lights, cosy seats and the screen seemed half-a-mile wide.

'Ever seen anything like it before, Omi son? Worth every penny.'

During the interval Satish brought Omi to the restaurant on the ground floor. It faced the afternoon sun and the smoked-glass windows filled the place with a strange light. Omi was uncomfortable, but impressed.

'Wait till you see the other,' Satish said and led him up a wide staircase.

The restaurant for the two-ten class dazzled Omi. Well-dressed men and women sat on sofas or leaned against the mirrored walls, or stood by the bay-shaped bar with their elbows resting on its polished surface. They spoke English. It was a kind of English Omi had never heard before.

'High society of the capital,' Satish whispered.

Omi took a deep breath.

'This is life,' Omi said to himself. 'The day I come to live in Chandigarh I shall sit only in this gallery, no matter what it costs. After all.'

'Want tea?' Satish asked.

Omi nodded. The man behind the bar looked them over and pushed two porcelain cups and a small pot of tea towards them.

'Ten annas,' the man said.

Satish gave him twelve.

'Why twelve? You gone mad?' Omi whispered.

'Tip. Got to do it here. Everyone does. Otherwise they will think you are jat-dhoosh uncultured type.'

'Twelve annas for this mean pot of tea! Mother-fucking thugs. In Panchkoola you can buy as many cups as annas.' Omi could not get over it.

The bell rang. Omi looked at the clock above the bar. Half-past-four. Omi and Satish hurried down to their ten-anna seats. The lights had gone and the screen was alive with a dance and a song. Vijayanti Mala was showing what the world had come to see.

'It was half-past-four when we came in. The film won't finish until six,' Omi said.

'Don't worry, yaar. We can leave in time if the film hasn't finished,' Satish said.

'Shut up, you fun-spoilers,' a number of voices shouted from behind.

Vijayanti Mala took over and they remained shut up till the end. It was six-fifteen.

'And my father?' Omi panicked.

'We'll say we got lost.'

But unknown to them, Khatri saw them coming out of the cinema.

'Let the bastard reach home,' Khatri said to himself. Nothing had gone right that day. He had hung around in the pillared verandah of the old Secretariat, pressed many a rupee in the palms of the peons to get his files moved from one desk to another. But it was one of those days. The burra sahib, the head clerk, simply wasn't interested. Even Gulati could not prevail upon him to listen to the pleas of a poor man like Khatri. It needed something more, Gulati had hinted, to Khatri's increasing dismay.

'What did you see, boys?' Khatri asked.

Omi did not know what to say. He hesitated between the truth and a lie. There was a look in his father's eye which only meant one thing.

'Whether Father suspects or not, there is a beating at the end of the journey anyway,' Omi reasoned. 'If our story convinces him it might be less severe, but if it doesn't . . . Better tell the truth.'

But Satish didn't give him a chance.

'I took him to see the High Court, the new Secretariat, the Assembly, the Lake . . .'

'Acchhaa? Yes? And did you like what you saw?'

'Very much, Father. Absolutely beautiful.'

'Really? Let's catch the bus, then — if we haven't missed it, that is. When we reach home we will listen to the rest of your story.'

The bus driver hooted twice as he recognised Khatri.

'But where is your bike?' Khatri said.

'My bike!' Omi cried.

The two boys ran to Annapurna. Khatri had a word with the driver and followed them. The bike was gone. They looked everywhere and asked everybody, but nobody had seen it. Khatri looked at Omi. Omi looked at his feet. Satish looked away. The three walked back mournfully to the waiting bus. Nobody uttered a word during the seven-mile journey. Everybody knew what lay at the end of it — a pair of broken legs. Khatri's face was dark and ominous like a menacing silent monsoon cloud, needing only a spark to blast it into the fury of thunder and storm.

Aneja stood in the headlights of the bus, scratching the middle of his sutthan.

'Took so long. What happened?' he asked Khatri. He was worried.

'Ask the boys.'

Aneja didn't have to ask the boys. He knew. He whacked Satish on the head.

'What did you do, you son of a bitch?' Aneja screamed.

'*Nagin*. Saw *Nagin*,' Satish shrieked at once. A moment's delay would have brought down a shower of blows.

The shower of blows came down anyway as Aneja caught his son by an ear and dragged him home, watched by a growing crowd of the Panchkoolans.

'Whose idea was it?'

'Omi's.'

'How many times have I told you not to waste time with that good-for-nothing two-time matric-sitter?'

More blows fell as Satish howled in pain and the size of the crowd increased. 'If I see you with him ever again . . .'

Khatri waited till they were inside the back room of his shop. Then, without a word, he began. His peshawari sandal rained non-stop. Omi howled in pain.

'Whose idea was it?'

'Satish's.'

'How many times have I told you not waste time with that son of a dog?'

Omi howled.

'And the bike. I spent ninety rupees on it only last year.'

Seva Singh intervened as usual and saved Omi. He offered him food. Omi refused to eat.

'Will you eat or not?' Khatri roared, giving him a couple of kicks.

54

It worked. Omi started to eat with a mouth full of sobs. To resist further could only result in more beating. Khatri was really furious. Everything had gone wrong that day. The treatment he had received at the Secretariat had made the prospect of getting even one shop in the capital uncertain. On top of all that was the loss of the bike.

'Ninety rupees!'

Khatri bought Omi an old bike so that he could continue his tuition.

'You lose this one and you will have lost your skin. I will simply peel it off you. Just like this . . .' Khatri showed him how.

'He won't. He is a smart lad, our Omi bau,' Seva Singh said.

'He is a bewakoof fool who doesn't know the meaning of the word money. He thinks it has no use unless it can be wasted.'

The net result of the capital adventure was that Omi started to study harder. Khatri noted it, but only from the corners of his eyes. Unlike Aneja, he had not laid any restrictions on Omi about seeing Satish. But he didn't allow him to have anything to do with the election campaign of Jan Sangh which the Sangh cadets supported. One day when he saw Omi with a Jan Sangh badge on his chest, his nostrils flared.

'Come here fatta-fatt at once, you Sanghi-bhangi untouchable,' he shouted. 'Where did you get that raddi rubbish?' Khatri was in a rough mood. He was going somewhere.

'At Sangh. To support Dev Raj Sharma,' Omi said.

'Take it off fatta-fatt and throw it away in the river, or . . .'

Omi took the badge off.

'I don't mind if you go to Sangh for games. But for their politics, I mind. Understand?'

'Father's politics are Father's. Mine are Mine. I am a Sanghi,' Omi said to himself and pinned the badge on again as soon as he saw his father board a lorry bound for Manimajra.

'What's this?' Satish asked, coming up to see Omi, in spite of his father's warning.

'Want one?'

'Yeah.'

Omi gave him several, as well as scented cards with Jan Sangh material on them. This was their first meeting since Chandigarh. The conversation naturally moved on to *Nagin* and sex.

'Fabulous tits those, weren't they? What did I tell you, Omi son? In that last dance when she bent down towards us, I really thought they would burst out of her blouse. My chap was up at ninety degrees and going cock-a-doodle-do. Absolutely berserk. Wasn't yours?'

Omi knew what he was expected to say.

'Mine too. Bilkul. Pukka ninety degrees.'

'How much of the ruler does it do?'

Omi did not understand. But Satish spelled it out.

'How long is it, you bewakoof fool?'

'Is it necessary to know?'

'Just curiosity, yaar.'

'How long is yours?'

Satish thought for a moment.

'Six inches. At least. And yours?'

Omi thought for a moment.

'Six inches. At least.'

'What we need is a ruler. A twelve-inch ruler.'

'Not a yard?'

'Maybe, in a couple of years — I'm still growing. But what about Chandi Mandir? Interested? Ideal day, today. Sunny and warm. They may be out there. Besides our fathers are away.

'Where has yours gone to?'

'To see an important man in the capital.'

That decided the issue. They went on two bikes. Near the spot they hid their bikes between the road and the river and made their way through the bushes like trained soldiers, noiselessly.

The afternoon was tense. The usual breeze, a notable characteristic of the valley, was absent today, making the sun sharper. The sound of little leaps of truant water breaking over the general hum of the river reached them clearly. There was also the slap-slapping of the Rajasthani women beating their washing with wooden bats. There were several of them — naked, half-naked and clothed in their colourful skin-tight blouses. As the boys got nearer, they could hear the sound of talk and laughter.

'Look, look, look,' Satish whispered.

Some fifty feet from them a young woman was getting out of her clothes. She removed her blouse revealing two fair breasts. She shivered as she anticipated the touch of the cold river water on her bare flesh. Then she released the waist cord of her skirt and let it fall with a jingle of tinsel bells at the hem. Unaware of the excited gaze of the two boys, she slowly entered the water. Feet, ankles, knees, thighs, hips and a part of her torso, just up to her breasts — the water was only that deep. She splashed water on herself, rubbed her breasts and, arching her spine, immersed herself up to the chin. A few minutes later she came out. Once outside the water she stood in direct view of the rascals, shaking her shivery body free of water. The next moment she was dressed and had walked away towards the other women down the river.

Omi and Satish withdrew in silence. They didn't stay for another such Godsend. It was enough. For the first time Omi had seen a completely naked young woman. He had seen his mother without clothes, but that was different. She was his mother.

'Well, what do you say, Omi son?' Satish said after a long silence.

Omi said nothing. He had felt an awakening in his shorts when the woman stood facing them, dripping with water. It was gone now. Now he felt flushed in the face.

'Fabulous . . .' Satish hissed.

Omi nodded in silence.

'. . . All my six inches cock-a-doodle-do. What about you?'

Omi said nothing.

'What about your Manimajra girl? Any progress?'

Omi shook his head.

'Didn't you write her a letter?'

'No point. What could I have written? How could I have given it to her?'

'Not seen her since? Not given her more tits-massage?'

'She looks and smiles. That's all.'

'They say if she gives you smiles, she'll give anything. Anything. It is up to you to take. Ask her to meet you at nightfall in the fields.'

A peacock flew past them over the bushes.

'You want me to look like his arse, no?' Omi said, pointing to the peacock. 'What if she hands the letter to her brother?'

'Child of yesterday, that's what you are. Why should she? If she let you handle her titties then she obviously wants it. Can't you see?

Perhaps you can't because OP Khatri, Vladivostok wallah, is fucking blind.'

'What shall I write?'

'Say, "there is no other way to meet you, unless you come to the sugar-cane field at such and such time today or tomorrow evening . . ." Give a tender touch and say, ". . . there is so much to say to you. I am dying to say it. Please let me . . . please." Change my name if she doesn't turn up.'

That night Omi composed a letter in Hindi, using the *we* and *us* of the great Urdu poets:

Ever since that moment, that day, we are not the same man. Our heart and soul, now no longer our own, are forever filled with your divinely lovely form. If our eyes do not behold you even for a single day, life becomes meaningless. We long for you so much . . . so much. There is only one way in which we can meet — in the fields behind your street after my lesson. Today. There is so much to say to you. I am dying to say it. Please let me . . .

Your devotee.

The letter was written. What was needed was an opportunity.

The opportunity presented itself. The election was only a few days away. Ashok was caught up in the election fever. He went to neighbouring villages to give speeches. He travelled in tongas and rickshaws with loudspeakers run on car batteries. He told the villagers of 'our past glory', 'our future glory' and 'our great destiny', all of which lay with Jan Sangh.

One day Omi arrived for the lesson and Ashok was not to be seen.

'Gone to a village to give a lecture. Back soon,' Ashok's mother said.

'Good. Today is your day, Omi son. Will she come?' Omi waited.

To kill time he opened and shut books. But he was ready, absolutely ready with the letter in the breast pocket. Sometime later there was a noise in the verandah. Omi craned his neck to see. Guddy stood at the hand-pump in the verandah, filling a bucket.

'Now, Omi son.'

He came and stood in the doorway with the letter in his hand, quite amazed at his own courage. Guddy looked at him with half a smile and went on jerking the pump handle. She was puzzled to see that silly look on his face. Then she saw the letter in his hand and shrank in terror. She shook her head. Sleepily Omi advanced, whispering 'for you', and stretched out the hand with the letter. Guddy had no choice — a minute longer and someone would see. She took it and pushed it down her bodice. Omi retired in the same daze in which he had advanced, and collapsed in the reading-writing chair. What now?

'Constipated or something, Om Parkash?' Ashok said, coming into the room a minute later. 'Your face is white as this wall. What do you eat in Panchkoola?'

'I am alright. Of course, bilkul. What do you mean, Ashok ji?'

The letter was delivered. Now it was a question of a golden era of happiness — or ruin. Total ruin more likely.

'What if she gave it to her brother, Ashok so-and-so, BA, LLB?' Omi would run away to Bombay.

'But what will I do if she does come?'

He would do the things that a man does to a woman. Man things. But Guddy did not come.

Omi was sick, love-sick. He was smitten with ishk love, the age-old enemy of poets and fools like him. The disease became worse as the days passed. For there was no sign from Guddy. As far as she seemed concerned, Omi simply didn't exist. It was not surprising, therefore, that Omi lost all love for life, including his father's goodies — barfi, pera, jalebi, gajerela, laddu and the lot — and tried to bury himself in his books. The change was remarkable and it was commented upon.

'At this rate he will not only pass, he may even get some good marks — a second division maybe, Lala ji,' Ashok said, after addressing old Panchkoola one day.

Omi was listening. 'At this rate I will not only pass, I will simply pass away. Cremation ground,' he said to himself.

Khatri did not comment. It might slow the boy down if he did.

'Omi bau only lives for his tuition, it seems,' Seva Singh said. He was surprised that Omi no longer took advantage of his father's visits to the capital. But he had a hunch. That night Khatri went home and Seva decided to cook Omi butter parathas.

'Another one, Omi bau?' Seva asked after the second one.

'No,' Omi said tragically.

Seva nodded to himself — this was serious. Omi saying no to a butter paratha?

'Omi bau, any girl-shirl doing this to you?'

'What sort of talk, Seva Singh? Do I look that sort of person?'

Seva Singh thought before answering.

'Yes,' Seva said.

'Shows you how little you know me,' Omi said.

'Omi bau, take an old man's advice. Women are not worth it.'

But better advice came from Satish.

'Majnu Romeo, listen to me and pass on another letter. You got to give a woman time. They have to think before they take the plunge. They are different, you know.'

'Go wash your face and get off my back,' Omi replied.

'I have so much love and she none at all? Not possible,' Omi said to himself. It was difficult to understand. He decided to give it one last go. If it didn't work, he would call it a day. Never again would he look at another woman for as long as he lived. He would become a brahmacharya, life-long celibate.

He wrote another letter.

'Balls to her brother and the world. I am going to deliver it, broken jaws or not.'

A couple of days later he saw Guddy in the bazaar. He rang his bicycle bell several times. When she looked up at him, he dropped the letter at her feet. Guddy looked to her left and right, hastily picked up the epistle and introduced it into her bodice with a terror-stricken face. Luckily no one was looking.

It was much the same sort of letter as the first one. But there was an important PS to it: *Should we perish before long, take the blame on your fair forehead which this sick heart kisses with more love than it has for its own life.*

Omi had written, signed and delivered the letter in front of the whole world, in a bazaar. If an answer did not come he would do what he had to do. He had no doubt about it.

An answer came. But not before a lot of suffering and some comments.

'Sure, sure. Give up this blasted exam if it is going to kill you to

pass it. Became an illiterate halwai like your father,' Khatri said
crossly.

'Omi bau, you are killing Lala ji now, you know,' Seva said.
Khatri was not eating very much now.

'Romeo died, Majnu died, Ranjha died. And you are a mere
Omi. Best suggestion — go unto a fast and lay down your breath as
a man's son should, with shaan dignity. At your funeral it will be
said *here goes a man who loved and died of it*,' Satish said.

'Go wash your face, you dog son,' Omi replied.

'Well-known fact that Romeos never listen to sense. If they
did . . .'

'I said go wash your face. Or else.'

'The Election is just round the corner. Martyrise yourself.
Become a shaheed martyr. Make headlines and beat Congress at its
own game. You'll become famous. Just like that.'

Election day came, changing the face of Panchkoola. There were
grand and colourful shamiana marquees everywhere. Everywhere
there fluttered little paper flags in all the colours of the rainbow,
between the shops and shamianas and between the shamianas and
the trees. People walked and talked with an air of urgency, for
Panchkoola was a polling station.

Congress and Jan Sangh had the largest shamianas with the
largest number of helpers. Congress was camped right near
the shops, Jan Sangh occupied the space between the shops and the
trees. The Akalis were near the river and the Praja Socialists were
next to them. The Communists were on the road to Chandigarh
and Sher Singh, a local jagirdar land-owner and the Independent
candidate who campaigned under the image of a tiger, was right
opposite the Communists.

In the middle of all this was stationed the Polling Officer who
represented the Government. This gentleman was actually a railway stationmaster at Dhulkote. This proved to be of interest to
Khatri. He was slightly acquainted with the man, Kandhari, from
his Camp days — Dhulkote station was only a stone's throw from
Camp Baldev Nagar.

Long before polling time, voters started to arrive. Party lorries
brought groups of families from the surrounding villages. These

families, voters and their children, sat on their haunches around the shop and stalls, waiting vacantly. The men, clad in tent-like khadi homespun, sat in groups pulling at hookahs. The women, half veiled by the dupatta breast-scarf or the sari, sat away from the men, minding the children. The policemen outside the Polling Officer's tent, their legs and calves wrapped up in khaki woollen bandage to keep the cold out, shifted their weight from leg to leg and eyed the village women lustily.

It was a *bumper* day for Panchkoola. Khatri loved a day when he was so busy that he did not even have the time to feel happy about it. It was like Diwali when everybody must eat sweets.

Without waiting to be asked, Khatri sent a tray of sweets and a pot of tea to his acquaintance in the Government tent. Kandhari, the Polling Officer, was flattered. At lunch-time Khatri waited for an order — it was owing to him. But it was not forthcoming. Instead of sending Seva or Bawa, he sent Omi over. It was good tactics.

'I was just about to send my man,' Kandhari said, taking a good look at Omi. 'Are you Lala ji's son?'

Omi said he was. Kandhari had another look at Omi.

'Come and sit down and tell me your name.'

Omi told him. He also explained that he was studying for his matric and only helping his father out that day, to make it clear that he was not a shop boy.

'What will you do after passing your exams?'

'College.' Omi had never really given it a thought. He said the first thing that came to him.

'Where?'

'Chandigarh.' Omi explained that the Khatris were on their way to the capital. 'The Government is giving us two shops there.'

'What will you read at College?'

'Science.' The subject that hurt his guts the most.

'To be an engineer?'

Everybody in India wants to be an engineer. Omi nodded. It was flattering to be a subject of interest to the Polling Officer, the boss of the whole Election tamasha spectacle.

'I want to sit for the army exams. I want to become an officer.' Omi knew he was lying through his teeth, but the Polling Officer was a stranger and strangers are a liar's best audience.

'You look just right for the army,' the Polling Officer said, echoing the words of the man from Ambala. 'A lot of English you need for that, though. How good is your English?' he asked in English.

'It is not bad for someone of my age and experience,' Omi replied in English, swaying his head from left to right.

'Excellent. If Lala ji is not busy, ask him to come and see me.'

Omi ran back and passed on the message. Khatri placed his son in his gaddi seat and gave him a warning.

'Don't put your mouth in the sweets or your hand in the galla, understand?'

'Don't worry, Father. You know me.'

'That's why I am warning you.'

Khatri walked off to the Government shamiana, unable to suppress a smile at his son's last three words.

'Your son is a delightful boy, Lala ji,' the Polling Officer said after the customary small talk devoted to each other's welfare. 'What plans do you have for him?'

Khatri instantly knew what it was all about.

'He is as yet a young lad, not sixteen yet. I want him to get a good education. At least a BA.'

'What do you want him to do afterwards?'

Khatri became alert.

'Business . . .'

'He seems interested in the army career,' Kandhari said.

This was news to Khatri. He smiled. 'Yes, but he is interested in so many things.'

'The point is to guide him into a decent career.'

Had the Polling Officer, in the middle of all that polling, called him here to tell him how to guide his son? Khatri gave him a searching look and waited for him to come to the point.

Kandhari wasted no more time. 'I have a daughter, Lala ji . . .'

So there.

'. . . She is as yet, like your Om Parkash, very young. But you know and I know how fast children grow up in this day and age of cinema and films. Therefore, perhaps it is wise to think of their future well in advance. You agree?'

Khatri nodded his head in agreement, his initial feeling of surprise transformed to a glow of importance. Kandhari might be a stationmaster — and he, Khatri, a halwai — but he, Khatri, had

63

the son. And what of Dhulkote? It was only a twiddle of a station where only a few trains stopped. But one day Kandhari might get a bigger one. Perhaps Chandigarh itself. Who knew.

'She is, like your Om Parkash, our only child . . .'

This was a welcome piece of news. One doesn't want brothers and sisters in the way when it comes to dowries.

'. . . and she is only fourteen. So there is plenty of time. And, if her mother approves, and you approve, perhaps we could talk further. We are, after all, the same biratheri, Khatris and Kandharis, the same cast unit.'

It was true and nobody from the unit married outside it. Khatri nodded his head thoughtfully and looked at his wrist-watch.

'Send us some lunch, Lala ji, and let me pay for the refreshments I had this morning.'

'No, no, no, Station Master Sahib.'

'Yes, yes, yes, Lala ji.'

'But.'

'No but-shut. I can't be in debt to someone who may become my daughter's father-in-law. I am a Hindu, not a mallachaa.'

Coming back to his shop Khatri dismissed his son by waving a hand.

'Been in the sweets, boy?'

'Father!'

'Been in the cash box?'

'Father!' How could he tell his father that he no longer cared for such mundane things as sweets (though he had transferred a few coins to his pockets — they might come in handy one day).

'Off you go to your reading-writing.'

Omi ran to his hut.

'Seva Singh, are you going to give your vote?' Khatri said.

'Forgot all about it. Might as well go along and put it in the tin.'

'Who will you vote for?'

'Haven't thought about it. The Akalis have been pressing.'

'Waste of time putting your vote in the Akali box. Put it in the Congress box if you want to listen to me.'

'Omi bau has been after me for Jan Sangh.'

'How many times have I told him to remain clear of their politics? It seems his arse is itching for my peshawari chappall.'

Ashok was seen coming towards the shop.

'Haven't you voted yet, Lala ji? Don't forget us. After all, if not friends like you, who else will help us?'

'Vote for *them*, the sanghi-bhangi leeches?' Khatri said loudly as Ashok disappeared.

He was among the last of the voters. After the vote Kandhari stopped him outside the tent.

'It appears as if I will not be able to get home tonight after all. The count will take a long time.'

'Lorries keep going all night.'

'We shall see.'

But Khatri knew he wanted to stay there for the night.

The day was done. The growing shadows of the tall mangoes were swallowing Panchkoola. The shamianas were taken down and loaded on to tongas to be carted away. Panchkoola was returning to normal. The Government sat down to open the ballot boxes and Khatri went to the back room of the shop to add up the day's takings. He folded the notes expertly and tucked them into the deep pocket inside his vest, next to his skin and entered the loose change in the long red khastar register.

The count took a long time. At the end of it, Khatri and Kandhari sat down to dinner inside the Government tent. Seva was cooking and Bawa ran between the shop and the tent with piping-hot chappatis, plates of goat curry and other things. Omi was with his books.

'Perhaps your wife would like to see our Munni. No problem. She is welcome at the station any day, less than a mile from the Camp. Any day. Ten minutes by rickshaw.'

Khatri nodded.

They spoke of Khatri's plans for Chandigarh, and of Omi's future.

'First thing, he should learn to speak English fluently. That will open doors for him. Get him a real College Professor to teach him English in the capital. Any assistance you need — I am not unknown there, you know — let us know. After all, he is almost our own son now.'

Congress won. Jan Sangh was second in the poll but the gap between them was vast enough to be humiliating. Omi was hurt.

He felt betrayed. But he didn't talk about it during his lesson with Ashok the next day.

'What's the point? What's done is done.'

Nor did Ashok refer to it until the end of the lesson.

'Congress won on false promises. We lost because we made true promises. In politics, no one believes you if you tell them the truth. We said India needs to be strong; Congress said India needs more agriculture, more factories and more education. Now, if you are strong, you will have all that anyway. No problem. Look at America, strongest country in the world and it has everything.'

'Will Sangh pack up now?'

'No, no, no, we have no direct connection. We were only helping . . . volunteers . . .'

Omi knew that Ashok was deluding himself. All Omi wanted to say was, 'Dear boring Sir, where is your sister?'

'. . . The Sangh meetings will go on as usual. You are coming today? But of course.'

'Father is not very well.' Khatri was perfectly alright.

'Ohho? But he looked alright yesterday.'

Omi had forgotten that Ashok was in Panchkoola doing last-minute canvassing.

'His back. Comes and goes.'

'Come for a few minutes . . . We could do with your moral support.'

Omi had to give in.

'Back in a minute,' Ashok said and ran upstairs to change into his khaki Sangh knickers.

While Ashok was upstairs, who should show up in the veran-dah? Omi's heart missed a beat. Twice Guddy crossed the verandah and as she went she darted glances into the tuition room.

Life returned to Omi. His heart beat as fast as the pistons of an express railway engine.

'She cares for you, Omi son. She wants you, boy. She does, she does, she does.'

Then all of a sudden his heart stopped beating. All of a sudden Guddy came right into the tuition room, took out a little square of a paper from her bodice and smacked it on the tuition table. Next moment she was gone.

'You taken ill or something, Om Parkash? Your face is white as the walls,' Ashok said, coming in after his sister. He felt his forehead and pulse. 'I think you better go home then.'

Talking with the wind on his bike, Omi read the letter twenty times: '*I know I should not be writing this, but I am. I cannot come to see you where you suggest. I have my shame to think of.*'

That was all. Omi was full of disappointment. He was full of happiness.

'My first love letter,' he said loudly to the lonely road with moist eyes.

That night he asked Seva for butter parathas and ate four of them.

'You celebrating your defeat or our victory?' Khatri said. 'Life isn't all that bad, Omi bau,' Seva said with a smile.

'The furnace is ready and yearning for your iron. Drop it in. Now,' Satish said.

'But how?'

'I don't know. Work out a way of meeting her yourself. You've got to do some work yourself, I can't do *everything* for you, not that I mind.'

Omi didn't know what to do. Something must happen.

'Something has got to happen. Otherwise.'

It happened.

One day, after his lesson, Omi decided to go to the newly arrived touring-talkie. It was showing a famous recent film, *Awara*, with two of the greatest names of the Indian cinema — Raj Kapoor and Nargis. Omi, who had no hope of being allowed to see it, wanted to look at the photographs displayed on the cinema's corrugated-iron walls. Khatri was away at the Camp and he could loiter there as long as he liked.

He spent some time looking at the photographs, and then some money at the stalls on things his father would have called 'rubbish' — such as channa-roasted chickpeas, phulian (roasted rice grains), marunda (a slab of roasted rice and sugar), nuts, boiled sweets and so on. Then, on an impulse, he decided to cut across the fields, avoiding the town centre and saving half a mile. As he approached the sugar-cane field behind Guddy's house, he caught sight of someone like her at the unattended well. Leaving his bike he ran to the well. It was Guddy, but there was another girl with her. On seeing him, this other girl gave a knowing smile and quickly put herself out of sight. Omi saw her disappear into the sugar cane.

Omi felt quite foolish. He did not quite know why he had come. He certainly did not know what to say. Guddy, too, was speechless. Usually pretty, she looked even more so in that confusion. She blushed deeply and bit at her dupatta scarf, shifting her startled eyes from Omi's to her feet. She looked very shy. Omi wished he had not gone that way.

They stood there for what was clearly an eternity. Finally Guddy broke the silence.

'Why did you follow me?'

'I didn't. I saw you and came over.'

'Go away, somebody will see us.'

Omi took her hand in his and drew her close to him. Guddy did not withdraw.

'Someone might see. Then what will happen?'

'No one will see us in the sugar bushes.'

Omi pulled her into the sugar cane. She did not resist. It was cool and green and there was no sound except that of the breeze whispering through the tall sugar cane. They held each other and stood cheek to cheek.

'I do love you. Very much. I can die . . .' Omi said.

'Please . . .'

Omi burned with an intense longing to put his hand into the bodice of her shirt. He tried. She let him. Her mango-shaped breasts felt warm like the meek doves he had so often brought down with his catapult in the Camp and on the river side. They always felt like that, warm, as they throbbed with dying life in his hands.

He kissed her on the cheeks, the forehead, the eyes, but couldn't muster enough courage to kiss her on the lips.

'I love you so. Not possible, so much love.'

'Om,' she said and suddenly she was crying. Two huge tear drops fell on his hand.

Omi too started to cry.

Guddy's friend made a sound of clearing her throat. It sounded like a warning. Guddy shivered in his arms and was out and gone in a moment. Omi wiped his eyes on his sleeve and waited until the girls were safely out of sight. Five minutes later he jumped onto his bike and cycled home in a trance.

At Panchkoola he was almost run over by Bhola Ram.

'Om Parkash, how can you sleep and cycle at the same time?'

Bhola Ram screamed from the cab of his lorry and slapped his forehead in disgust.

'Didn't see you, uncle Bhola Ram.'

'The youth of today, their brains are in their ankles.'

'Honest, uncle Bhola Ram, didn't see you.'

'Honest, nephew Om Parkash, I thought you had some sense in that head of yours. My fault, I was wrong.' Bhola Ram slapped his head again and drove off.

Omi looked out for Satish as he crossed the shops. He even called out to him, a thing he would not normally do, for that would get Satish into trouble with his father. But Satish was one of those people who were never there when you wanted them. And he had never been wanted more than today. Omi had to talk to him.

Seva knew where he was.

'Gone to Chandigarh with his father. They have gone to get their shops. They will be back on the last bus.'

Later when Omi heard the bus arrive, its doors open and shut, he ran out and stood half-way between the bus and the Aneja shop. Satish was walking by the side of his father. The boys pretended they had never seen each other before. Aneja realised that a silent signal had passed between them and he tried to ignore it. But he gave Omi a long dirty look.

'Studying hard, Om Parkash? Must pass the matric this year. Can't go on failing every year. Bad influence on other people,' Aneja said, passing Omi.

Omi hated Aneja. He smiled foolishly and called him a mother-layer inside his throat.

After dinner, as Omi lay in his bed reading about the third battle of Panipat, Satish tapped on his window. Satish knew, as he knew everything, that *it* had happened.

'Put it here,' Omi said, throwing out a hand. The two boys had a hearty handshake.

'Shabas, shabas, bravo, bravo — Ustad Guru.'

'I got her today.'

'You mean you laid her?'

Omi did not answer.

'On your knees to Mahaguru Satish, on your knees. Has she got a friend? How about me? After all.'

Omi told him the story.

'You fool. You utter and total fool. You mean you had her there in the sugar cane and you didn't ground her? Oh God, what sort of a man am I dealing with?'

'But we are in love with each other.'

'Don't give me that lidd horseshit. There is no such thing as love. Besides, everything is fair in love and war.'

Omi didn't know how to explain what it meant being in love.

'What could I do?'

'You could have done what a man would have done. But you are not a man, you are an insect. Even insects do it. Never mind. Behave like a man next time. That's all. And tell me, is her friend good-looking?'

Omi couldn't remember what she looked like.

'Never mind, yaar. As long as she is not one-eyed or one-legged. Ask her to bring her friend along next time. Perhaps a foursome will strike a better bargain. I will kindle the fire and light the way. You just follow the leader. You do to your girl what I do to mine.'

'But how the hell am I to ask her to meet me first? And where?'

Satish looked up at the starry sky.

'Oh God! You gave a starving man a bowl of rice pudding but didn't teach him how to eat it. Tragedy of tragedies. Our tragedy — India's tragedy — we simply don't know how to help ourselves.'

A lorry came to a halt and Omi heard his father murmur his thanks to the driver.

'Piss off, Mahaguru Satish Kumar, if you don't want an arse-splitting beating from my old man.'

'Oh God!' Satish muttered, looking up at the sky, and disappeared in the darkness of the bus stand.

Khatri was in a good mood. Omi knew he had had a peg or two on the way. But he was surprised that he had not stayed the night at the Camp.

Khatri carried a basket.

'What have you been doing, boy?'

'Reading-writing, Father. I thought you would stay with Mother tonight.'

'Road Ways on strike tomorrow. That's why. Here, take this.'

Omi looked in the basket. Sweets.

'Sweets?' Omi said. It was like carrying bamboos to Bareily or coal to Newcastle.

There was also a blue poplin shirt and a fountain pen.

'All for you.'

'For me? But.'

Khatri changed the subject.

'Your mother says you should be going home soon for your exams. Today I made arrangements with your school. You sit as a private candidate and you better pass this time. Otherwise you will blacken my face . . .'

'But the sweets and the shirt and the fountain pen?' Where had they come from? Khatri ignored the question.

'. . . We have so many plans for you. In our new capital you will live like a man's son. Proper. Like a gentleman. We'll hire a pukka College Professor to teach you to speak English like the sons of officer people, the burra saabs. But you must pass matric exam this time. Don't blacken my face. Understand?'

Omi was puzzled.

'Perhaps Father had more than two pegs?'

Omi fell in love with the shirt. Blue was his favourite colour and the poplin was soft. He tried it on. Just right. Omi would wear it for Guddy tomorrow. Wait till she saw him. She would be drawn to him by invisible threads.

'When are we going to Chandigarh, Father?'

'God willing, soon. Soon. Two months, three months.'

So soon! And Guddy?

'But you go home as soon as this tuition is over.'

'No hurry, Father. Six whole weeks to the exams.'

'When do you have to pay Ashok?'

'On the fifteenth.'

'You better go home on the sixteenth then. We will see how Ashok, the sanghi-bhangi, worked for his hundred rupees.'

So Omi had only ten more days with Guddy. What would she think when she found out that he was being sent away from her? Would she be sad?

'Ten more days for man things.'

But the next day Guddy was not to be seen. Omi pricked up his ears like Dabbu, his companion in distress, listening to every sound. listening for a sound of her. But Guddy didn't come.

'Please come, my dearest. Come to your Omi, your servant for life.'

He looked at his shirt and thought of the invisible threads.

'Aré Om Parkash, where is your mind today?' Ashok said looking at his new shirt. 'Are you preparing for your exams or for a film auditioning?'

Omi delayed his departure by engaging Ashok in a bout of unnecessary questions, hoping Guddy would show up. Ashok, somewhat surprised at Omi's ardour for his studies, and equally bored by it, idled through the answers. Finally he suggested that it was getting late.

'We will go into all that tomorrow.' Ashok dismissed Omi.

Because Omi was late getting back, Satish drew the natural conclusion.

'Well done, hero. Shabas. Did you speak to her about the other girl and me?' Satish asked.

'Didn't even see her.'

Satish's face hung in disappointment. He looked sorrier than Omi.

'Maybe tomorrow. But don't forget,' he said hopefully.

'And if she still doesn't come?'

'Then we sit on the bank of the river and wank.'

But the next day Guddy did show herself. She had been ill, in bed with fever. And yet she came downstairs.

'What are you doing here? Back to bed upstairs, silly girl. You still have a high temperature.' Ashok rebuked her.

'This stupid country! I can't even ask him what is wrong with her.' Omi slapped his forehead in disgust.

'You see, what could I do?' Omi said to Satish back home.

'Invisible threads. At least she came down. For your bloody sake. She is in love with you, rat-face.'

Love! The word of the films. Whatever did it mean? Catching her in the fields, holding her against your body, caressing her mango-shaped breasts, and wanting to do it again and again? What now?

Nothing. Nothing happened during the following days.

'She must still be ill,' Satish said.

Omi certainly was. He pined away his last days in Panchkoola. He couldn't do anything. Asking Ashok about her would result in a broken jaw.

Guddy did get well before he left, but Omi noticed something different about her behaviour. She came and went, but she did not look into the tuition room. Omi could not understand.

'This is love, Omi son. You are smitten with ishk. Only way to put an end to this misery is the river. Drown yourself. Martyrise yourself. At least you'll have become famous,' Satish said.

Omi even refused to go and look at the naked Rajasthani women, and felt disloyal to Guddy for having looked at one.

The day of the last lesson arrived.

'Here,' Khatri said and gave him five ten-rupee notes. 'Pay off the sanghi-bhangi. If you don't pass the exam, I will break his legs also.'

Omi wore the blue poplin shirt and arrived at Ashok's much too early, hoping that Ashok would not be there and he would be able to see Guddy — maybe even talk to her. But Ashok was there.

'Early today, Om Parkash! Never mind, we will finish early. By the way, big big congratulations! You have scored over all of us.'

'Congratulations? For what?'

'Go on, go on. Don't hide it from your friends. Even if you kept it a secret, other people have kept us informed.'

What the hell was Ashok talking about?

'I have no idea what you are talking about, Ashok ji.'

'Is it possible? Your marriage and you know nothing about it?'

'*Marriage?* Mine?'

Ashok was obviously joking. But what a joke! Marriage!

Ashok realised that the surprise on Omi's face was not feigned. He became serious. Suddenly his tone changed.

'Haven't you been told?'

'Told what?' Panic took over Omi.

'That they have arranged a match for you.'

'Who?'

'Lala ji and the stationmaster of Dhulkote.'

The Polling Officer!

'When did they do so?'

'A couple of weeks ago.'

So that was it. That was why Guddy had vanished. Oh, that bastard stationmaster! What could Omi do now? He could not even tell her that he had been the last one to know of it. And that too through her brother, *her* brother.

'Marriage? For when?' Omi knew that instant what he was going to do. He was going to run away. For good.

'Oh, not for the near future. They want to give you a good education first . . . in the capital.'

So that's what the coals-to-Newcastle sweets and the shirt and the fountain pen had been all about. That's why a 'pukka College Professor' and English tuition in 'our new capital'. That mother-laying stationmaster of Dhulkote. That mother-laying know-all Bhola Ram. That mother-laying Election. That mother-laying Tirath Ram.

'I say,' he said to himself. 'Don't let them tie you down like this. You are so young and not without promise. Fight it off like the Punjabi that you are. Don't let them tie a rope around your neck so early in your life.'

Omi felt broken in two.

As he peddled back to Panchkoola for the last time, it became clear that life for him was over.

'Aurangzeb was less cruel to the Hindus and the Sikhs than they have been to my Guddy and me. Hitler was less cruel to the Jews. But what am I to do now?'

It was a straightforward thing. He could not lay down his arms. He had to take revenge.

'I will teach that Ma chod mother-laying stationmaster a lesson. I will, I will, I will.'

TWO

The first to greet Omi as he got off the bus was Dabbu. Omi didn't know how much he had missed him till he saw him. The bus stop was at the junction of the main road and City road, a hundred yards from the level-crossing. Dabbu sat outside one of the many wooden shacks and stalls halfway to the level-crossing. He went berserk when he saw Omi. He came running and wanted to climb Omi as if he was a tree. Dabbu barked and jumped and went mad with joy, wagging his tail so furiously that people feared it would drop off.

'There, there, there.' Omi hugged Dabbu.

A number of people stopped by to watch this touching reunion.

'Wah wah, wah wah! What love!' they said.

'There, there, there,' Omi said.

'This is love, true love,' the people said.

Ram Rakha, the tonga driver, offered to take Omi's things home in his tonga for nothing — it was only a few hundred yards away. They loaded up the tonga with Omi's trunk and bedding. Omi accompanied Ram Rakha on his bike, holding the side of the tonga with one hand. Dabbu ran alongside, his pink tongue darting in and out of his mouth, looking happy.

'Air is full of stories of your shops in the capital. Don't forget your poor old friends in your rich days, Om Parkash,' Ram Rakha said as he chucked at his horse through a missing front tooth. 'Tut, tut, tut, tut, tut . . .'

'Never, Ram Rakha, never. How are your mother-father and kid-kiddies?'

'All is well except for this poor animal. Need a young new horse to bring about a change in my kismet.'

'One has got to wait for the good things in life.'

'That's what I am doing — waiting. Horses come to those who wait.'

At home Paro was doing someone's hair. But it was not Banto. It was a young woman Omi had never seen before, a very beautiful young woman. Omi's heart missed a beat.

'It can't be!'

Paro hugged her son and started to cry.

'Fine welcome, this, Ma,' Omi said, stealing a glance at the beautiful young woman. It was difficult to look elsewhere. She looked at the mother and son with great interest.

Banto and other ladies from the street arrived to see Omi. They tried to calm down Paro, but Paro could not stop crying.

'I am coming home, Ma, not going away. There is a difference.'

Paro was interested in the difference. She sobbed. Banto boiled water for tea. Other ladies fussed over Omi. Omi had eyes only for the young woman.

'Grown taller, hasn't he?' Banto said.

'What, in two months?' Omi said.

'And fairer,' Banto said.

'I only went to Panchkoola, auntie, not Simla.'

Finally Paro stopped crying. She blew her nose, undid a knot in her dupatta breast-scarf, took out a half-rupee coin, waved it around Omi's head three times and gave it to old Thakri, the untouchable bhangi woman who was at that moment cleaning the latrine. This would keep the evil eye away from her son for some time.

Tea came. But who was this beautiful moon face?

'It can't be!' Omi's heart missed several beats as several thoughts crossed his confused mind.

It wasn't. It was the wife of the new neighbour. If Omi was relieved to know this, he was also disappointed. While he was in Panchkoola, a young married couple had come to live in the house of the lullaby-singing mother and her heavy-breathing child.

The moon face was also a very sad face, Omi thought, especially the eyes which seemed to be at the verge of tears. Her name was Rani. Omi was supposed to address her as Bharjai, which in Punjabi means brother's wife. Who this *brother* was did not matter. It was a custom, a minor but important safety device to prevent ambiguity in social relationships.

Omi did not know who this *brother* was, but he was grateful to him for coming to live next door. Omi learnt that *brother* had a clerical job at Dhulkote Power House and he saw him later that day as he arrived home from work on his bicycle.

Omi did not like him.

Brother was tall, thin and angular. He had a long face, a longish nose and protruding teeth. Omi did not like people like that. His name was Chaman Lal. Omi did not like that either.

The boys welcomed Omi back, though he felt there was a difference. They seemed to treat him differently than before. Was it because he had been away, while they had stayed where they had always been? The tuition with Ashok did not seem to have done him any harm at all. Once Omi was famous for his lack of information, now he seemed to know everything.

'Omi only had to go to Panchkoola to return an abler man,' Bhajju said.

'As if it were England,' Bali said.

'But Panchkoola-Returned, he is abler than he was. You must admit,' Des said.

'People travel seven seas to reach England. Why they do that, the fools?' Harpal said.

'Our Omi only had to travel twenty-odd miles on a lorry . . .' Bhajju said.

'. . . And come back on a bus like one of the *England-Returned*,' Bali said.

'Omi son, you want a queue of rich fathers of beautiful daughters outside your house? Then print on your door, *OP Khatri, Panchkoola-Returned*, and see,' Punnu, the one-legged said.

'Bewakoof fools. If Mahatma Gandhi was still alive, he would have shot himself out of shame on hearing you like this — with three bullets,' Omi said, giving Punnu a friendly kick in the arse.

'No harm trying, is there? You never know,' Punnu said, hopping away on his crutches.

'Punnu, I am going to chop your *second* leg off. I am telling you.'

Omi had forgotten the sound of Kailash's sad whistle. On his first night back home he heard it. It sounded so near, that groan.

Another night it sounded even nearer and full of greater pain. Omi heard it every other night, even when Kailash was not driving the train. Then one night Omi woke up and sat in his bed and listened. The heavy-breathing child was gasping for breath and choking, as if it was being smothered.

'Open up you useless barren bitch.'

A bad dream. Omi returned to sleep.

The same night a swarm of locust settled on the Camp and the countryside.

'Up, up, up,' Paro shouted early next morning. 'Come out and see.'

Omi rubbed his eyes and couldn't believe what he saw when he opened them. A carpet of these abominable creatures outside the house.

'Locust!' Omi had never seen the locust before.

When the sun rose, it was still dark. The air was thick with this giant-sized grasshopper. It looked like a small green corn with spindly legs, its leaves flapping like wings. It seemed to be raining and the rain was giant caterpillars with eyes like buttons. It was an incredible sight.

'This mother-laying locust,' Omi muttered.

Everybody was out in the street making a lot of noise. They were killing the creatures with their shoes and anything else they could lay their hands on.

'This mother-laying . . .'

Bhajju passed on his bike with a badminton racket in his right hand.

'Ninety-nine,' Bhajju said and stopped.

'Ninety-nine what?' Omi asked, rubbing his eyes.

'Ninety-nine my score. Top scorer.'

'You playing cricket on a day like this, you fool?'

'Ninety-nine locust I killed,' the top scorer said and completed his century with a brilliant stroke. 'There.'

The sun was fully risen, but it was still dark, like twilight. The boys came, all of them. They came with drums, trumpets, cymbals, bugles and the rest of the paraphernalia of the HS High School band.

'The crops!' they shouted. 'Got to save them. Otherwise there will be a famine.'

Men followed, led by Chandi Lal, the headmaster of the local primary school and a pillar of the local society. He was handing out things to make noise.

'Everybody out in the fields. Everybody,' Chandi Lal shouted urgently, handing Omi a dholuk drum. 'Make much noise. Drive the tiddi-dal locust away. Save the crops. Otherwise.'

The Camp had a population of five thousand, today it sounded like ten. Hundreds of volunteers — men, women and children — spread out into the fields. They carried empty ghee canisters, tin boxes, broken bicycle rims, dholuk drums, rickshaw and lorry hooters, and anything else that would make an unpleasant noise. Marching ahead of them were the boys with the equipment of the school band. They marched through fields of wheat, corn, choliya green barley, sugar cane and fruit orchards. They had a field-day helping themselves.

Chandi Lal was heard regretting his idea.

'Boys doing more harm than the locust. They are eating up everything,' Chandi Lal shouted with a pained faced. But nobody heard him. There was too much noise.

The day wore on, but there was no respite. The locust came. One by one the people went back home, worn out. Only the boys remained. Near dusk-fall they found themselves in a fruit orchard with much of the fruit destroyed by the locust. They decided to have a rest there and sample the fruit. The owners of the orchard were elsewhere, driving locust away from their more valuable crops of wheat and corn. Therefore the boys could eat as much as they liked.

'Omi says the Japanese eat snakes. I wish they ate locust,' Bhajju said, repeating his century-making stroke. 'We could export them. Become millionaires.'

Omi had had enough of fruit, choliya green barley and the vegetables. He longed for normal food, cooked food.

'Not even a ghoogi dove in sight I could kill and roast and eat,' Omi said, showing off his catapult. There hadn't been a bird in sight all day long.

'Why not roast a few locusts? I hear they taste finger-licking good. I hear from a reliable source. I also hear from the same source that they eat them in Vladivostok. True.'

'Why not roast a whole lot of them — quite a few of them

around — have a party and invite your reliable source?' Omi said.

The invasion started to subside as it grew darker. The boys marched back home, singing songs. A few hundred yards from the fruit orchard Omi realised that he had left something behind, Chandi Lal's dholuk. But no one would go back with him.

'Bastards. May snakes bite you on your way back,' Omi said crossly. He threw stones at them. The boys laughed and disappeared in the growing darkness.

It was pitch dark when Omi got to his dholuk.

'And now I have to walk back all by myself. This Ma chod locust and those Ma chod friends!'

It was about two miles from the Camp through bush and fields.

'What if a tiger comes along?'

The tiger no longer roamed these parts. Once upon a time it did and so the legend was still there.

'I will beat the dholuk so loudly that it will frighten the shit out of his arse and he will run away.'

Omi picked his way carefully, making the least amount of noise, not to attract the tiger and his fellow creatures of the wild. Half a mile from the fruit orchard Omi came upon a well-known shrine, an ancient marri tomb. A Devi Goddess or her ashes were supposed to be buried under it. It was an eight-foot-high pyramid of little red bricks. Childless women were known to pray here to conceive. Men were not supposed to come there, or even near it — that would be interfering with god — and they never did.

Omi knew this and hurriedly tried to withdraw when he realised where he was. Just then he heard the same sounds he had heard in his sleep last night, someone groaning. He hid behind a bush and listened. He saw a dark shadow by the pyramid, a human shape. His heart almost stopped beating: a ghost.

The shadow lit a little earthen lamp and placed it at the base of the pyramid. In the dim light of the earthen lamp Omi saw that it was a woman. She took off her clothes and started to dance slowly in front of the pyramid, wailing softly. She went around the pyramid three times and started to dance wildly, wailing louder and louder. She tore at her hair and beat her naked breasts and Omi thought she was a daian witch. Suddenly she stopped. She raised her arms towards the dark sky and looked towards the bush where Omi was hidden.

'Come, come, my God. Come . . .' she shrieked and started to shake her body violently, her legs and breasts and arms.

Something happened to Omi. God came into him. He removed his clothes and, beating his dholuk drum madly, leapt into the dim light of the earthen lamp cock-a-doodle-do and ninety degrees, and started to dance wildly like the unknown woman. The unknown woman came and clasped him and dragged him down to the earth made barren by the locust.

'I say, stay at home this evening. They are coming. Don't just slip off like a piece of soap,' Paro said to her son one day.

When Omi had protested to his mother about 'this marriage story which is bound to have a tragic ending', she had slapped her head in disgust at his stupidity.

'Good family. Stationmaster. Income over and above his salary. Free house. Free servants. Free travel. Any amount coal, iron, wood and what-not. What more you want? Besides, she is the only daughter. All their wealth will come to you. What more you want?' she had said.

'Who is coming, Ma?' Omi asked innocently. He had earlier seen a railway peon come and deliver a message to his mother.

'*Them*, who else?'

'What time?'

'Five.'

Good. Omi knew what he was going to do. He was going to teach that Polling Officer a lesson. He would vanish in thin air. And that is exactly what he did.

Omi posted Banto's ten-year-old son, Lallu, at the bottom of the street. He gave him half an anna and told him he would get the other half if he did as he was told. Lallu was to spot the railway couple descending the slope from the highway in the rickshaw, then come running on the double to tell Omi.

'In absolute secrecy.'

Lallu kept his part of the bargain. In due course he came running and stood outside Omi's house with his hand pushed through Omi's window for the remainder of the promised anna.

Omi paid and slipped out. He went to Bali's house. Bali's mother said Bali was dead.

'Don't call for him again,' she said without even looking at Omi.

He went to Des's house. Des's father asked if Omi had any serious intentions of passing his matric on his second go. Omi did what he was expected to do, kept his mouth shut and went away.

He went to Bhajju's house and was greeted by his elder brother who had never like Omi nor ever made a secret of it.

'Second time matric-sitters should not be loafing at five o'clock,' the man said.

Only Harpal's mother was helpful.

'Playing tree cricket, what else can he be doing,' she said.

A Camp sport, tree cricket was an unconventional game by all accounts. First, for reasons unknown to anyone, it was played only during this time of the year, just when the matric exams were due. Second, you ran the risk of breaking a leg or your neck if you weren't absolutely first class at it. Happily everybody was absolutely first class at it. All that was needed was two able-bodied teams and an old tennis ball. After the toss, the batting side went up into a mammoth banyan tree between the market and the shops. The fielding side remained on the ground and tried to get wickets by hitting the batsmen in the tree with the tennis ball.

The condition was that the batsman must be hit on the body. If he stopped the ball with a hand or kicked it away with a foot he was not out. To score, the batsman caught the ball and threw it away as hard as he could. The member of the batting side nearest to the ground jumped off the tree and ran between the great tree trunk and a brick placed at twenty-two yards from it while the fielders chased the ball. The batsman was run out if a fielder hit him with the ball while he was running between the wicket. The rules for four and six were the same as ground cricket. They were the same for catch-out — that is, if one punched, kicked or threw the ball and a fielder took a catch. The batsman was clean bowled if a fielder hit the stumps, the great tree trunk or the red brick, while he was running between them.

Like everybody else, Omi loved tree cricket and loved batting more than fielding. A match had just started and he begged his way into the batting side, wondering what his mother would say when she found out he was missing from home.

At home Paro had put on her peacock-blue sari embroidered in gold and silver thread. Earlier in the afternoon Banto had washed her hair with dehi yogurt. After it was dry, she had oiled it with mustard oil as usual and combed it till it glistened.

'Big day,' Banto had said.

When the railway couple got off the rickshaw Paro was standing in the doorway with a pot of mustard oil. She poured the oil on either side of the threshold in welcome as Kandhari and his wife stepped over it. A servant in railway blue, carrying on his head a basket big enough to hide a man in it, stood outside.

But where was Omi?

'He was here only a moment ago. Oh, that boy. He can slip away like a bar of soap. Our boy is so shy,' Paro said, shyly.

She gave Lallu a shout.

'Lallu, son, go and call Omi. He must be at the kirket tree. Go tell him they have arrived,' she said, giving Lallu an anna.

'They have arrived. Auntie is calling you,' Lallu said to Omi under the banyan tree. Omi was batting somewhere in it.

'Go tell Ma you can't find me. Say I am not here.'

Lallu went back.

'Auntie, Omi says he is not there.'

Paro could have killed her son.

'I will go and bring him,' Kandhari said.

When Omi saw the Polling Officer he decided to run and hide. But it was too late. Kandhari was there, right under his batting position.

'Come on, Om Parkash. Your mother is worried.'

Omi gave up. He caught hold of a hoary whisker of an ancient tree and slid down like a monkey.

'Dangerous game, no?' Kandhari said.

'Who is that?' a batsman in the tree asked. 'Where is Omi going?'

'His father-in-law. Omi is going to his father-in-law's house,' Bali said.

'But he is the Station Master of Dhulkote,' Bhajju said.

'Stationmasters can also be fathers-in-law,' Harpal said.

'Our Omi will get free train rides at least, if nothing else,' Bali said.

'If I were him I would insist on a railway trolley in the dowry,' Punnu, the standing umpire, said.

The boys laughed and Omi could hear them. The bastards. Even he laughed to himself at the situation. He had not expected Kandhari to come to call him. He would have run away had it been anyone else. It was not Kandhari's fault really. Having a daughter he was bound to be on the look out for a nice, promising boy. Nice, promising boy! Flattering thought, but Omi did not want marriage.

'I want to be free. I don't want to be dragged into the butcher's back yard to come out clean and washed through the front door as dead meat — that's what marriage does. I want to be free. No ropes around my neck. Free, free, free. Besides, I am so bloody young. But for all this, who knows what might have happened with Guddy. The fire was hot. All I had to do was drop my iron in. Never got a chance. This bastard came and threw cold water instead. Never mind. I'll teach him a lesson yet. I'll teach them all a lesson.'

Omi's mother wore an expression which was louder than any words: *wait till your father comes home*. Luckily his father was not coming that night.

'Omi son, we've come all the way to see you. Don't be shy, and sit down. No difference between your parents and us now. What difference?' Kandhari's wife said.

Omi noted that she was flat-chested and thin as a bamboo stick. Her voice was shrill as the whistle of a railway engine. Omi would have liked to tell her that he was not shy at all and that if her daughter was half as ugly as she was then they could put her neck on the line. He, Omi, would give the green flag to the engine driver.

'Fine boy though,' Kandhari's wife went on, addressing no one in particular. 'A little shy, but no more than he should be.'

So that was expected of him. Shying from elders was a sign of the respect one had for them.

'If only you had taken to the fields instead of going to the cricket tree, Omi son. This bitch of a bamboo stick would not be saying all this,' Omi said to himself.

'Fine lad. Intelligent lad,' Kandhari said.

'As he grows up he will understand his responsibilities. Won't you, Om Parkash?' Kandhari's wife said.

'Like hell I will, bamboo stick,' Omi said to himself.

Kandhari's wife then opened a tiny purse and reached out a hand to Omi. She was holding some money out.

'Take it. Small thing, but it is in the name of the sacred tie between your mother-father and us. Besides, I am meeting you for the first time. Can't leave without placing something on your palm.'

Obscenities longed to shoot out of Omi's throat. But he kept quiet.

'Take, it. Om. Your natural right,' Paro said.

But Omi sat still, shaking his head. Kandhari's wife pushed the notes into his shirt pocket and, caressing Omi's cheek gently, urged her husband to rise and leave. But Paro had prepared some refreshments.

'Ram, Ram, Ram!' Kandhari's wife said in consternation and touched the lobes of her ears. 'Eat in the house of my future son-in-law?' It was out of question. 'We are Hindus, you know, sister. Not mallachas.'

At the door Paro asked her son to touch their feet, the normal thing. It showed filial respect. Feeling embarrassed, confused and above all blackmailed, Omi lowered his right hand towards the floor and in one go swept it a few inches above the four railway feet. The couple pretended not to notice his perfunctory manner. Paro blushed deeply and bit her lower lip in shame.

'Omi,' she said.

'Shy lad,' Kandhari said, justifyingly.

'But no more than I should be,' Omi said to himself, feeling pleased with this slight defiance.

Kandhari's wife caressed his cheeks again before leaving.

'I'll have to wash my face twice now,' Omi muttered as soon as the Kandharis were out of sight.

'How much did she give you?' Paro said, extending a hand for the money.

'Ninety-one.'

'Can't be, you cheat. It is either fifty-one rupees or one hundred and one. Come on, give it to me.'

'My natural right, you said. So I'll keep the money.'

'Don't waste my time. I have a lot to do . . .'

'After all, it is me who is supposed to, *supposed to*, wed that bitch of a bamboo stick's daughter.'

'Hai, my mother! What did I do in my past life to beget a monster like him for a son? Hai, hai, hai! My karma. O God, what did I do? Please tell me.'

'O God, what did *I* do in *my* past life to be caught in this trap?'

'Hear him talk. Just like his father — feelingless. Shut up and hand me the money.'

Crossly, Omi smacked the money on the bed where Kandhari's wife had sat. Paro picked it up, licked her finger and counted it.

'Just what becomes of their status,' Paro said.

'Status! What status? What status is there in being the Station Master of Dhulkote where hardly five trains stop, where even dogs won't pee, where even crows won't drop their droppings?'

'O God, what did I do?'

Omi rushed up to his mother and snatched the wad of notes. He peeled off a couple of tenners and returned the rest.

'What, robbing your own mother now? Wait till your father gets home. Panchkoola air has made villain of you. Return the money at once. Or . . .'

'It's for me. After all I am the goat who is being taken to the butcher's shop. It is me, your own son, who is being martyred.'

'May snakes bite me to hear such talk from my own flesh and blood. You will bring us laurels and a name. Pass on the money. Or . . .'

Omi did not stay for further dispute. He was back at the cricket tree and asking the score.

'Omi son, what these secret-secrets going on?' Bhajju said.

'What you talking about, yaar?' Omi said.

'The badmash scoundrel. Want to get married in secret in the godown warehouse of Dhulkote station? Full of rats and scorpions. True. Ask Harpal,' Bali said.

'True,' Harpal said.

'Whatever you do, don't forget to ask for a trolley in the dowry. Important to have your own railway transport these days,' Punnu said.

'And don't forget to invite us,' seven sisters' brother said.

'When is the big day? Before or after the exams?' Des said.

'Tirath Ram coming to the wedding?' Bali said.

Omi's nostils flared.

'No. But he is going to your mother's. I hear she is leaving your father. Is he a gandoo queer then, your old man? Must be,' Omi said.

Bali picked up the red brick at the other end of the wicket and simply aimed it at Omi's head. Omi ducked in time.

'Watch your big mouth, Omi son. Next time I will split your head,' Bali said.

'Watch your big queer mouth. I am going to fix you one of these days, once and for all,' Omi said.

The boys kept them apart and no blood was spilt, but the fight throbbed in Omi's limbs. It was only postponed.

Bali's father was an 'industrialist' as the boys termed it. He had an industry 'growing' in their back garden. He manufactured buckets in the back yard and sold them from the front. The back garden was five yards long and four yards wide. Their front wall always had a number of buckets of varying sizes hanging from nails.

He also made canister lids. People brought their empty ghee canisters with labels of dalda and other brands of ghee and oil and he charged them one-eight for providing a lid, material and labour included. Unless the customer asked for the labels to be left on, Bali and his brothers pulled them off and glued them into an album. They had the only collection of its kind in the Camp or elsewhere in the country.

A few canister lids and a bucket or two a day kept the family fed and clothed. Bali's father had no complaints really — he wasn't a greedy man — but, like everybody else, he wouldn't mind a little bit extra. Besides, he had three daughters to think of. Last year a very holy swami had told him that something would happen this year. So he took an expensive decision and sent off his tender to the Air Force base in Ambala Cantonment. It was a daring gesture because it had to be accompanied by fifty rupees, a lot of money. The Air Force wanted five hundred buckets and it had invited quotations from manufacturers.

The gamble paid off and the Air Force accepted the tender. Bali's father got the contract and the news travelled fast.

'Getting rich, Bali son. Won't recognise us now, won't talk to us now,' Punnu said early one evening as Bali passed him in the market without seeing him under the sack-hood of Harbans Singh's vegetable shop.

'His father got contract for five thousand canister lids from the Air Force. True,' Punnu told Harbans Singh.

'Our Air Force gone nuts or something? What do they want so many canister lids for? Doesn't make sense,' Harbans Singh said.

'Not five thousand. Only five hundred,' Baldeva, the telu oil merchant said from his shop next door.

'But where is he going to make so many of them? Inside his arse?'

'Inside your mother's cunt. It must have plenty of room if all your vegetables came out of it,' Bali said.

The Sikh temper flared. Harbans Singh leapt from his seat and was upon Bali. Bali was a boy. Harbans, a four-times matric-sitter, a man. But anger and insult know no age barriers. The two rolled in the dust of the market.

'Oi, oi, oi . . .' the whole bazaar shouted as they separated the combatants.

'You struck your twelve o'clock or something, Harbans Singh? Want to kill the boy?' Bhaia, the paan wallah, said.

But Bali hadn't appeared to be an easy kill. He had fought well and knew it.

'Off you go, tiger son,' Bhaia said to Bali.

Bali spat at Harbans' shop and walked off to the great banyan tree. A few boys sat under it, talking. They were discussing the bucket contract and Omi's engagement.

'There he is, the bucket master,' someone said.

'Shut your arse, Parduman,' Bali said.

'When you go to deliver your buckets take us along, will you? We want to see their jets.'

'I will show you one right now — a kick in your fat arse will . . .'

Omi was seen coming from the main road.

'Here comes OP Khatri, *PR*,' Des said, changing the subject. It had reached a crucial stage.

'Coming from Dhulkote, Omi son?' Parduman said.

The boys laughed. Omi's nostrils flared.

'I say, when is it, then? Before or after the exams?' Des said.

'Printed the invitation cards yet? Don't forget to ask us old pals,' someone else said.

'He won't bother. Why should he? All he wants is a wife and a trolley. Isn't that so, Omi?' Des went on.

'Des, don't try to be too clever. It might prove harmful for you,' Omi said.

'Anything wrong in wanting to be invited to a friend's wedding? Not asking for a ride with your wife in your trolley, am I?'

'Shut up, Des. Or it will be the worse for you.'

'How worse?' Bali butted in. 'How worse?'

'Bali!'

'No, tell me. How worse?'

'Bali, you are being a fool. Keep your arse out of it.'

'Me being a fool? Who the hell are you to tell me what to do?' Fight hadn't gone out of Bali's limbs.

'You really want to know?'

'Yeah. That's why I am asking. So speak unless you don't have an answer. I am not asking where Vladivostok is.'

The boys roared with laughter. Omi reached out and landed his right fist on Bali's jaw.

'You Panchkoola-Returned son of a bitch . . .!' Bali shrieked and fell on Omi.

Bali was taller and broader. The boys thought Omi had had it today. But Omi was too swift for the big-boned Bali. He lashed out in full frontier temper. He hit Bali in the face, the stomach and the sides. Beaten, Bali tried the last resort. He went for Omi's testicle. He tried to catch them in order to squeeze the life out of his enemy.

'My balls! Is that what you want? Who for? Your sisters?' Omi roared and hammered Bali's head on the dusty ground.

The boys intervened.

'Anyone got anything more to say?' Omi said, looking at Des. Des looked away.

Omi felt as much bewildered by his victory as Bali did by his defeat. His prestige rose sky-high. Bali's suffered a steep decline. Since his father's bucket contract a certain arrogance had come into Bali's manner. Some boys thought he had started walking as if he was the Nawab Latti Khan himself. So nobody felt sorry for him. But Omi was sorry, not for Bali, but for something he had just learned — that they were all really quite silly.

91

It was an unnecessary fight and winning it had not brought him any joy. His shirt in shreds, Omi walked home slowly, followed by a number of little boys who had turned up to watch the fight.

'Who beat you up this time?' Paro said as she pushed his food towards him.

Omi neither answered nor ate the food.

'Bloody fool,' he swore at Bali, not for fighting with him, but for something else. 'We Indians are stupid.'

Satish would have understood.

'You better eat. Your father is coming home,' Paro said.

That was different. Omi started to eat. He had just finished eating when he heard Dabbu bark furiously in the street. A lorry came to a halt outside and Omi recognised it from its brakes. It was Bhola Ram's.

'Father,' Omi shouted and ran out to greet him.

Khatri alighted from the cab of Bhola Ram's lorry and Satish jumped out of the back. The boys shook hands and had a hearty hug. Satish had returned to the Camp for the exams.

'Aré Ustad Guru, going to be family man?' Satish said and hugged Omi again. Dabbu barked and jumped and wanted to be included in the embrace.

'I am going to shoot this dog one day,' Satish said, embracing Dabbu.

Khatri left the boys and dog and went inside with Bhola Ram.

'No, serious, yaar,' Satish said. 'True, you getting a wife?'

'Don't know why, though. We Indians special people. God made us special.'

'She got a sister or a friend?'

'She got a mother alright. Beautiful. Beat Vijayanti Mala tits any day. I can fix it if you like.'

'And who is this beauty we hear of, come to live next door?'

'No idea. But how do you know about her?'

'Everybody knows her husband beats her. We know everything.'

'What else?'

'That he is a mean son of a bitch, that they are an odd couple — they never go anywhere and no one come to them. That sort of thing.'

'What is *that sort of thing*?'

'You know. He is worried that the whole world is after her.'

'Some world, this, our Camp.'

'Oi,' Khatri shouted from inside the house. 'Come in at once.'

But before Omi went in he asked Satish about Panchkoola.

'Panchkoola? Panchkoola is finished as it was. Finished for us at any rate. Next stop Chandigarh.'

Seeing Satish had brought back Panchkoola to Omi. He knew life there was over for his father and so it was over for him too. He would never go there again. He would never see Guddy again.

Alone in his room with his books, Omi brought out Guddy's letter, read it several times and cursed the Election.

'My fucking karma.' Omi felt like kicking or breaking something. He crushed a cockroach under his feet the way he had crushed scores of locusts that day.

The locust! He must never think of that day again. He had interfered with God. He must never think of that day . . . Never. Omi crushed another cockroach.

Chaman Lal snored next door and Omi felt like kicking the wall and telling him to shut up. But that might wake up Rani.

'How can she sleep with all this snoring anyway?'

The wall was obviously thin enough, for he heard their door creak — it must be Rani *going out* — but the snoring continued. She did not come back and Omi fell asleep. A few hours later he was woken up by her screams. Chaman Lal was beating her with a danda stick. This time Omi picked up a shoe and started hammering the wall with it.

'Shut up, you Khatri dog,' Chaman Lal yelled and beat his wife more. Her screams woke up Omi's parents and other neighbours. They came out in the street and stood outside the couple's house. The door opened and Chaman Lal came out, brandishing his danda stick.

'Go away, you vultures. Leave us alone,' he howled.

In the electric light inside the room Omi saw that Rani stood naked, with blood on her body. *Brother* shut the door in his face.

A few days later, Omi contemplated his future.

Next stop Chandigarh, the elegant new capital of the Punjab, where elegant people spoke elegant English and made him feel ashamed of himself. If his father did arrange for him to have English lessons, as he had said, that would give him the start he wanted. Other things would follow.

But that was Chandigarh, our new capital. This was the Camp, where real life was. Omi felt locked into it by the railway station of Dhulkote on one side and his old school on the other.

'I might as well go along and see what the bitch of a bamboo stick has got for a daughter. Won't it be wonderful if she does look like her mother? Then no one will blame me for breaking the "sacred tie".'

But how was he to get close enough to have a look at her?

'If that owl-faced Polling Officer saw me around the station he would think that I was dying to see my future woman. The double-triple bastard. It would never occur to him that I might be there to reject her because she looked like her mother — ugly. If I was seen there, I would seem too eager, willing and available which I am not.'

The only alternative was to find out about her movements and try to see her away from the station. But how?

'You need help, Omi son — some spies.'

But who?

Satish was obviously his man.

'No. Not this time.'

It had to be someone neutral, someone not from the Camp. Omi clicked his fingers — he knew his man.

'Bakshi.'

Bakshi was an old classmate who lived in the Power House in front of Dhulkote station. Omi decided to take a trip there, it was only a few minutes by bike. He went one evening.

The Power House, right opposite Dhulkote station, housed its employees in a small colony by its side. Omi went looking for his old classmate. Bakshi was not at home.

'Must be playing volleyball, what else? He is going to fail the exam,' Bakshi's mother said to Omi.

'Omiii . . .' Bakshi shouted as he saw Omi. He abandoned the game and came running. They shook hands and embraced each other several times.

'Big big congratulations, man. Going to be family man, eh, Ustad Guru?'

Omi looked away in answer.

'And stealing our own stationmaster's girl from under our very noses. First-class badmashi rascalship I call it.' Bakshi said.

'I dropped by to see what you were all up to. Where is Monga?'

'He must be cramming at home. You know him. This bloody exam. It has sucked all my blood. See?' Bakshi pinched his cheeks. 'Nothing left. How about you?'

Omi pinched his cheeks.

'Nothing left here either.'

'Why God made exams? Just to torture us? Don't understand.'

Bakshi took him home and gave him a cup of tea and all the news since the Vladivostok episode. Then Omi was leaving and he hadn't said a word about the real reason for this visit. But Bakshi knew. He put an arm around him and walked him back to the main road.

'I say, why not take a little walkie-walkie to the railway station?' Bakshi whispered with a wink at the gates of the Power House.

'What for?' Omi said innocently.

'To see if we can catch a glimpse of our bharjai. I'll come with you. Only behind the station.'

'No,' Omi said and touched the lobes of his ears in consternation. 'What are you saying, Bakshi? You crazy or something? Striking your twelve o'clock or something?'

'No harm done. Time for the Kalka Mail. The stationmaster will be at the station, her mother at home. Perhaps our bharjai is playing outside and perhaps we get a chance to see her. Quick look only. Quick, quick, quick look.'

Omi said no, but followed Bakshi to the railway quarters. There was no one playing outside.

'That must be your in-laws',' Bakshi said, pointing to the biggest of the five railway houses. The front door was half open, but there was no sign of activity, inside or outside. Nor any sounds.

'We will walk past and then walk back. Bharjai may come out,' Bakshi said.

'What if that son of an owl was to see me here?' Omi wondered and tried not to think of it any more. He shielded himself behind Bakshi as they came in line with the half-open door of

Kandhari's house. He looked in, his heart rising to his throat. There was no one within the few feet of vision. After twenty yards Omi sighed in relief.

'Let's turn back,' Bakshi said. He seemed more anxious than Omi to see the daughter of the stationmaster.

'Forget it, Bakshi.' Omi couldn't go through it again.

'No harm done, man. What's the matter with you?'

They were ten paces from Kandhari's house when the door opened fully and out stepped Kandhari himself. After a casual glance at the boys Kandhari walked towards the station. During the split second Omi thought that his heart had stopped, that he was going to die. Till that moment he did not know that shame could kill. When Kandhari turned away Omi's heart started to beat again, albeit still loudly. He was not recognised.

'Phew,' Omi sighed loudly. He was not recognised.

But that very second Kandhari stopped, turned towards the boys and gave the large water-melon smile which Omi first saw in Panchkoola.

'Om Parkash!'

Om Parkash wanted to sink into the earth.

'How come you here? Mother-father well? Reading-writing well?'

'Why didn't Kalka Mail run me over? What have I done to deserve to be alive?' Omi said to himself when he got home.

'What is the matter, oi? Your face is dark as a railway engine,' Paro said.

'The Kalka Mail,' Omi said.

'What about Kalka Mail?'

'It was late.'

'So?'

Omi didn't answer. Paro looked outside the door at the starry sky and raised her eye brows.

'What did I do, God?'

'One thing I want to tell you, Ma. Call this "sacred arrangement" off, or it will be her neck or mine under the Kalka Mail. I am telling you now.'

'Ram, Ram, Ram . . .!' Paro pinched her ear lobes. 'Call yourself a son? Pukka rakshas demon you are.'

'Ma, I have seen her. She is uglier than her mother.'

96

'Munni? Munni is beautiful as a rose. What's more, she is docile as a cow. She will make a dutiful and an obedient wife. What more you want?'

Khatri arrived unexpectedly.

'What is he burr-burring about? What is he moaning about?' Khatri asked as he sat down to dinner.

'Says he wants a different wife.'

'True, oi?'

Omi didn't answer.

'Your marriage is not your business. Your business is reading-writing. Understand?'

Omi did not answer.

'Understand or not?' Khatri raised his voice.

Omi still did not answer. Khatri's nostrils flared — it was touch-and-go. Khatri let it go and blew his anger away with a loud sigh.

'I got married when I was eighteen and your mother sixteen.'

'Those were old days, Father.'

'Old days or new, marriage is marriage.'

'These days people like to know each other before they get married.'

'Plenty of time for that. All your life.'

Khatri recalled how he had protested when his parents had arranged his marriage.

'All boys do that sort of thing,' Khatri said to himself and dismissed Omi to his books.

Banto, Banarsi and some other neighbours came. It was warm now and they sat on charpois out in the open verandah. They laughed and talked. Omi could hear every word they said. They only talked of one thing, Rani and Chaman Lal.

'We must do something before it is too late.'

'Husband and wife. What can we do?'

'Call the police next time.'

'Husband and wife. Even police can't interfere.'

'Anyway, PC Chandu knows. But he says, if they were to arrest all the wife-beaters in the Camp, they would need a prison as large as the Red Fort of Delhi.'

'Why doesn't she leave him?'

'And go where? Hindu woman. She is married to him for this life and all those to come.'

Satish knocked at Omi's window. Omi left the light on and slipped out. Dabbu came from the darkness and joined them.

'Chaman Lal,' Omi said.

'The husband of . . .?'

'Yeah. He needs a fix.'

'What sort of fix?'

'A fix he'll remember forever.'

Satish understood. They talked about it.

'But he is big. We need to be more than two.'

'We'll wait.'

They went to the market and found Harpal and Bali at the paan shop. Omi and Bali looked away when they saw each other.

'You two got to make up,' Satish said, putting his arms around them. 'Something has turned up, something important. Need solidarity. now. Come on, shake hands.' Satish pushed them against each other. Bhaia offered paans on the house if they would make up. He begged them. Reluctantly they shook hands.

'That's no good. We want a proper embrace,' Bhaia said.

Omi and Bali embraced each other reluctantly.

'Special silver paan for the new friends and their friends.' Bhaia went mad and made them four paans. Satish took him into their confidence.

'End of your shop if you open your mouth, Bhaia ji,' Satish said.

Bhaia understood and agreed. Not only that, he gave them a valuable piece of information. 'I saw him *going out* only a few minutes ago.'

The four boys covered their heads with guinea sacks, armed themselves with danda sticks and went into the *going out* field. Dabbu followed them. They did their best to send him back, but Dabbu was one of those dogs; he persisted. They found Chaman Lal sitting behind a bush near the camel bridge, humming a film tune. They beat him into the shape of a peacock's arse, poured water from his brass gadva over his head and rolled his face in his own shit. Dabbu barked furiously. Without uttering a word they left Chaman Lal groaning on the ground as his wife often did in his bed in the middle of the night. They took his dhotti leg-wrap with them and threw it away in a pool of muddy water on their way back.

Next morning Omi woke up to a stir outside. A murmuring crowd had gathered outside Chaman Lal's house, including Khatri who had made an exception and delayed his return to Panchkoola to find out what it was all about. The uniformed figure of PC Chandu presided over the proceedings. He stood in the doorway with one hand on his hip and the other holding a wooden baton, twirling his moustache.

'Very lucky, Chaman Lal, if you ask me. At least no broken bones. Only the face, and the face doesn't matter. A few stitches here and there and it will be as good as new, no?' Chandu said in a loud police voice.

Chaman Lal said something from inside the house which no one could hear.

'Yes, yes, yes. Law and order in the Camp. That's alright. But you can't expect the police to guard the *going out* area. What you want — a police guard each time you *go out* for a pee?'

Chaman Lal's answer was inaudible.

'Yes, yes, yes. But the question is why four men and a dog should want to break your face while you were doing it — not for your dhotti. The answer is well known to you, as it is to the rest of the Camp.'

Chaman Lal moaned.

'Yes, yes, yes. Family is family. But.'

Another policeman arrived on a bicycle, followed by an empty rickshaw. They helped the heavily bandaged Chaman Lal into it. Rani, her face covered with her dupatta scarf, sat next to him.

'Philadelphia Hospital,' Chandu ordered the driver.

'Chaman Lal deserved it,' Banto said to Paro.

'You should keep your nose out of these things, you husband-eater,' Banarsi whispered to his wife.

'Wonder why didn't they do it earlier?' someone said.

'They chose the best place for it, though,' someone else said.

The Khatris withdrew.

'Fools,' Khatri said and took leave of his family.

'I wish I was there when they did it,' Omi said to his mother. 'I hear they bashed his head in his . . .' Omi didn't finish the sentence because he realised that he had made a mistake.

'How do you know? You've just woken up,' Paro said and fixed his gaze with hers.

'Just overheard someone say so outside,' Omi said, looking away.

'Where were you last night, badmash scoundrel?'

'Ma! You know me!'

'That's why I am asking. I know my bewakoof son.'

'And I know my Nobel Prize mother.'

'What's that?'

'Best prize white English people give for the greatest achievement.'

'And look at my achievement!'

As the exam got nearer, Omi took to praying. Early every evening, just after sunset, he sat down cross-legged on the floor in his room and read a chapter of *Bhagavad Gita*. There were two copies of the *Gita* at home, in Hindi and Sanskrit. The Hindi one was long, with an elaborate explanation of the text. The Sanskrit one only had the original text. As a result it was about six times shorter. Omi read the Sanskrit *Gita*.

'Bribing God, eh? But God knows you don't understand a word of Sanskrit,' Paro said.

'Hindi or Sanskrit, *Gita* is *Gita* and God knows that too.'

He read a chapter a day. At the end of his recitation he folded his hands on his chest and shut his eyes.

'Please God, don't forget your little son Om Parkash on the day of the results. Please, not like last year.'

HS High School had closed down to give the examination boys time to prepare. It was a habit of the Camp boys to go and read in the fields. They went in groups of two or more, pacing up and down, mugging up. The railway track, which ran parallel to the highway, was a favourite. They just kept walking along it, reading out aloud, and stopping at bridges. If no one was looking, it was alright to do a bit of poaching of the seasonal fruit and vegetables growing in the fields around the track.

Omi, Satish, Harpal and Bali were walking along it one fine morning. They had started from the Primary School, passed the level-crossing on the road to HS High School and Ambala City, and stopped at Banwari Wala Bridge. It was nine. They wouldn't be going home for another couple of hours, when it would be too hot to be strolling in the sun. The radishes and carrots in the fields across the bridge were very tempting. They went across and, after some minutes of successful poaching, came to the next bridge which was only a couple of hundred yards or so from Dhulkote station itself. At their end of the bridge stood an unattended trolley. A sola-hatted Overseer was under the bridge on the dry sandy river bed, giving orders to two labourers. The labourers were taking measurements with a long metallic tape while the Overseer took notes.

'Want to try it?' Satish asked Omi.

'As if it was his father's,' Harpal said.

'Father's or father-in-law's. Same thing,' Bali said looking in the direction of the station and laughing. Satish and Harpal laughed too. Omi found himself joining them.

'Go wash your face, bucket master,' Omi said, giving Bali a gentle kick in the arse.

The men of the trolley were hidden under the bridge so the boys saw no harm in just sitting in it. It was one of those motor-driven things, with spacious seating which the boys found to their liking. Omi fiddled with a knob, Satish with another, Bali with a handle. No one knew who touched what, but the engine started up. The trolley began to move with the boys in it. They tried every instrument, but they could not stop it. It was going faster and faster.

'Oi, oi, oi . . .!' the two labourers screamed as they ran after the run-away vehicle.

'What the hell are we going to do?' Omi asked in panic.

'Stop the fucking thing,' Bali answered in panic.

'How?'

'Go ask your father-in-law.'

On another occasion Omi would have broken Bali's jaw, but today, in this trolley, things were different. Panic prevailed.

'Shall we jump out?' Harpal said.

'No. We got to stop it or we will cause an accident. We may collide with an oncoming train,' Omi said.

'Stop, stop . . .' the labourers screamed as they ran after the trolley. But it had gone a good couple of hundred yards towards the Camp.

'Do something, then, you Panchkoola-Returned son of a bitch. You started it up,' Bali said in total panic.

'I didn't, you did, you mother-laying bucketeer.'

'Stop this you-you-me-me,' Satish said.

'I am jumping off,' Harpal said.

'I can hear a train coming. I am jumping off. I don't want to go to jail. You started it, you stop it. Coming, Harpal?' Bali said, jumping off. He rolled over on the grass on the sloping sides of the track.

'Me, too,' Harpal said and leapt out. He fell safely, got up, felt himself, dusted himself and vanished into the fields.

'Let's jump, Omi,' Satish said. 'Otherwise.'

'We simply got to stop it.'

'Jump,' Satish said and baled out.

Omi tried pulling this and that. Nothing worked.

'Fair-weather friends,' he screamed and tried every lever and button again. The trolley went faster and faster. He did what he had to do. He too jumped out and ran away from the Camp, towards the City. He bumped into the other three at the Grand Trunk Road. They were too bewildered to accuse each other any more. What if it causes an accident? What if someone gets killed? It was all too frightening. The four held a brief conference, took an oath never to tell anyone or to admit it if caught, and decided to move off individually in different directions. Omi decided to get lost in the little alley lane of Ambala City and wait for a while.

The trolley sped on towards the Camp. The level-crossing attendant saw it when it was barely fifty yards from the gate. He shouted a warning to the tonga driver who was about to cross it. But it was too late. The trolley crashed straight into the horse, severing it from the tonga and carrying it twenty yards before toppling over the line. The driver and the passenger fell out, unhurt. The horse lay covered with dust and blood.

'My horse, my horse!' cried the tonga driver, Ram Rakha.

Ram Rakha ran to the hut of the level-crossing keeper, Hans Raj. He got the bewildered Hans Raj by the throat and dragged him to the scene of the accident.

'Son of a bitch!' Ram Rakha said.

People came running from all directions.

'Son of a bitch!' No other words came to Ram Rakha.

People saved Hans Raj from being strangled and held Ram Rakha back.

Words finally came to him.

102

'Were you sleeping, son of a bitch, that you left the gate open like your mother's chut? Look what you have done to my animal!' Ram Rakha started to weep. 'You have killed my animal.'

In a sudden surge and a sudden burst of energy, Ram Rakha broke loose. He pierced his way through the dense crowd and was upon Hans Raj's throat once again, determined to kill him.

'Listen. Listen. I done nothing. Swear on my mother's head. It's true, Ram Rakha,' Hans Raj managed to say.

People pulled Ram Rakha back and let Hans Raj give his account of the event.

'I thought I was seeing things. Only half an hour ago I had seen the Overseer sahib going down in it. And there it was, coming up, without the sahib, without his men and without warning . . .'

'Stuff your warning.'

People tried to explain, but Ram Rakha wept.

'How will I feed my children, mother-father and wife? If this mother-layer hadn't been snoring my animal would still be alive.'

'But your horse is alive. It is only slightly injured,' someone said.

The horse had stood up, dripping with blood and shivering and neighing. There were a few cuts on his body.

'My poor horse! What has the keeper done to you?' Ram Rakha embraced the horse and sobbed.

The two labourers arrived.

'Where are the boys?' they asked breathlessly. They had come running.

'Which boys?' Hans Raj asked.

The Overseer and Kandhari arrived on bicycles. The Overseer had gone to the station to borrow a bike to give chase and Kandhari had offered to go with him.

The crowd grew and the sweet-vendors, the channa, chooran and kulfi wallahs, thrived on it. PC Chandu arrived with his assistant and a photographer. He went up to Hans Raj and handcuffed him.

'I done nothing, Chandu. Ask anyone,' Hans Raj said and started to weep. His wife and two small children also started to weep. The people begged Chandu to be merciful. 'You got kids too, haven't you?'

The sola-hatted Overseer called to Chandu.

'Release the man,' the Overseer said.

Chandu did not like being spoken to like that in front of everybody.

'I keep law and order in the Camp. I give orders here, Sahib,' Chandu said with one hand on his hip and his baton in the other.

'True, true,' a few voices said.

Kandhari put an arm around Chandu and took him aside. A minute later Chandu came back and unlocked the handcuffs.

'First it was Pakistan and now it is our own railway,' Ram Rakha wailed. 'Look at my horse. Just look at him.'

'The railway will give you compensation, Ram Rakha,' Kandhari said.

'I don't want compensation. I want a horse.'

'We don't keep horses in our stations.'

'Ask for a train, Ram Rakha,' Punnu said from the crowd.

'Or ask for an engine,' Bhajju said.

The crowd laughed.

'Joke with us. Go on, joke with a fate-smitten man. First it was Pakistan and now . . .'

Ram Rakha's wife had come running to the scene with an infant on her breast. The child was howling.

'What have you done to my man?' she addressed the crowd.

Seeing her, Ram Rakha started to weep again. 'Ruined, ruined, ruined. We are ruined, woman.'

Finally it was the Overseer who pacified Ram Rakha. 'You either claim compensation or go home and forget it.'

The police photographer cleared the crowd and took shots of the tonga, trolley and the horse. Then Ram Rakha asked his wife to sit on the tonga to keep guard while he took his horse to a vet in the city. The horse limped, but it walked reasonably well. A number of friends walked with him and his animal, followed by a number of little boys. Ram Rakha threw stones at them to make them go back, but they kept on following.

Omi passed the procession near his old school.

'What happened to your animal, Ram Rakha?' Omi asked innocently.

'My rotten karma!' Ram Rakha grumbled and walked on.

That night Omi surprised his mother by not going out to eat the air of the Camp.

'How will you digest your supper then?' Paro said.

'Exams, Ma, exams,' he said and shut himself in his room. There was a knock at his window. It was Satish.

'Chandu has special orders to catch the trolley hijackers. Too much crime in the Camp suddenly. We better lie low and not be seen together,' Satish said.

Half an hour later there was another knock at the window. It was Harpal.

'Chandu is looking for us. We better not be seen together again.'

A little later there was another knock. It was Bali. He delivered the same information and made the same recommendation.

Omi was sorry for Ram Rakha who had given him many a free ride in the past, and therefore felt twice as guilty about the accident.

'I will make it up to him one day.' How, he did not know. 'I will one day, somehow.'

In the meantime he had to lie low, not go outside. He might be recognised. But if he stayed in all the time, his mother would become suspicious and find out. He knew of a trick that might work, but he had never tried it before. He had only heard of it from friends.

'Nothing like trying.'

Before going off to sleep, he strapped two medium-sized onions inside his armpits. When he woke up next morning he carried a strong smell of onion, but the trick had paid off.

'Ma, I think I got a temperature.'

Paro felt Omi's brow and went to Banto's house to borrow their thermometer.

'Hundred! It is all your loafing. You set one foot outside this house and I will have your head shaved off by your father. He is coming home tonight.'

But Khatri did not come home that night, nor the next. In fact he did not come until the end of the week. He had been very busy, making visits to our new capital, seeing Gulati and others like him.

Bhola Ram gave him a lift. He dropped him at the main road, at the junction of the road that led to the City near the level-crossing.

They both noticed a corrugated-iron construction in the waste land by the level-crossing.

'The touring talkie that was playing at Manimajra,' Bhola Ram told Khatri as he got off. 'Take Bharjai there to celebrate.'

'Left us to dogs for a whole week! Who do *they* think they are?' Paro said as she saw Khatri. She had had her hair oiled and combed by Banto and it glistened. She wore the sari he liked best, a red silk banarsi sari with silver stars and a broad silver-thread border.

Khatri grinned.

'Work, Begum, work. We don't sit on our arse wearing out the sutthan. We work in Panchkoola.'

'You work at lies. I know.'

'Not easy, you know, Begum. Our capital is a city of a rare breed of crocodiles — they *don't* cry as they swallow you. Where is the boy?'

'Playing with Lallu.'

'Playing with Lallu?'

Omi had been reduced to playing marbles with Lallu in the immediate vicinity of their houses. Chandu wouldn't come there twice.

'Been ill, the boy, and you leave us to dogs. A whole week.'

Khatri hung his turban on the wooden peg in the verandah wall and slapped Paro on the buttocks.

'Prettier than Rani.'

'Liars.'

'What news of them?' Khatri pointed to the house behind theirs.

'All too quiet. He doesn't let her out of the house. She is withering away like a flower. She is either going to run away or kill him.'

'Did Chandu find out who beat him?'

'He didn't, but I did.' Paro leaned over and whispered something in his ear.

Khatri slapped his thigh and laughed as he had never laughed before.

'Our own Omi?' Khatri laughed and couldn't stop laughing. He laughed louder and louder. People in the street stopped to listen. Banto and Banarsi came running and stood around him.

'Somebody told you some real joke,' Banarsi said.

Khatri nodded, slapped his thigh and went on laughing. Banto and Banarsi looked at each other and then at Paro. Paro went red in the face and they thought they had guessed the reason. Banto's mouth fell wide open and she covered it with a hand.

'Why you not tell me? Another one at your age!' Banto said.

'No joke, this,' Banarsi said and the husband and wife went back.

'Oh God,' Khatri said and looked at the sky. 'I know you got to make some people thick, but why do you send them to live next to me?'

Khatri slapped Paro again and let his hand remain on *that* roundness. He caressed it, and her thighs, and moved closer.

'I say. Go on and feel it,' Khatri said and took Paro's hand to his sutthan. 'Full seven days' long it is.'

'That charra place Panchkoola is making you a pukka badmash randy type. Just look at the size of it! Why don't you lay it across the Jhajjar? Make your own bridge. Charge toll tax.'

Khatri was double hungry as usual.

'I say. You think we can . . . before the boy comes back?'

Paro let go of the toll bridge and held her ears.

'Ram, Ram, Ram! Shame on you.'

'Alright, alright, alright. What's on the menu?' Khatri was dying for a home-cooked meal.

Paro had a surprise. Ladies' fingers. Khatri rubbed his hands in delight like a boy. Ladies' fingers were out of season, but a neighbour had managed a crop somehow and, knowing her husband's passion for them, Paro had asked for a pound.

'Wah wah. Wah wah,' Khatri said ten times during the meal.

'As if *they* have never eaten them before,' Paro said.

'I say. How about the late show? A touring talkie has come to the Camp,' Khatri said while gargling after dinner.

Paro looked puzzled. What had come over her husband tonight? She had never been to the cinema since Partition, and only once before that — soon after they had got married. Women didn't go to the cinema. It was wicked to do so.

'I am decent woman with a son.'

'Come, come. A touring talkie doesn't come here often, besides we don't get ladies' fingers at this time of the year.' Khatri leaned over and whispered that the shop in the capital was almost in the bag. 'Special day.'

Paro agreed.

'But you stay at home with your books,' Khatri said to Omi when he saw the boy putting on his shoes.

'But Father.'

'But Father what?'

'I have been cooped with my books all these days. The film will relax me, refresh my brains.'

'Stay home and read.' It was final.

Paro took a shawl, Khatri a blanket. The nights were still cold.

'Ma, I want to go with you,' Omi said.

'Do as you are told. Or . . .' Khatri said from the door.

'Ma,' Omi pleaded.

'You heard or not?' Khatri raised his voice.

'Read and write. Don't just doze off,' Paro said from the street.

Left alone, Omi burned with anger. The moment his parents were out of the street he switched off his light and jumped into bed. In ordinary circumstances he would have stayed up another two or three hours to study.

But Omi could not sleep. He was too angry for that. When lying down in anger became unbearable, he got up, switched on the light, put on his shoes again, took out the railway ten-rupee notes and went out of the house. He locked the door and stood facing the street, feeling free to do whatever he liked.

But where would he go? Omi did not know. There were not many places. The touring talkie was the only one within a reasonable distance. But there he would be seen by his parents. His father would give him a beating there and then. He could go to Ambala City, though. He could get there, see a film and be back before his parents. The touring talkie his parents had gone to only ran on one projector and this meant a number of intervals. They would not be home for another four hours. Omi would be back ages before that.

But going all by himself in pitch darkness was easier said than done. It was not yet nine now, not very late, but coming back would be. Midnight. Cycling back at midnight!

Omi put the key back in the lock and opened the door.

'Chickening out, Omi son?'

Omi stopped to think.

'Of course bilkul not.' He was his father's son, afraid of nothing.

An idea came to him and he put the lock back on the door. He would take a rickshaw. That would deal with the midnight darkness. He had plenty of money, railway money. He stopped a rickshaw at the main road. Dabbu barked from the dark roadside and joined him. 'City,' he ordered the man. 'And Dabbu, you go back.'

Dabbu ran after the rickshaw to the level-crossing, but turned back when the rickshaw picked up speed.

At the cinema in the City the rickshaw driver did not have change for a ten-rupee note.

'Going to cinema by yourself, boy? Where did you get all that money? Steal it?' the rickshaw driver said.

'Mind your own business. The money is my own.'

'Is it?' the rickshaw driver said with a smile on his face.

The show had started. Omi wanted to go in in style. He bought a first-class ticket for one-four, a quarter of a pound of peanuts and a silver paan, and went in. He had hardly been there ten minutes when a hand tapped him on the shoulder. Omi looked up. A policeman stood behind him.

'Come outside, boy.'

Terror struck Omi. Ram Rakha's horse! Was he caught after all?

Outside, the incandescent glare of the naked lights of the eating stalls and rehris blinded his eyes. The lean black face of the tall policeman looked ugly and dangerous.

'Where is the money, boy?' The policeman slapped Omi round the face.

Omi was dumbfounded. Tears rolled down his cheeks, not so much because of pain as because of a painful shock. The policeman thrust his hand in Omi's pockets and brought out the rest of the money and his peanuts.

'Where have you hidden the rest?'

'Hidden what?'

'The rest of the money. Come to the lock-up house. We'll make you talk.'

Omi began to cry loudly. A crowd gathered around them.

'Thief, the boy is a thief,' the policeman said to the people and whacked Omi on the head. Omi was speechless. He sobbed loudly. The policeman dragged him off, followed by a score of spectators.

'Get lost or I'll take you in as well,' the policeman yelled at the spectators. They dropped off.

'Tell me where you have hidden the rest and I'll let you go,' the policeman said.

Omi pleaded. He told him the money was his own. Given to him by his own mother-in-law, the wife of the Station Master of Dhulkote.

'Bakwas and Lies. Don't drag the wife of a respectable man into it.' The policeman whacked Omi on the head again.

It was unheard-of for a young boy to go to a late-night show on his own. And sitting in first class could not be on the strength of his pocket money. The policeman, tipped off by the rickshaw driver, was sure he was onto something. There was all that money to confirm it.

Omi cursed Kandhari for having come to Panchkoola. He cursed his wife for giving him the money. He cursed the touring talkie for coming to the Camp. He cursed the neighbour who grew that unseasonal crop of ladies' fingers that put his father in such a good mood. Above all he cursed himself for being so stupid.

'It must be Ram Rakha's horse.' Omi was convinced God was punishing him. 'Serve you right, Omi son. You never learn. Six months inside will teach you just what you need to learn.'

The policeman whacked Omi again.

'Where have you hidden the rest of the money? I'll let you go if you tell me,' the policeman said.

Omi knew that the policeman meant it.

'But there isn't any more money,' Omi said through his sobs.

'Tell me and you are free.'

Khatri and Paro spent a miserable night. They did not sleep. The terrible mystery of the locked door led to a night-long search for Omi. They woke up all Omi's friends. With them, their fathers and brothers and other volunteers, they looked for Omi everywhere. They shouted his name in the night, in the dark alleys of the Camp and the fields around.

'Omi has run away from home,' Bali said.

'He has run away from the exams,' Punnu said.

'Doesn't make sense. He knew everything this time,' Satish said. He was puzzled. Everybody was puzzled.

'Bombay,' somebody said.

Whenever a young man from the Camp ran away from home he was usually found in or on the way to Bombay, to become a film star.

'He must be on his way to Bombay,' the search party agreed unanimously and retired.

Khatri slapped his forehead and Paro sobbed into a hankie.

Early next morning a policeman appeared at the Khatris' door.

'Is this the house of Om Parkash Khatri?' he asked the crowd of friends and sympathisers who had come back and now stood outside the house.

The demented Paro dashed outside.

'What has he done?' she asked. Her sobs became uncontrollable when she heard that Omi had spent the night in the jailhouse.

Khatri recalled that Kandhari had a relation in Ambala City police. He felt awkward about having to ask his help in this delicate matter, but it was an emergency — and a mistake on the part of the police.

Bhola Ram arrived to pick up Khatri and they went in his lorry — Khatri, friends of Omi, their fathers and the policeman. They went first to Dhulkote station to see Kandhari. Kandhari then went with them to the City.

Unslept, pale, with eyes swollen with weeping, Omi broke down at the sight of his father and Kandhari. Kandhari had a few words with the inspector. Omi was released instantly. Bhola Ram drove them back.

At home Paro sat on a charpoi in the verandah with Banto, Rani and the other ladies of the neighbourhood. She held a hankie at her nose and stared blankly at her feet.

'They are here,' Banto said and they heard the lorry hooter as it turned into the street. Satish and Harpal helped Omi down and placed him in front of his mother. Paro clung to her son and the two of them wept bitterly. Khatri stood away at a distance, talking with Kandhari and Bhola Ram.

'Do you think he will ever act like a man?' Khatri asked Bhola Ram.

'He will, he will. The day he gets his own family,' Kandhari said.

'And sooner the better,' Bhola Ram said.

Omi looked around at the faces. His eyes rested on Rani's and he saw tears in her eyes. In that instant he recognised the woman of the tomb of the Goddess Devi. Their eyes held each other's and he knew she had recognised him too. Later that afternoon when his mother was having her daily siesta like the rest of the Camp and Omi was with his books, he heard someone come into their house. He turned and saw Rani standing in the doorway of his room. Speechless, he stood up in disbelief. Rani came and put her arms around him. She hugged him tight, as his mother had done in the morning, and cried silently. It was not a lover's hug.

There was nothing left for Omi in the Camp now. Only the exams. All his friends had disappeared from sight, cramming at home. Only those known to be *guaranteed failures* still met at Bhaia's paan shop or under the great banyan — Harbans, Bhajju, Punnu and some others. It was said in the Camp that these boys were *born to fail matric*, no matter how many times they took the exam. So far Omi had only hovered on the borderline of this definition; but to prove to himself that it was wrong, he stopped going there. Satish and Harpal met him occasionally, but things weren't the same between them. The Camp seemed to have changed for Omi since that afternoon.

It was a lonely time. Even his father was coming home less and less, which only meant one thing — that he was getting nearer and nearer his dream, Chandigarh, our capital.

'Chandigarh. Our capital. That's where my life will begin. All that has taken place so far has been incidental — except for a thing or two.' Guddy was one, and the other . . .? Omi was never to think about it.

Omi never thought of how the new life would begin, nor what it might entail. It was an area of time which he hoped to fill with different things than he had been used to.

'Big things.'

But what if he failed the exam like last year? He would run away.

It was an unhappy period. The only consolation was the news that the railway were paying out the compensation to Ram Rakha. His horse was hale and hearty and still ran the tonga. But the vet had given a favourable report, according to which the animal would have to be put down. In the light of this report the judge awarded Ram Rakha the handsome sum of five hundred rupees, a small fortune.

'All's well that ends well.' But Omi had not been able to forgive himself. He still said he would make it up to Ram Rakha one day.

'I will. Somehow or the other.'

And Rani?

Omi knew he was not to think about her. He knew that the only thing he was to think about was the exam.

The first day of the exams arrived. Paro gave him a breakfast of yogurt and dry chappati. Omi hated both, but yogurt and bread were supposed to be auspicious. He recalled the quantities of yogurt he ate last year.

'A lot of fine yogurt down the drain.'

As Omi took a step across the threshold, Paro undid a knot in her dupatta scarf, took out a rupee note, waved it around his head three times and gave it to Thakri who *happened* to be around at the time. Banto came out and, as a gesture of her blessings, patted Omi on the head.

'Can I go now, Ma?' Omi asked.

But the ritual was not over. Paro fed him a spoonful of sugar and sprinkled a handful of rice on him.

'Nation of fools.' Omi said. 'Nation of beautiful fools and I love you, Ma.'

Tirath Ram was invigilating in the examination hall and Omi made the mistake of arriving a few minutes too early. He ran straight into him.

'Lala ji, if you fail — and I know you will — and return to the school for your third year, I will make an omelette of you.' Tirath Ram said.

'He will be in the capital, Sir, next year,' Harpal said.

'And I will be able to buy and sell three masters like you, Tirath Ram,' Omi said.

Tirath Ram's nostrils flared. The boys thought he was going to beat up Omi. But Omi was an outside candidate. Tirath Ram shut up. He just fumed. The boys laughed.

The exams lasted three exhausting weeks. Equally exhausting was the increasing heat. The short-lived Punjabi spring had abruptly changed to summer. The wheat fields, depleted by the locust onslaught, were ready for the farmer's sickle. Soon he would reap the meagre harvest he had tended with trepidation for months, load his bullock cart and make trips to the grain markets in cities like Ambala.

On the day of the last paper it was hot beyond belief. But the Camp matric-sitters took no notice of it and, after the exam, they pedalled off to the Cantonment to see the matinee show of the current hit at the Royal. It was a ritual — they did so every year. Omi went with them. Like the rest, he felt he had earned this treat, and for once his mother did not object.

'Don't land up in jail again,' Paro warned.

The film they were going to see was *Nagin*, still a box-office hit.

'But we have seen it, Satish,' Omi said.

'When you get tired of seeing those tits, you are tired of life,' Satish said.

The Royal was full house. They went to see a circus instead, the Greater India Circus. It turned out to be a good one — from its vast tent to its enormous tigers. But most of the performers turned out to be non-Indian, in spite of its name. Pink-skinned girls in bulging bikinis acrobated dangerously to the English music of the Goan band from behind the arena. An English-looking driver of an American World War Two jeep made it leap fifteen feet in the air amid screams from the canvas amphitheatre. The clowns had no skin visible. They were either painted or powdered. Omi could not decide on their origin.

'They are all acrobats or other performers,' Satish told him.

The Goan band, dark-faced men in Edwardian regimental uniforms of red and gold, played music of a byegone age as the fairy-white horses galloped in formation to the whip of a pink-skinned young woman in mauve satin briefs.

'Lovely tits. Better than Vijayanti Mala's. And it's the real thing,' Satish said and reached out with his hands to catch them.

'That's the one to ride,' Bali said.

'She got a whip. She will make you gallop like a horse,' Satish said.

'Look how she moves her bum. She is itching for it.'

'I am going cock-a-doodle-do,' Punnu said, and proved it.

The boys started clapping in unison with him. As the girl went faster and faster, Punnu followed and the clapping grew louder and louder. The boys sat on benches high up in the circus tent, the cheapest class. The finale of the act came with the girl standing astride two riders on their shoulders. The Goan band went wild and Punnu even wilder.

The animals came and Omi felt happier. At least these would be Indian.

'Tiger shit,' Satish said and pinched his nose.

The circus ended with Punnu's girl in the tusks of an elephant, with a tiger on the back of the elephant and a chimpanzee on the back of the tiger.

At the camel bridge on the way back home the boys climbed up to a halt to watch a train pass underneath.

'Next stop Dhulkote,' Bali said, looking slyly at Omi.

'Why not jump in, Omi son, and take a ride to your station. Maybe your-in-laws aren't home, and you can go and give your compliments. Maybe something else also,' Des said laughing.

'We will follow on bikes and bring you back home in garlands,' Harpal said.

'Go on, if you are a man,' Bhajju said.

'He is not a man. He is an insect,' Satish said and told them of Guddy.

So it was out.

'Were her tits nice and firm?' Des asked.

'Did you venture down below?'

'Did you actually ground her?'

'How long did it take?'

'How many times?'

'Did she twist and jerk like in the *Kama Sutra*?'

'Got her photo-shoto?'

'Let's see.'

'Oh boy. I am going to wank as soon as I get home,' seven sisters' brother said, making *that* gesture. 'I am going to wank to your Dhulkote woman.' He hadn't understood that the girl of

Satish's story was not the same as Omi's betrothed one.

Omi went red in the face. The fact that he was not going to marry her was not the point. The point was that seven sisters' brother had spoken like that and that was quite enough.

'Why not ask one of your seven sisters to lend a hand?' Omi said and kicked seven sisters' brother in the arse.

The seven sisters' brother went mad.

'You jail-going Panchkoola-Returned son of a randi whore . . .'

The seven sisters' brother went for sure victory, Omi's testicles. But Omi put his bike between the enemy and his jewels. The boys did the rest. They took the enemy away. He hurled a few obscenities at Omi, Omi hurled an equal number back at him and they pedalled back to the Camp in twos and threes, exhausted. Omi found his father sitting on a charpoi outside their house in the street, shaking his left leg and reading *Milap*. Everybody slept outside now and they put out their charpois early in the evening, lining the streets. Inside, his mother cooked a dinner of ladies' fingers, now well in season. Omi winced. Ladies' fingers meant trouble.

'How did you fare, boy?'

'Lovely film, Father. You should see it. Such character acting.'

'I mean the exams.'

'Oh, very well.'

'That's what you said last year.'

'Last year was different, Father.'

'Every year is different, boy.'

'I simply can't fail. You'll see.'

'That's just what I want to see.'

'You can't see what isn't there. The exam-passing line doesn't exist in his palm. Only loafing is written there,' Paro said.

'Your habit, Ma, to speak like that of everybody. You become a palmist or something?'

'You better pass your matric this time, boy, or you will blacken my face.'

'Of course, Father. Bilkul. You saw me working in Panchkoola.'

'And I saw you working here.'

'Different this time, Ma. I have become more intelligent. Ask anyone in the Camp if you don't believe me.'

'Hear the Sheikh Chilli talk,' Paro said.

'We shall see. Ready for our capital?'

Omi wanted to dash off to the market and buy everybody a special silver paan and announce the news. But it was difficult just now. He had just come home. Immediately after the ladies' fingers dinner he hopped onto his bike and cycled through the dark streets of the Camp.

'Goodbye. Permanent goodbye from Omi,' Omi said every time he saw a contemporary. The streets were cluttered with charpois, but Omi was an expert cyclist. It didn't matter if there were no street lights. He could cut sharp angles without touching anyone or anything. If the Camp had taught him anything, it was to cycle.

Omi came upon a group of boys.

'Adieu, adieu. Permanent alvida,' he said.

'Running away to Bombay, Omi son?' Bhajju said.

Omi did not even look back. He just rode on.

When he got back after a special silver paan, he found his parents, aided by Banto and her Banarsi who lay in their respective charpois a few feet away, fanning themselves with rush punkhas and counting names of cities which ended with Pur, such as Kanpur. There was a total lack of breeze that night and on such nights that's what the people did; for the general belief was that, if you managed to count twenty-four such cities, you would be rewarded by a gust of fresh breeze.

Omi joined them and together they counted thirty such cities, well known, little known and unknown. But no gust of breeze came. What came instead was (and it sent a murmur of applause through the street of the Camp) a sudden rain storm.

'Wah wah, wah wah,' people muttered thankfully. They rolled up their dhurrie bedding, picked up the lightweight string charpois and ran inside their houses.

It rained heavily and delightfully for a couple of hours, guaranteeing a good sleep for the rest of the night. Omi heard Kailash's train come and whistle and go past the Camp. He also heard the other noise behind his room, someone gasping in pain, someone being smothered.

'Open up, you useless bitch.'

There were slaps and muffled cries.

'Open, you useless barren randi slut whore. I am your husband.'

There was a shrill cry which was instantly muffled up. Then something happened — Rani bit him or pushed him away — and Chaman Lal fell off the bed with a thud. He went mad. He beat Rani with a wooden rod and Rani screamed loudly in pain, waking up the entire neighbourhood. Everybody came out. Khatri and Paro decided against going out to watch the tamasha fun like the others. But Omi picked up his mother's washing bat and was the first on the scene, hammering hard on Charman Lal's door. People thought that the Khatri boy was going to kill Charman Lal. Dabbu barked by his side.

Chaman Lal opened the door and gave two full-bodied slaps on Omi's face. Omi went reeling to the muddy earth and Dabbu went wild. He bit Chaman Lal on the ankle. Chaman Lal screamed in pain, snatched Omi's wooden bat and struck Dabbu hard with it.

'What is it to you, you son of a dog? She is my wife. Don't interfere. Go away, you vultures,' Chaman Lal yelled and slammed the door on the people.

Omi stood up, his ears ringing with a whistling noise, and wiped the mud off his face with his sleeve. There was a trickle of blood from his nose. Somebody handed him a piece of cloth to wipe it.

'Husband and wife. Shouldn't interfere, Omi. She is his wife, he can do what he wants,' Banarsi said.

'Go and sleep now, Omi. We will have him arrested tomorrow,' someone said.

'How can we? He is her husband,' someone else said.

People went back home. Omi slipped back to his room.

'What's going on, oi?' Khatri said from his room.

'Nothing, Father. Chaman Lal.'

'You keep out of it and go to sleep now.'

But Omi could not sleep. He lay awake, his ears still ringing with that whistle. His cheeks throbbed with pain. All was quiet again, except for the distant howl of jackals. Omi lay in his bed and looked out at the sky through the rectangle of his open window and heard his pulse beat in his cheeks. He did not know how long he had lain there. Suddenly he heard a familiar sound next door, the creak of the door as someone opened it. Omi got up and looked out of the window. He saw Rani carrying a large can and hurrying away towards the fields. Omi jumped out of the window and ran after her. A hundred yards into the bushes, Rani stopped and struggled to open the can. Omi reached her and snatched the can away from her. It was full of kerosene oil. He also took away the box of matches she carried in the other hand.

Next morning when Khatri learnt of the events of the last night from Banarsi, his first impulse was to take the wooden bat and beat up Chaman Lal. But he thought for a while and then he took Banarsi with him to go to see Chandu. The three of them talked for a long while.

'Go fetch Ram Rakha,' Chandu ordered his assistant.

A little later the assistant returned, seated at the back of Ram Rakha's tonga. A young new horse drove it. Khatri and Banarsi sat in the tonga. Chandu and his assistant rode on two bicycles by their side and they went to Power House in Dhulkote where Chaman Lal worked. Chandu handcuffed him and bundled him into the tonga in front of a surprised crowd of clerks and engineers.

'What has he done?' they asked.

'Tell them what you've done, Chaman Lal,' Chandu whacked him on the head and ordered Ram Rakha to drive back.

At the City road junction he stopped the tonga and ordered Chaman Lal out. He unlocked the handcuffs. Chaman Lal looked surprised.

'You crawl from here all the way home,' Chandu whacked Chaman Lal again. 'Start crawling.' Chandu gave him another whack.

Chaman Lal started to crawl. Every time he straightened up Chandu gave him a kick with his army boots. Chaman Lal crawled all the five hundred yards from the main road to his door, followed by a large crowd. Rani sat on the verandah floor surrounded by a few ladies of the neighbourhood. Her mouth fell open when she saw Chaman Lal crawling.

'Somebody bring some water,' Chandu said.

Somebody brought a bucket of water.

'Wash her feet now,' Chandu ordered Chaman Lal and whispered something to his assistant. The assistant went away hurriedly.

Chaman Lal washed Rani's feet.

'Apologise to your wife.'

Chaman Lal muttered something.

'Say it loud and clear for everyone to hear. Say it with folded hands.'

Chaman Lal folded his hands and apologised.

'Now, if you ever touch a single hair in her head, by God I will take you in for five whole years. You understand?'

Chaman Lal said that he understood.

'Say it loudly.'

'Yes, I understand,' Chaman Lal said loudly.

'And now you have to apologise to the rest of the Camp and this is how you are going to do it.'

Chandu's assistant returned with a donkey and a garland of old shoes. They blackened Chaman Lal's face, with shoe polish, placed the garland of shoes around his neck and mounted him on the donkey. Somebody produced a dholuk and pounded on it as the procession went through the streets of the Camp.

'Total fools,' Khatri said to his family and slapped his forehead in disgust. 'That's what we are.' Then Bhola Ram arrived with Seva and Bawa to take the Khatris and their belongings to our new capital.

THREE

I

Paro wanted to go to Chandigarh through Panchkoola. Having lived with the name for so long, she wanted to see the place for herself. She wanted to see its tall trees, the river Jhajjar running by it, and to hear the cooing of its water mill.

But Panchkoola turned out to be a disappointment — a mere bus stop in the middle of nowhere. Paro shook her head. After a minute of having been there she wanted to move on. She wouldn't stop there even for a pee. Panchkoola was not worth it.

'Let's move on to the next surprise,' she said.

Chandigarh proved to be more than a surprise. It was a shock. Paro slapped her forehead and shook her head each time she looked out of the cab of Bhola Ram's lorry.

'What sort of houses are these cement boxes? Are they for people or pigeons?' she said, referring to Le Corbusier's buildings.

'They got an Angrez to design them,' Bhola Ram said.

'Couldn't they get hold of an Indian?'

'The contractors were Indian.'

'Then these buildings won't stay up for very long. I can tell you that.'

'If anyone heard you speak so ungratefully the Government would take both the shops back,' Khatri said.

'But you know very well what our contractors are like . . .'

'When I want a lecture on them I will ask you. In the meantime . . .'

'. . . But it's true. Our contractors. Utterly useless. Just like our Government. Before Independence Nehru said he would give us milk-and-honey Ram Raj. Lo and behold our Nehru's Ram Raj! Prices four times what they were — wheat, rice, milk, ghee . . . Four times more than what they were when the Angrez ruled. And now these pigeon-holes for houses. Nehru's Ram Raj.'

In Sector 23 there was a large roundabout. On one side of it was a new Hindu temple. On the other, under the shade of a cluster of trees, was the shopping centre for this area. The Government had given Khatri a two-storey building there — shop downstairs and a two-roomed flat upstairs.

Reaching the shop, Paro's mouth fell wide open. She held a hand to it.

'*Capital Sweets*' was printed in capital letters across the shop front. It was repeated in Hindi, Urdu and Punjabi in small letters.

'Hai, my mother!' Paro muttered in amazement. 'What was the need for such a big shop? Are we going to sell sweets or horses?'

'If I had listened to you, I would still be sitting in that wooden dump,' Khatri said.

'At least there weren't the worries you had getting this stable, and those you will have running it. Why didn't you do what Aneja and Juneja did, *buy-and-sell* the shops, make a profit and settle down in the Camp? Commonsense.'

'I want progress.'

'And the other shop — another stable?'

'It is Chandigarh, you know, woman?'

'I know. Better even than Vilayat England.'

'Here you will have to behave differently.'

'I know, I know. Talk differently, walk differently, eat differently, belch differently, even shit differently, no?'

'Paro, like the buffalo, you are happy only in the muck of the village pond. This is Chandigarh, repeat Chandigarh, our new capital. Not your father's village.'

'Hear *them* talk, as if they always lived in *their* father's palace in Patiala!'

Omi, Seva and Bawa brought in the belongings. But there was someone with Omi, getting in the way.

'Dabbu!' Paro shrieked and slapped Omi on the head. 'I am not having him in the house, do you hear?'

'Why did you bring the dog, oi?' Khatri said. He also gave him a slap.

'Couldn't leave poor Dabbu behind, Father. Not after what happened.' Omi had smuggled Dabbu on board the lorry at the very last moment.

'I am not having him in the house. Over my dead body. Either he goes back or I, back to the Camp.'

Paro did not like animals in the house. They were impure, especially dogs. Paro would sooner touch an untouchable bhangi latrine-cleaner than a dog.

'But he is my best friend, Ma.'

'A dog is a dog.'

'He saved my life, Ma.'

'Dog is dog and I am not having him in the house.'

Bhola Ram solved the problem.

'I will take him back next time I go south,' he said.

But Seva Singh made a sensible suggestion.

'Lala ji, big shop and house. Dog is useful to have around. Thieves and robbers don't go where dogs bark.'

Even Paro couldn't disagree with that. But she was still cross.

'With a son like you I am sure to reach heaven,' she said to a smiling Omi.

The flat upstairs was spacious, clean and unlike anything Paro had lived in before. She liked it. She opened and shut built-in cupboards and switched the lights on and off in every room, shaking and nodding her head alternately.

'Come here a minute, Ma,' Omi invited her to the star attraction, the lavatory. 'Pull the chain.'

Paro pulled the chain and ran out in fright as water flooded the bowl. She gave Omi a slap on the head.

'Why couldn't that Angrez design a proper one on the roof or outside the house? Perhaps the Englishmen cannot smell,' Paro said.

'New city, new designs, new ways. People get used to them,' Bhola Ram said.

'Kaliyug, black age, this — having the latrine next to where you cook and eat and sleep.'

Khatri was downstairs while the settling down took place upstairs. He had insisted on opening the shop even if there were no customers. It was a beginning.

'It is only the beginning,' Khatri said to his wife that night.

'Yes, the beginning of our end. I watched all day with both my eyes. Not one customer.'

Khatri tried to explain. But would Paro listen?

'Why couldn't we *buy-and-sell* the shops like the others and settle down in the Camp like the others?'

'Still the silly girl of your father's village. This is not his village.'

'I know. Our new capital.'

'It is here we are going to build our lives and that of our son. It will be unlike anything you or I have been used to.'

'It is not burfi, laddu or jalebi that is the Khatri speciality. It is Sheikh Chilli talk, building castles in the air.'

'Capital Sweets going to work, woman.'

So it began to prove. The shop picked up business. But neither Khatri nor Paro would admit to each other that it had. It would offend God if they did. Only silence pleases God, and thanks said in silence.

Paro made a couple of friends, Satya and the Doctorani. Satya, a lady of her own age, lived next door on the right. Satya's husband, Ujjagar, owned a small shoe factory. The Doctorani, a few years older, lived next-door on the left. Her husband, Dr Devan Chand, was a homeopath. Every other day Paro went with her new friends to the temple two hundred yards away to offer sweets to Lord Krishna. The temple was new and beautiful. It was quite a change from the Camp where there had been no proper temple. Sitting in a proper temple made all the difference. It made praying easier.

Khatri went to the temple less often, but thanked Lord Krishna every day. Every day he would look in the direction of the temple, take a little bow and thank Lord Krishna for *all this*, as he would say — the shop, its contents and the house above it.

'I wasn't starving in Panchkoola. But . . .'

But there was no comparison with *all this*. A real brick-and-cement house. Customers coming and going. What more did he want? Nothing.

One morning, as Paro came down to take a handful of bundi for the temple, Khatri surprised her by giving her a whole trayful of it.

'God is God, but what is the meaning of this?' Paro said.

'Begum, it is He who gives it to us anyway. Take some back.'

Paro was sure that there were less expensive ways of thanking God. But she took the tray. Outside the shop she met a woman clad in a white sari and white blouse. The woman wore wooden sandals that made a loud slap-slap noise as she walked, and carried a small basket on her head. She had come to their house to ask for handha, spare food, what some poor Brahmin widows live on. It is their natural right. As a good Hindu you give them something every day.

Paro and the woman looked at each other, recognised each other and got locked in an embrace. Then they started to weep.

'You ruining my business,' Khatri said.

'What has happened, Ma?' Omi said.

The woman in white turned out to be a friend of Paro's from the past, from the pre-Partition days. She sobbed. Paro sobbed. Only they knew why.

'The Musalmans killed him in the train from Lahore. They hacked him to pieces, Paro. To pieces.'

'My poor Chatkarni! Now reduced to this,' Paro said.

'Paro, they came. Tall, tall Musalmans on high, high horses. They had sharp, sharp swords and long, long lances. They laid down big, big trees across the line and stopped the train and hacked everybody to pieces — three thousand men, women and children. Hindus and Sikhs. Chopped heads and legs and arms outside and inside the train and blood, blood, blood. They hacked my house-wallah — an axe through his head, a sword through his neck and a spear through his body. In front of my eyes. What more can I tell you, sister Paro? They hurled the bodies and limbs into the train, upon me, and I hid under a mountain of chopped limbs, in a mire of blood, red and thick. They dragged off young women and girls by their hair. They tore off their clothes and raped them in the fields. They cut their breasts off and pushed their spears through where they had raped them and filled up the train like a butcher's wagon. What these eyes saw no rakshas demon can ever imagine. The cries these ears heard . . .! They spared the driver, cleared the track and sent the train of thousands of chopped-up bodies and limbs to the border at Attari. To freedom, to Ram Raj in India . . .'

'Come, come, now. Go upstairs and dry your tears,' Khatri said. He had heard a hundred such stories, each one more heart-rending than the next. He also knew Chatkarni and remembered that she liked to add a bit of spice to her stories.

Chatkarni came every day for her handha, her natural right. Paro spent an hour or more talking with her of the good old pre-Partition days and the year of the holocaust, 1947, when her own sisters and Chatkarni's husband were killed. Chatkarni was impressed by the way the Khatris had made their new life.

'And now you have not one but two shops!' Chatkarni said.

The other shop, a much smaller one, was in Sector 15 a couple of miles away. It was near the new University Campus. It was slow. It worried Khatri.

Chatkarni had an idea.

'Sub-let it, Paro,' Chatkarni said.

'Sub-let it. Rent it out,' Paro said to Khatri.

Khatri shook his head. He knew what he was doing. 'No, Begum. When the University gets going, students will flock to it.'

'Students? They only eat rubbish, like your son. Give him a rupee note and see what rubbish he will buy with it. Sub-let it.'

'Paro, if your mother-father put some sense in that head of yours, perhaps you would have been able to understand my plan.'

'I know. Once the University gets built, once the students start coming, they will come and sit in your shop instead of doing their lessons. I know.'

'Oh God! What did I do?'

But with or without returns from the little shop, as it came to be called, Khatri had no complaints.

'Only been here two months.'

If he missed anything, anything of his recent past, it was his morning dip in the Jhajjar at Panchkoola. Standing there, knee-deep in water, with the great mountains on one side and the rising sun on the other, had a special meaning — he was a Hindu and the sun and the water therefore were important. Why they were important was not the point. The point was, they were there. Every morning. And he got a good feeling being there with them.

'Only been here two months.'

There was one thing, though, that worried him. His son. Khatri would like to find a real College Professor to teach him English, good English. Khatri himself had attended school up to the middle level, till the eighth class — five years of the primary school and three years after that. In his school they only taught Urdu. He couldn't even remember what other subjects he was taught. He was a 'middle pass', as it was called — eight years of schooling, from the age of five to thirteen. But he wanted his son to be a 'BA pass'. At least.

'I must find a College Professor. A real one.'

Khatri spoke to a young man, Dev, a collegiate customer. Dev loved Khatri's lassi yogurt drink and came every day to drink it.

'No problem, Lala ji. I know the very man. Professor Bhatnagar. He speaks better English than any Englishman. He speaks it so well that you can hardly understand what he says.'

Dev brought Professor Bhatnagar to the shop one morning.

'It is not for ordinary tuition,' Khatri said. 'I want my boy to speak English well and fluently. Just like you, Professor Sahib.'

The Professor gave Khatri a searching look. He was hurt.

'I am not only a matriculate, but an FA, a BA, an MA, and a senior lecturer at the famous Chandigarh College. I did not learn to speak English as I do from tuition in two months, Lala ji.'

'Not two months, but say four, six, twelve or even more. That is not the point.'

'What is the point, Lala ji?'

'The point is my boy should speak English fluently, like you. Real and proper stuff.'

Professor Bhatnagar looked puzzled — he hadn't said a word in English. He nodded thoughtfully and looked at Dev. What had he landed him into? Like other teachers, he had always given private lessons, but always for poetry, prose, drama and that sort of thing — for examinations. But what would he do with this one? How would he start?

'Alright, Lala ji. We'll give it a try.'

'How much a month?'

Professor Bhatnagar thought for a moment.

'Hundred.'

'I am poor man, Professor Sahib.'

'I got you the best man, Lala ji,' Dev said.

'But this is cruel,' Khatri said, scratching the middle of his sutthan.

There was a compromise. Seventy-five rupees.

Although Omi would have loved to be able to speak English, he found the idea of more tuition so soon after the exams rather tiresome. It was a holiday period — waiting for the results — and whoever had heard of taking tuition during such periods?

'Couldn't it wait a while, Ma?' Omi addressed himself to his mother knowing she would be sympathetic, although for different reasons.

'Ask *them*. *They* have got strange ideas in *their* head ever since *they* set foot in this city full of pigeon-holes.'

'Thank God someone has got a head in this house.' Khatri said. He was adamant. He was anxiously waiting for his son's 'English speaking' tuition to start. He liked the jovial-faced young Professor and hoped he would succeed in making the boy rattle off English as he had heard important people do.

But Professor Bhatnagar was uncomfortable about it. How was he to go about it? That was the question. The answer to it came from a colleague.

'Give the boy comics to read.'

This proved to be something even Omi found interesting. Professor Bhatnagar bought comics from the English Book Depot in Sector 22 and they read them together. Omi thought it was fun. He had never thought it would be all pictures, stories and just talk.

'You should let me see English films now, Father,' Omi said. English films were shown at the Kiran cinema in the smart neighbouring Sector 22, Omi's cinema.

'They show kissing and other *such* things in English films,' Chatkarni said.

'True,' Satya said. 'English films are only good for bad purposes.'

'And you want to see them? Ram, Ram, Ram!' Paro held her ears in consternation. 'You want to become a lafanga-badmash decadent-type loafer? Ram, Ram, Ram!'

'Ram, Ram, Ram,' Chatkarni and Satya said together.

'No, boy. They are not fit for a decent lad from a decent family,' Khatri said. He had heard that they showed half-naked women in them. Even when they were clothed, you could still see a lot.

'Father, 1955, this. Not the nineteenth century. Professor Bhatnagar says they are the best way to learn to speak English. Ask him.'

'What sort of teacher is he?' Chatkarni said and pinched her ears.

Khatri asked Professor Bhatnagar.

'It will be good for Omi to hear English spoken by English people,' Professor Bhatnagar said.

That Sunday, Khatri gave Omi his ticket money. Omi wangled some more for refreshments in the elegant restaurant during the interval.

'Did you understand?' Khatri asked as soon as he got home after the show. 'Tell us the story.' Khatri wanted to make sure that he was getting his money's worth.

It was a Hollywood film and Omi had not understood the dialogue. But he managed to guess the story. He recounted the film, filling in the gaps with his own imagination.

'Sure you haven't cooked the whole thing up?'

'Father, you know me!'

'That's why.'

'Ask Dev. He was there too.'

Khatri checked Omi's version of the film against Dev's. It did not clash too seriously. Khatri was pleased. He let Omi go.

'See, Lala ji! Not doing too badly for a matric boy,' Dev said. 'Professor Bhatnagar best man.' Dev wanted to be given credit where it was due.

Khatri understood.

'All your meharbani kindness, Dev bau,' Khatri said handing him a glass of sweet lassi on the house.

'Another few months and your boy will be speaking English like a real gentleman,' Khatri said to Paro when he went up for lunch.

'Waste of money if he is going to be a halwai. Waste of time and money teaching him English ways. He will slip out of our hands. He won't recognise us — our fate in our old age. Teach you a lesson.'

'But he is not going to be a halwai like me. That's the idea.'

'I know your ideas . . .'

'The education I did not get, I am going to give him. It will make a man out of him, a big man. Whatever it may cost.'

'And who will look after this stable and the little shop?'

'When he becomes a big man there will be no need of shops.'

'Sheikh Chilli talk.'

'Paro, you will remain the village woman I wedded. Fit only to live in dung heaps like the Camp.'

'*Their* habit to speak thus of *others.*' *Others* was Paro herself.

'Won't you like to see your son a big man, an officer?'

Of course. But what sort of officer?

'He can't even pass his matric.'

'He will this time.'

'That will surprise me.'

When the results appeared in *The Tribune* one morning, it surprised not only Paro, but everyone else as well. Omi not only passed, he got a First. He was taken aback.

'The university made a mistake,' Omi feared.

'Told you. Our boy is not a bewakoof dud after all. He only looks it,' Khatri said. Paro was happy. She stained her lips as she bathed and wore the star-spangled red sari her men liked. She also put on a bindu red dot in the middle of her forehead, something she did only on very special days.

'I want to send laddus to the neighbourhood. One hundred and one laddus,' she said. One sent sweets to friends and neighbours on happy occasions, usually laddus, the golf-balls of bundi made twice as attractive by bits of edible silver paper. Their number depended on the importance of the occasion. If Omi had passed last year, the Khatris would have sent fifty-one laddus. An extra year for the same exam increased the importance of its result. And then a First!

'Send two hundred and two. Your son, your laddus,' Khatri said, slapping her on her rump.

'Send some to his master in Manimajra. Let Bawa take them,' Paro said.

'Ashok? Of course, bilkul. Om, you better take them personally — your teacher. Go down and make a nice package of twenty-five laddus and take the first bus to Manimajra.'

'No, take fifty-one. Becomes our status. After all. Beside, it is all because of him that you've passed,' Paro said.

Manimajra! Guddy! Omi jumped. He tried to remember what time Ashok was usually out. He might get a chance to see Guddy all on her own.

People came from the neighbourhood to congratulate the Khatris. Chatkarni undid a quarter-rupee coin from a knot in her sari, waved it around Omi's head three times and gave it to Rano, the young untouchable bhangi girl who did the Khatri house and who happened to be doing it just then.

'Ashok did his job, Bhatnagar will do his,' Khatri said to Paro as Omi left.

'Took the boy two years to pass.'

'Not the same thing, this. And once in College . . .'

'Once in College he will get the College airs and show you what two and two make. Already he can't live without seeing those shameless films on Sunday. Once he is in College . . .'

'Anybody from your family ever set foot in a College?'

'*Their* habit to humilate the *others*. What have we done to you?'

Far from his parents' discussion, Omi sat in the blazing-hot interior of the Manimajra bus. Twenty minutes later he was in Manimajra. The sun bit him at the shoulders through the freshly ironed blue poplin shirt as he walked to Ashok's house. He hoped that Ashok wouldn't be at home. He hoped only Guddy would be there. But everybody was at home.

'Well, well, well. Welcome and congratulations, Om Parkash,' Ashok said, embracing him and relieving him of the parcel of laddus as if he was expecting them.

The verandah was hot, its brick floor reflecting heat. Ashok took him straight to the tuition room. His mother and Guddy sat there in front of an electric fan that swayed slowly from side to side. Omi was given a chair and entertained with a glass of lassi and small talk. But Omi had come for Guddy. She had looked at him from time to time and Omi had wondered if there was any love in those glances.

'Whether it is there or not I will never get a chance to say anything to her with all these guardian angels around. Better forget about it, Omi son, and . . .' Omi stood up.

'Out of the question, Om Parkash. You will have lunch, wait for the heat to pass, and then take a bus home,' Ashok said, pushing him down in his chair.

'Roti lunch,' Ashok's mother said and went up with Guddy to prepare the food.

Omi was pleased with the treatment. Why not? He got a First. After lunch Ashok said he had to go somewhere, but would be right back.

'Why don't you have a nap, Om Parkash?' Ashok said.

So Omi was going to be alone in the tuition room. Maybe he would get a chance. Left to himself Omi felt a stranger in the old familiar room. Would she come? There had been no hint in her eyes. They hadn't once given him that devastating look he was the happy victim of in the good old days.

'But will I have enough courage to speak to her if she does come down? My only chance. If she does I will. I shall say whatever comes to my mind.'

Omi lay on a dhurrie on the floor in front of the revolving fan, waiting.

Half an hour later there was a movement in the verandah. Omi's heart leapt to his throat. He sat up and looked out. Guddy was crossing the verandah to go to the other room.

'Now, Omi son. Push open the door, and . . .'

Omi started to feel a streak of disobedience in his legs.

'Move, you insect.'

Omi crossed the hot verandah, looking right and left. Finding her door open, he walked in. His heart had stopped beating long ago.

'Come to see your lovely face. That's all,' Omi said.

Guddy lay on a dhurrie on the floor, reading *Chanda Mama*, a children's story book. She looked up, but said nothing. She seemed to have been half expecting him to come to her room. She arranged her dupatta scarf on her bosom and looked bashful.

'Do you dislike me so?' Omi said.

She did not reply, but kept looking at him.

'I just came to see your divine face. I had to come.'

Omi knew he was saying something that was not strictly true. What if his father had decided to send Seva or Bawa instead? What if he hadn't passed?'

Guddy stood up. She rearranged her dupatta scarf on her breasts and looked him full in the face. For a moment Omi thought he saw that devastating look.

'I was pining away. I was perishing. Dying,' Omi said.

'Go, someone will see. My brother will be back any moment,' Guddy said.

'I will go if you say so. Never to return.'

Saying this Omi advanced and kissed Guddy on the lips as he had seen in the English films. He pressed her fragile body against his troubled heart.

'Why do you hate me so?' Omi said.

'What is she like? Is she pretty?' Guddy said, disengaging herself from his embrace. Again she rearranged her dupatta scarf.

'Not my fault. I didn't even know about it. My karma.'

Guddy looked away. The old look had gone from her face.

'There is nothing between us — God doesn't will it. Please go.'

Omi tried to take her in his arms again. But Guddy turned her back to him.

'Go, think of my shame. If someone saw you here it would ruin me. There is nothing between us. There can't be anything between us — God doesn't will it.'

'How do you know what God wills or doesn't?'

'Ask yourself. Ask your parents. Ask *her*, whoever she is.'

'I ask you — do you will it?'

She turned.

'Go, please.'

Omi went back. He did not wait for Ashok to return, nor for the heat to pass. He walked away at a half-running pace. He wanted to put as much distance as possible between him and Ashok's house and as quickly. He couldn't wait to get on the first bus to Chandigarh. As it was, he had to wait a long while, until the third bus came. All the others were full. Even the third bus was full up, but the conductor took pity on him.

Omi squeezed in next to a young village girl — and then an extraordinary thing happened. In spite of the tempest in his heart, Omi suddenly became aware of her. His right elbow was in contact with her left breast and it had taken him all that time to realise it. Omi sat up and looked to his right. The girl was well built and a few years older than he. Next to her sat a boy of Omi's age and Omi was sure he had seen him around at the cinema. This had an inhibiting effect on Omi. But the girl seemed unconcerned.

'What a day? A First in the morning, a brush-off in the afternoon, and now this. What a day? God, you are quite extraordinary.'

Omi looked at the boy next to the girl, their eyes met and Omi thought that he saw him smile faintly.

Omi thought of the last time he had made this journey and felt a ripple of shame over his cheeks. A little later the girl raised her arm to give more room to Omi's elbow. Omi thought of Satish and of what he would advise under the circumstances. He smiled to himself as Satish's advice flashed across his mind, and extended his left hand. The breast was firm and round. The girl, like all village girls, did not wear a bra.

'What a day? A First in the morning, a brush-off in the afternoon, and now this.'

Omi discovered that there was an open vent in the kamiz shirt of the village girl. Would she let him put his hand through it? Should he try? It was an agonising decision. Time was passing — they were only a mile or two from the Chandigarh bus stand.

Omi tried. She let him. He caressed her beautifully shaped breast and was gone cock-a-doodle-do and ninety degrees. Then something else happened. Omi tried to reach the second breast. As he did so, his hand met another and the girl slapped Omi's face with one hand and that of the boy on her right with the other.

'What is going on here?' the conductor said.

'These lucha badmash bad men on my sides!' the girl said and started to cry loudly.

'I done nothing,' the other boy said quickly.

'You done something to the poor girl?' the conductor said to Omi, whacking him on the head before he could even open his mouth.

Omi was too confused to answer. The conductor slapped him on the head again, stopped the bus and put him outside in the blazing sun.

'You eat the white heat for the rest of the way home,' he shouted at Omi.

There was not even a tree in sight to rest under. The pink and cement-grey distant buildings of Chandigarh looked very distant indeed. They shimmered like a mirage in the June heat of the Punjab. The Kasauli mountain loomed on Omi's right, but home was far, far away, past several mirages that he saw as he cursed himself and Satish and the fifty-one laddus.

'If I don't die of sun-stroke, I will certainly die of cursing Satish.'

Omi wanted to cry. He couldn't, because he was laughing.

*   *   *

New clothes, fashionable clothes, the sort collegiates like Dev wore, were ordered for Omi. A white shirt to go with white trousers and a check shirt to go with check trousers. A pair of new shoes was also thrown in.

Chatkarni was the first to notice them.

'College doesn't educate boys. College ruins boys. And all these clothes will ruin Omi double, double quick,' Chatkarni said to Paro.

'*Their* idea. What can I do? You tell me.'

'All I can say is that you are witnessing the ruination of your boy.'

'You are ruining the boy,' Paro said to Khatri.

'Anybody from your family ever go to College?' Khatri said. 'And I don't want that handha Brahmini poisoning your ears. Tell her to keep her arse out of it.'

'Ram, Ram, Ram!' Paro said and pinched her ears. 'Talk like that of a poor Brahmin widow and invite the wrath of God.'

Omi was dying to start College, the famous Chandigarh College with its six hundred boys and three hundred girls, all under the same roof and most of them, as was well known, devoted to one thing — looking beautiful. The boys were known to dress with care, the girls to kill. Omi was simply dying to get there and start living.

On his first day, Omi cycled into an ambush, a reception committee of older boys. At the College entrance — a glass and concrete structure — he was met by a beautiful boy in a beautiful bush-shirt. He wore the fashionable Ray Ben American sun-glasses and carried about him an air of importance. There was a sweet smell of perfume about him also.

'Name, please?' the sweet-smelling boy said in posh English.

'Om Parkash Khatri.'

'Follow me, please.'

Omi was taken to the back of the College building. There it overlooked a mango grove a couple of hundred yards away, just across the road to the University. They were met by a number of beautifully dressed boys who talked in posh English. They were speaking to another newcomer. Omi thought he had seen him somewhere.

'May I introduce Mr Khatri Sahib to you, chaps?' the sweet-smelling boy said.

'Welcome, Mr Khatri Sahib,' the boys said.

'Meet your colleague—Mr Kapoor Sahib,' one of the boys said pointing to the other newcomer. 'And shake hands.'

137

Omi shook hands with Kapoor. Omi was sure that he had met that hand before. In the bus from Manimajra?

The senior boys broke up into two groups. One group took Omi a few yards away.

A Professor in black robes passed by.

'Ragging, eh? Don't overdo it, boys,' the Professor said and walked away.

'What is ragging?' Omi venture to ask.

'Part of First Year Induction.'

'What is Induction?'

'It is you do as you are told. Understand? What are you wearing under your shirt?'

'Nothing.'

'Oh, good. Take it off.'

'Why?'

'This is the world-famous Chandigarh College, Khatri boy. You don't ask questions here. You do as you are told.'

Omi shook his head.

'Come on, boy.'

Omi shook his head again.

'Give him a helping hand, somebody.'

Help came willingly and a number of hands took his shirt away.

'What are you wearing under your trousers?'

'Nothing.' Omi wished the boys didn't speak English.

'Oh, marvellous. Take it off.'

'No.'

'Most important. First Year Induction. Most compulsory.'

It was the boys' English that made it so confusing.

'No,' Omi said and held his belt firmly.

'First Year Induction, yaar. Most compulsory.'

The boys were obviously experts at First Year Induction. Some held Omi's arms, others his legs. And off came Omi's beautifully ironed white trousers.

'You Ma chod mother-laying bastards,' Omi screamed in Punjabi, the only language which could express what he felt now. 'Go lay your mothers and sisters . . .'

'Temper, temper . . .'

Omi held his genitals in his hands and looked around in panic. A few yards away Kapoor, divested similarly of his clothes, held his genitals in his hands, showing bits of his pubic hair.

'A race for you two — up to the mango grove. He who gets back first gets his clothes back. He who comes last . . .'

'. . . On your marks. Get set . . .'

Another Professor in black robes was seen approaching. The boys formed a ring around the two naked boys so that they wouldn't be seen.

'Professor Bhatnagar, Professor Bhatnagar . . .' Omi yelled.

Professor Bhatnagar stopped. He shook his head and slapped his forehead in disgust.

'Tut, tut, tut,' Professor Bhatnagar said. 'College of fools.'

'Only joking, Sir.'

'Give them back their clothes. Puri,' Professor Bhatnagar said to the sweet-smelling boy with the American sun-glasses. He shook his head and slapped his forehead again.

'What use was our Independence? It only produced fools like you — India's future. Oh, God. Foreign yoke was better than living with fools.' Professor Bhatnagar waved the older boys away.

Omi picked up a stone as large as a laddu and aimed it at the sweet-smelling Puri. It knocked off his fashionable sun-glasses and shattered them to pieces. It was a near thing. It could have been his eyes.

'Teach you a lesson, Puri,' Professor Bhatnagar said.

Puri and the other boys did not look back.

'I don't think they will bother you now,' Professor Bhatnagar said and left.

Omi and Kapoor dressed quickly and shook hands again, though neither of them knew why.

'I say, we can't go on meeting like this,' Kapoor said.

'Good thing no one knows us here,' Omi said.

'Now everyone will. Don't worry.'

At home Khatri waited eagerly.

'How is the new College, boy?' he asked from his seat in the shop as soon as Omi alighted from his bike.

'Beautiful building. Brand new. Even the furniture.'

'What about the people? Anybody noticed you?'

Omi thought for a moment.

'Quite a few, I would say.'

'Good, good, good.'

Omi knew what he had to do. That night before going to bed

he strapped two medium-sized onions to his armpits.

'Ma, I think I have got something. Fever. Can't go to College,' he said in waking up next morning.

'It's all your loafing in the fashionable Sector 22. And *they* say nothing,' Paro said.

Khatri took Omi's hand and felt his pulse.

'Nothing wrong with you,' Khatri said.

'Bawa, go borrow Doctorani's thermometer. Hakim Doctor Khatri Sahib knows as much about pulse-taking as elephants know of flying,' Paro said.

The thermometer came.

'98.4,' Khatri said. 'Go bath under the tap and off you go to College.' Khatri wanted his money's worth.

Boys at College ignored Omi, the girls wouldn't notice him and he had yet to discover anything about himself to commend to the world at large. Life was difficult. But it was equally difficult to believe that he really had nothing to give, for he had, something important — friendship. He was overflowing with it. He was dying to give it and he was dying even more to receive it.

Every morning Omi dressed with care, hoping that today he would strike a lasting friendship or that some girl would notice him and look him in the eye meaningfully and give him a smile.

Omi did not strike a friendship, nor did any girl look him in the eye. The College over, Omi pedalled back dolefully and waited for the evening, to stroll aimlessly in Sector 22 with Kapoor and Shambhu or whoever else he ran into. Soon he came to realise how insignificant he was in the glamour world of Chandigarh College.

There were about forty girls in Omi's class of over a hundred. Only for English, which was compulsory for all, did the whole class sit together in the grand Lecture Theatre — everything about the College was grand. Girls sat in the front rows, boys in the rear. Professor Gupta, a junior lecturer, took them for English. Professor Gupta's lectures were the most popular. They started in pandemonium, continued in pandemonium and ended in pandemonium. The grand Lecture Theatre, with all those paper aeroplanes flying during his lessons, looked like a busy miniature airport. Boys wrote declarations of lifelong love on them. Some made master drawings of their genitalia. The girls never touched the aeroplanes.

'Anyone I catch disrupting class discipline will go straight to Principal Varma and be fined fifty rupees, if not get rusticated,' Professor Gupta said throughout every lecture.

'Can you pay a fine of fifty rupees?' Professor Gupta asked one day of a boy he caught doing something (the boy did not know what).

'See me after the lecture,' Professor Gupta shouted at the boy and tried to resume the Shakespearean sonnet, the boys' favourite: 'Let me not to the marriage of true minds . . .'

After the lecture, Professor Gupta took the boy by the hand and took him to Principal Varma. Principal Varma, a pleasant-faced fifty-year-old bachelor, looked harrassed. He was dealing with two other similar cases: two other Professors and two other boys stood around his table. He took a quick look at the frightened boy.

'Alright, son. Wait outside,' Principal Varma said and waved him away. 'You can't fine a boy fifty rupees for making a noise, Gupta ji. Fine him a rupee or two at most,' he said to Professor Gupta.

'The Principal leaves it entirely to me,' Professor Gupta said to the boy. 'I am not cruel. I don't want to crush your father with a fine of fifty rupees. Then how do you want me to treat you? Think hard.'

The boy thought hard. He found the answer in History. When the vanquished Indian king Porus was presented to the victorious Alexander the Great, the latter had asked a similar question.

'How do you want me to treat you?' Alexander had said.

'As one king should treat another,' Porus had replied and won the Greek over.

'As a teacher should treat a pupil,' the boy said to Professor Gupta.

Professor Gupta smiled.

'But, Sir . . . What did I do?'

Professor Gupta did not really know. 'I'll let you go if you apologise in writing,' he said.

'But, Sir . . .'

'It's either that or fifty rupees . . .'

141

The boy wrote out an apology in his worst handwriting and made his escape.

'Bastard,' the boy shouted when he was out of ear-shot.

The next day Professor Gupta called the boy to the stage of the Lecture Theatre and produced the letter of apology.

'Read it aloud, Om Parkash,' the Professor said.

This was too much. Omi took the letter and crushed it into his pocket. The girls giggled, the boys laughed. The air traffic multiplied.

'Get it out and read it to the class,' Professor Gupta said.

Omi shook his head. A struggle began. Professor Gupta tried to get the paper out of Omi's pocket. But Omi moved faster. Omi did a smart thing. He put the paper in his mouth and chewed it up. The class roared. Even Professor Gupta could not stop laughing. He waved Omi back to his seat in the last two rows.

'First it was Ma chod mother-laying Tirath Ram, now it is Gupta!' Omi muttered to himself.

That night Omi strapped two large onions to his armpits. But the Doctorani's thermometer refused to be persuaded.

'98.4. Go bath under the tap,' Khatri said.

Omi took the thermometer and examined it.

'Made in India,' Omi read. 'What do you expect?'

Omi realised that he had made a mistake about the subjects he had chosen. Just because of his First, the fool had chosen Economics, a difficult subject. History was what he should have gone for. It attracted the girls — it was an easy subject. Out of the forty girls in his class, about thirty read History. That's how easy it was.

Glamorous girls, fashionable girls, girls from the rich north-end of Chandigarh, girls in skin-tight clothes of imported materials and exhaling the sweet smell of imported perfumes, all read History. They were ravishingly different from any girl Omi had passed by in the Camp. After the English lecture they would walk briskly across the mirror-floored corridors to do History with Professor Raj Kumar. Omi, left with a score of dull and studious-looking boys and girls, would walk slowly to the Economics lecture. Almost all of these girls wore glasses.

'Glasses on girls don't go. The pretty ones become plain, the plain ones become plainer,' Kapoor said. He read History.

Besides, Professor Raj Kumar was the only *Cambridge-Returned* on the staff. He wore cotton suits and was highly popular, especially with students from the rich north-end, the boys and girls with public schooling; they flocked to him like moths to a flame. He was young, in his mid-twenties, beautiful and spoke English beautifully.

'Speaks English like an English Lord,' everybody said. 'You can hardly understand what he says.'

It was a treat to hear Professor Raj Kumar speak English, he never spoke in any other language. By comparison English spoken by other Professors, including Professor Bhatnagar, sounded like Anglicised Punjabi or vice versa. In fact there was no comparison and it was obvious.

'That's it,' Omi said to himself. That was the English he had to learn to speak.

Kapoor confimed this view.

'That's the English you have to learn to speak if you want to get anywhere in life,' Kapoor said.

Omi had an idea. It would kill two birds with one stone. 'What if I changed Economics for History?'

Then he would not only be with the girls without glasses, but also hear Professor Raj Kumar's beautiful English every day.

Omi needed his father's signature on a form for this.

'If Father guessed it was because of the girls . . .' Omi separated two imaginary pieces of paper glued together. 'My skin will come off just like this.'

It was a serious matter which required serious thought. Omi gave it serious thought and quickly arrived at a conclusion.

'Father doesn't have to know about it. Anyway, History or Economics — one and the same thing for him. College subjects.'

He got a form from the College office, filled it in and asked Kapoor to sign his father's name at the bottom.

'On one condition — you call me Dad from this day on,' Kapoor said.

'Alright, Dad.'

The boys shook hands and Kapoor forged Khatri's signature.

Omi sold off his Economics books and bought *The Golden History of India* with the proceeds. He still had to buy *The Golden History of England*.

'Just a question of cash. A bit of it. Let me lay my hands on it.'

Omi was waiting for an opportunity to *sit* in his father's *seat*. Such opportunities came but rarely, for Khatri never left the shop except to go briefly to the little shop which Seva looked after.

However, a couple of days later, the opportunity presented itself.

Khatri had been somewhat restless for the last few days. When Omi questioned his mother about it she shook her head and lowered her voice.

'God has come into *them*,' Paro said.

Omi did not understand. But late that afternoon, as Professor Bhatnagar left after the English-speaking tuition, he saw his father make a basket of his sweets and send Bawa for a cycle rickshaw.

'Where is Father going?' Omi asked his mother.

'Kalka. To see his guru.'

'I didn't know Father had a guru or needed one.'

'Everyone needs a guru. Ours is Gokul Baba.'

'You seen him, Ma?'

'No.'

'Then how can he be your guru too?'

'Don't torture me with your silly questions.'

'But what is Father going there for?'

'To thank him.'

'For what?'

'For all this . . .' Paro said with the sweep of a hand, meaning the shop and the house above it, '. . . and the little shop.'

Khatri gave a shout for Omi from downstairs.

'Mind the shop while I am gone. And don't put your mouth in the sweets or your hand in the galla. Do you hear?'

'Yes, Father. You know me.'

'That's why.'

That evening Omi bought *The Golden History of England* from the English Book Depot in Sector 22. It had a picture of a young Elizabeth II on the cover with all the crown jewels. Omi thought she looked very pretty.

'Now all I have to do is to learn to speak like Professor Raj Kumar. Then there will be no difference between me and those "imported shirts".'

Omi was thinking of the sons and daughters of the elite of the

Punjab who brought glamour to Chandigarh College. These people were called 'imported shirts' because of their attachment to imported goods. They had all spent a number of years in the same public schools in the mountains. Thus they distinguished themselves from the others, the 'ordinaries', by a healthy pink in their cheeks which only the mountain air and water gives. This colouring, loosely called Simla Pink, showed immediately who was who.

The Simla Pink crowd spoke excellent English, almost as beautifully as Professor Raj Kumar. The staff of Chandigarh College were particularly friendly to them, even though some of them seldom attended any lectures — they were known to be doing more interesting things like picnicking in Kasauli and elsewhere in the hills. Even when they did attend classes, they read English novels and comics during them.

The Simla Pink boys and girls came and went in cars and motor bikes that roared noisily and were seen every Sunday morning at the cinema for the English films. Most of them had English nick names. They talked and laughed loudly. Most of them smoked, even some girls and many Sikh boys too. Rumour was that they also drank.

Omi and boys like him, the 'ordinaries', seemed a different race. They couldn't speak English, they didn't have the beautiful Simla Pink in their cheeks nor did they wear imported shirts, jeans, jackets, shoes or perfumes. Instead they came to College in pyjamas, many of them. After the lectures, or during free periods, the 'ordinaries' stood in knots at a distance from the Simla Pinks and moved aside whenever a group of them passed. Omi worshipped the Simla Pinks.

One day Omi told his father about the public schools.

'Costs three to four hundred a month and they only speak English there,' Omi said.

'Big shops sell the same stuff as small shops for double the price. You are learning English from Bhatnagar, aren't you?'

'Not the same thing, though, Father. You don't understand.'

Khatri whacked his son on the head.

'See how your son talks to his father now?' Khatri said to Paro. 'The bastard has only been at College for a few weeks.'

'All your own fault. Those clothes and those shameless films

145

. . . Wait another few and he will show you what two and two make.'

Omi knew the comics off by heart. Professor Bhatnagar had started him on English novels. He was on his third now.

'Get him the English newspapers as well, Lala ji,' Professor Bhatnagar said.

The Tribune started to arrive every morning.

Omi preferred comics to any other kind of reading material, but Khatri saw to it that he read the newspaper.

'Not only will your English improve, but you will also learn about world affairs. Besides, it costs money.' *The Tribune* cost money, so it had to be read.

The point was to learn to speak English. What had world affairs to do with that? The comics were fun. The novels, though difficult to read, had their advantages. It made an impression at College to be seen with one in your hand. It was something in common with the Simla Pinks. But *The Tribune* was a bore.

Paro had her own opinion about it.

'Unnecessary expense. What has the boy got to do with news and newspapers? Why has he to know of a murder in Ambala or a rape in Patiala? Newspapers are meant for grown-ups,' Paro said.

'Any grown-up in your family ever read an English newspaper?' Khatri said.

'*Their* habit to speak like that of the *others*. As if I were the untouchable bhangi girl Rano,' Paro said and started to cry. It was unusual.

'Mother!' Omi said.

'Come, come, Begum. You know better than that,' Khatri said. He went up to her and slapped her on her bottom. It was only then Khatri noticed that she wore her red sari and that her lips were stained orange. He smiled and slapped her again and felt a slight stirring in his sutthan.

'Go and bath, boy,' Khatri dismissed Omi and caressed Paro's bottom. 'I say, got a yaar-shaar here also?'

'Since you set foot in your capital how many times have you opened your eyes?' Paro said wiping her tears with the end of her red sari. 'You don't look at us any more. It is always money, money, money.'

Khatri put an arm around her and felt her thighs. The stirring in his sutthan had increased. But Paro was in no mood to be trifled with.

'Leave us alone and go back to your galla. My family neither went to College nor read English newspapers. What do you want from us illiterates?'

Khatri took her hand and tried to take it to his sutthan, but Paro disengaged herself. She shed another tear and blew her nose.

'How many times since you've got here?' she said and went to the kitchen to make breakfast.

Khatri closed the shop at quarter to eight in the evenings according to the regulations. But it was still daylight. In Panchkoola there had been no regulations and he had kept the shop open until much later. There was nothing else to do, and besides, odd lorries stopped by. In Panchkoola he had kept the shop open for small amounts of money that trickled in slowly. Here in the capital he did not have to do this. There was less work and no mad rushing about. No shuttling between the Camp and Panchkoola. No Aneja and Juneja to worry about with competition. Here it was peace and quiet.

But there was something irksome about this peace and quiet.

In Panchkoola, Khatri had never doubted that every penny he earned was well-earned. Here in Chandigarh at the end of the day, when he sat down to count the day's takings, he did so with a foreign feeling, with a sort of lump in some socket of his lungs, that it was only half-earned. At such moments he missed Panchkoola, its cool breezes coming from the Kasauli mountain and the sense of urgency the buses breathed into his business life there.

That evening he sent Bawa with a five-rupee note to buy a quarter bottle of the Red Fairy and went up to the roof of the house to drink it. Normally, Paro would have grumbled. But today she did not. She saw Bawa sneak up the stairs to the roof with the little red bottle, a bottle of soda water, a glass and some savouries, but pretended not to have seen him.

An hour later Khatri came down with a smile on his face. He

147

rubbed his hands and slapped Paro on her bottom.

'Double, double hungry,' he said.

Paro ignored him.

'Absolutely bilkul true. Double hungry,' Khatri said and put both his arms around her and moved closer.

Paro remained quiet and remained where she was, standing by the window of the kitchen, looking out at the trees of the nurseries behind the row of their shops.

'Come on, Begum. Relent a little,' Khatri said and took her hand to where he took it in such circumstances.

'Ram, Ram, Ram! What if the boy saw you with your tent peg sticking out?'

'Where is he?'

'As if you don't know. He is loafing in Sector 22.'

'Let him loaf a little longer,' Khatri said and undid her sari.

'Shame on you. What if the boy comes back?'

'It won't take long,' Khatri said and led her to the room next door. Paro followed holding the peg in his sutthan, her sari trailing behind her.

Ten minutes later they were back in the kitchen.

'And now you won't look at us for another few weeks,' Paro said.

'Same time same place tomorrow and every day.'

'Sheikh Chilli talk.'

Omi arrived, singing a film song.

'The University is starting soon I hear, Father. Our little shop will be alright then,' Omi said without giving his father the opportunity to question him about his loafing.

'So what? Shops are not left to servants to run,' Paro said making a reference to Seva Singh.

'I can't be at two places at the same time, can I?' Khatri said.

'Why not put the boy there?' Paro said.

'Told you a hundred times — I don't want him to end up a halwai like me.'

'Oh no, you want him to be a Dipty Commissioner.'

'We are not starving without him being the second ox on the harness. With God's grace we will give him a proper education and let him make his life.'

'Or ruin it. He is already catching the airs of the College. He won't wear the same trousers for more than two days running. He says they get dirty. And he won't let me wash them either. He won't even carry a hankie unless it has been washed, starched and ironed by a proper dhobi.'

Khatri was secretly pleased at this delicacy his son was acquiring. He smiled to himself.

'You seem amused. Wait until he learns the ways of the English speakers. Just wait another few months. Then he will wrap you around his little finger. Don't say then that I didn't warn you. You better put him in the little shop. Anyway, how do you know that Seva is not cheating you?'

'Seva is a trustworthy man. That's why I keep him there. Besides, I make him account for each and every ounce of stuff in the shop. I am strict with him.'

'They don't cheat when you are looking.'

'Well then?'

'Then rent out the little shop.'

'That handha Brahmani has been poisoning your ears again. Don't you realise that when the University gets going, that little shop is going to run twice as fast as this big stable?'

'Then have someone of our own to *sit* in it instead of a servant.'

'Aha, I know what is on your mind. Your sister's husband. As if I haven't had enough of the bastard. Open your ears and listen to me carefully. I can take care of cheating servants, but God save me from dishonest relatives.'

'*Their* habit to run people down. He is not really like that.'

'Isn't he? The son of a bitch cheated me of hundreds. If he wasn't your sister's house-wallah I would have hung him on the kirket tree and have everyone in the Camp come and spit on him.'

'He was only a boy then. I will see to it that he behaves like a man this time.'

'The question will not arise. I don't want to see him anywhere near Sector 23 or Sector 15. Get it out of your head.'

Paro shut up, but let a few silent tears run down her cheeks. She took up the lethal weapon of silence and remained quiet all through dinner and after, sighing from time to time.

'What is eating you? I have told you I would rather leave the little shop to Dabbu than that scoundrel badmash. Be thankful that I did not hand him over to Chandu like that Chaman Lal.'

When Khatri had moved to Panchkoola, before giving up the shop in the Camp, Paro had got her sister's husband Bhajjan to mind it. Bhajjan was active, energetic, respectful and ready to please. But Khatri was suspicious of him. Bhajjan was a trifle too respectful, too agreeable and too ready to please. It took Khatri three months to prove his hunch. He caught Bhajjan red-handed. He had been using two registers, showing more expenses than sales. One night Khatri, tipped off by Ram Rakha, arrived unexpectedly. He fished out the original register from under Bhajjan's pillow. Khatri had given him a beating he would never forget, with his peshawari chappal, in front of the whole bazaar and sent him back to Pipli near the famous Kurukeshtra, where he had come from. That was the story.

With a wounded look on her face, Paro went on with the washing-up. Slowly she rubbed the brass utensils with ash from the choolha kitchen fire, and washed them under running water from the tap. Her silence, even though Khatri knew it was calculated, hurt him. After a long day in the shop, especially after a quarter of Red Fairy in him, Khatri needed conversation. Usually she provided it in abundance. But today Paro burnt inside.

Suddenly Khatri felt angry. In spite of the quick ten minutes next door before Omi's return, and in spite of the food inside him, the Red Fairy still glowed in him.

'Where have you been all this time?' Khatri said to Omi.

It was an unnecessary question. Omi hesitated.

'Where the hell have you been?' Khatri thundered. 'Have you both lost your tongues, mother and son?'

Paro looked at her son and opened her mouth at last.

'*They* know very well where he has been — loafing after girls in Sector 22. Then why *they* ask?'

'You go vagabondising tomorrow and I will pluck the skin off your body.'

Omi knew where safety lay. Up on the roof, where they slept in the summer. He hurried upstairs and counted the stars, waiting for sleep. His parents joined him and went to their respective beds without a word. All three tossed and turned in silence but for different reasons.

*   *   *

As Omi sat cross-legged on the kitchen floor one morning eating his breakfast paratha, a crow as black as coal came and perched on the verandah balcony. It started crowing loudly.

'Look,' Paro said with a glint in her eyes. 'A crow!'

'No, Mother. It is a peacock.'

'Shut up and listen. It is crowing.'

'So?'

'A letter is coming to us.' The Khatris never received any letters.

'Superstitious nonsense, Ma. No wonder India doesn't make progress. How can you believe it? Who told you crowing crows bring letters?'

'You'll see.'

Sure enough there was a letter in the first post that morning. It fell into Omi's hands as he was about to leave for College.

'A letter, Father, a letter!' Omi shouted excitedly.

Khatri took the letter, ground his jaws and looked at it carefully.

'I thought so,' Khatri said with a nod and handed the letter to Paro.

Omi snatched it away from his mother and tore it open.

'"My dearer-than-life sister Parvati . . ."' Omi read in Hindi.

Khatri shook his head and slapped his forehead.

'Waste of time. I know what's in it,' Khatri said and went back to the shop.

Paro took the letter from Omi and started reading it. As she read, her heart rose to her throat and two large tears trickled down her cheeks.

'What does aunt Vidya say, Ma?'

Paro did not answer. She read the letter silently and cried silently. Chatkarni came for her customary handha and Omi took off for College. Paro gave the letter to Chatkarni to read. Chatkarni also started to cry. When she had finished reading the letter the two women embraced each other and wept for a long time on each other's shoulders. Paro did not say a word to anyone for the rest of the day.

'What was in the letter, Ma?' Omi asked after dinner that night.

'I only have one sister left now!' Tears came into Paro's eyes and she choked for breath.

'Silly woman,' Khatri said.

'Your father's heart is made of stone. It was made by a stonemason,' Paro said.

'But what was in the letter, Ma?'

Paro did not answer Omi's question.

'How can *they* enjoy their prosperity here when the only sister I've left now is starving in Pipli?' Paro said instead, burying her head in her pillow.

A few days later another letter came and there were more tears. But Khatri was unmoved.

The day the third letter arrived, Paro stopped eating.

'Hunger strike, eh? Mahatma Gandhi stuff, eh? I am not a fool like Mountbatten. I won't give in,' Khatri said that night on the roof.

Paro sobbed.

'Go on, starve yourself to death. Better still, go drown yourself in the lake and take your dearer-than-life sister and that bottle of poison Chatkarni with you. I will pay for the taxi.'

When Omi woke up next morning his mother was not in the kitchen making breakfast. She was not anywhere in the house. He looked at his father inquiringly.

'Don't look at me like that, boy,' Khatri said.

'But where is Mother?'

'Gone to Pipli.'

'What for?'

'To fetch her dearer-than-life sister's husband to ruin the little shop.'

'Again?'

'Yes, that's your mother — a thick-headed Punjabi jatni. She says he is a member of the family. The bastard cheated us of hundreds the last time, this time he will cheat us of thousands.'

'Why did you let her go, Father?'

'Peace, boy, peace. That's what I want. Not the rivers of rain which flowed down her cheeks every night all these nights. And still I said go to hell. No, I said. But she went at the first cry of the cock. I told her as she went that I would break Bhajjan's legs if he set foot in my house. She heard, but still she went. I am telling you now, boy, I will break both his legs.'

Omi knew that his father would do nothing of the kind. But he shared his loathing of Bhajjan. He could not understand why his mother wanted him to work for them again. He had read all the three letters. Each one of them spoke of the hardships of penury in Pipli and the famine-like conditions there. Each letter ended with blackmail:

'In the barren desert of our lives, the only cool breeze of solace is the sure knowledge that at least my dearer-than-life sister enjoys a life of plenty.'

When Omi returned home from College in the afternoon, his face red with heat and the effort of cycling in it, he felt miserable. The house was lonely. Dabbu, usually not allowed upstairs, rose to the occasion and mounted the stairs boldly — as if he owned the house. Bawa served Omi his meal. Omi shared it with Dabbu. Then, after a cool and long drink of lassi, he settled in his parents' room for the daily siesta under the electric ceiling fan. Dabbu spread himself on the floor at his feet. It was Professor Bhatnagar's bicycle bell that woke them both up a couple of hours later. Omi put his head under the bathroom tap and shook himself free of slumber. While combing his hair in the mirror next to the window he saw two rickshaws pull up at the back door of the shop. One contained his mother and aunt Vidya, the other Bhajjan and their luggage. This meant that they had come to stay.

Dabbu barked furiously and shot down the stairs.

'Hell,' Omi said in English and hurried next door to his own room where Professor Bhatnagar was waiting.

'Come to live off us, the bloody chor thief,' Omi swore at his aunt's husband. 'He will eat our salt and betray us!'

Paro and Vidya came straight up, leaving Bhajjan to pay off the rickshaws and follow with the luggage.

'Where is my nephew Omi?' Omi heard aunt Vidya ask his mother in a fragile voice. She was ten years younger than Paro and quite beautiful. His mother shooed her into silence.

'At tuition. With his master. Very expensive master.'

'And brother?'

'Down in the shop.'

'Good arrangement. Shop and house under one roof. Wah wah, wah wah! Come and go when you want. Rain or sun, no worry. Wah wah, wah, wah.'

Bhajjan brought up the luggage, making much noise on the

stairs. He passed the tuition room and Omi had a closer look. In a striped pyjama the colours of which were half faded, and a greying white shirt with the crease of the washing line in the breast and the sleeves, he looked shabby.

'Guests? Relations?' Professor Bhatnagar said. He, too, had a look as Bhajjan passed by the door.

Omi felt ashamed.

'He used to work for Father at one time.' Omi denied all relationship and felt ashamed of himself for doing so.

'Hell!' He swore between his teeth and wondered if his father downstairs knew that the Pipli people had arrived.

Khatri knew everything. Dabbu's furious bark had alerted him, Bawa subsequently had informed him. He hoped that Vidya and her husband would not come down to inspect the shop and to say namastey greetings. Nor, Khatri had decided, would he himself go up until quarter to eight.

Dabbu barked furiously again and Khatri realised that they were coming down. But it was only Bhajjan and Dabbu nearly bit his legs off. Bhajjan came and stood in the door-way with downcast eyes and hands folded on the middle of his greying shirt. He was saying namastey to Khatri without actually saying it.

'How the hell can he face me after the beating I gave him? Shall I not tell him to get the hell out of here?'

'You have come? Wife well? Mother-father well?' Khatri said instead.

'Everybody is very well,' Bhajjan said, looking at the floor near Khatri's feet.

'The son of a bitch is ashamed of what he did to me. That's why he won't raise his eyes from the floor,' Khatri said to himself, inside his burning throat.

'You better go up and ask your sister to give you something to eat. I will come when I can. Busy time, this.'

It was not true, but Khatri had said so to deal with his embarrassment.

'The cheating dog. If only a man could talk to his wife sometimes!' Khatri said after Bhajjan.

'Is brother coming up?' Vidya asked her husband as he got upstairs.

'He is busy.'

'Five onwards is a very busy time on Tuesdays. Temple-going day, Tuesday,' Paro explained, though she knew it was rather early. People started going to the temple only after six.

When Professor Bhatnagar got up to leave, Omi followed him downstairs and went into the shop instead of going up to meet the guests.

'Met your uncle?' Khatri asked.

Omi answered with an uneasy look on his face. Both father and son realised that each was as reluctant as the other to go upstairs.

'Your mother! Would she listen? He cheated us once, he will cheat us again. But you try telling her. "My sister. When she is starving in Pipli, how can I rest in peace here." You try telling her. Can't fight a Punjabi jatni. You try.'

Vidya hugged Omi and spoke to him as if he was her own boy. Omi quite liked that. She had the charm and figure his own mother must have had at twenty-five. Omi thought she was wasted on Bhajjan.

'A matter of karma,' he said to himself.

'Go and tell your father,' Vidya said.

'Father is busy at this hour.'

'This is not the Camp, you know. This is Chandigarh. Our new capital,' Paro said. She sounded apologetic.

Khatri finally appeared.

'The pursuit of money swallows you so completely that your only sister has no place in your thinking. What sort of a brother are you?' Vidya said.

'Work, work, work. It is not money, it is work,' Khatri said. Vidya was young, firm of figure as Paro was ten years ago, and quite beautiful. It was difficult to ignore it.

'We are here only to help you,' Vidya said.

'Or to ruin me,' Khatri thought.

'There was no need to uproot you from your work in Pipli, though. I said so to your dear sister,' Khatri said pointing to Paro.

'Family is family. After all. The mistakes of the youngsters have to be forgiven by the wise elders,' Vidya said, looking from her own husband to her sister's.

'Family is family. After all.'

'*They* only want the little shop to be run the way *they* want it,' Paro said.

Bhajjan cleared his throat as if he wanted to say something. But he remained quiet, his eyes glued to the floor. Khatri looked at him, but quickly turned his eyes away and looked at his son who was gazing out of the window, looking bored.

'Tell him that you forgive him,' Paro urged her husband. This was the first time she had spoken to her husband publicly.

'Mistakes of the past are things of the past. Elders have to forgive. Who else have we to look to in our hour of need?' Vidya said. She sounded both angry and hurt saying so.

With his gaze still fixed on the cement floor, Bhajjan cleared his throat again.

'I made a grave mistake and I have suffered much,' Bhajjan said.

'Serve you right,' said both Khatri and Omi simultaneously to themselves.

'I have brought him here so that he can apologise. He has suffered much for his mistakes. Can't you see that? Look how much weight he has lost!' Paro said, looking both at her husband and her son.

'Yes. He was much fatter when he was feeding on our food,' Khatri and Omi thought simultaneously.

'Tell *them* again, tell *them* again how sorry you are,' Paro urged Bhajjan.

Tall and thin and full of shame, Bhajjan crossed the length of the room in long strides and looked at Khatri.

'Forgive us, brother,' he said, bowing to touch Khatri's feet.

The sight of a grown man cringing killed Khatri's anger. He stopped Bhajjan before he actually touched his feet and, feeling as embarrassed as he thought the other must feel, he let it pass at that.

'All an act,' Omi thought, though he also felt embarrassed by the whole thing. 'All an act,' he said to himself as he ran downstairs, hearing Dad Kapoor shout for him from the courtyard.

'Hell!' Omi said to himself as Dabbu jumped on him. 'And you behave yourself, Dabbu boy.'

One good thing came out of Bhajjan's arrival — Khatri started to take greater interest in the little shop. He started to go there more often. But he was worried about Seva Singh.

'Not our responsibility. Let him go where he came from.' Paro had the ready-made answer to the problem.

Khatri ground his jaws and scratched the middle of his sutthan. Then he shook his head. He could not find it in him to throw out a trusted servant for the sake of a brother-in-law he loathed. He was angry with himself for having succumbed. 'I should have let her go on with her monsoons and her rivers of rains.'

As Vidya and Bhajjan moved to the litle shop, Seva came back to the Sector 23 and shared a back room with Bawa. Khatri felt glad about it. So did Omi, he liked Seva — he had saved Dabbu from being deported to the Camp. He had also cooked him some memorable butter parathas back in Panchkoola. That seemed a long time ago. Yet it was less than nine months ago.

During his first month, Bhajjan showed more profit than Seva Singh used to.

'Told you. Seva was cheating us,' Paro said.

'It is only because of the Congress Conference that took place in Sector 15,' Khatri explained. 'Wait and see.'

'A snake will remain a snake, Ma,' Omi said.

'Shut up, you son of your own father.'

'Professor Gupta taught us new English proverb today, Ma. You cannot change a leopard's spots.'

'It is family. And family is family,' Paro said. 'I only have one sister left now.'

'He is not my family. He is a snake. Any hanky-panky this time and he goes inside. You better tell Vidya,' Khatri said.

'Tell her yourself.'

'Alright, I will.'

And when the two sisters were together again two days later, Khatri went up in the afternoon to give Vidya a piece of his mind. Vidya washed clothes for her sister in the bathroom. The door was closed, but not bolted from the inside and Khatri, thinking it was Paro, pushed it open and went in. He wanted to tell his wife what he was going to say to her sister.

Vidya wore only a muslin kurta shirt. It was wet, and so transparent. It clung to her shapely breasts, which seemed almost naked. She stood up, looking for her dupatta scarf, which was on the drier part of the floor by the door.

A warm flush spread over Khatri's face.

'Where is Paro?' Khatri asked meekly instead of giving her the rebuke he had prepared and rehearsed.

'Gone to buy some soap,' Vidya said, bending down to pick up her dupatta scarf, and offering a deep view of her breasts through the neck of her shirt. She stood up full length, taking her time to cover her almost naked bosom.

Confused, Khatri withdrew. Back in his seat in the shop he was quiet — the warm flush had spread to the whole of his body. He wished he had not gone up then and seen her almost naked. She looked so young, fresh and desirable. She reminded him of Paro when they were just married, when all that Khatri could think of was her body. Youngest of the four sisters, Vidya was also the most attractive — the other two sisters had been murdered with their husbands by Muslims during the holocaust of 1947. When she was married off to Bhajjan in the same year, her father-in-law was not poor. It was Partition which ruined him. And he was less fortunate than the other refugees fleeing from Pakistan in reestablishing himself in India. After several abortive attempts at various places he had dwindled to a wayside shop at Pipli. Bhajjan and Vidya lived with him. Married for eight years, Vidya was still childless.

Khatri's ears burned with the sight of her almost naked body, and he felt ashamed.

'Ram, Ram, Ram! Aren't I a bit old for such things?'

Khatri tried to dismiss her from his thoughts, but the image of her wet body kept emerging in his mind. He knew he would not be able to say anything to her now.

The day had been cloudy. Over the clay hills, before the Kasauli mountain, there had been flashes of lightning. But it did not rain in Chandigarh. At six in the evening Khatri left Seva in charge of the shop and took off on Omi's now-dilapidated bike — its saddle was in bad shape, the brakes hardly worked and its carrier at the back was broken — to visit the little shop, two miles away.

At the roundabout by the temple it occurred to Khatri that it might rain — the sky did not look good. But he was on the bike now and he might as well carry on. Besides, Vidya was still up in the house and he did not want to run into her again, at least not today.

Khatri had gone barely half a mile when the flashes of lightning suddenly grew nearer. At Sukhna Cho, the seasonal river that passed through Sector 16 and skirted his own Sector 23, a few drops of rain fell on him. A few hundred yards more, by Omi's College, a great thunderstorm broke over Chandigarh and it started to rain furiously. The day became dark and bleak.

'I was a fool. I shouldn't have come today.'

Khatri still had over a mile to go.

'I should have listened to myself and waited till tomorrow.'

A fierce wind blew against him, making cycling a struggle on the deserted road. There was not a single living thing in sight.

'Who would be about in this forbidding storm? Only a fool like Shadi Lal Khatri.'

He was exactly halfway. Whichever way he went, it would be the same storm and the same amount of rain to drench him.

'Forward, then.'

There was another fool about, a solitary figure trudging along in the rain on the lonesome road.

Vidya!

'What on earth are you doing here in this weather?' Khatri said, hopping from the bike.

'I couldn't get a rickshaw, so I had to walk home,' Vidya said, hugging herself.

It was clear what Khatri had to do. He had to give her a lift on the bike. But where on the bike? The carrier was broken. There was only one place where she could ride with him.

'Alright then,' Khatri said.

Vidya sat on the cross bar, between Khatri and the handlebars. The incandescent whip of the lightning cracked thunderously overhead and the storm raged as Khatri struggled forward. The warm flush of the afternoon reappeared in his face and limbs and a stirring suddenly started in his sutthan. Khatri felt ashamed of himself.

'Hai, my mother! what a big, big . . . storm!' Vidya said.

Khatri said nothing. Cycling had become very difficult with a passenger on the bike in that wind. He had to push himself forward to pedal.

Vidya's breasts rubbed against his arms accidentally, making the stirring in his sutthan quite uncontrollable. The tent peg rose.

'Ram, Ram, Ram!' Khatri said to himself. What was he doing? Had he, Shadi Lal Khatri, a twice-born high-cast Hindu, no shame, no honour, no fear of God? Where was his izzat self-respect?

The tent peg rose. Lightning sizzled and thunder clapped only yards above them.

'Please God, let the lightning strike me dead here and now. Please save me.'

Khatri was saved. An empty rickshaw came from the darkness of the storm. He jumped off the bike and let Vidya get in it. Then he hung his head in shame and guilt and pedalled back home furiously. He ran into Paro at the shop.

'Any man going anywhere in this weather would only have one reason to go there,' Paro said.

'Pray tell us what that reason would be?' Khatri said, handing the bike to Omi.

'He must have a randi whore mistress there.'

'Dead right,' Khatri said and went out in the rain again. He took with him a handful of sweets and went straight to the temple.

'What's wrong, Shadi Lal?' Ram Narayan, the Pandit of the temple, said.

'Nothing, Pandit ji,' Khatri said and sat down in the crowd. Only when he rose to leave an hour later did he realise that Omi sat behind him.

'God's really come into *them* this time,' Paro said when she served dinner to her men.

Khatri did not answer.

'Men become fools when God enters them,' Paro said.

Still he did not answer. Nor did he eat very much.

'Alright, alright. If you are going to sulk like this every day, I will send Vidya back to starve in Pipli. The Muslims killed the other two, you can kill this one. You shouldn't have any problems with your stonemason's heart.'

Omi was puzzled. Something mysterious was going on. The mystery deepened when his father announced the next day that he was going to Kalka.

'Can I come too, Father?' Omi said.

'I am going to see my guru, not a randi whore's nautch dance show. I am going to my guru.'

'*Our* guru, Father.'

That did it.

'Alright. But we won't be back till tomorrow.'

That was quite alright. Tomorrow was Sunday.

*   *   *

The journey to Kalka in a 'matchbox' bus was a bore. The only highlight was passing by the famous Pinjore Gardens where Omi saw a bunch of the Simla Pinks getting out of cars and jeeps with hampers. But instead of going into the delectable gardens which had once belonged to the Moguls and then to the Maharajahs of Patiala, they went down a heavily wooded khud ravine down the hillside, down to the Jhajjar. Minutes later the 'matchbox' bus arrived at Kalka and stopped in its drab bazaar. But Khatri made no effort at getting off.

'Another few miles. A place called Dhalli,' Khatri said.

The great Kasauli mountain rose abruptly where Kalka's bazaar ended. Suddenly they were in the mountains. The light was different, the air was cooler and it smelled fresh and delightful.

The name Dhalli rang a bell. Omi had heard it mentioned in College, though he had forgotten in what connection. It turned out to be a shop in the mountainside a couple of miles inside the Himachal Pradesh border. Behind it were a few huts. The shop was famous for two things. One was pickles, especially of pork. The other was liquor — beer, brewed in Solan in Himachal, midway to Simla. The Punjab and Himachal had different excise duties, making it attractive for Chandigarhias returning from the hills to take advantage of it. The octroi post at the border never checked. They just waved people on in either direction.

The Khatris got off here. Omi saw another Simla Pink jeep and two boys in blue jeans hauling a sack full of beer bottles down to it from the shop. They ignored Omi.

'Ah, Lala ji,' a man from one of the huts said.

'Is Billa around?' Khatri said.

Billa, a boy of Omi's age, was around. He was their guide. He led the way along a narrow footpath downhill through thick jungle. As they advanced, the path grew narrower and the growth thicker. Only when they came to a clearing did they glimpse the stupendous view of the valley and the river at its base. For an hour they walked and then stopped for a rest. They had come a long way down the valley and could hear the river now, though they could not see it yet. Suddenly the foliage thinned out and the river came into full view, a few hundred yards away. Clear blue water lapped against rocks and boulders. On a raised clearing by its bank stood two huts. They had arrived.

As they neared the huts, Omi panicked.

'Look, look, look, Father!' Omi cried and pulled his father back.

Outside the huts sat a large leopard, staring straight at them. Omi was sure he had eaten the guru and that he now awaited them, the shishya disciples.

'Don't worry, babu ji. It is only Mohan,' Billa said.

There was another strange sight. A cow, a calf and couple of goats stood by idly, munching grass.

'Ram, Ram, Shadi Lal. Ram, Ram, Om Parkash,' Gokul Baba greeted them with a toothless grin, coming out of a hut.

Omi was too overwhelmed by this strange menagerie to wonder how the holy man knew his name. He looked at his father.

'Ram, Ram, Guru ji,' Khatri said and bowed down to touch his feet. Omi did the same.

'Mohan recognises you now, Shadi Lal. He came to tell me it was you.'

Omi was dumbfounded.

'I have brought him up as my own son since he was a little kitten,' Gokul Baba said to Omi. 'Go and give him some milk. He likes you. Billa son, bring Om a bowl of milk.'

Billa brought Omi an earthenware bowl full of milk.

'There. Don't be afraid, Mohan loves you,' Gokul Baba said.

Omi took the bowl to Mohan. Mohan looked up at him — straight in the eye — and yawned, showing Omi what he did not want to see, those teeth. Omi almost dropped the bowl. He simply could not bend to place the bowl in front of Mohan.

'Shadi Lal, you show him,' Gokul Baba said.

Khatri took the bowl of milk from Omi and gently placed it in front of the leopard. Mohan slowly started lapping up the milk, making a slap-slap noise as he drank. Gokul Baba invited the father and son to bathe with him in the river. Mohan watched as they splashed the fiercely cold water on themselves. Night came down with an extreme abruptness as nights do in valleys. Suddenly it was dark. There was a noise in the dark foliage. Mohan, as if he knew what it was about, disappeared in the jungle. Soon the bushes parted and a number of men, women and children appeared. They brought flowers, food and a dholuk drum.

'Full moon. It is the kirtan holy singing night,' Gokul Baba said.

They sat down with the mountain village folk and the kirtan began. Gokul Baba sang and clapped two tiny brass cymbals. Everybody sang after him. A woman played the dholuk drum rhythmically. Their singing and the dholuk echoed in the great valley. Omi also sang and shut his eyes like the others, but when he did so he saw the leopard stare at him. He quickly opened them again. Gokul Baba swayed from side to side, so did his father. Omi had never seen his father like that, so engrossed in singing.

When the kirtan was over, Gokul Baba distributed the sweets Khatri had brought. Somebody served Omi food, two chappattis and dhal in a white enamelled plate. A little later, Gokul Baba gave him a blanket and sent him to one of the huts. There were two charpois string beds in it. Omi laid down in one and looked out where Gokul Baba and his father sat by a fire under the stars and a waning moon. He saw Mohan come and sit by them. Tired and bewildered, Omi soon fell asleep. Gokul Baba and Khatri talked until the moon dipped over the mountain.

Next morning, the father and son touched Gokul Baba's feet again before setting out to catch a 'matchbox' back to Chandigarh.

At home Paro wore her peacock-blue sari and a red bindu dot in the middle of her forehead. There was something else, something which made the father and son look at each other. Paro wore real English-style lipstick. Khatri looked away to hide his smile and Omi gave out a loud, shrill whistle.

'What did Gokul Baba say to you, oi?' Paro said to Omi.

'He said don't be afraid of leopards, he said,' said Omi.

Paro slapped her forehead in disgust.

'True, Ma. That's just what he said. Ask Father.'

'And what did he say to you, Mr Khatri Sahib? You look happy. Must have said *something*.'

'We talked of what we had to talk of.'

'But what? Anything special?'

'Gokul Baba said what he had to say.'

Omi's friend Shambhu called for him from the courtyard and Omi ran downstairs.

'Stay away from the jaloos march, do you hear? It is dangerous,' Paro shouted after her son.

'What jaloos march?' Khatri asked, hanging his turban on the turban peg.

'For the Punjabi Suba. The Akalis want an independent Punjab for themselves, don't they?'

'And is that why you are done up like a doll? Got a yaar-shaar among them?'

'Did Gokul Baba say that Mr Khatri Sahib is allowed to look at his wife?' Paro said, turning away and giving him her profile.

'Yes,' Khatri said, slapping her on her bottom and pulling her into the palang bed.

'Can't be a bad guru then, eh,' Paro said and allowed herself to be pulled into it, though it was early in the day.

The great procession was a mile long. It started from the Sikh Gurudwara in Sector 22 and took the same route the Panchkoola Traders Union had once taken — through the fashionable shopping centre to Sector 23. There it turned north.

Everybody turned out to watch. Street pavements were packed, balconies full of men, women and children, all leaning forward eagerly to see the tamasha fun. The Khatris came too, with all their neighbours and Dabbu who had a field day barking his head off. Thousands of bearded Sikhs in blue turbans, the agitating Akalis of Amritsar and Sikhs from all over the Punjab, marched leisurely past them. They carried banners saying: *Khalistan for the Khalsa — Home for the Sikhs*.

And they shouted: 'Punjab for the Punjabis.'

They wore swords in old scabbards — some held naked ones in their hands. Invariably, everybody wore the legendary Sikh kirpan dagger by the waist and a few thousand, the Nihang Sikhs, carried fierce-looking lances and spears — the very arms the Sikhs had taken up against the mighty Aurangzeb and other tyrants of the mighty Mogul Empire in the seventeenth and eighteenth centuries. And so the tradition of carrying arms, begun as a matter of daily necessity by the great Guru Gobind Singh three hundred years before, was paraded in all its glory past Sector 23.

There was a vast police presence. Hundreds of policemen, Hindus and Sikhs, equipped with wooden lathis, accompanied the procession. By contrast, they looked poorly armed. In the event of a collision, the outcome was a foregone conclusion. A sheer massacre.

'Look at the sea of black beards and blue turbans,' Omi said.

'Turbans, turbans everywhere, but not a head underneath them,' Kapoor said in English in the inimitable style of Professor Gupta.

'They have struck their twelve o'clock and lost their senses. Why do they want an independent Sikh state? And right next to Pakistan, their greatest enemy. Doesn't make sense,' Paro said.

'All a Sikh can run is a taxi, not a country,' Kapoor whispered in Omi's ear so that Seva wouldn't hear.

'No, Ma. They want Punjabi as the official language for the Punjab.'

'What is the official language of the Punjab?' Paro asked Khatri. Khatri did not know.

'Anyway, what difference does it make what it is?' Khatri said.

Paro asked Satya and her husband. They did not know either.

'Ask Seva Singh. He should know,' Satya's husband said.

'It is certainly not Punjabi,' Seva said with a smile.

'But what is it? Do you know, boys? You go to College,' Paro asked Omi and his friends.

Omi, Kapoor and Shambhu did not even know that there was such a thing as an official language.

'I'll ask Dr Devan Chand,' Omi said. 'He should know. A doctor.'

Dr Devan Chand stood next to them in the crowd with his wife, the Doctorani and their six children. The eldest, a girl whose name was Sarla, was in Omi's class. But she never looked at Omi in College or outside it. She only looked at Satya's brother, Romesh. Romesh was a senior student, a Third Year boy. He was very studious and very distant and he, too, never looked at Omi and his kind, the First Year insignificants, but only at Sarla.

'They send love letters to each other through their eyes, you know. They have their own sorting office,' Kapoor had once said.

But Romesh and Sarla had never been seen talking to each other, in or outside the College.

Omi went and asked Dr Devan Chand. Dr Devan Chand was not sure.

'Ask one of the marchers,' Dr Devan Chand said.

Omi stopped a ferocious-looking Nihang Sikh. He had a long black beard reaching his navel, a long 1857 vintage sword rattling by his legs, and a very long spear with a yellow handkerchief tied to the blade. Dabbu alone was not intimidated by his outlandish appearance. In fact he did not like it at all and took it upon himself to show his dislike of him.

The Nihang Sikh was taken aback by the strange question.

'Hindi,' the marching warrior said and marched on.

Romesh was seen making his way towards them. He looked at the Devan Chands and then at the others. He looked at the Devan Chands again, at Sarla this time. He ignored Omi and his friends and went up to his sister. He told them what the official language was.

'English,' Romesh said.

'Doesn't make sense. We speak Punjabi at home. Children speak it at school, boys and girls at College, men in offices. Why can't we write official letters in it?' Paro said.

'Doesn't make sense,' everybody said.

'Right. Let's join the march then,' Omi said. Everybody laughed.

A few days later, Omi woke up in the morning to a murmur down by the shops.

'Mother-laying hell!' Omi said at what he saw.

Under the trees in front of the shops, and everywhere else as far as he could see — on the street pavements, on the grass of the big roundabout and inside the grounds of the Hindu temple — was a sea of saffron. Thousands of Brahmins in orange-coloured robes and with clean-shaven heads, squatted leisurely. Next to them lay their crash-helmet-like hollowed-pumpkin begging bowls. They wore chains of rosaries and beads around their necks and across their shoulders.

'Father, Father!' Omi yelled and ran downstairs. He had to check himself at the shop door, for it was full of the same people.

'What is going on outside, Seva?' Omi asked Seva in an urgent whisper.

'They are agitating for Hindi,' Seva whispered back in an urgent whisper.

But they did not look the agitating type. Omi thought they looked rather passive, almost half-asleep.

As the day advanced, more holy men arrived — swamis, sadhus and gurus and disciples of swamis, sadhus and gurus. Thousands of them. There was going to be a counter-demonstration. Omi had seen a headline in *The Tribune* to that effect, but who expected this sort of turn out?

The great Hindu march also took the same route. And everybody came out to watch the new tamasha fun. Instead of last week's blue turbans, today there was a sea of clean-shaven heads shining in the afternoon sun. The holy men chanted Sanskrit mantras. Some carried banners and some shouted slogans. Dabbu did not like them either. He barked.

'*Mother India Speaks Hindi.*'

'*Matri Bhasha, Hindi Bhasha — Mother Tongue, Hindi Tongue.*'

Some half-naked sadhus with long beards and unkempt hair carried the trishul trident. Invariably, everybody clutched a crash-helmet begging bowl. They walked slowly and looked half-asleep, as if they had breakfasted on opium. By contrast, the policeman looked sturdy and veritably menacing.

'They have miles to go and they already look tired,' Omi said.

'Ten of those Nihangis could have demolished a hundred of these sleep-walkers,' Kapoor said.

'But what do they want?' Paro asked.

'They want Hindi as the official language for Punjab,' Omi said.

'What is wrong with Punjabi? We are happy with it. Doesn't make sense.'

'Ask them, Ma.'

Paro stopped a humble-looking young shishya disciple with a clean-shaven head and a long bodi topknot.

'Pray holiness, why do you want Hindi?' Paro asked most humbly.

'*Matri Bhasha, Hindi Bhasha,*' the young shishya chanted and shook his little dumru hand-drum. '*Matri Bhasha, Hindi Bhasha.*'

'Pray holiness, what is the official language of the Punjab?' Omi asked as humbly as his mother had done.

'Punjabi,' the disciple said, adjusting his bodi topknot.

'Where do you come from, Guru Maharaj?' Omi asked, detecting a slightly non-Punjabi lisp about his speech.

'Benaras.'

'But that is in UP. And this is Punjab.'

'Everybody knows that,' the holy shishya disciple said, shook his dumru dum-dum and walked on.

'What is the bastard doing in Chandigarh then?' Khatri said angrily.

'Ram, Ram, Ram! Speak like that of a Brahmin and invite the

wrath of God,' Paro said and pinched her ears.

'Crooks in disguise.'

'Brahmins, Brahmins everywhere, but not a man among them,' Kapoor the poet laureate said. 'At least the Nihangis looked like fire-eaters. These fellows look like mere kheer rice-pudding eaters.'

'Brahmin pandit types. What do you expect them to look like? Samson?' Shambhu said.

'What caste are you, Shambhu?' Khatri asked. He did not like his son to mix with lower-caste boys. It was not a question of money, it was a question of caste.

'Malhotra,' Shambhu said.

Malhotras were high-caste Kashatriyas, the kings and warriors of the past, like the Kapoors. In fact higher than the Khatris, as far as it went.

'That's alright then,' Khatri said and turned his eyes upon the marches.

'*Bharat Varta, Arya Varta — India, land of the Aryans*,' a bunch of marchers shouted gently past them and Dabbu nearly bit the leg off one.

'When the Englishman ruled, there was none of this nonsense. Everybody did as they were told and everybody was happy. No, Lala ji?' Dr Devan Chand said. A heavy-set man, he was a few years older than Khatri.

Khatri chose not to answer. He was a Congress man. Like most Indians he loved the English, but he did not like them.

'Gandhi and Nehru promised Ram Raj — milk-and-honey Utopia — after Independence. And look at this. Akalis yesterday, Brahmins today. Prices sky high and this is Independence. Ram Raj indeed bilkul! I tell you we were better off under him.'

'Under who, Doctor Sahib?' Omi asked.

'Him, the Englishman, of course.'

'Oh him? I thought you were talking of God.'

'God in India doesn't work. Only fools do. Look at the marchers — they don't know what they are saying. Look at us — we don't know what they were saying. Country of fools, ours,' Satya's husband said.

Omi was a bit surprised to hear Satya's husband offer an opinion. He was usually so quiet.

'Must be a communist,' Khatri whispered in Omi's ear.

'What is a communist?' Omi asked his father in a whisper.

'A troublemaker.'

Next day during Professor Raj Kumar's lecture, Omi dared to do something he had never done before. He raised a hand to ask a question. Professor Raj Kumar was talking about the wives of Henry VIII.

'What is a communist, Sir?'

Everybody was taken aback. Every head in the class turned to look at Omi.

'But . . .!' Professor Raj Kumar was more taken aback than the others. '. . . but what has it got to do with Anne Boleyn . . .?'

The class laughed. Omi felt foolish.

'. . . Well, never mind,' Professor Raj Kumar said. 'Anyone here who can answer Mr Khatri's question?'

A Simla Pink hand went up.

'Ah, Sally. Yes?'

'Communists live in Russia. They had a revolution in 1917,' Sally said. She was a robust Sikh girl and her real name was Salvinder Kaur. But as with many Simla Pinks it had been shortened to an English nickname.

'That still doesn't answer the question,' Professor Raj Kumar said. 'Any takers?'

Another Simla Pink hand went up.

'Yes, Harry?'

'A communist, Sir, is a member of the communist party,' Harry said. Harry's real name was Hari Hardas.

Professor Raj Kumar shook his head.

'Any more takers?' he asked the class.

There were no more takers. Professor Raj Kumar explained.

'Common, community, commune, communism, communist. Follow? Common property in the community — you share the work and the proceeds equally. Communism. Follow? The Communist party is dictatorship of the proletariat. Do you understand, Khatri?'

'Yes, Sir,' Omi lied. He wanted to say something, but decided to keep his mouth shut. He had a terrible feeling that if he opened it, he would say something silly and everybody would laugh. He always had this feeling whenever he wanted to say something in the class.

'Any questions?' Professor Raj Kumar asked the class.

There were no questions. Everybody had understood.

'Unrelated though your question was to ol' Henry and his various ladies, I am awfully glad you asked it. I like people to have an inquiring mind, ask intelligent questions. Do you follow?'

Omi felt a pleasant flush creep over his cheeks.

'Ma, Professor Raj Kumar was pleased with me today,' Omi said at home over lunch.

'What did you do?'

'He said I had an inquiring mind. He said that I was very intelligent.'

'He needs to have his head tested,' Paro said, tossing over a chappati to him.

Omi told Professor Bhatnagar about it as they sat down to read *The Tribune* that afternoon.

'So my tuition is doing you some good after all,' Professor Bhatnagar said and asked Omi to translate the headlines: *HINDU SIKH LEADERS FOR DELHI TALKS*.

'Does that mean there won't be any marches any more, Sir?' Omi asked.

'Not unless the talks break down. Not for some time at any rate,' Professor Bhatnagar said.

'Pity,' Omi said to himself.

Omi told Kapoor and Shambhu about it when they met for their evening constitutional in Sector 22.

'Pity. It was such fun — those blue turbans and those shiny egg-heads.'

'Best way to waste an afternoon, it was. Better than any mela fun-fair,' Shambhu said.

But Omi had discovered other ways of wasting an afternoon or even a whole day, and they were far more interesting.

He discovered that nobody cared if he missed a lecture or two or more — nobody even noticed it. The way to achieve this was quite simple — by 'proxy' as the system was called. A friend obliged and said 'Yes, Sir' when the Professor called out the register at the beginning of each lecture. It was much more interesting to pass those fifty-five minutes in the tuck shop or at the Dhaba tea shops behind the College by the mango grove.

There was something exceedingly boring and soporific about the teachers. The only exception was Professor Raj Kumar. Every other Professor was a 'bore'. Anyone who listened to them was also a 'bore'. Omi had for long been a great 'bore'. But now, nearing the end of the first year of his College career, he was trying hard to discard that label. He now spent much of his College time outside the College.

He also attended the special but secret readings of Pondies.

Pondies were novellas in English published by anonymous publishers and written by anonymous authors. They were written and published before 1947. Rumour was that that their authors were either English or Anglo-Indian. They were stories of sex in which the highly imaginative authors left nothing to the imagination of the reader. Their appeal lay in their explicit descriptions of the act. Often, if not always, they ended in delightful orgies with the young white sahibs performing sexual acrobatics like trapeze champions with slightly darker-skinned girls — the Dollys and Mollys and Pollys of the Anglo-India of the '30s and '40s. *Kama Sutra* paled before them.

Nobody knew why they were called Pondies, but that was the name under which they circulated. They were collectors' items, avidly collected by Simla Pink boys. They turned up now and then at Chandigarh College, often accompanied by fading picture-postcards of naked European ladies and gentlemen.

It took Omi all this time to become aware of this important contribution by the British Raj to twentieth century Indian literature. Whenever a new Pondy turned up, many a proxy 'Yes, Sir' was said. On such occasions, Simla Pinks and the 'ordinaries' sat together in the open air under the warm autumn sun. A Simla Pink, renowned for his elocution, read it out loud with as much feeling as Laurence Olivier would have read *Hamlet*.

Some boys said 'wah wah', others professed to have 'killer erections'.

Time, predictably, passed quickly.

The annual internal exam turned up.

When the results came out, Omi only displayed the English one. He had a First in it. He had failed in all the other subjects. But he did not tell his father. He said the other results had not yet come out. But one day Khatri found out the truth for himself from Dev.

When Omi returned from his usual promenade in Sector 22 that evening, he ran straight into his father. Khatri sat waiting in an armchair by the stairs, his peshawari chappall in his right hand.

'Son of a bitch!' Khatri roared. That was all he could say, he was so angry, and he let his peshawari chappall do the rest of the talking.

'Son of a bitch! Lied to me, your own father! Failing in all the subjects!' Khatri finally managed to say.

Omi cried out in pain, but Khatri went on relentlessly.

'If you go out again watching girls, wasting my money, I will break both your legs. I will hang you upside down by your ankle at the door shop.'

This beating surpassed any Khatri had given his son in the past.

'Leave him. Do you want to kill him? All your own fault anyway. I told you that he would get out of your hands once we came here. Didn't I? Get him another English tutor, a real English mem sahib this time. Go on! Go on!' Paro shouted from the kitchen.

'Shut up, foolish woman. I got him tuition to make his life, not ruin it vagabondising and girl-watching.'

Next morning there was a letter from Mr Varma, the Principal of the College. It was in English. Khatri sent for Romesh. Romesh came and translated it. Mr Varma said he was sorry that Mr Khatri had not answered his first letter sent three weeks ago which had drawn attention to his son's poor exam results. Mr Varma went on to say that unless Om Parkash showed better results in the forthcoming special tests, he would not be allowed to go up to the Second Year — this was a condition he had to fulfil.

'Son of a bitch! Ate up the first letter! Son of a bitch!' Khatri said, grinding his teeth. He was seething as he had never seethed before.

'Told you, didn't I?' Paro said.

Fortunately for Omi he had already left for College — he had missed the postman by a minute. Khatri was in full frontier temper. He would like to fly to the College, catch the bastard by his hair and give him the beating of his life in front of the whole of the College.

'How many times haven't I told you to put the boy in the little shop? But who listens? We can go on barking our head off, but who listens?'

'Shut up, bewakoof woman. How do you know what I had in mind?'

During the lull after the early-morning rush, when many came to breakfast, and the temple-goers to buy sweets for Lord Krishna, Khatri sat quietly and thought about his son. He wished he could talk to Gokul Baba about it. But Gokul Baba was far away in the mountains. He tried to think what Gokul Baba would say to him. Suddenly his anger started to subside. The more Khatri thought about it, the less he felt angry.

'Anger won't solve the problem — it never did. Patience and coolness. Money, tuitions, beatings won't solve everything.'

When Omi alighted from his bike, his face glowing with the exertion of competitive cycling with other boys, Khatri ignored him and let him climb the stairs. He came after him several minutes later.

Paro had warned Omi. So Omi knew what was coming. In shame he lowered his head, and like a good Hindu, resigned himself to his fate.

But Khatri said nothing. He went straight to his bed and lay down on it. He never did so during shop hours.

Omi was puzzled. His mother was equally puzzled. She had stopped doing what she was doing in the kitchen and was ready to intervene and stop her husband when she thought the beating was enough.

'Aren't you well?' Paro asked, putting her head round the door.

Khatri did not answer, but called Omi to him. Omi went in, shivering. Khatri looked at him for a long time.

'You stole the letter the College sent?'

This was a moment for truth. Omi nodded.

'You were afraid?'

Omi nodded.

'Why do you think you failed? Were the questions too difficult?'

Omi nodded.

'Is that the only reason?'

Omi did not reply.

'Do you find the work at College very hard?'

Omi nodded.

Khatri fixed his eyes on the ceiling and stared at it for several minutes. Omi gazed at the floor, waiting.

'Do you want to do something else instead? Sit in the little shop with uncle Bhajjan?'

'No,' Omi said at once. Heavens!

'Then you better pass these special exams that are coming up.'

Omi gazed at the polished cement floor and twitched his toes. The matter was serious.

'Start working right away,' Khatri said and rose from the bed and went downstairs.

When Kapoor came to call for Omi in the evening, Omi shook his head.

'I am studying, Dad,' Omi said.

Dad Kapoor thought Omi had gone mad.

'Sector 22 gone dead without you, yaar,' Shambhu said a few days later in College.

'Girls don't go there any more because there is no Omi around. That's cruel, yaar.'

'I hear there is going to be another jaloos march soon,' Kapoor said.

'What other jaloos march?' Omi said. He hadn't seen anything of the kind in *The Tribune*.

'All the girls of Chandigarh marching this time. Protest to the Governor. They don't want Hindi, they don't want Punjabi. Only their Omi,' Shambhu said.

Omi gave him a kick in the arse.

'Got to pass this fucking *condition*. Otherwise they will pull me out of the Second Year.'

'Bullshit,' Kapoor said.

'Tell Varma to stuff his *condition*,' Shambhu said.

Kapoor and Shambhu too had this *condition* on them. Their nonchalance about it impressed Omi. However, he did drop out from the evening rounds of Sector 22. It was painful. 'But . . .' Omi said to himself and worked. He scraped through the exam. So did Shambhu. But Kapoor failed. He was very angry.

'Fucking Varma,' Kapoor said crossly, as the three of them stood on the College lawn, analysing the marking. He tore his papers to bits and fed the bits to the cool breeze from the Kasauli mountain, which obligingly spread them far and wide on the lawn with *No Litter Please* sign.

Khatri was pleased. He bought Omi a wristwatch from the Big

174

Ben Watch Stores that day.

'What did you get him such an expensive watch for? Watches are for grown-ups,' Paro said.

'I felt like it,' Khatri said.

'Father and son! Looking at the two of you, I can't tell which one is the greater moorakh fool.'

'You are witnessing the ruination of your son, Paro,' Chatkarni said.

Vidya did not agree with Chatkarni.

'College boy. Handsome College boy needs handsome watch,' she said, hugging Omi.

Omi forgave Bhajjan that instant for all he had done to them.

A debate was coming up at College.

'Why not have a go?' Professor Bhatnagar said.

Clearly Professor Bhatnagar was joking, Omi thought. Whenever he had attended debates in the past, it had been to boo someone else, or simply to stare at girls — the two main reasons why boys attended them. Speak in one himself? Clearly Professor Bhatnagar was joking.

But Omi did not want Professor Bhatnagar to think he was afraid.

'What could I say?' Omi answered just as casually.

'Leave it to me,' Professor Bhatnagar said and wrote out a paper.

'Now mug it up. Drink it down your throat word by word. And then smack it down at the audience from the stage,' Professor Bhatnagar said.

Omi started learning it. He went to the Public Nurseries by the swimming pool behind the shops. He addressed a big mango tree as Mr President, and all the other trees as Ladies and Gentlemen. He spent four afternoons with Mr President, Ladies and Gentlemen. On the fourth afternoon he felt he was ready.

'Let's hear it,' Professor Bhatnagar said.

Omi spoke it over.

'Good, but don't stop going over it ten times an hour until the debate. A debate is a debate. You follow me?' Professor Bhatnagar said.

Omi followed him. He went over it ten times an hour until the hour of the debate. He felt ready. Though he couldn't deny that he was a little nervous.

'But everybody is. All great actors and statesmen are.'

Omi recalled Professor Bhatnagar's words as he went into the hall with his friends.

A smart girl from the smart north-end went on to the stage before Omi and thundered out her piece in Simla Pink English. She made it look so easy.

'See? Piece of cake,' Kapoor said.

'Mr Om Parkash Khatri,' the President called from the microphone.

'Mr President, Ladies and Gentlemen . . .' Omi began in Professor Bhatnagar's clear-cut English. Then he paused, according to Professor Bhatnagar's instructions. But Omi could not get out of the pause. He had forgotten the opening lines of his speech.

Boos, loud and clear, rang out in the College hall. They hit the empty pit in his stomach.

'Mr President, Ladies and Gentlemen . . .' Omi started again, pulling the mike nearer. The hush returned. Omi spoke a few lines and took another pause. Once again he got stuck. Booing and hissing started from the side of the hall where Kapoor, Shambhu and all his other friends like Pritam Singh and Tully were sitting. Omi could recognise Kapoor's voice in spite of the butterflies in his stomach.

'The bastard!' Omi yelled. The loudspeakers carried his voice across the hall. Suddenly there was much laughter amid all that booing and hissing.

'Never mind, yaar. You got stage-fright. Happens to everyone. Try again,' Kapoor said after the debate.

'Try, try again. Don't forget Bruce and the spider,' Shambhu said.

'I was afraid you might get stuck somewhere, but to stop after the first four words . . .!' Professor Bhatnagar said. 'Make sure you don't the next time.'

As if there would be a next time.

'But I can't let the bastards have the laugh on me . . . I'll teach them a lesson.'

Omi tried again. This time he stopped only a couple of times. They booed, but this time it was less painful.

'Are you aiming to be Nehru or Churchill or something?' Kapoor said.

The third time Omi went right through his speech without forgetting a single word.

'Shabas bravo, son Churchill. Shabas bravo,' Kapoor and Shambhu said, embracing him. 'Our future Prime Minister.'

'That's it. Next time you might win yourself a prize,' Professor Bhatnagar said.

Omi did. A litle silver-plated cup on a black wooden base. He gave it to his father.

'See? He is not a dud bewakoof after all,' Khatri said to Paro.

'Now don't go and give him more presents. He is too spoiled as it is. Besides, it is only a little egg-cup,' Paro said.

'Anybody in your family ever won a cup?'

Vidya hugged Omi when she saw the cup. Even Chatkarni was impressed. But Satya was not.

'Our Romesh has many such cups. He won them for good exam results,' she said.

'He would, wouldn't he? A born "bore",' Omi said to himself. He had a mild surprise the next time he passed by Romesh in the shops. Romesh looked at him this time.

'Well, well, well,' Omi said to himself.

Omi won a cup in every debate. He could even write his own speeches now. As the end of Omi's second year at College and the university exam approached, Professor Bhatnagar asked him if he wanted to carry on with the English lessons.

'You speak English as *good* as I do now,' Professor Bhatnagar said.

Omi spoke English fluently. Not only that, the two years of Hollywood Sunday mornings had done their bit — they had taken out much of Professor Bhatnagar's Punjabiness from Omi's English.

'I don't believe it is necessary,' Omi said in English.

'Think carefully, boy,' Khatri said, when Omi consulted him.

'The rest depends on me,' Omi said.

'Alright,' Khatri said.

'Alright,' Professor Bhatnagar said.

'Now send in the application for the military exam,' Khatri said.

But Omi liked College life. With his knowledge of English and English films and his debating success, things were changing. They had never been better.

'I ought to do the BA at least before doing anything else.'

'Why not? Why not?' Kandhari said, coming unexpectedly, late one morning, with a huge basket of all sorts of fruit and other gifts. There was cloth for a shirt and a pair of trousers, and a necktie for Omi; a piece of silk cloth for his mother, and a hand-embroidered muslin kurta for Khatri.

'Station Masterani well? Daughter well?' Paro asked.

'Very well. Thank God.'

Lunch was being made. After the usual chit-chat that goes on between parents-in-law, Paro announced food.

'Ram, Ram, Ram! Eat in the house where my daughter is going to be daughter-in-law? Out of the question,' Kandhari said, touching the lobes of his ears.

'Come on Station Master Sahib, times are changing,' Khatri said.

'But a daughter is still a daughter.'

'I know. But.'

After a certain amount of fuss which the Khatris were expected to make, and a certain amount of reluctance which was expected of Kandhari, he agreed to share the Khatri fare.

'Well, I will have to pay for it,' Kandhari said, sitting down on a six-inch-high peeri kitchen stool.

Clearly Kandhari was happy to see that Omi had grown taller and that he spoke English so effortlessly.

'And all those silver cups!'

Clearly, some change had taken place between that boy of Panchkoola Polling Station and this youth who spoke better English than the ex-Polling Officer himself. And what about the shop and the house? Every room, every cupboard smacked of prosperity. Mrs Kandhari would be delighted to hear all about it. Kandhari rubbed his hands with joy.

'Let him do the BA. Let him do the MA. There is no reason why Om shouldn't try for the Civil Service. Who knows what lies ahead for him and for us? He may well become a Deputy Commissioner. After all, it is from boys like him that DCs are chosen. No, Lala ji?'

'We will see, we will see,' Khatri said noncommittally. He knew his son.

Kandhari had instructions from his wife to give twenty-one rupees to the boy as he left. But at seeing Omi and hearing his beautiful English which had won him ten cups, Kandhari pushed fifty-one rupees into Omi's shirt pocket.

'No, no, no. What are you doing?' Khatri and Paro said in unison. They were expected to protest, Kandhari to disregard them.

'It is the first time I have seen him for two years. I can't go away without leaving something in his palm. Don't let a policeman catch you this time, Om Parkash,' Kandhari said and laughed.

Kandhari also deposited a five-rupee note on the sill above the choolha cooking fire in the kitchen.

'For the food I have eaten in the house of my son-in-law,' he said.

Paro fussed and tried to return it. Kandhari wouldn't listen. It was only normal. No self-respecting father would eat in the house where he was giving his daughter in marriage.

The Khatris let the note remain on the sill. Kandhari was leaving. His rickshaw had arrived. Bawa had been sent to fetch it. (He had returned sitting in it.)

'It is no more than becomes his status. He could not have given less,' Paro said, counting the money.

'Status, my foot,' Omi said, snatching the notes back.

'Give me the money,' Paro ordered.

'As if it was yours.'

'Of course it is your parents'. You are our son, or aren't you?'

'Here, take the rupee note. I'll keep the rest. After all it is me who is to marry this girl. What if she turns out to be deaf and dumb?'

'What do you think you are? Actor Raj Kapoor from Bombay? The girl is right for you. Come, give me the notes.' Paro advanced and took the money from Omi.

'Fifty-one,' she counted. 'Becomes his status.'

'Status, what status? That of a stationmaster of Dhulkote where not five trains stop all day! Even dogs don't cock their legs there — you will have to pay them to make them piss there . . .'

'Listen, listen to the Maharajah of Patiala . . .'

'. . . How would I dare show myself at College if they found out I was betrothed to the daughter of a stationmaster? And of Dhulkote at that! Even the crows don't drop their droppings there, Ma. It is true . . .'

'. . . Listen to Nawab Latti Khan . . .'

'. . . Am I to be packed off and married so young? Are any of my class-mates engaged? I don't have to follow in your footsteps. Things are different now. This is the new India, not the old marriage-making factory.'

'Listen, listen. I told *them*. This is what comes of modern education. Teach him more English!' Paro addressed herself to her husband, who was down in the shop.

'You'd better break off this engagement, Ma. I don't want a stationmaster and his rails around my neck for the rest of my life.'

'Where was your tongue when you were in the jailhouse at Ambala? Who else would have got you out?'

Omi slapped his forehead, shook his head and went to his room.

II

Omi often read *The Tribune* to his parents. On Sunday mornings, neighbours often came along to hear him read the news. They sat on charpois in the courtyard and basked in the warm winter sun.

'*Harijans to March on Capital*,' Omi read out the headlines one morning. Harijans, which literally means Children of God, was the name given by Mahatma Gandhi to the untouchables of India who form a quarter of the population of the country.

'What, another jaloos? What language do the Harijans want?' Paro said.

'*Protest Against People and Government*,' Omi read out and translated.

'What do they want? An independent state? Muslims wanted Pakistan — they got it. Sikhs wanted Khalistan — they did not get it. What do Harijans want? A Harijanstan?' Chatkarni said.

'Who will clean our latrines then?' Satya said.

'*Protest Against People and Government*?' Satya's husband said. 'Very interesting!'

'What do they want from *us*?' Satya said.

'From the people they want a wage increase,' Omi translated.

'My Basanti is not having anything from me,' Satya said.

'How much do you pay her?' Paro asked Satya.

'Five rupees a month. She is lucky — flush system. She doesn't have to carry *it* away on her head as they do everywhere else.'

Satya was right. Chandigarh was unique in this respect. It was completely sanitised, the only city in India — there were no dry latrines as in other cities. So the Harijan untouchable bhangis of Chandigarh, like Rano and her family, did not have to cart away the night soil on their heads as bhangis elsewhere had to. Chandigarh had a modern sewage system. No open sewers and drains ran through its streets as they did in other cities and towns. The Harijan untouchable bhangis here did not have to clean them, nor scoop out the filth from them by hand as they did elsewhere.

'Chandigarh bhangis may be luckier than the others, but still. Still they are bhangis — untouchable,' Ujjagar said.

'What do they want from the Government?' Khatri asked.

'Ten per cent of all jobs. Mind you, Father, twenty-five per cent of the population is untouchable, did you know that?'

'Well, it is a matter of karma. It is their karma,' Chatkarni, the high-caste Brahmin, said.

Omi carried on.

'Ten per cent jobs, ten per cent seats in State Assemblies and National Parliament, free education, better housing. . . .'

'They are just demands . . .' Khatri said.

'And when they get educated and rich who will clean your latrine? Who will clean *their* latrines? They will make *you* do the job *they* were born to do. Absolute total kaliug black age this,' Paro said.

The other ladies agreed with Paro. They nodded heavily.

'But Ma, you don't understand. This is democracy.'

'What's that?'

'Equality and equal opportunity for everyone.'

'That is stupid law — no wonder India doesn't make any progress. You can't make a bhangi sit on the same table to eat with another Hindu. Ten per cent seats and ten per cent jobs, yes. But . . .' Chatkarni said.

'But what?' Omi said.

'But you can't eat with him.'

'Why not?'

'Because.'

'Because of what?'

'Because he is an untouchable bhangi — he touches human filth, he cuts up dead animals for their hide, he makes your shoes with their leather, he burns unowned human corpses — and because you are a caste Hindu, not a polluted mallachha outcast type. That's why. It is written in all the holy books.'

It so happened that Rano walked into the courtyard at that moment to do the Khatris' house. She was often late on Sundays.

'Sorry, Ma ji,' Rano said to Paro. She called her Ma ji. 'There is so much work on Sunday mornings. Double work some people make me do.' Rano said and went past them to go upstairs.

'Rano,' Khatri called her.

Rano stopped, looking surprised. Khatri had never spoken to her before, nor ever called her by her name. Her kamiz shirt was soiled and dirty. Her duppatta breast scarf had holes in it. And she was barefoot, as she always was, summer or winter.

'You are getting a rise from today,' Khatri said.

'What did you say, Lala ji?' Rano could not believe her ears.

'You deaf or something? I said a rise.'

'How much?'

'How much do you get from this house? How much does Ma ji give you?'

'Five rupees a month. Standard rate.'

'Seven and half rupees from this day on. Alright?'

'*They* have gone crazy. Utterly crazy, squandering money like that. What does she have to do in this house? She only sweeps and cleans twice a day. She doesn't carry *anything* out — everything is flushed out anyway. In the Camp, Thakri had to carry it on her head and she only got three rupees a month . . . Why not send her a money order to cover the arrears?'

Khatri stood up from the charpoi, slipped into his peshawari chappalls, and went upstairs.

'Father and son, why don't you two walk hand in hand with Rano in the Harijan jaloos procession?' Paro said to Omi.

The jaloos procession, of fifteen thousand Harijan untouchables from all corners of the Punjab, started from the Harijan colony behind Sector 23. It took the usual route, but nobody turned out to watch it. Business did not stop as it had done during the last two marches. Men, women and children did not crane from the balconies to watch the tamasha fun. Street pavements were not packed this time. Only a few people, mostly College boys and other idle young men, came. They came to see the Harijan women. These women were poor and could not afford bras. When they walked in the breeze, their flimsy kamiz shirts clung to their bosoms. Their breasts bounced up and down. The College boys came to see the bouncing breasts.

Chandigarh ignored the great march. The people and the Government rejected the Harijans' demands. The Harijans took the matter in their hand. They went on strike all over the Punjab.

'*Punjab Stinks*,' *The Tribune* headlines said.

The Punjab stank. City centres stank the most. Though people had started *going out*, still the cities were shrouded in the lingering smell of human excrement. The streets of old cities, dirty at the best of times, became hovels of filth and devastating stench. Drains overspilled and sewers burst open.

But the new capital of the Punjab, because of its prized flush and modern sewage systems, did not suffer. It only had pyramids of uncollected rubbish at street corners.

There was another Harijan march. This time everybody came out to see it.

'*The Government Stinks, the People Stink*,' the marching Harijans shouted.

The Khatris and their neighbours stood at their usual place.

'Look, our Rano,' Paro said, spotting Rano in the vociferous crowd.

'And my Basanti,' Satya said.

Rano and her friend Basanti carried a long banner between them.

'What does their banner say, Omi?' Paro asked.

'*Freedom Was Assassinated on 30 January 1948.*'

Paro stopped Rano. Every untouchable in the capital was on strike, like his or her colleagues in the rest of the Punjab, but Rano still came to do the Khatri house. She came secretly, if only once a day.

'What happened on 30 January 1948?' Paro asked.

'A Hindu killed our Mahatma Gandhi with three bullets,' Rano said.

Shambhu leaned over and whispered in Omi's ear.

'I say, your untouchable is highly touchable. She got good ones.' Kapoor was listening.

'Wait till you see our Kali's,' Kapoor said. 'Absolute killer tits.'

In the language marches no women had taken part. Hindus and Sikhs don't like their women to be on parade like that. They like them to remain out of sight, out of the public's eye, away from the lustful eyes of other men. The Harijan women are on parade all the time, they work. But they don't matter, they are Harijans. So they can march and they marched today with their men.

'Best way to beat the Government — give them stinking hell,' Paro said.

'We will, Ma ji,' Rano said and walked on.

'There she is,' Kapoor whispered.

'Who?' Omi said.

'Our Kali. Just look at those tits! What did I tell you?'

Kali was very dark, as most of Harijans are by comparison with Hindus and Sikhs of the Punjab. They carry in their veins the blood of the original dark-skinned inhabitants of India, the Indoriginals whom the fair-skinned Aryans conquered and enslaved at the dawn of Hindu civilisation four thousand years ago.

'Pity she is so dark. Almost black,' Shambhu said. 'But so what? Tits are tits.'

'And hers are made of silk. Black satin,' Kapoor said. 'They are silk, satin and honey.'

'How do you know?' Omi said.

'I'll tell you another day,' Kapoor said with a wink.

Wave after wave of dark-skinned Harijans came.

'At this rate they will bring the Government to its knees,' Paro said.

The Harijans did. The Government gave in.

'*IT IS TEN PER CENT*,' *The Tribune* headlines said one morning.

The Government agreed to the ten per cent demand and it made a recommendation to people: *Give A Conscientious Wage Rise*. The Government hinted at a twenty-five per cent rise. But the people refused to give it. After much bickering they agreed to ten per cent.

'All that stink for a mere ten per cent! They shouldn't have accepted it,' Omi said.

'Better than nothing,' Paro said. 'At least they got something.'

'The trouble with us Indians is that we settle easily for crumbs. That's why we don't make progress. We are a nation of crumb-takers,' Omi said.

'Listen to the only wise tongue in this country of crumb-takers,' Paro said to Khatri.

Khatri slapped his forehead and shook his head.

Omi was putting in a lot of work for the university exam. So were all the other boys, all except Kapoor who was not taking it. Walking Sector 22 had stopped once again, but Kapoor came to see Omi now and then and Omi quite enjoyed wasting an odd hour with him. Early one evening, Kapoor came again and gave Omi a surprise with his turn-out. He wore a tie.

'Do you like good food?' Kapoor said.

'Stupid question. Who doesn't?' Omi said.

'I mean *best* food. *Best* and free.'

'Another stupid question.'

'Then come with your Dad. You are invited to a party. The only condition is you must wear *best* clothes — necktie and all.'

Clearly, Kapoor was joking. But Omi saw no harm in taking an evening off. He went and changed into smart clothes and the Kandhari tie.

Kapoor took him to the wilderness behind Sector 23. There was nothing there except open fields, a few mango orchards and the bhangi untouchable colony, a shanty town of mud huts.

'But this is the bhangi colony. Where is the party?' Omi said.

Kapoor smiled in answer and kept walking along a kucha earth-track through the fields.

'What the fuck, Dad? Why the neckties?'

Kapoor stopped by a sugar-cane field and looked back. Someone was coming towards them through the milky haze of the country-side. It was a female figure. At a hundred yards Omi saw that it was a very dark girl. Kapoor's girl of the Harijan march!

'Son of a bitch,' Omi said, giving Kapoor a kick. 'But why the tie?'

'The tie is for the party . . .'

The girl joined them.

'Kali, meet my best friend Omi. He was dying to meet you,' Kapoor said.

Kali smiled. Omi had never seen teeth whiter than hers. She was so black that she looked almost blue. And she was very beautiful. Omi never knew that black people could also be beautiful. If one was black, one was ugly. His parents and everybody else here in Chandigarh or back in the Camp wanted fair-complexioned brides and grooms for themselves and their sons and daughters. If the girl was fair, she was alright. If not, she was not alright. It made the prospect of finding a husband for her difficult. If she was very dark, as Kali was, the chances of finding her a husband were bleak indeed. Her father would have to dangle the carrot of a disproportionately lavish dowry But if the boy was dark-skinned, it was not that bad — wasn't Lord Krishna himself dark? A good job still got him a fair-complexioned bride from a good family. That was life. But none of this affected Kali, for all untouchables were dark.

Kali leaned over and whispered something in Kapoor's ear.

'Kali says you are good-looking,' Kapoor said to Omi. 'She needs glasses.'

Omi blushed and felt foolish.

Kali laughed. She leaned over and whispered something else in Kapoor's ear.

'Kali says she can fix you up,' Kapoor said.

Omi blushed some more. Kali laughed again.

'I know just the girl for you,' Kali said. 'Pretty as you are, Omi bau.'

Kali's forthrightness impressed Omi. He could not get over the fact that a girl as black as her could be so beautiful.

'Alright, son,' Kapoor said, putting an arm around Kali's shoulder and walking away with her into a sugar-cane field. 'Guard the fort.'

Kapoor and Kali disappeared into the sugar cane. Now and then Omi heard Kali giggle. Omi worried. What if someone came along? What if they went and told his father that he was seen outside the bhangi untouchable colony, standing guard over a bhangi untouchable girl and a Hindu boy doing God knows what in the sugar-cane field?

Some time later Kapoor and Kali came out of the sugar-cane field.

'Don't worry, Omi bau. We done nothing wrong. Only a bit of messing about,' Kali said. Then she undid a packet of ten cigarettes from a knot in her dupatta breast scarf and gave it to Kapoor.

'For you both,' Kali said. 'And now I must go back. Or else my father will come and skin you both alive. Until next time. And you come too, Omi bau, I'll fix you up. The girl is pretty as you.'

'So, pretty boy!' Kapoor said, as Kali went back.

Omi kicked him in the arse.

'Bastard,' Omi said. 'Why bring me here? And why in a tie? Beats me completely.'

'The tie is for now. For the party, you fool,' Kapoor said.

Kapoor took him to Sector 16, an affluent part of the city. It was more than a mile away and by the time they got there it was quite dark. Kapoor bought Omi a Vimto in the shopping centre and lit two cigarettes.

'So you are fixed, eh?' Kapoor said.

'But why make me wear a tie? Where is the party?'

Music could be heard in the distance. It got nearer. Soon a marriage procession came in sight — first the band in Edwardian regimental uniforms surrounded by men carrying gas-lights on top of their heads. Then the bridegroom mounted on a horse — both the bridegroom and the horse were heavily decorated with flowers and other devices. Behind the mounted bridegroom marched, quite slowly, a couple of hundred smartly dressed people — the family, the relatives and friends of the family of the bridegroom.

The torch-bearers and the band took a turn at the shops. The mounted groom and his entourage followed. Life in the shopping centre of Sector 16 came to a standstill. Everybody came out to watch the marriage procession on its way to the bride's house for reception and dinner. The band players warmed up under the gaze of so many onlookers. They stopped and played their favourite number — a tune from the current box-office hit, 'Shree 420'.

Kapoor finished off his Vimto with one deep intake from the drinking straw and winked at Omi.

'Come. Our party.'

Kapoor took Omi's hand and joined the well-dressed wedding guests.

'Look normal,' Kapoor whispered.

'I can't.'

'You said you like *best* food.'

'I do. But this is . . .' Omi could not find words to describe it.

The food was superb — it would be in Sector 16. But Omi was too afraid to be caught out. He hardly ate.

'Fool,' Kapoor said. 'Enjoy yourself. Take life as it comes, as Byron said.'

But Omi could not take life as it came. He was sure that each one of the two hundred diners, under the grand shamiana marquee with rows upon rows of multicoloured lights, knew that he was an interloper. He could feel their eyes boring holes in his back. It was only a question of time before they would be apprehended and thrown out unceremoniously. They might even get a beating.

Dinner over, the sweets came. They came in great variety and abundance. Must be a rich man's daughter getting married.

'Pockets,' Kapoor whispered.

Omi did not understand him.

'Party is over,' Kapoor whispered again after a while.

Outside the great shamiana, they were offered cigarettes and paan — special silver paan. Omi thought of Bhaia and Harpal and Bali and Des and Punnu and Bhajju and the locust.

'Omi,' someone said from among the hosts. Omi shrank in terror. They were caught.

'Bhaia! What are you doing here?'

'I got a paan shop in Sector 17. My first wedding contract, this. Come for a paan tomorrow.'

'Exams now. I'll come another day.'

'Fucking idiot you are Nearly ruined everything. Such *best* food and sweets. You constipated or something?' Kapoor said as soon as they were at a safe distance from the wedding house.

'Such *best* sweets. See?' Kapoor said and, one by one, brought out the goodies from his pockets. Omi suddenly felt very hungry.

'Don't look like a fool at the next party,' Kapoor said giving him the sweets, and a kick.

'No next party,' Omi said. 'I say, the sweets are not bad, Dad.' They tasted just like his father's stuff.

'Father, why don't you do marriage contracts?' Omi asked at home.

'Of course I do. If you took interest in the shop you would know. I did one today in Sector 16.'

The days passed. The exams came and went.

'Father, can I go swimming?' Omi asked, on the afternoon of the last paper. He always asked his father now. It pleased Khatri and he seldom refused.

'Be careful,' Khatri said, giving him a chavvani, a four-anna coin. It cost four annas to get into the pool.

The afternoon was coming to an end, but it was still hot. The water, especially at the shallow end, was lukewarm.

'It's like swimming in a cup of tea,' someone said to him. It sounded like Simla Pink English.

Omi turned around and saw it was Arun, a boy from the College, one of the 'imported shirts'. Omi knew him well by sight. Omi had often seen him going and coming in cars with his mob.

Arun was friendly. They spoke of College, the exams and girls. Omi was shy because of his homemade swimwear: it was an old striped pyjama which had worn out at the knees. Aunt Vidya had cut it above the knees neatly and done a hem. But inside the water Omi felt alright. In the water no difference could be noticed. Omi thought he spoke English as well as Arun.

'I say, can I drop you somewhere?' Arun said at the end of the swim.

'Oh, I haven't far to go. I'll walk.'

Omi did not want Arun to know where he lived. He was ashamed at being the son of a shopkeeper. A halwai at that.

'I say, can't we get something to drink to cool us down? Are you in a rush?'

Omi wasn't.

'Then let's go to Sector 22. We'll get something there.'

Omi had left home with only the chavvani which he had paid to get in the pool. But he did not want to refuse or to say that he had no money. In Arun's open-air MG it felt beautiful and cool as they raced towards Sector 22. Sector 22 bustled with life and Omi felt good. He had never sat in a car before.

The air-conditioned Savoy looked intimidatingly elegant and glamorous. The door waiter greeted Arun with deference and Arun asked after him in return. Although the door waiter was an old man, Arun patted him as if he was a child. Inside the restaurant, another waiter hurried up to them and salaamed Arun.

'Get me a nice table, Johnnie,' Arun said to the waiter.

'What are you having, Aimie?' Arun asked Omi, calling him Aimie instead of Omi, giving an English twist to his name. It sounded like a Simla Pink name. Omi liked it.

They sat there for an hour, sipping cold coffee from tall glasses, and talking of girls and films. Then Arun signed to Johnnie for the bill. When it came Omi fumbled with his pockets, making a show of wanting to pay the bill.

'Go to hell,' Arun said and leaned over to one side of the table, looking at the bill. He settled the bill out of Omi's sight. Johnnie salaamed enthusiastically.

'Rich man's habit to keep money matters outside friendship,' Omi said to himself.

'Coming for a swim tomorrow?' Omi asked outside the restaurant.

Two beggars assailed them and again Omi fumbled with his pockets. But Arun quickly gave one of them an eight-anna coin.

'Share it between yourselves,' Arun said to them in Punjabi. Even his Punjabi had something special about it, something aristocratic.

'Don't know what I'm doing tomorrow. Tell you what. Why don't I give you a ring?' Arun took it for granted that Omi had a telephone at home.

'What would he say if he saw my place?' Omi wondered and wished they had a house in the north-end, a telephone and a car.

'We are not on the phone.'

'Never mind. Leave it to me. I'll come if I can, and I'll pick you up.'

But Omi did not want to be picked up. It meant that Arun would find out that he lived on top of an ordinary shop, and that he was the son of a halwai.

'I shall go in any case. Do come if you can. I'll look out for you.'

Arun did come. They went to the Savoy again after the swim. Omi had brought money today. At the end of an hour and a packet of Char Minar (a cheap cigarette which even the rich of India smoke for some reason, even if everything else must be imported) Omi signed to Johnnie for the bill. They quarrelled over it.

'Go to hell,' Arun said.

'Go to hell,' Omi said.

Arun told Johnnie not to take the money from his guest and folded a note into the bill. When they were getting up, three girls came in accompanied by Bill, a tall Sikh boy whose real name was Ballinder Singh. They came straight to their table.

'We missed you at Harry's. What happened?' one of the girls asked Arun.

'He had gone off with someone, hadn't he?' Bill said with a smile.

'Where is she?' the girl asked.

'God knows. By the way, this is Aimie. Nina, Leela and Baba. You know Bill, the bugger. We were just leaving,' Arun said.

'Stay a bit longer, unless she is waiting,' the girl said.

They stayed and the girls teased Arun about this girl who remained unnamed. Most of the conversation was incomprehensible to Omi. He sat quiet and laughed from time to time at jokes he did not understand. But it did not matter. What mattered was that Omi was there. It was a privilege.

'Lovely bitches,' Arun said outside the restaurant. 'Anglos, from Miranda House. They will give, if you know how to take.'

Omi did not quite know what Arun meant. He had never met girls so lovely. Miranda House of Delhi University had an aura which only the film world of Bombay could match.

When Omi met Arun the next time, Arun was beaming with a mysterious smile.

'I say, you made a hell of an impression on Baba, the little one in the green dress,' Arun said. 'She said you were gorgeous.'

Omi was puzzled.

'Yes?' Omi said, blushing. He recalled Arun's words — 'they will give . . .'

'Don't go red in the face. I'll fix up something.'

'Can you? Will you? How?' Omi said.

'Look at the bastard! Love at first sight or something? Forget all that. She is an Anglo, not for loving. But she is game. Just remember that.'

The only thing Omi knew about the Anglo-Indians was that they looked, dressed and behaved like the British whom Omi had never seen. He nodded to Arun, as if to say he would remember.

'Leave it to me. I'll fix up something when I come back,' Arun said.

'Where are you going?'

'Sorry to be a bore. But it was there before you saw her. I am going to Simla for a few days. Why don't you come too?'

Omi wanted to laugh. Who would let him go? He could see his mother pinching her ears and hear her and Chatkarni mutter 'Ram, ram, Ram!' in consternation at the mention of Simla. Simla was the pleasure ground of the rich. All sorts of things happened there. 'All sorts of badmash wicked things,' Omi could hear his mother and Chatkarni say in unison.

At home Omi thought of Baba, the lovely Anglo-Indian girl in the green dress.

'Can it be true? Is it possible? I didn't say a word. It must be my looks,' Omi said to himself studying his face in the mirror. 'I am better looking than Arun and Bill. All they have is rich fathers and an accent. Not long ago I sat in that hovel of a shop Father bought from Hari Das, selling shrivelled vegetables and licking pieces of gur sugar. And now? Ah! All I've got to do is polish up my accent a bit. Then we will see what two and two make and what this Bill and Arun look like beside me.'

But the shop worried him. He could improve his accent, but what about his home?

'If only I could persuade Father to bring about a few changes in the shop. Give it a bit of polish and so on. Much better to be called a businessman's son than be labelled as the son of a halwai.'

'Father, I have an excellent idea.'

'What about?'

'About our business.'

'You mind your own business and let me look after mine.'

'But it can only be good for us, Father.'

'How?'

'Let us make our shop more attractive.'

'What's wrong with it?'

'Nothing. But . . .'

'If there is nothing wrong with it, then why the hell change it?'

'If we make it look better, we will attract more customers.'

'Make it look better, how, boy?'

'Have a proper counter. Decent chairs and tables and table cloths. A few good lights instead of those naked bulbs. And a little office for you in the back.'

'What else?'

'Better crockery. Have cardboard boxes with our name printed on to take away sweets in.'

'What else?'

'A telephone for you.'

'What else?'

'Get Seva and Bawa to wear uniforms instead of dhotti and pyjamas.'

'Yes? And who the hell will pay for all this?' Khatri said and scratched his sutthan.

Omi scratched his head.

'The money we spend initially would be recovered by increased sales. And once it gets going we will have it all back in no time.'

'Achaa? And if it doesn't?'

'We can't fail, Father. The city is growing. It is one way of making a penny.'

'You want to ruin your father. You are one of those sons who don't want to see their fathers happy.'

'Father, what I suggest can only bring more happiness. Better and best days.'

'What, buying a new counter and patloons for Seva and Bawa?' Khatri told his son to get lost and stop torturing him.

'The boy isn't talking complete nonsense, Lala ji,' Pandit Ram Narayan said. He was in the shop at the time. 'It may cost a bit of money — a thousand or so — but no risk, no gain. Remember, the capital is growing.'

This piece of advice coming from the temple priest had a meaning for Khatri.

'It is a lot of money, Pandit ji. And the boy is full of dreams. I can't follow them blindly.'

'It deserves a thought though,' Pandit Ram Narayan said.

'Father, I have another idea.'

'Keep it to yourself. You want to ruin me.'

'Why not make it a proper, a real restaurant? It would cost a bit, but there is no restaurant in our part of the capital. It would be an instant success.'

'You mean stop selling sweets altogether? You are mad, like your mother.'

'Think, Father. There would be no rivals. Once it gets going . . . we would be made.'

'And if it doesn't get going . . . total ruin. That will be for being greedy. God kicks those who ask to be kicked.'

'Think, Father. We have the swimming pool, the temple and the evening market. A proper restaurant is badly needed. If we don't open it, someone else will. Then we will repent and regret for the rest of our lives.'

'Now get lost and leave me alone. And here comes your idiot friend. Go waste your time with him. Don't waste mine.'

Kapoor arrived. He had a funny look on his face. He wore a tie and looked smart.

'What badmashi pranks are you up to today, Kapoor?' Khatri said. He gave the boys a laddu each and dismissed them.

'Omi bau is changing, Lala ji,' Seva Singh said. 'He is getting commonsense.'

Khatri was not sure of that. The only thing he was sure of was that he was not going to sink even a single rupee in any silly ventures. God had been kind to him and Khatri was not going to abuse God's kindness.

Khatri folded his hands on his chest and took a little bow towards the temple.

'I am honest. My prices are fair. I only use pure ghee.'

Pure ghee and fair prices were partly responsible for his shop's popularity. Quality completed his reputation. Quality was his pride. And while Paro too was proud of the quality of their sweets, she was always critical of his prices.

'In Sector 22 the price of everything is twice than ours. No wonder they mint money there, while we remain as we are,' Paro complained regularly.

'A little more sense in that head of yours and it would have done the trick. Then you would have known, woman, that I beat them all by keeping my prices lower. I get more customers.'

'What is more important? Money or customers? If our prices were right we would get more money. It is commonsense. Ask anybody.'

'I am glad I don't have your commonsense and I don't want to ask anybody.'

And now his son was showing signs of commonsense.

'*Best* wedding taking place in Sector 10 this evening,' Kapoor said.

'So?' Omi said.

'So go and put your *best* clothes on. Tie and all.'

Omi shook his head.

'What if we get caught?'

'Why should we? Why should anyone even think that we are not invited? Did you think that the people sitting next to us at the last wedding were all invited? Do you ever consider that the chap next to you in a bus might be travelling without a ticket? Did you think whether I had a ticket or not in that hand-shake bus? No, you didn't. You didn't because one doesn't think of such things. In a civilised world we don't think we are living next to a thief.'

It was convincing, but not convincing enough. Omi shook his head.

'Besides, this is an ideal wedding from our point of view. The girl's family and friends have come from Amritsar, the boy's from Delhi. Only a few locals are involved and the whole thing is taking place in a school. The girl's family will think that we are from the boy's side and vice versa. The girl's father is very rich. The food will be better than *best*, out of this world. What more do you want?'

Omi still wasn't convinced.

'But how did you find out all this, Dad?'

'Dads know everything.'

Reluctantly, Omi went and got changed.

'Long way, Section 10. How are we going to get there?' Omi said.

'We'll go in style. We'll go in a rickshaw.'

Kapoor was right about the wedding. Obviously it was a rich man's daughter's wedding, for dozens of cars were parked on both sides of the school gate. There was another, an even surer sign to confirm this. Behind the dozens of cars, in the rough area between the road and the low school wall, sat scores of beggars and untouchables with empty tin cans and empty earthenware pots,

195

watching the tamasha fun and waiting — the richer the wedding the larger their number at it. They sat on their haunches and listened to the loud-speaker blaring famous film songs, the best of the Binaca Geet Mala, the Indian Top Ten, of the last several years.

The school gate was buried in rich exotic foliage. It was bedecked with flowers and twinkling lights. Two huge banana trees on its sides supported a large sign which said WELCOME in glittering lights. The drive to it had a ceiling of row upon row of multicoloured paper flags. They stretched as far as the eye could see. When the two boys alighted at the gate, they were welcomed with garlands and ushered in with great politeness.

'What did I tell you, Omi son?' Kapoor said in a whisper, drawing Omi's attention to the fairytale setting.

It looked just like a film set. The school building and the colourful shamiana marquees in the school grounds, and every bush and tree there wore necklaces of thousands of coloured light bulbs. Hundreds of well-dressed men, women and children strolled around or sat on sofas under the shamianas. Silk saris shimmered, jewellery glittered, paper flags fluttered and the air itself was perfumed with rose-water attar.

'What did I tell you?'

Waiters in red coats with gold brocade moved around urgently with silver salvers, offering refreshments. Kapoor was quite choosy. He advised Omi to be equally choosy and gave him a useful bit of advice.

'Save your appetite for the real thing.'

Omi was afraid that every pair of eyes was focused on him. He was sure that at least one pair of eyes watched him wherever he went, that of a heavily bejewelled lady of about fifty in a green silk sari.

Kapoor selected a sofa in a corner of a shamiana. The two boys sat down and munched at salted pistachio nuts sipping Coca Cola. The lady in the green sari came and sat down next to them. Omi's face went yellow.

'Where are your parents?' the lady asked Omi in English.

Omi's heart stopped beating. Kapoor nudged him, urging him to keep his calm.

'They are in the other shamiana,' Omi managed to say.

'What is your father's name?' the bejewelled lady said.

Omi was convinced that he was going to die. It was worse than at his first College debate.

'Shadi Lal Khatri.'

'Ah! So you are the Khatris of Jor Bagh,' the lady said giving a gentle slap on Omi's arm. 'We live in Lodi Road, you know. So near. But Delhi is so big. One hardly gets to know one's own neighbours even. My sister knows your mother very well, she knows you too. Savitri, she looks just like me, only younger. But you can hardly tell the difference. People are always mistaking us. Remember her, no?'

'Oh yes,' Omi said, remembering Savitri.

'She couldn't come. She had to go to Ahmedabad with her husband Bodh Raj. Big big trouble at their cloth mill. Big strike. Indian workers! Never satisfied. They want more, more, more. You must know — you had a strike at your mill last year, didn't you? Indian workers! They want more, more, more, no?'

Omi nodded gravely. He knew all there was to know about strikes.

'You managed it alright, your strike. Your father is a clever man. Our Bodh Raj is not. He is a fool. No, not really. But.'

A waiter came and held out a silver salver to her. She took a handful of pistachio nuts and munched at them noisily.

'And you go to St Stephen's. Best College in India. As good as Oxford or Cambridge if you ask me. You must know our daughter Indira, no? She goes to Miranda House. Don't know her? Well, you must meet her then. I am going to do bathroom. I'll bring her back and introduce you.'

The lady in the green sari handed Omi her uneaten pistachio nuts and went away.

'Phew!' Omi said, breathing out loudly. 'Wish she had told me where our cloth mill was. But what the hell did she mean by, "I am going to do bathroom"?'

'She meant she was going for a pee. And we better piss off too. She has designs on you, Omi son.'

They moved to another shamiana where people were settling down to the real thing, a Maharajah's dinner: partridge, quail, chicken, fish, mutton, guchchi (the wild morel mushrooms from Afghanistan, eaten in these parts only at weddings) and a large variety of other delicacies. But before they could find somewhere to sit, the bejewelled lady found them. She was accompanied by a plain girl with an impressive amount of jewellery around her neck, ears and wrists. She was about eighteen.

'Ah, here you are. I was looking all over the place for you,' the lady said. 'Our Indira. Surely you have met in Delhi, no?'

The lady left her daughter and Omi staring at each other and disappeared into the crowd once again. Kapoor nudged Omi. Omi knew he had to say something, but the question was, what? 'Son of a bitch,' Omi called Kapoor inside his throat and wished he had stayed at home.

'I am Indira Mehra,' the girl said in Simla Pink English.

'This is Shiv Kapoor,' Omi introduced his friend, but forgot to introduce himself.

A silent pause followed. Kapoor pushed a finger in Omi's arse, urging him to open his mouth.

'Splendid wedding. All these decorations. Mummy said you are at St Stephen's. I haven't see you around the Campus . . .'

'Big place,' Omi said.

'Surely you know my brother Bobby . . .'

'I am sure I do . . .'

'. . . He is somewhere around. Let's go and look for him.'

'No, no, no. I'll go,' Omi said and slipped away. He went straight to the school gate and blew out a sigh of relief.

'Son of a bitch,' he called Kapoor inside his throat. 'I'll never listen to him again.'

Just then there was a hand on his shoulder. Omi shuddered.

'Where are you going? You can't go away like that, without trying the best food in the world.' It was Kapoor.

'No, Dad.'

'Yes, sonny boy.' Kapoor put an arm around Omi's shoulder and led him to a shamiana where there were only two seats left. We won't be disturbed here.'

The food came. It came in great quantities. The guests were served liberally. Just when everybody was about to start eating, there was a loud noise behind them, from the five-foot-high canvas wall of the shamiana which separated the wedding feast from the rest of the world — the cars, the beggars and the untouchables. Everybody looked back. Fifty or more dark faces were staring at them from above the canvas wall and fifty or more bodies were leaning against it. The supporting pegs flew up out of the earth under their weight and the canvas wall flopped over flat, onto some of the wedding guests. There was a great deal of commotion and noise as servants chased the beggars and the untouchables away with lathis and sticks.

'Kali,' Omi and Kapoor whispered to each other. She held an empty tin can in her hand as she ran away from the collapsed canvas wall.

Within minutes, the canvas wall was back in position, between the marriage guests and the untouchables. People starting eating. The food was, as Kapoor had anticipated, out of this world.

'What did I tell you?' Kapoor said as he tore apart a partridge expertly, as if he ate it every day. Omi had never eaten partridge or quail before.

But people around them were hardly eating. They ate only a quarter of what was heaped on their plates. When the meal was over, servants came with large steel buckets and emptied all the half-eaten food into them. They took them across the school grounds and laid them down in a straight line in front of the untouchables. The untouchables fought and pushed each other to get a hand in the buckets. More buckets came with half-eaten biryanis, pillaus, nan, meat, poultry, game and vegetables and the beggars and the untouchables settled down to a feast. What they could not eat they took away in the tin cans and earthenware pots they had brought with them to the rich man's daughter's wedding.

'*Best* wedding,' Kapoor said after the sweets, nudging Omi, meaning it was time to go.

From the corner of his eyes Omi saw Indira's mother eyeing him. But luckily, according to the custom, everybody rose from the tables at the same time. The boys got lost in the general confusion that followed. At the school gate the parents and the family of the bride were saying goodbye to the guests. With their mouths full of a very special silver paan (Omi could tell it wasn't Bhaia's , for it was much richer), they folded their hands in respect to the father and the mother of the bride, Seth and Sethani So-and-So of Amritsar. Then they shook hands with her brothers who insisted on embracing them as they were embracing all other male guests.

'Thank you for coming,' one of the brothers of the bride said.

'A memorable wedding. No Maharajah could have put on a better show,' Kapoor said.

'All your meharbani and kindness.'

'Kapoor bau ji, what are you doing here?' a voice came from nowhere.

Kali stood by the gate, ten feet from them, looking quite surprised to see the two boys. Everybody turned their heads. First they looked at the untouchable girl in tattered clothes, then at the elegantly turned-out Kapoor and Omi. If Kapoor had ignored her and kept his cool, it might have been different. But Kapoor panicked and did a foolish thing.

'Run,' Kapoor whispered to Omi and took a leap over the three-foot-high school wall, only to trip and fall. Two waiters in red and gold pounced on him and led him away somewhere behind the main shamiana.

Omi was caught like a rat in a trap. The partridge, quail and the rest suddenly rebelled in his stomach.

'Pray who are you, Sir?' asked a young man from the wedding line, firmly laying a hand on Omi's shoulder.

'Why I am a guest, Sir. What an extraordinary question?' Omi said in his best English.

'On whose invitation, may I ask? That dog-tailed interloper's?'

'No, no, no,' a familiar voice said. 'Om Prakash is with me. He is like a son to me.'

A few smiles broke out on the paan-stained lips, for everybody knew the truth.

'Ah, Uncle Kandhari Sahib! Good thing you told us. We were about to educate this young man in the art of guestmanship, like the other guest . . .' the man said, rubbing his hands.

Omi heard someone cry out in pain behind the great shamiana. Kapoor was being educated in the art of guestmanship. Omi would have preferred that to being rescued by Kandhari.

Kandhari took him back to the party.

'Don't worry, Om Parkash . . .' Kandhari said with a know-all smile.

Omi wished that the earth under his feet would open up and swallow him. It was shame of a kind which makes a man think that the only thing he wants from life is death, instant death, there and then.

'Son of a bitch. Why does he have to be there every time I am in the shit?'

'. . . Don't worry, Om Parkash. Not a word will pass these lips. Who hasn't attended a wedding party in your capacity? I did it when I was your age, and surely your father too. The only difference was that we did not get caught. Now go home.'

Omi went to a dark corner of the school playground and leapt over the wall. Out on the road he wished a car would run him over. Omi was ready for it. But everyone was driving intelligently that night.

Khatri was doing some hard thinking. He ground his jaws and shook his legs. Should he try one of the boy's ideas?

A couple of days later Khatri took a bus to Manimajra. He went to a printing press whose owner he knew from his Panchkoola days, and ordered two hundred cardboard boxes to pack sweets in to take away.

'Eye-catching design and first-class printing,' Khatri said to the printer. 'It is for our new capital, you know.'

Paro grumbled the day Bhola Ram brought the boxes in his lorry.

'More expense. Unnecessary expense. Other people run their shops for profit, my house-wallah runs ours for loss,' she said and slapped her forehead.

'Wait and see, Ma.' Omi was triumphant.

'Wait and see what? Our ruination?'

In two sizes and two colours, pink and blue, the boxes looked pretty. The name of the shop and the address were enclosed in a wreath of flowers in the middle of the lid. A beautiful young Lord Krishna played his flute to a sad-eyed cow and a baby calf on each of the four corners.

'It is the fashion, Ma. Big shops in Delhi and Bombay sell sweets in these.'

'Big shops in Delhi and elsewhere make big profits and put them in their pockets. Your father wants to throw his away in these boxes.'

But people liked the idea of taking sweets home in nice boxes instead of having them loosely packed in brown paper bags. The boxes did a good job too. They travelled far and wide. In every corner of Chandigarh, Omi spotted them lying on top of garbage cans or peeping at him through heaps of rubbish. They were an excellent advertisement for the shop, as was seen in the 'month of marriages'.

This was the marriage season, when most Hindu marriages take place, as laid down by the pandits. Every season Khatri, like all halwais, was very busy. But this year Seva and Bawa were unable to cope.

'It is our boxes, Father.'

'I need another servant,' Khatri said.

'Why incur more expense? Get your loafer son to help. He isn't doing anything these days.'

Khatri was annoyed.

'Keep the boy out of it. I have told you one hundred and one times that I don't want him to follow in my footsteps — either you have no ears or no head. I don't want him to do a servant's work when I can afford a servant. He is not to be a halwai.'

Bhajjan was there. For once, Khatri found his presence less irksome, even welcome. And Bhajjan worked hard with Khatri in the fury of production to meet the demands of the 'month of marriages'. Sometimes there was more than one marriage party to provide for in the same day.

Nanda, the Hospitality Officer of Governor House, was so pleased with the quality of Khatri's catering at his daughter's wedding that he called him aside to have a word with him in private.

'The Governor House contract is finishing shortly, Lala ji. Why don't you take over supplying us regularly and for our At Homes.'

The Hospitality Officer explained what the contract involved.

'You will no doubt revise the price of tonight's work, Lala ji,' an assistant of the HO said to Khatri later.

'Naturally, naturally.'

Naturally. The contract was a gift of God. If it involved lowering that night's quotation, Khatri wouldn't fuss. He wasn't a fool. On the contrary. Khatri beamed with satisfaction.

'It is our boxes, Paro. The boxes that hurt you so much when they came. They won me this contract,' Khatri said when he got home.

The contract wasn't enormous, but it was for Governor House and that meant a lot. Khatri took another trip to the printer in

Manimajra with a chit from Professor Bhatnagar. He ordered
another batch of boxes with a new notice:

By appointment
Governor House
Chandigarh

This was printed in gold letters with the official three-headed lion
capital over the wreath encircling the name of the shop. He had it
painted on the shop sign as well. Then he folded his hands on his
chest and took a bow towards the temple.

'Now the furniture, Father,' Omi said.

One morning Omi came down and found a bullock cart parked
behind their house. It was loaded with a new showcase and a new
counter. Another day Omi came down and found his father being
measured up by a tailor master from Sector 22. A few days later two
silk kurtas, a silk waistcoat with twenty-one buttons and a Nehru
durbar coat were delivered by the same tailor master.

'Hai, my mother!' Paro said and nearly pulled her ears apart
when she saw Khatri in his new clothes. 'Are you taking up randi-
bazi whoring or something?'

Omi smiled. The Doctorani, Chatkarni and Satya sniggered.
Vidya laughed.

'All your doing,' Paro said to Omi. 'Why don't you, father and
son, start walking Sector 22 hand in hand, ogling College girls?
Why not catch a few of them and open up a cosy little chabara dance
house for your delectation?'

'This is not the Camp, nor your father's village. This is
Chandigarh, our new capital. I have to meet big officers, go to
Governor House. I can't go in rags.'

Khatri was negotiating another Government contract with the
help of Nanda, the Hospitality Officer. Now and then he had to
visit the Secretariat. On one of these visits, Khatri noticed a mirror
in one of the ante-rooms of a burra sahib's personal office and looked
at himself in it.

'It is the same Shadi Lal Khatri — of Panchkoola or of Chandigarh,' he said to himself. But there was a difference. Khatri was
impressed by the difference.

'It must impress the others as well.

But somewhere in himself Khatri was ashamed of his vanity.

'Khatri, old cock, do you need all this silk and so many buttons on your waistcoat?'

Khatri knew that he did.

'I have to at this time of my life, my grahasta domestic period. I must fend for my family and fight for a better existence for them. This silk is a part of the fighting kit.'

Khatri decided he would go to Kalka soon.

It pleased Omi to see his father's new look. He would look like a Congress leader if he wore a Congress topi instead of the peshawari turban. But Omi did not mind the turban, it gave his father shaan dignity and a presence. Omi would feel proud to stand in the middle of the College with his father now. He wasn't sure about this before. He wondered what his father would look like in European clothes.

'Father, why don't you try a proper English-style suit?'

'Ganging up with your mother against me? I don't wear these clothes for the love of them. I wear them out of necessity. Necessity. Understand?' Khatri said sharply, not realising that Omi was genuinely impressed. Unlike Paro.

'Oh, necessity. Necessity to look life a lafanga badmash pimp,' Paro said. 'You are blackening my face in front of all the women of the neighbourhood. Do you know what Satya said to me in front of everybody? She said — Parvati, your man is getting new feathers. Take care he doesn't fly away from you.'

'Silly husband-eaters. The bitches have nothing else to talk about. I am surprised your Chatkarni hasn't said anything so far.'

'She has. She says you are already flying.'

Khatri laughed.

The new contract came through and Khatri announced that he was going to Kalka.

'Next Saturday. You come too, boy.'

Omi shut his eyes before answering. He saw Mohan stare at him. He opened them again immediately. On Friday night he selected two onions carefully and strapped them to his armpits.

'If it doesn't work this time I'll never touch an onion again.'

Omi held his wrist in his hand when he woke up next morning, feeling his pulse.

'What now? You got fever again or something?' Paro said.

'It is nothing, Ma. I am perfectly alright,' Omi said without letting go of his wrist.

'Let me see,' Paro said and took his hand. She felt his pulse and then his brow.

'It is burning. Bawa, go borrow Doctorani's thermometer.'

'I am alright, ma.'

The thermometer came. Omi prayed.

'One hundred and one! Hai, my mother!' Paro said. 'You set one foot outside this house and I will break both your legs.'

Khatri had a look at the thermometer.

'Humm,' he said and sent Bawa to fetch a rickshaw for the bus stand. An hour after he left, Chatkarni arrived for her handha. She felt Omi's forehead.

'Give him a good cold drink of nimbu pani lime water with a pinch of rock salt and plenty of sugar,' Chatkarni said.

Satya came to inquire after Omi.

'Give him a good hot drink of green herbal tea without any sugar,' Satya said.

Aunt Vidya came and took his temperature again.

'One hundred and two! Hai, my mother!' Vidya said, holding a hand to her wide-open mouth.

'You've overdone it this time, Omi son,' Omi said to himself. The fucking onions.

The city was growing. People with and without money were flocking to it from all parts of the Punjab. Some came even from beyond. Those who came here with money came to make more. Those who came without came to make some. The skeleton of the new capital of the Punjab was fast acquiring flesh. There were more buildings, more people, more hustle-bustle raunak, more traffic and more business.

'It was my idea of the boxes, Ma, which won us the Governor House contract. If Father hadn't listened to me we would have remained what we were — ordinary sweet-sellers. Now we are famous. Ask anyone,' Omi said to his mother.

'See, Father? My idea worked. It did more. I am telling you, we should convert the shop into a proper restaurant. We can't go wrong. It will be like having our own mint. A private gold mine,' Omi said to his father.

'Go, go, go and stop poisoning *their* head with greed,' Paro said.

'Go, go, go and worry about your exam results,' Khatri said.

'We simply can't go wrong, Father. I am telling you.'

'And I am telling you to shut up,' Paro said.

'Paro, Begum Madam, your son wants to ruin me.'

'Just don't listen to him, the barking dog. Don't think about it.'

But when Khatri was alone he could not stop himself thinking about the restaurant idea of his son.

'It is a snare, a trap that I am setting up for myself. I have become too vain and greedy as I approach old age. Even the threat of losing all that I have made for myself and my family doesn't stop me from craving for more. Is this what the Hindu grahasta, living a worldly life, is about?'

If it was, it was painful, for it involved painful decisions. The elders said that at the age of twenty-five a Hindu would get married. The elders said that during the next twenty-five years he would go through his grahasta period and lead a worldly existence to the full: become a family man, preferably with several sons, and devote himself to their welfare and to the pursuit of success and wealth. During this time, the elders said, he must enjoy the fruits of his success. What the elders did not say was that greed was seldom removed from the struggle for success.

Khatri ground his jaws and shook his legs and scratched the middle of his sutthan. Paro saw him do all that. She knew that he was torturing himself.

'Just don't listen to that greed-tongued son of yours,' Paro said.

Of all the crucial decisions Khatri had been faced with in his life, this seemed to be the most difficult.

There had been a moment in Peshawar in August 1947 when he and his relatives had sat with their heads in their hands thinking of life and death. Hindus and Sikhs were being slaughtered every day around them as Muslims were being slaughtered elsewhere in the Punjab. They were huddled together in a strange mesmerising immobility. All they did was pray for life. The decision to leave home and property still would not come. Where would they go? To freedom in India? But Peshawar was in India and they did not know what freedom meant. The provincial government was still pro-Congress despite being entirely Muslim. Nehru had come. Mountbatten had come. But theirs were empty visits. Partition was inevitable. The Hindus and the Sikhs had to go. Where? Nobody knew. So they all stuck to their homes and possessions and let uncertainty paralyse them. It was then that Khatri had told Paro to pack up a bundle of essentials and flee with him in the name of God. Some others had followed him. But many, like Paro's sisters, had remained and were never heard of again.

'It was my decision that saved us and those who came.'

But this time it was different. Then, life had been at stake. Now it was money. And that made a difference.

'What will be, will be,' Khatri said loudly, and wanted to see his son. He wanted to speak to Omi. To hear him talk about his ideas for the restaurant. He sent Bawa to fetch him. When Omi came, however, Khatri first kept him standing and then spoke of this and that.

'When are your results being published, boy?'

'Next week, Father. You know very well, Father.'

Omi knew he had not been summoned for small talk. He knew his father well. Before his father could, he came to the point himself.

'Father, have you thought any more about the restaurant?'

'You talk without knowing what you are talking about. Have you any idea what a restaurant is likely to cost to make and then to run?'

'I do. But we can afford it, if we decide to.'

'But can we risk it? It may well break my back.'

'We simply can't fail, Father.'

Khatri was full of admiration for his son's blindness.

'But you must pass your exam, boy.'

'I will, Father.'

Omi did, though only just.

Khatri consulted his friends and well-wishers.

'It is not a bad idea. If it works, it will make your future,' Nanda said.

'It is bound to succeed, Lala ji. You can't be doing the wrong thing,' Professor Bhatnagar said.

'The city is growing. You have some chances of success. But finally it is in His hands,' Pundit Ram Narayan said, looking towards the temple.

'It is a gamble, Lala ji. Don't forget you are a family man. Your son is going to be a family man. You have to think about all this,' Bhola Ram said.

'You may be building your own tomb, your own Taj Mahal, by building the restaurant,' Satya's husband said.

'How can you become so reckless with our lives? Why don't you simply drown us in the lake?' Paro said through her rivers of rain.

'Father, it is the best chance for us to make real money. It is a Godsend . . .'

'It is a thunderbolt . . .' Paro said from her veil of monsoon.

'. . . If we don't, someone else will come up with a restaurant next-door one of these days and we will cry for the rest of our lives . . .'

'I would rather cry than die . . .'

'. . . Our restaurant will mean real money, big money. Forget the Camp, forget Panchkoola, forget Capital Sweets and think of . . .'

'. . . And think of an early death. The Muslims spared us, now we can do it ourselves through our son's kindness and your blindness.'

Khatri felt and looked harassed. His son's optimism and Paro's pessimism had the same effect on him. Khatri started to avoid them. One evening, just before closing the shop, he sent Seva Singh with a fiver to buy a half bottle of the Red Fairy, the ruby-red whisky from Karnal. Seva smiled as he put on his shoes. Only on rare occasions did Khatri send him on such a mission, when Lala ji was thinking or worried or celebrating.

'And what do you think about it, Seva Singh?' Khatri asked.

Seva scratch his head. As a poor man he was not supposed to have an option.

'I am poor man, Lala ji, what can I say? But Omi bau does say intelligent things from time to time. If it was not a question of so much money I would say yes. But.'

'It is a question of a lot of money.'

Seva had hardly gone twenty paces when Khatri called him back.

'Bring a half bottle of Solan Number One instead,' Khatri said, giving him another fiver for that expensive Indian whisky which the British had endeavoured to substitute for Scotch. It cost twice as much as Red Fairy.

'Why shouldn't I drink the better stuff? I don't make money for the mere sight of the bank notes.'

Khatri closed the shop when Seva returned, and came upstairs with the Solan Number One in one hand and a soda in the other.

'Are you taking to the bottle now, then?' Paro said, holding her ears. 'All that silk and twenty-one buttons and now whisky. What next? A randi whore, no doubt.'

'Give us a glass, Begum,' Khatri said and slapped her on the bottom.

Khatri took the glass and went up to the roof.

'It is such risk, so much expense. It will have to succeed.'

Khatri poured himself a finger of Solan Number One and raised the glass to the darkening Kasauli mountain.

'The boy's restaurant will have to succeed.'

There was one more thing he had to do. He had to see Gokul Baba. If Gokul Baba said yes, then Khatri would go ahead with it.

Gokul Baba said yes.

III

Omi saw Arun at the English film one Sunday morning. The English film-goers liked to arrive early. Smoking and sipping soft drinks, they made conversation, saw each other and were seen. The boys dressed with care, the girls to kill. The boys numbered a few 'ordinaries' among them, the girls not one. They were all Simla Pinks, the progressive type. 'Ordinary' girls never came to see English films — English films showed all sorts of wicked things. 'Ordinary' parents preferred their daughters to remain unprogressive.

Omi was as much a regular as anybody. He, too, arrived before time, lit a cigarette, bought a Coca Cola and sought out someone to talk to. Usually at least one of his friends, Kapoor, Shambhu, Pritam or Tully, was there. But while his friends and the other 'ordinaries' sat downstairs, Omi, because of an old promise with himself, sat upstairs in the two-ten gallery, the smart class.

Arun was chatting with some Simla Pink boys and girls. Omi thought he would catch him on his own during the interval and went in. He had a shock. In a dark corner of the gallery he saw two other 'ordinaries,' Romesh and Sarla. Speechless, Omi looked away.

'Long time no see,' Omi said to Arun, catching him by the arm during the interval.

'Wish you had come. Had a roaring ball,' Arun said and embraced Omi. 'Simla was packed with females. Lovely Anglo and Parsee girls from Bombay, the giving type.'

Arun told him about the fête at Shelley's and the ball at the Cecil, but Omi did not know what Simla life was like. All he knew about Simla was the story of Scandal Point, where a playboy Maharajah had kidnapped a British Governor's daughter, for which he was banished from Simla to build his own summer capital elsewhere in the hills. He also knew that before Independence all the Englishmen in India went up there and did wicked things, and that now the rich Indians went there and did the same things.

'Let's lunch together. I've got so much to tell you,' Arun said as the bell went. He did not mention a word about Omi's Baba.

The lunch at the Savoy was superb. Arun told stories of Simla, of this dame and that, of this party and that dance. Omi was dying to ask about Baba. At last he did.

'Ah, the bugger's been pining away. Well, she was there too and she is here now . . .'

'Where?' Omi said, looking around.

'Not here, you fool. I mean she is in town and she is coming on the thirteenth. You are too.'

'Where?'

'My place. I'm having a party.'

'What party?'

'Nothing much. My birthday.'

'Ah, a birthday party,' Omi said to himself. He had never been to one. The 'ordinaries' here did not have birthdays, nor did anyone else back in the Camp.

'Lots of girls coming. You come too and make hay while the sun shines. Right?' Arun said, wiping his mouth with a corner of the milk-white napkin. He looked very elegant doing that.

'Right,' Omi said, wiping his own mouth with his napkin like Arun.

At home, Omi ran into Romesh at the door. Romesh ignored Omi as usual. It was clear that he had not seen him in the cinema. Upstairs, Omi found his mother fuming with anger. She was telling Chatkarni that God had given her a hurricane instead of a son. 'Others beget sons for comfort and joy, I got mine for worry.'

Khatri was in his room, reading *Milap* under the ceiling fan and listening to her.

'Where have you been, loafer? The food is cold and good only for Dabbu,' Paro said.

'I ate with a friend in a restaurant, Ma. I wanted to find out about their food and decor, now that we are going to have our own restaurant.'

'You are the one who is going to pull this house down on our heads, brick by brick.'

'Ma, do you know how much they charge for a meal for two? Twelve rupees.'

'And who paid?' Paro's eyes popped out.

'My friend.'

That was alright.

'Twelve rupees for two? Ram, Ram, Ram!' Chatkarni said, pinching her ears.

'Think, Ma. If we charged two-thirds of that and fed fifty people a day, think of the profit. Over two hundred rupees a day! Just think of it.'

'Stuff more greed in your father's head. Go and bring this house down on it, brick by brick. Chatkarni, I must have killed a Brahmin in my past life to get him.'

Khatri, sitting in the next room and listening, did not participate in this discussion. Omi knew what it meant. It meant that his father was thinking. Omi knew that whenever his father was like that, an important decision was on its way.

'Ma, it is not greed. It is sense.'

'Father and son, that is just what you both don't have. Sense.'

'Ma, shave my head off, if what I say doesn't come true.'

'And shave mine off, if what I say doesn't come true — our ruination.'

Khatri was making calculations and sighing from time to time. He had discussed it with everybody he knew. After all that they had said, he was back where he had started. He was terrified. He ground his jaws and scratched the middle of his sutthan.

'Two hundred rupees in notes. Every day, Ma. We will have a car inside six months. We will go to Simla every summer — take auntie Chatkarni with us. We will take you both to Benares,

211

Hardwar, Amritsar or any other holy city you name. What more you want?'

Sarla came to borrow their new electric iron, putting an end to this mother-and-son discussion. It was clear to Omi that she had not seen him in the cinema either, for she did not look at him. Omi went to his father's room.

'Father, the Savoy crockery is something you simply must see.'

'Why?'

'It has got their name on it. We got to have it too, when the time comes.'

'Which time, boy?'

'Father! Our restaurant.'

'Get lost and stop torturing me.' Khatri dismissed his son with the flick of a finger.

'And their decor, Father. You simply must see that too. An absolute must.'

'Go look at your books. You are starting College tomorrow.'

Omi was looking forward to starting his Third Year. For some reason it was supposed to be the best of the four College years leading to the BA exam.

'Life begins in the Third Year,' everybody used to say, though no one knew why.

It began well, with a beautiful Pondy someone had brought back from vacation in Simla. Nobody attended the lectures that day and there were a score of killer erections under the laden mango trees.

Omi was also looking forward to something else, to Arun's party and seeing Baba again.

'But perhaps she has forgotten all about you, Aimie son.'

Omi was right. Arriving late on his new green Robin Hood bike, he saw her in the large crowd talking to an 'imported shirt' known as Duke, a well-known lady-killer. Baba looked at Omi, smiled and then turned her back to him. For the rest of the time she remained with Duke, playing with his shirt buttons from time to time.

'But you knew it would be like this, Aimie son. So.'

Arun introduced him to Duke's brother Count, an equally well-known lady-killer, and Betty, Veena, Meera and Sue. Count was telling the girls what was obviously a hilarious joke, for the girls could not stop laughing. Nobody talked to Omi. He was an outsider. He walked away.

Time passed slowly. Omi drank two Coca Colas, smoked a few cigarettes and came to the conclusion that this was not the place for him, an 'ordinary'. At the door, he collided with Arun.

'Nobody leaves my party like this. Nobody,' Arun said, giving him a jab in the side. Then he turned to a new arrival. 'Ah, there. Come and meet someone special. Aimie — Indira.'

This was too much, much too much. What was Omi going to do? He looked towards Arun. But Arun had disappeared.

'Hello again,' Indira said after what seemed a long pause.

'Splendid party,' Omi said, recalling what she had said at the wedding. 'All those people.'

'Did you not say you were from St Stephen's in Delhi?' Indira said after another pause.

'I didn't . . . Your mother assumed I was . . .' Here was an opportunity to change the subject. '. . . Oh, by the way, how is she?'

'She'll be here soon — you can ask her yourself . . . But why did you let me believe . . .?'

'How do you know Arun?' Omi said, interrupting her.

'Met him with Titli in Simla. Do you know Titli?'

Who didn't? Titli, which in Hindi and Punjabi means butterfly, was the darling of Chandigarh College. She was a tennis star. Boys skipped lectures to watch her frolic about in her sexy kit with racket and ball. Yes, Omi knew Titli.

'Yes, I know of Titli. But how do you know her?' Omi said.

'We were at school together in Simla and we competed with each other in everything.'

'In everything?' Omi asked as they went to get some food.

'I got prizes in school, she got them outside . . . Do you know someone else here — Baba?'

'Yes, slightly. She likes shirt buttons. Look.'

Indira laughed.

'You know something . . .' Omi said, not really knowing what to say, '. . . I've never been to Delhi or Simla . . .' It sounded like a criminal confession.

'You don't mean it. Liar.'

213

'. . . True. And you know something else? I am a poor boy really . . . Not like these "imported shirts" and Simla Pinks . . .' Omi didn't know why he had said that. He was quite amazed at himself. But he felt relieved in a strange sort of way.

'What?' Indira said.

Omi explained and Indira laughed loudly. She liked these names.

'So you don't wear imported shirts,' Indira said.

'My shirt is pure Indian cotton. Probably made at your aunt Savitri's mill in Ahmedabad. . . . Incidentally, is their strike over?'

'How do you know all this?'

'Your mother thoughtfully informed me of all that.'

'How come you speak such excellent English for a starving non-Simla Pink?'

'Ah, that!' Shabas bravo, Professor Bhatnagar! Wouldn't he love to know it? Wouldn't his father love to know that he had got his money's worth? Omi changed the subject. 'How long are you staying in Chandigarh?'

'Going back tonight. By the night train. Mummy is coming to pick me up from here.'

Arun came and asked why they weren't dancing. Omi didn't know how to dance.

'Piece of cake. Indira will show you a couple of steps . . .' Arun said.

People were dancing to western music on the back verandah. 'One, two, three . . . One, two, three . . .' Indira showed Omi how to waltz. While dancing she asked the question he was most afraid of being asked in that party.

'What does your father do?'

Should he tell her that he was a halwai? Omi thought fast.

'He is in catering,' he said. It sounded much better. 'We are opening a restaurant.'

'Oh really. What are you going to call it?'

'The Pall Mall.' Omi had been playing Monopoly at Shambhu's place earlier that day and the name had got stuck.

'Nice name. It is that of a famous street in London,' Indira said. She seemed to know the game. 'Right next to Piccadilly.'

Indira's small breasts touched Omi now and then as they danced. Omi felt some excitement in his body. Just as he was beginning to enjoy himself her mother arrived. Now Indira would go away and he would be left by himself again.

'My mother,' Indira said. 'And look who is with her!'

Titli. She came straight to her school-friend, with a searching look which seemed to say: and who is this?

'He doesn't know how to dance. I was teaching him a few steps. Don't you know Aimie? From your College?' Indira said.

'Of course I know Omi,' Titli said, throwing her head back haughtily.

The regression from Aimie to Omi hurt. He smiled foolishly.

'Is our Indira a good teacher?'

'Depends on how good a pupil I am really.'

'Does it?' Titli said, looking Omi up and down. 'I suppose it does. I hope you are a good pupil. When you've learnt a dance, take me to the floor, won't you. I would like to know how good a teacher my dear Indira is.' Titli gave him a long look. It made him a little uncomfortable. But he also liked it.

'One, two, three . . . One, two, three . . .' They danced and Omi thought that it was not that difficult after all.

'Piece of cake. Told you,' Arun said, dancing past them with a beer bottle.

A little girl came to say that Indira was wanted by her mother. Indira went away, saying she would be back in a minute — she did not come back. Something else also happened, which led to the lights being dimmed: Arun's parents left for their club. The servants were dismissed. The atmosphere changed. It became intimate. Omi saw Titli's eye on him from time to time. He thought he saw a flicker of a smile on her lips once or twice.

'Suppose I took up her invitation?'

Next time Titli smiled, Omi went and asked her.

'Why not?' Titli said.

'An historic moment,' Omi said as they danced.

'What?'

'You dancing with me — history in the making.'

Titli laughed.

'You are a fast learner, Omi. Oh sorry, I mean Aimie.'

Omi felt hit below the belt. He said nothing.

'Good teacher, my school-friend eh? But she didn't teach you to dance slow, now did she?'

'I don't know the difference.'

'You want to learn?'

As they danced, Titli's breasts brushed against Omi all the time. But she seemed unaware of it.

'Of course, it is accidental. She is not that sort.'

In that intimate atmosphere dancers shuffled on the floor. They 'sorry'd', 'beg-your-pardon'd' and 'my-fault'd' each other. Someone with imagination switched off the main lights, leaving only the feeble spotlights in the garden which were directed at flower bushes and trees.

'I did not know you were called Aimie,' Titli said.

'I did not know either. Not till recently, that is.'

'I like the name. Aimie. Pretty name. Suits you.'

'I like your name. Titli — butterfly. Are you one?'

'Yes, I fly from one flower to another,' Titli said and laughed, hugging him — accidentally, Omi thought. 'Do you like tennis?'

'Only when you are playing.'

Titli laughed loudly and hugged him again. This time they remained in that position for a while. The couples around them were hardly moving, clinging to each other, as if the music was an adhesive.

'Funny boy. And when I am not playing tennis . . .?'

'I never think about it.'

Omi saw a few lady-killers steer their ladies to the flower bushes in the garden.

'Hot in here, isn't it?' Titli said softly.

But Omi did not hear her.

'Hot in here . . . you deaf or something?' she said in his ear, touching it with her lips.

'Isn't it?' Omi said, sounding very casual. Was she hinting that they should follow the lady-killers and their ladies?

'No, she can't be. She's only being polite. It is only my dirty mind, always having ideas.'

The music stopped, but people were still dancing, clinging to each other. Titli blew out a sigh. Omi did the same and waited for a new record. Then Titli spoke.

'Very hot in here. Do you have any qualms about going to the garden? Lovely garden.'

The garden was beautiful. A light breeze made it even more so. Far away the Kasauli mountain formed a dark, high wall on the horizon.

'Umm . . .! Lovely. Told you,' Titli said, breathing in the perfumed air of the garden.

Every bush was trimmed to perfection in the soft spotlights. Other couples were grouped together as single ghostly shadows in the bushes. Omi and Titli danced cheek to cheek. Omi knew he had to do something, but what? With Guddy it had been easier, he had been in control of things. With Titli he was not.

'Please God, help,' Omi begged. He was reminded of the saying that God helps those . . . But he did not know how to help himself. He knew what would happen if he tried anything foolish. Titli would kick him in the balls and just walk off.

But something happened. Titli steered him to a corner thick with bushes. There she took his mouth in hers and simply took his breath away.

Early one morning, a building-contractor's lorry arrived and deposited the materials for conversion in the Khatris' back yard. Paro was looking from the first-floor balcony, her chin cupped in her hand and her elbow resting on the balcony.

'All the provisions for our ruin. All his doing. Sons bring prosperity to others. Mine can only bring ruin to us,' she said to Satya and the Doctorani who stood on their balconies with their chins cupped in their hands like her. Their children stood around them, watching the tamasha fun.

Omi was downstairs in the yard. He had instructions to check up with his own list and he bossed about with a pencil and a notebook in his hands. Having checked every item twice, Omi made his way to the shop to see his father. Just then, Bawa came running out and whispered something urgently in his ear. Omi hurried to the shop and found his father, very pale in the face, talking with difficulty to a young man Omi had never seen before. Something was wrong.

'. . . It is your own fault. You can't fool the Government all the time . . .' the young man was saying. He was dressed in a khaki shirt and trousers. He had a stern face and the menacing look of a policeman.

Omi ran up and stood next to his father. Behind them stood Seva and Bawa.

'. . . If not, then it will be jail. Think carefully, Lala ji . . .' the man said harshly.

Omi felt the floor slip from under his feet. His face went white with fear.

'. . . Serious matter, this. Very serious. Refusal to show your books . . .'

Khatri ground his jaws and scratched the middle of his sutthan.

'. . . No wonder India doesn't make any progress, what with people like you cheating the Government right and left . . .'

Omi was puzzled that his father let the young man talk to him like that.

'. . . You say you haven't got any books. It is the same thing as refusing to show them. Everyone keeps some kind of books — the crooks keep two sets. But you say you haven't got any. Amazing. Do you think we are fools? Clearly you do. But we have caught up with you, at last.'

Khatri still said nothing.

'Oi, you two,' the young man shouted authoritatively at Seva and Bawa. 'Back to work.'

'Your son?' he asked, looking at Omi.

Khatri did not answer.

'Besides the figure the Department fixed, there will be the fine. It could be any amount. How much? I can't tell. I can't help. I am only a small fry in the Department, a very small fry if you ask me.'

'Can I ask you if we can come to some arrangement between ourselves?' Khatri finally said. 'Surely. Anything you say.'

'I am from the Anti-corruption Department, Lala ji, Anti-corruption. We are incorruptible. Don't offer us any bribes. I know this is India, but. We are Anti-corruption. We put people inside first and ask questions later.'

'What shall I do then?'

'Pay up. Fine and all. Or eat the air of the jail.'

'How much will it be?'

'Maybe five thousand. Maybe more. I can't tell. I can't help. I am only a small fry, a very small fry if you ask me.'

'Five thousand!' Khatri said to himself. Half his savings.

'Think, Lala ji, think. I'll be back on Monday,' the young man with the police looks said, and left.

'Skip the College, boy, and sit in the shop. I am going to see Nanda in Governor House,' Khatri said gravely, walking out of the shop. Omi saw him mount a rickshaw.

'Income Tax,' Seva said to a bewildered Omi.

Inside an hour, Khatri was back, sweating.

'Nanda wasn't there. Go fetch Dr Devan Chand,' Khatri said to Omi.

Dr Devan Chand was busy. He had a number of patients waiting in his shop. But Omi whispered in his ear that it was urgent.

'Very urgent.'

Dr Devan Chand left the patients waiting and came. He nodded gravely and went on nodding for a long while.

'Bad, Lala ji, very bad. Anti-corruption people are very cruel. Their job is to ruin families. My advice — just pay up,' Dr Devan Chand said.

This was not what Khatri wanted to hear. He sent for Satya's husband. Satya's husband shook his head and said the same.

'Pay up.'

'Go fetch Pandit Ram Narayan from the temple, boy. Perhaps he knows someone in Anti-corruption.'

Pandit Ram Narayan did not.

'But,' Pandit Ram Narayan said. 'But my wife's nephew is in the police,' Pandit Ram Narayan took him to the police station in Sector 17.

'Yes, Uncle. I know a couple of chaps in Anti-corruption. We work hand in hand, the police and them,' the nephew of Pandit Ram Narayan's wife said.

Pandit Ram Narayan whispered something to his wife's nephew.

'Yes, yes, yes, Uncle. I know it is important. I'll take you there just now. Bad people though, Anti-corruption. Don't we *know*?'

Khatri shuddered.

The three men went to the Anti-corruption Department's offices in Sector 22. The police officer left Khatri and Pandit Ram Narayan at a street corner nearby. Ten minutes later he returned with his friend.

'What is the name of the officer who saw you, Lala ji?' the friend of Pandit Ram Narayan's wife's nephew said.

'Mr Phulka,' Khatri said meekly.

'Phulka? You don't stand a chance with him. He is . . .' The man leaned over close to Khatri's ear and whispered, '. . . he is a pukka communist. He will either put you inside or . . .' The man leaned close to Khatri's ear again. '. . . or settle for not a penny less than half the actual amount in question.'

Pandit Ram Narayan looked at Khatri. Khatri nodded softly.

'Have a word with him. Ask him what he wants to drop the case,' Pandit Ram Narayan whispered.

'I will try, Pandit ji. But a very difficult man, Phulka. Nobody knows what makes him tick. Sometimes it is money, sometimes it is his ideas.'

The man went back, leaving the other three talking in hushed voices by the street corner. Fifteen minutes later he returned, accompanied by Phulka.

'You are wasting your time, Lala ji. I told you then and I am telling you now. No bribes. Think of India and pay up,' Phulka said and walked off.

Khatri and Pandit Ram Narayan returned to Sector 23. At home Khatri found Paro sobbing into a hankie.

'Were we unhappy in the Camp? Were we starving there? What was wrong there? Why didn't we buy-and-sell the shops like Aneja? Why did we take this stable? Why did we come to this city of misery?'

Khatri sat down on a peeri kitchen stool, his head in his hands. When Paro brought the food he shook his head.

'Eat a little. What will be will be,' Paro sobbed.

Khatri shook his head. Five thousand! He would rather go to jail than pay.

'Whatever I do, I must see Nanda first. He is a big shot. Then Gulati in the Secretariat. Then, if all else fails, the Station Master. He has relations everywhere. That's what family is for,' Khatri said to himself and called his son.

'Anything happened with Pandit Ram Narayan's wife's nephew, Father?'

'Go to the Post Office and telephone Governor House. Ask if Nanda Sahib, is back.'

Omi went to the Post Office a few doors away and was back within minutes. Nanda was not there.

'Mind the shop, boy. I am going to the Secretariat to see Gulati. I will also look for Nanda on my way back.'

'Eat a morsel at least. It is so hot. The blazing hot air will go to your head if you go out on an empty stomach . . .' Paro said.

Khatri shook his index finger and walked into the blazing sun.

'The Anti-corruption Department is worse than our police. It was only created to destroy happy families. You should have paid some tax, a bit of it at least like everyone else, to keep the tax vultures happy. You know,' Gulati said.

'But what to do now?'

'We've got to get somebody big. Big.'

'Who?'

'I am thinking . . .' Gulati said, scratching the middle of his trousers. '. . . Leave it to me, Lala ji. I'll get someone.'

'The man is returning on Monday and it is Friday today. Not much time left.'

'All I can do is try, try hard. I will, and I will come to your shop after work. It will cost God knows how much — these things cost a lot as you know. How much have you got on you, Lala ji?'

Khatri felt uncomfortable. He always did in Gulati's presence. It always resulted in the same thing: Khatri's money going from his pocket into Gulati's.

'Fifty,' Khatri said with a pained face.

'That will do for the moment . . .'

Khatri felt very unhappy parting with the money.

'. . . Don't worry too much. This is India. God looks after everything here. Everything works out alright in the end here,' Gulati said.

On his way back to Sector 23, Khatri called at Governor House. Nanda was back.

'Delicate matter, Lala ji. I work in Governor House. If I got involved and the word got out, you know what would happen . . . You understand?' Nanda said.

Khatri understood.

'You should have been paying some sort of tax, at least a bit — like everyone else. My advice is: just pay up.'

'No one is going to get involved. It has to be someone of one's own people,' Paro said at home.

'Om, slip on your shoes and take the next bus to Ambala. Go to Dhulkote and ask the Station Master if he has any suggestions. Come back by the next bus.'

Omi had a date with Titli later on. She would have to wait, he thought, as he stood for the bus.

Omi got off the bus outside the Power House and crossed the half-cultivated land to the station. Nothing had changed during all this time. The last time he had come here, Bakshi was with him. It was not a happy memory.

'How come, Om Parkash? Mother-father well? What's wrong? Your face is white as this wall,' Kandhari said.

Omi explained.

'This is serious,' Kandhari said, looking up at the slow-moving blades of the fan slung from the high ceiling of the railway office. 'Very serious. I think I better return with you to Chandigarh. Wait here. I am going home to tell Munni's mother. You can't come because it is the custom. Young men don't go to the house of their betrothed. You understand?'

Omi understood.

Twenty minutes later Kandhari was back. He called his subordinates, gave them strict instructions about how to run the station in his absence and walked with Omi to the Power House to catch a Chandigarh bus.

They found Gulati at the shop. He was just leaving. By the look on his and his father's faces Omi knew that things were still the same as they had been that morning. Paro was watching from an upstairs window, still sobbing.

'Never mind. What has happened has happened — everything will be alright in the end. It would have been better had you been paying some sort of tax regularly, just to keep them quiet. But never mind. What is done is done. We'll see what can be done now,' Kandhari said as they all assembled upstairs.

'How were we to know about income tax and all that?' Paro said.

But it was not true. Khatri had received letters regularly from the tax department, letters that made ridiculous demands for money. He had done with them what he thought best, fed them to the rubbish bin.

'Did anyone pay it in Panchkoola or the Camp? You earned what you earned and you kept it,' Paro said.

'Never mind, sister. We will do something about it. I am going to Sector 4. A cousin of the Station Masterani lives there. He is in the Excise Department, but he is well-placed, a burra sahib. He should be able to do something. And you better come with me, Lala ji.'

Kandhari left Khatri outside the main gate of his wife's cousin's big house. A great boxer barked at him from the inside. It was seven, the best time of the day for business. Khatri wished he was back, weighing out sweets and taking in money, waiting for a quarter to eight when he would lock up. Today he would have given a ten-rupee note to Seva for a *half* of Solan Number One.

Fifteen minutes later a servant came and said he was wanted inside. The boxer barked its head off as Khatri shied past it.

'It will cost you something like a thousand, I am afraid, Lala ji. We will have the case dropped,' the Station Masterani's cousin said. 'It is not for me. You understand? These men don't do anything for nothing.'

Khatri understood. He knew it well. He took the glass of orange squash from the outstretched tray of the servant.

'But Mr Phulka said he would be coming on Monday . . .'

'He won't now. I have sent for him. Five hundred will look after him. The other five hundred will look after the others.'

'I shall have the money here first thing in the morning.'

'Right. And in the future, do pay some sort of tax, like everyone else. Understand?'

Khatri sipped his drink and nodded his head.

'We are doing all this for the sake of our brother and sister of Dhulkote. Otherwise we don't do such things, we are Government people. You understand?'

Khatri understood.

At home, Paro was waiting anxiously.

'I want to send sweets to the temple,' Paro said as soon as she saw her husband. 'I made a promise to God this morning.'

'Do what you like. Send what you like. Your sweets,' Khatri said.

'There, I don't think there is a bus going at this time. I'll take the ten-twenty Mail then,' Kandhari said.

'Out of the question. You are staying with us overnight,' Khatri said.

Kandhari did not fuss. He thought it would be a good idea to stop for the night and not only learn more about Khatri's plan for the restaurant, but also to see how much Omi had advanced since his last visit. His lips remained sealed about the last time he had met Omi.

Omi had a date with Titli for eight. But it was gone half past seven now and the Station Master was still around. How would he get away?

'Just slip out.'

He saw his father give Seva Singh a ten-rupee note and heard him invite Kandhari to the roof.

'Back in an hour, Ma,' Omi said to his mother and slipped out. He returned home at eleven and received a searching look from Kandhari. That look was still on Kandhari's face next morning. Omi decided to take refuge in College and left home in a great hurry.

The Pall Mall Restaurant was inaugurated by the Minister of the Bridge. Khatri had him approached through Nanda. The Minister was delighted to accept. He ate a piece of Pall Mall cake and sipped tea from a cup which had Pall Mall printed on it.

'Long way from Panchkoola, this,' the Minister said, looking around the inside of the restaurant. 'Must have cost a lot of money, Lala ji.'

'What doesn't cost a lot of money these days, Excellency?' Khatri said.

Khatri looked as much a Congress leader as the Minister. They were both dressed in much the same way, except for Khatri's new peshawari turban, specially starched for the grand occasion.

Everybody wore new clothes. Paro and Vidya had washed, oiled and combed each other's hair and they both wore English-style lipstick. They also wore identical silk saries with silver borders and little pink flowers printed all over. Omi had a new raw-silk jacket and a matching tie. Seva, as Head Waiter, sported a milk-white coat with shiny brass buttons. His face looked smaller and younger with his beard fixed with *Fixo*, the beard-starch of the Sikhs. With some difficulty, Omi had managed to persuade him to invest a rupee in this popular male cosmetic.

'A rupee well spent is worth ten. *Fixo* will make you look like a gentleman for as long it lasts. All Sikh gentlemen use it,' Omi had said.

It was true and Seva knew it. He looked handsome, a new Seva Singh.

'Wait till the customers see you. With the tips they leave in your palm you'll be laying the foundation of a two-storey house in the capital inside six months,' Omi had said.

Seva was pleased with himself and full of admiration for Omi bau. Omi bau, the kid of the Panchkoola of yesterday, was responsible for it all.

'Don't let even your little finger touch my coat if you want your face to remain as it is,' Seva had warned Bawa and the other two waiters. They, too, were dressed in white.

Bawa was by far the best-looking of the four. Tall and straight, he beamed with pride at the turn his fate had taken. Each time he passed the Ladies or the Gents, if no one was there he peeped in to look at himself in the new mirrors imported from Delhi. He loved his uniform and those brass buttons and, more to the point, he loved himself in it.

There were two dark-faced Goan cooks, Francis and Henry. Francis was the pastry cook, but he also worked the Expresso machine. They mostly talked in English. When they chose to speak Hindi, they sounded like black Englishmen.

The staff of six had caused much consternation among the ladies. Paro, Vidya and Chatkarni had pinched their ears and shaken their heads every time the subject had come up.

'Which tree is the money to come from to pay six servants?' Paro posed this simple question to her men daily.

But the father and son had ignored Paro. They worked as a team now. They did things together. Omi had persuaded his father to accompany him on a tour of the fashionable restaurants of the capital. Omi wanted his father to see how it was being done elsewhere, how money was being made there. Each time they got dressed up to go somewhere, Paro had slapped her head in disgust.

'A brothel, that's where you father and son are going to end up with a common randi whore. Shame on you both,' Paro had said each time.

The father had smiled and the son laughed, but neither had stopped to explain. They went ahead with their conversion plans with Bassi, the 'America-Returned' architect, a nephew of Nanda's.

Bassi had done a good job. He pulled down the walls to the kitchen, bathroom, toilet and store room. He even included a part of the back verandah, and provided a new kitchen and toilets in the yard.

The day the walls came down, so did Paro's great monsoon — one glistening tear after the other.

'Some kind of fungus or mould has taken root in your head. Otherwise you wouldn't have done this to us . . .' Paro had said to her husband.

'If I had not given birth to you myself I would have sworn that you were not born, that you grew up in a cabbage field,' she had said to her son.

Again, the father had smiled and the son simply laughed.

'Yes, go on wih this tamasha fun and have the whole house broken down. Why not? Why not? We can live on the roof or pitch a tent in the yard,' Paro had said to both of them.

'Wait and see, Ma. Inside six months we will be buying you a car. Just wait and see. Only six months.'

'I will hold you, no one else but you, responsible for our destruction. First you put greed in *their* head, then you bring this destruction on it.' Paro knew what she was saying. She had seen her husband pay out bill after bill.

Khatri's own calculations had proved painfully wrong. He had been relying on his son's. This worried him twice as much.

'We must give the very best, Father, to expect the best for ourselves,' Omi had said to his harassed father.

Khatri now had this permanent harassed look. For weeks now he had not made any of his masterpieces. The thought that he might have to stop making them completely bothered him. It did more than that. It made him wish that he was making barfi, bundi, gajerela, jalebi, chum chum and the other things he was famous for. He wished he could do that and wait for the customers to come and take them away so that he could make more, more and yet more. He was proud of his stuff and knew it was the best. Khatri was an artist. He loved money, but he also loved his art, making sweets.

Khatri had been following his son.

'Alright, alright. Do what you want,' Khatri would say inside himself. 'It is all for you anyway. You are going to be a family man. It is you who will need all this. Not me.'

Khatri had to borrow money from the bank.

'Don't let your mother get a wind of it. Otherwise . . .'

Omi knew what his father meant. He had felt bad about the fact that his father had to borrow money. He felt worried about the risks his father had taken. In fact he was frightened. But he kept a straight face in front of his parents.

'It has got to run and run well,' Omi had said to himself every hour of the day and night. 'Otherwise . . .' Omi really did not know what it would be otherwise.

But they, father and son, never told Paro that Khatri had borrowed nearly five thousand from the bank to make the place look as it did, to make the Minister of the Bridge say: 'Long way from Panchkoola, this . . .'

Only Khatri did not feel that it was a long way from Panchkoola.

The Minister had been gone an hour. Khatri sat by himself in the little office which the clever nephew of Nanda had cleverly designed under the triangle of the stairs. From time to time he looked up at the old Nehru calendar and the garland the great man had given his son some three years ago. The garland, the only relic of his past and perhaps the only visual link with it, had gone brittle and crumbly. No one was allowed to touch it and nobody did. Not even Omi. He knew his father was a Congress man. More than that. He was a Nehru man, a Gandhi man.

Khatri listened to the murmur rising from the restaurant where the last of the official guests were lingering. It was a great change from the air of urgency which business used to breathe into that old dump, Panchkoola. The hissing and the purring of the Expresso coffee machine and other gadgetry were foreign sounds to him. They conveyed a strange feeling of discomfort. Khatri thought of the old days in Panchkoola and suddenly missed its pleasant breeze and the rustling-whistling noise it made as it pierced its way through the tall mango trees. He also missed the chatter of the stream and the song of the mill where the villagers brought grain to be crushed into flour.

'I was not unhappy there.'

But that was not the point. The point was his son.

'Let the boy get married. Let him get settled and I will feel my work ended. Then I will go. This is no place for me. This is not my garb — this silk and twenty-one buttons.'

Khatri did not really know what he meant, but in a way he did. It was there, before him, around him. This was his place and there was nowhere else he wanted to go . . . and yet. And yet there was this something that had left a hole in his heart. It was a strange kind of loneliness that he had never felt before, a loneliness he could not share with anyone, not even Paro. Especially Paro. Only when he saw his son, felt him near him, did his heart feel a little lighter. But such moments came and went. The fact remained. His work was not ended.

The telephone rang. A woman spoke in English. Khatri called his son and heard him talk English in the phone.

'All for him, all for him,' Khatri said to himself, listening to Omi without wanting to know what he was saying in English.

'Father, do you feel alright?' Omi said when he put down the receiver.

'Yes, yes.'

'You look tired.'

'Yes, I am.'

'Come and see how the people have started coming.'

The public had started coming. One of the first arrivals was Arun, with a bunch of his friends. Ever since Arun's return from Simla, Omi had become very close to them. Titli's interest in him had made him acceptable to them. It had made him almost one of them.

'Damn good show, Aimie, old chap,' Arun said, hugging Omi. The other boys said and did the same.

'Beats the Savoy any day,' Bill said.

When they got up to leave, Omi refused to take the money from them.

'What? Do you want to go out of business on the first day?' Arun said.

A waiter dropped some plates in the kitchen. Omi heard Seva bark at him and whack him on the head. Omi rushed out to shut them up. This was not Panchkoola, not the village they had come from. This was Chandigarh.

'Your voices should not be heard by the customers. You should only be seen, not heard. Understand?' Omi was furious.

'Father, come and see how it looks with real customers,' Omi said, going back to the office. 'It is our publicity. It is paying off after all.'

The Pall Mall had been well publicised.

'Publicity is the soul of business. A restaurant won't last a day without it,' Bassi had said.

They had had a slide running in the cinema for two weeks before the opening. They had huge painted wooden boards on all approaches to the city and at other prominent spots, including the lake. *The Tribune* had carried announcements for three weeks running before the inauguration.

'It won't go in vain,' Bassi had promised.

He seemed to have been talking sense.

'You watch them and deal with them. I am going upstairs for a lie-down,' Khatri replied.

'What are you doing up here? It is only ten minutes since you opened the place. Left it to dogs to run it?' Paro said upstairs. She looked at Vidya and shook her head.

Khatri did not answer. He went straight to the bedroom, took off his turban and shoes, and spread himself on the palang bed. A minute later Paro popped her head in the doorway.

'I have been saying again and again, again and again — don't work so hard, don't work so hard. But who listens to us in this house? Shall I send for Doctorani's thermometer?' Paro said.

'Nothing wrong with me . . .'

'Then go down and look after the cash. The public is coming. I have been watching the tamasha fun from the window.'

But Khatri remained. He shut his eyes and turned over.

'One hundred and thirty-nine rupees in notes, Ma,' Omi said, coming up after lunch. 'And the evening is yet to come.'

'Don't open your mouth too wide. Come and tell me after all the expense and the servants' salaries how much you are left with,' Paro said.

'Father better?'

'I am perfectly alright,' Khatri shouted. 'Why don't you mother-and-son stop torturing me?'

'I *must* have killed a Brahmin in my past life,' Paro said, looking out of the window at the sky.

Khatri went down late in the afternoon. A few customers sat in the darkened interior with the hum of the air-conditioner. When he heard Vidya leave for Sector 15, he went back up.

Omi worked all day and came up only when the last of the

customers had gone, well past midnight. His parents slept in their room. Omi looked in and saw his mother stir and look up at him.

'Two hundred and ninety-three rupees, and sixty-seven naya paisa, Ma,' Omi whispered in his mother's ear. 'Father better?'

Khatri stirred and Omi saw that his father was wide awake. But Khatri did not say anything. He just turned his back to his wife and son.

'Father better?' Omi asked his mother as he woke up next morning.

'Yes, *they* are alright. *They* are downstairs.'

'Two hundred and ninety-three rupees! The very first day, Ma. Just think where we will be in six months.'

'Go and bath and stop torturing me. You'll be late for College.'

A little later Bawa came running up.

'Telephone for you, Omi bau.'

Khatri had taken the phone. It was the same voice as yesterday.

'Who was it?' Khatri asked after Omi had spoken his English into the phone.

'Mother of a friend of mine.'

'What did she want from you at nine in the morning?'

'She wanted to know if I knew where Dalip, their son, was.'

'And what did she want from you yesterday?'

Omi had forgotten that it was his father who had taken the phone yesterday when Titli phoned to congratulate him.

'Oh, some trouble there, Father. Dalip has failed an internal exam and he hasn't been home for two whole days.'

Khatri nodded his head as if he found this information very interesting.

'But how did his mother find out about our new telephone?'

'Oh, somebody must have told her about it. I was surprised myself that she should know. Quite amazing.'

'Is that so?'

'You better watch out, boy,' Khatri said to himself as Omi ran up to have his bath, 'Your father wasn't born yesterday. I don't have to know English to know what you've been talking about.'

'You better watch out, Omi son. Father wasn't born yesterday. He doesn't have to know English to understand your love talk,' Omi said to himself, as he sat under the bath tap, shivering in anticipation of the cold water.

All Khatri wanted to do in the office was to look at yesterday's accounts. Having done that he wanted to go back upstairs and have another lie-down. But the phone call changed his mind. He spent the entire morning in the restaurant, keeping one eye on Francis and Henry, the other on Seva and the other waiters. He inspected every nook and corner of the Pall Mall and all its crockery and cutlery. He went up for fifteen minutes only to have a quick lunch with Paro. He surprised her by eating one chappati more than his usual two. Paro was pleased, but she decided not to show it.

In the evening Omi's friends, Arun and Co, came. A number of girls were with them. Khatri watched them with interest. He saw Omi go and sit with them. He thought the girl he sat next to was particularly attractive, and that her eyes sparkled each time she looked at his son. Through the corners of his eyes Khatri noticed that his son's hands were under the table all the time.

Days passed. The Chandigarhias liked the Pall Mall. It became the talk of the town.

'Told you, Ma, didn't I? Told you, Father, didn't I?' Omi said every day.

Paro told him not to open his mouth too wide, nor to draw in too much air. Khatri did not answer, but he worked hard with his son. They worked day and night, the father keeping a close eye on the son. But in spite of all that, Omi managed to slip off every now and then. Khatri ground his jaws and scratched the middle of his sutthan. He wanted to know where his son went. But each time Omi had a water-tight explanation. Either a world-famous professor was giving a lecture on How to Think Rationally Without Trying, or an even more famous musician was giving the one and only once-in-a-lifetime recital in the College hall.

'The great swami Kumarananda of Madras is giving a talk this evening. Can I take a couple of hours off, Father?' Omi said one day.

'And what is it about this time, boy?'

'It is about how to enrich your mind and soul through simple living and simple thinking. Can I go?'

'Alright,' Khatri said, grinding his jaws. Later, when he saw Omi dress up with care, he drew Seva aside and whispered something in his ear.

When Omi said he was off, Khatri made a sign to Seva. Seva dropped everything and followed Omi at a distance of a hundred yards. Omi took the road between Sector 23 and Sector 22, humming an English song. He hailed a rickshaw and told the man to drive north. Seva too hailed a rickshaw and told the driver to follow. At the end of the road Omi's rickshaw, instead of taking the left turn towards his College, turned right and took the main road that ran through the heart of Chandigarh. Seva nodded his head gravely and told the driver to keep following.

Omi's rickshaw was heading for the lake. Halfway down the lake road, a car coming from behind stopped in front of it. Omi's rickshaw stopped. Omi hopped out of it smartly, paid the driver — obviously more than the actual fare, for the man salaamed heavily — and got into the car. The car drove off along a kucha dust track that led to the wilderness before the clay hills. Seva had seen all that he had been sent to see.

'A friend picked up Omi bau in a car and they drove off to the College,' Seva said to Khatri back in the Pall Mall.

'Was the friend a boy or a girl?'

Seva scratched the middle of his snow-white trousers, his face fixed with *Fixo* showing signs of pain.

'It was too far for me to see, Lala ji. My eyes are not as good as they used to be. But I have no reason to think that it was not a boy.'

Khatri knew his servant. He also knew that there was nothing wrong with his eyes. But he decided not to torture him further by asking him more questions about his son. He waved him back to work.

'Omi bau, you made me lie for the first time in my life,' Seva said to Omi with the same pained expression outside the Pall Mall door as soon as Omi got home, three hours later.

Omi was puzzled.

'You striking twelve o'clock or something, Seva Singh?' Omi said, putting an arm around him affectionately. 'What is the matter?'

'The matter is serious, Omi bau . . .'

'But what is it?'

'Ask yourself, Omi bau . . .'

Omi asked himself and was even more puzzled.

'. . . Lala ji thinks you are taking steps in the wrong direction . . .'

'What sort of talk is this, Seva Singh?'

'. . . Lala ji thinks you are up to some badmashi hanky panky . . .'

'Do I look the kind of person who would get up to your hanky panky?'

Seva scratched his trousers as he searched for an answer.

'Yes, Omi bau . . .'

'But you know me, Seva Singh!'

'. . . That's why I am saying this. Think of your father. Think of the wound it would cause in his heart if he found out: I was sent after you this evening to find out. But I did not tell him what I saw. I said to myself: Seva Singh, you must have a talk with Omi bau first. For me, Omi bau, you are still the kid of yesterday who liked my butter parathas . . . You better mend your ways, Omi bau . . .'

Omi felt ashamed of himself. He hung his head down in shame and went in. The Pall Mall buzzed with life.

'How was the lecture boy? Took a long time!' Khatri said, without looking up at his son. He appeared to be engrossed with a bill that he was writing out.

'Incredible man, this swami. You should hear him, Father. You would love the sort of things he has to say.'

'I am sure. But what sort of things?'

'Oh, highly philosophical . . .'

'Just the things I want to hear these days. Take me along next time he gives a talk.' Luckily for Omi, Nanda walked into the restaurant with somebody important.

'Trouble at the home front, honey,' Omi said to Titli next time they met. 'Father suspects. He had me followed by the head waiter the other evening . . .'

'Gosh!' Titli said with a hand on her wide-open mouth, her eyes sparkling.

'But Seva Singh is quite sensible. He did not say anything.'

'Good. But what if he had?'

'Then they would be making arrangements for my marriage.'

Titli laughed heartily.

'I don't believe you. I can't imagine you a married boy. What, at twenty! And married to someone you've never even seen!'

One day, during an unguarded moment, Omi had told Titli the story of his engagement. He hadn't meant to, but it just slipped out as they talked about the future, when they would both leave College and start life.

'This is India, you know.'

'But still. Twenty is too young. You have your whole life in front of you. You should fight it for your own sake.'

'How can you fight with your own father?'

'You can talk to him.'

'You can't talk to my father — you don't know him. My parents are Hindus . . .'

'So are mine.'

'Yours are progressive. Mine are orthodox. That's the difference between them. Your Dad is a retired general, mine is a retired halwai . . .'

Titli laughed at the drollness of the comparison — a general versus a halwai.

'So what?' Titli said. 'All the girls still look at you, whatever your father is.'

'And all the world looks at you, including me.'

'The funniest boy I ever met.'

'The prettiest girl I ever saw.'

'Liar.'

'I only lie when I have a reason to lie.'

'What is your reason to lie now?'

'Now there is no reason to lie. So I tell the truth, which raises a question. What are we going to do?'

'We'll just have to be careful.'

But it was difficult. Khatri kept a close check on Omi. He increased his vigilance. Omi started to skip lessons at College to meet Titli. Going out in the evenings had become impossible.

Word reached Khatri that Omi was seen in strange places, usually in the wilderness around the city but sometimes as far away as the hills around Kalka, in a car with an attractive young lady at the wheel. Khatri ground his jaws but kept quiet about it.

'What is eating you now?' Paro said. Everything was well with their world — money was coming in at the end of each day, the boy was working hard both with his books and at the 'shop', as she called the restaurant. Why then this dark cloud on her husband's brow? 'Are you paying the tax vultures regularly or not?'

Khatri was.

'Nothing is eating me, woman,' Khatri said.

Khatri was quite unable to take her into his confidence. He simply did not know what to do. Four years ago he would have given his son a good shoe-beating, which would have sorted out everything. But now the boy was too big for that — he stood a head above him. Omi was now a man, sitting for his BA exam in a few months. Nor could he talk to him. What was Khatri to do?

Omi had a feeling that his father knew everything. There was that look on Khatri's face, something about his eyes. They were not accusing him, they were searching him. It was only when Omi discovered that his father was eating only one chappati instead of his usual two that he started to get worried.

'Honey, Father knows. I am sure,' Omi said to Titli one day.

'Oh, damn. I am a bit tired of your father-and-son saga . . .' Titli sounded rather offhand. Omi did not like it. '. . . What do you want me to do? Go and ask him for your hand in marriage?'

Omi did not like that at all.

'Titli . . .' Omi said angrily.

'You have a choice — either stick around and have fun or run back to your mummy and daddy like a good little boy,' Titli said.

'Titli . . . Don't speak like that of my parents. You speak like a general's daughter now . . .'

'And you speak like a halwai's son . . . Stop moaning. Stop worrying. Just be more careful. Let's carry on. We will have fun.'

'But what about the future? What is our future?'

'Why are you so worried about the future? Let's live now. Let's have fun now.'

Arun was giving another party. But it was a party with a difference. It was going to take place during the day.

'What sort of party can it be in broad daylight?' Omi said. Parties should be in the evenings, in the dark.

'You wait and see. A special party,' Arun said.

Every Simla Pink party Omi had been to was a special one. But he had never been to one in broad daylight.

'You wait and see, Aimie, old chap. A party to remember,' Arun said.

Even Titli could not tell him anything more than that.

'You know Arun. Likes to give surprises,' Titli said.

'At the last one my surprise was you . . . I wonder what it will be this time,' Omi said.

'Tits last time, maybe balls this time,' Titli said and laughed heartily at her own joke.

The party was to be held on a Sunday, which was lucky, for the restaurant was closed on Sundays. Therefore there wouldn't be any problem for Omi to get away. But he decided to make double sure that there wouldn't be any. He took to studying hard, late into the night. Both Khatri and Paro noted it, but they both decided not to comment on it — it would go to his head and he might stop working so hard.

Someone else noticed it too — Romesh. He even spoke to Omi this time.

'Burning the midnight oil then, are we?' Romesh said to Omi one day, as the two of them met each other in the paan wallah's booth in the shops. Omi did not answer, but he wondered how Romesh knew. Their shops were adjacent to each other and they could not see each other's window. But Omi found out.

One night Omi retired early from the Pall Mall to spend two or three hours with his books. About 10.30 or so, he heard what sounded like someone running on his roof. Omi sat up to listen carefully. Someone was up there. A thief or a burglar?

Omi picked up a stick and ran up to the roof in two leaps to catch the thief. There was nobody on the roof. But before returning to his room he decided to have a look over the wall at Satya's roof. Maybe the fellow had gone there. When he found that, too, empty, Omi leaned over to look at Dr Devan Chand's. In the covered part of Dr Devan Chand's roof, Omi saw two figures locked in an embrace.

'Son of a bitch,' Omi said to himself and came back to his room.

Then every other night he heard Romesh cross his roof to go to Dr Devan Chand's .

'Son of a bitch,' Omi called him every time.

One day Omi heard his mother, Aunt Vidya and Satya talk in whispers in the kitchen. There was no need for them to talk in whispers, for there was no one else around — Omi had just come up the stairs. He went straight to his room, but curiosity made him tiptoe to the kitchen door and listen. He nearly burst out laughing when he found out what they were whispering about — Satya was

236

persuading his mother to undertake the role of mediator, or negotiator, of a delicate matter.

Later the same day Omi saw his mother and Aunt Vidya adorn themselves as they did on important occasions and call on the Doctorani next door. He was sure that they would be gone for at least a couple of hours. But Omi had a surprise. They were back inside fifteen minutes, Paro looking unhappy.

'What, did the Doctorani say no, Ma?' Omi said, laughing.

Paro was not amused. She undid her jutti shoe and hurled it at her son. Omi caught it in mid-air and laughed.

'Mission's failed, Ma? Never mind. Try elsewhere.'

'How do you know about it, Om?' Vidya said.

'This owl-face, loud-mouth and long-ears knows everything. Like his father,' Paro said.

Khatri was furious when he learnt of his wife's match-making efforts.

'You keep your arse out of such things. What do you know about these things anyway? Silly woman.' Khatri said.

'Satya begged me,' Paro said.

'That husband-eater! Why does she have to drag us into it?' Khatri said.

'Anyway, who would give their daughter to that owl-son? I don't blame the Doctorani, Ma, if you ask me,' Omi said.

'I am not asking you. Therefore.'

'Therefore what, Ma?'

'Therefore shut up.'

Omi shut up. But that night when he heard Romesh walk past their roof, he decided to let him know that he knew. But something was wrong upstairs, on Dr Devan Chand's roof. There was much shouting and screaming going on there. Dr Devan Chand was beating Romesh with a stick, the Doctorani was trying to pull him away and Sarla, her head buried in her arms, was sobbing. All four of them were making a lot of noise.

'Son of a bitch, son of a bitch . . .' Dr Devan Chand shouted, as he beat Romesh with the stick again and again.

'Let the randi whore's brother go . . .' the Doctorani said repeatedly, as she tried to drag her husband away.

It was a strange sight. It was equally strange that the other neighbours hadn't appeared on their roofs to watch the tamasha fun.

Suddenly Omi felt sorry for Romesh and wished that he could do something for him.

After taking several blows of the stick, Romesh, twice the size of Dr Devan Chand, decided to escape. He jumped over the wall and landed on the Khatris' roof. Dr Devan Chand then turned to his daughter and started beating her with the stick. The Doctorani fell on her husband and took several blows herself. She snatched the stick from his hand and flung it away into the night. Then she caught her daughter by the hair and dragged her away down into the house.

Shaken, Omi stood on his own roof, face-to-face with a bewildered Romesh. Romesh pleaded, first with a look and then with words.

'Don't tell anyone. Otherwise.'

Omi did not tell anyone. But for days he thought about it. For some reason he also thought about Rani of the Camp and wondered what became of her. He also wondered what would become of Romesh. He did not have to wait long — only till the day of Arun's special party.

Only a day before the party did Arun tell Omi that it would be an outdoor party, somewhere in the hills.

'Need an early start, Aimie. Get to my place by eleven,' Arun said.

That night Omi made up a few boxes of Pall Mall goodies for the party. He told Seva to hide them until the morning — Lala ji was not to know. He might get angry, lose his frontier temper and refuse to give him permission to go. But Khatri found out. He spotted the hidden boxes and surprised Seva when he said nothing.

'Don't tell the boy that I know,' Khatri said to Seva.

Seva laughed when Omi came to pick up the boxes next morning.

'Omi bau, it is like stealing your own goods, isn't it?' Seva said.

'I didn't want Father to know. That's all,' Omi said.

'But he does. Not to worry though. He told me not to tell you.'

'Then why are you telling me?'

'I don't know . . . I think you better be going, Omi bau. I just saw Lala ji send Bawa to fetch a rickshaw. He is going somewhere and he'll be down in a minute. Then he is bound to ask.'

Omi wondered where his father was going. It was unusual for Khatri to go out on a Sunday morning. But Omi did not ask Seva, though he asked him if his mother was also going. Paro was not going. She was not going for the simple reason that Khatri did not want to take her with him. So she was telling Khatri upstairs what she thought of him, and his son for that matter.

'Like father like son. Come and go when you please. The son goes off, God knows where, to waste his Sunday. The father *to his guru*—if you please — leaving me to dogs!'

'I am only going to see my guru, not a randi whore.'

'But what will I do all day long? Sit on my arse and kill flies?'

'Why not go and see your dearer-than-life sister? Why not?'

'Why not this? Why not that? Why not take me with you? I won't eat your guru.'

'Where I am going is in high, high mountains and thick, thick jungles. Full of tigers and leopards.'

'I would rather be eaten by a tiger than die of loneliness.'

'I'll only be gone for a few hours. Back before nightfall.'

'Come back tomorrow, or next week or next month. What is here to keep you . . . obviously not your wife . . .'

'Stop this you-you me-me nonsense. You'll make me miss my bus.'

Bawa returned with the rickshaw, sitting in it.

'Rickshaw, Lala ji,' Bawa shouted from the stairs.

'There,' Khatri said, taking leave of his wife. He got to the bus stop in Sector 17 before his son got to his friend's house in the north-end. Khatri's bus was there, and so were his son's friends — outside Arun's house, the assembly point. Khatri knew where he was going, but his son did not.

'Where the fuck are we going, Arun?' Omi asked getting off his rickshaw, clutching the Pall Mall boxes.

'Pinjore,' Arun said.

'But won't the Pinjore Gardens be full of tourists? It's Sunday, yaar.'

'There is a stunning beauty spot near there. You wait and see.'

'Let us go then. What are you waiting for here?'

'For the Walia sisters, Sally and Betty.'

'You folks go ahead. I'll wait for them,' Harry said. He drove a jeep. 'Aimie can wait with me.'

'No, Aimie is coming with me, and we are going before you all — advance party,' Arun said, relieving Omi of the boxes. He gave them to a servant to put them inside his car, which the servant was polishing with a rag.

Another servant came from inside the house to say that there was a phone call for Arun sahib.

'The blasted phone,' Arun said and went inside. A couple of minutes later he was back. 'Those blasted girls. They've got a cousin chap staying with them and they want to bring him as well. They also want to be picked up.'

'I'll go,' Harry said.

'Right, then. See you later, folks. Come on, Aimie, old chap,' Arun said.

Omi went with Arun, but they did not stop at Pinjore.

'But . . .' Omi said.

'We've got some shopping to do,' Arun said. 'Some booze from Dhalli. Only a few miles from here.'

'Oh yes!' Omi knew Dhalli. But what he did not know was that he would miss meeting his father there by a mere five minutes.

It was a miracle. Clearly God was on Omi's side this morning, for who knew what his father would have said (or more appropriately, done) had he seen him there, buying booze.

Khatri had got off his bus only minutes before Omi arrived there. With his guide, Billa, he had walked off along the heavily wooded mountain track leading to Gokul Baba's ashram in the belly of the valley. When the boys got out of the car, Khatri was a mere two hundred yards from the liquor shop.

Arun bought three cases of Golden Eagle lager.

'Try our new pickle, Sir,' the shopkeeper said to Arun. 'Our new onion pickle.'

'Another day. I am going somewhere today,' Arun said.

But Omi could not resist. He ate two medium-sized pickled onions and thought them delicious.

'So many bottles!' Omi said, as they loaded up the car.

'They will go. There are more than twenty people. They'll want more. Good thing some others are also bringing some booze.'

'What about the octroi post near Kalka?'

'Not to worry. They won't bother us.'

240

Arun was right. The man at the octroi post just waved them on.

At Pinjore everybody had arrived, everybody except the Walia sisters. Everybody wore jeans and open-necked shirts. The girls had their cardigans slung loosely around the shoulders. Omi felt somewhat foolish, because he was the only one wearing a tie. Titli made a face which made Omi take it off instantly.

'Do you know this place?' Omi asked Titli.

'Been here lots of time with Aru,' Titli said. She often called Arun that, affectionately.

'Where are we going to have the party?'

'Down there,' Titli said, pointing to the bottom of the wooded khud ravine where the Jhajjar glistened in the warm and pleasant sun.

'Beautiful day for a party like this. Let's get a move on.'

The expedition started.

'But what about Harry and the girls?' someone said.

'They will have to find their own way,' Arun said.

Arun's 'stunning beauty spot' was stunning. It was a flat green clearing the size of their College Lecture Theatre, with thick bush and shrub on three sides and the calm Jhajjar and the vast valley in front of it. Food and drink was laid on. The gramophone, an oldtime His Master's Voice type, came alive with an English song. Beer bottles were popped open, boys laughed and the girls giggled. The party had started. Arun set off the proceedings by dancing with his lady. Everybody followed him.

'All your school-friend's fault,' Omi said, as he danced with Titli.

'What?'

'She taught me this nonsense and then you came along and wanted to know how good a teacher she was.'

'You stink of onion,' Titli said loudly. 'Why did you eat it before coming here? You know I hate the smell. You should never eat onion or garlic before going to a party.'

Duly chided, Omi felt foolish, but also angry. Who was she to tell him what to eat and what not to eat?

They danced in silence. Omi was worried about his breath. He avoided talking because it would oblige him to open his mouth. But he burnt inside. So what if he had eaten an onion? She should not have put him down like that in front of everybody.

'She is supposed to be my girl, dammit,' he said to himself.

But he realised it was his own fault.

'You've got a lot to learn, Omi son.'

'Humm . . . thinking of somebody?' Titli asked after a long pause. 'Who is it? Not your father again?'

'Madam General, I don't like you to speak of my father like that . . .'

'Don't be so touchy. I only asked.'

Omi wondered what his father would have said (or more appropriately, done) if he saw him now, sipping beer and dancing with a girl in his arms — little knowing that his father was on the same side of the same river at another stunning beauty spot a few miles upstream, sitting at the feet of Gokul Baba and being gazed at by Mohan.

Titli stopped dancing in the middle of a record.

'I want to eat something. I'm starving,' She said. She went to where the food was and left Omi standing by himself by the river bank. Omi picked up a stone and threw it across the river as far as he could. He knew he was sulking.

'She is behaving like a general's daughter — spoilt.'

He threw another stone into the water.

'And you behaving like a halwai's son — stupidly. You are sulking.'

Omi danced with other girls in silence, trying not to open his mouth. It was not for an hour or so that Titli danced with him again.

'Still sulking?' Titli said.

Omi did not answer.

'I wonder what happened to Harry and the girls,' Omi said instead.

Just then the bushes behind them parted and Harry appeared with the Walia sisters. There was much jubilation. But there were two other chaps with them, not one as Arun had been told on the phone. They were both in their early twenties and both were strikingly handsome. Only one of them was the Walia sisters' cousin, the other was a friend of his. Both were tall and erect and they walked and stood like soldiers.

'Lieutenant Lali,' said Sally introducing her cousin. 'And Lieutenant Babar.'

Omi saw Titli take a deep look at Babar, the more dashing of the

242

two. He thought she looked at him in just the same way as she had looked at him at that fateful party, Arun's first party. He saw the young officer look Titli up and down, from head to foot, and smile.

A knife passed through his chest. Why had she looked at him like that? So what if the son of a bitch was so handsome?

Beer bottles were passed around. Omi saw Titli down half the contents of one in one go. Suddenly she had become very gay. She was talking a lot, laughing a lot.

'You alright?' Omi asked Titli in a whisper when he got the chance.

'Perfectly alright. I am having fun. I want to have a swim. Do you want a swim?'

'Isn't it a bit chilly for that?'

'Maybe for you, but not for me. Anyone for a swim?' Titli said, looking into the eyes of the dashing Lieutenant Babar. Clearly it was an invitation, a clear invitation.

'Love to,' Lieutenant Babar said, baring his broad hairy chest. Omi felt what a mongrel must feel at the sudden appearance of a fully grown alsatian.

Titli went with a bag into the foliage and returned clad in a one-piece swimsuit.

'Wow . . .!' a number of male voices went up, as Titli threw herself in the water.

Lieutenant Babar had come prepared. He wore his swimming trunks under his trousers which he discarded in haste as he jumped into the water after Titli. The water was only four or five feet deep, but deep enough for a good swim. They swam out of sight, into the bend in the river.

'Balls,' Omi said to himself, his heart pounding against his chest with anger and despair. 'My surprise!' Omi knew he had lost Titli. 'The bitch!'

Everybody else also stripped and followed them into the water, leaving Omi on the bank. Omi had come unprepared — he hadn't brought anything to swim in. In due course, everybody came back, all except Titli and the young Lieutenant. They had simply vanished. They returned an hour later, took a few bottles of beer, some food and towels and disappeared again. This time, into the foliage lining the bank of the river.

The afternoon wore on. Omi, sick at heart, realised what he had to do.

'Call it a day, Omi son. This is no place for you. You better take your arse home.'

Just as he was about to quit, Arun came and put an arm around his shoulder.

'Blast her. You knew what she was like. Forget her. Grab someone else,' Arun said.

Khatri had promised Paro that he would be back early. He took leave of Gokul Baba in the afternoon, feeling lighter in the heart than he had when he came. Gokul Baba had been pleased to see him and also pleased to hear of his progress. He even promised to visit him in Chandigarh one of these days.

'Very soon,' Gokul Baba said when he heard from Khatri that Paro wanted to come with him today.

'That should please her a lot,' Khatri said to himself as he boarded the bus at Dhalli. He knew that it would also please her to see him back sooner than he had said. But the bus broke down at Pinjore. The gear-box broke.

'I have to go back to Kalka to get the part,' the driver said.

'How long will it take?' the passengers asked.

'Maybe an hour, maybe more.'

The passengers did what Indians do under such circumstances. They sat down on their haunches by the roadside and waited. Near by were the five cars and jeeps of the party-makers. Khatri was sure he recognised them. He had often seen them parked outside his restaurant. He ground his jaws and scratched the middle of his sutthan. Then, for reasons unknown to himself, or for reasons which he did not want to admit to himself, Khatri stood up and ambled down the hillside towards the glistening Jhajjar.

He took a direction other than the boys and girls had earlier taken and so he ended up several hundred yards away from where the party was taking place. There was nothing to see there, only the calm waters of the Jhajjar he loved. It suddenly occurred to him that he was looking at the wrong place.

'They must be in the Pinjore Gardens.'

Khatri turned back from the river, taking a slightly different direction. A few yards into the foliage he came upon a stark-naked couple — sleeping in each other's arms, with empty beer bottles beside them. The naked couple stirred and looked up. Titli and Khatri looked at each other, and recognised each other.

'Get lost, old man. What the hell are you doing here?' the young Lieutenant said coarsely in Punjabi, with a soldier's arrogance.

'Oh, no! I don't believe it,' Titli said in English, throwing some clothes on her naked body.

'Do you know the bastard?' Lieutenant Babar said in English, throwing a stone after Khatri.

'No,' Titli said.

The stone hit Khatri on the back, but he did not feel it. He just walked away in a daze.

He walked parallel to the river and in a few minutes reached a bump in the hillside from which he could see the party. While some boys and girls danced clutching each other, others (many half-dressed) lay in each other's arms, in the tall grass or among the bushes. Away from them all and by the bank of the river, sat a solitary figure with his chin cupped in a hand and his elbow resting on a knee. It was Omi. He was throwing pebbles in the water. God was not on his side this afternoon. Or perhaps God was on his side, for Khatri, whose hands had itched to pluck the skin off his son's body, decided against it. Instead he decided to beat a hurried retreat and withdrew, climbing the hill as fast as he could, gasping for breath.

Khatri got home at dusk-fall. A small crowd stood idly outside the Pall Mall — mostly servants and other people who worked in the shops there. Khatri's heart missed a beat. Something had happened, something bad. But what? A fire or something?

Actually the crowd was not directly in front of the Pall Mall, it was around it, stretching on both sides.

'Bad, Lala ji, something bad happened . . .' Seva said, running up to him.

There was no sign of any fire. Khatri was sure that it was Paro. Something had happened to her . . . Khatri's heart sank.

'What, Seva Singh? What?'

Seva leaned over and whispered something in Khatri's ear. Khatri slapped his forehead, shook his head vigorously and touched his ear lobes.

'Ram, Ram, Ram . . .!' Khatri said and went up.

'Did you go to your guru or to a funeral?' Paro said when she saw his ashen face in the new neon light.

Khatri did not answer.

'Have you heard the news? Romesh and Sarla . . . Ram, Ram, Ram! The poor Doctorani! She took a whole bottle of poison when she found out. Lucky her husband is a doctor. He pumped it out. Lucky she is still alive. But what a thing to do — running away and getting married! What a thing to do to your parents! Total, absolute and bilkul pukka kaliyug black age this . . . Thank God our son is alright . . .'

Khatri did not say anything to his wife. He did not say anything to his son either when the latter got home an hour after him. The Khatris had a sombre evening — Omi did not even switch the radio on, a thing he usually did the moment he got home. Paro put it down to the tragic news of Romesh and Sarla first running away and then getting married. She did not press her husband and son for an account of their day.

Khatri retired early and rose early the next morning and broke an important Indian social rule. He took a bus to Dhulkote to see the future father-in-law of his son. Custom demands that it should be the other way round, that it should be the girl's father or relatives who should undertake such a journey for such a purpose.

Kandhari saw the point. He said yes and embraced his daughter's future father-in-law with great fervour. Then he, too, broke an important rule. Against all railway regulations, Kandhari broke open a bottle of Solan Number One in his office. The two men shook hands, raised their glasses and toasted Omi and Munni and their forthcoming marriage. They fixed it for the week after Omi's BA exams, in three months' time. The pandits would find the exact and auspicious day for the wedding after consulting the charts and after looking at the stars.

'I will not, I will not, I will not. I will run away from home . . .' Omi said.

'Do anything silly and you will kill off your father,' Paro said. She was delighted.

'Everyone gets married, Om. Are you an exception?' Aunt Vidya said. She, too, was delighted.

'I am so young. My whole future will be ruined.'

'When do you want to get married? When you are an old cock of thirty?' Paro said.

'You are destroying my life.'

'Listen to him talk, listen to him talk. Anyone would think we were putting him in jail,' Chatkarni said. She was delighted more than anybody else.

'It is worse than jail. I don't want the rails of that crooked Station Master around my neck for the rest of my life.'

'It was he who got you out of jail. It was he who saved your father from going to jail. Haven't you got an ounce of gratitude left in you? Is this what we gave you all your education for?' Paro said.

'He bought you with one hundred and one rupees, and I am being sold for free. I will run away a day before. I will drown myself in the lake the very day.'

'Om, you are a grown-up man now . . .' Vidya said.

'You are no longer the little boy I have to ask your father to smack. Behave like a man,' said Paro.

'Ma, I am telling you. Don't say after the horse has bolted that I didn't warn you. Break this damned engagement. Let me pass my BA. Now we are not the sweet sellers of the Camp. We have a first-class restaurant. In a few months we will have a brand-new car parked outside. Next year we can start building a three-storey house in the north-end. Then you will have rich families chasing you. We have plenty of status now, Ma, plenty of status.'

'Status my foot. A promise is a promise. Do you want the world to spit on our faces by breaking it? Ram, Ram, Ram! What a son! What did I do in my last life, Chatkarni? I must have killed several Brahmins.'

'I am warning you, Ma.'

'Go away and stop torturing me. Go and order the clothes. Go and choose the materials for your suits. Tailors these days are not what they used to be. They have become slow and unreliable. They take weeks to stitch up a single shirt these days . . .'

Omi heard his father climb the stairs. He hurried off to his room.

'What is the boy burr-burring about? What does he say, Paro?' Khatri said.

'He does not want to get married . . .'

'Come here, oi,' Khatri shouted.

Omi came back.

'You don't want to get married? What do you want to do then?

Sit by the bank of the Jhajjar and throw pebbles in it for the rest of your life?'

Omi got a shock. What did his father mean?

'But, Father . . .'

'There is no but-shut. Run downstairs and look after *your* restaurant . . .' Khatri waved his son down the stairs.

Shell-shocked, Omi hung his head and went downstairs.

'But how can Father know?' Omi wondered.

'Take him to the Cloth Palace tomorrow to choose cloth for his suits. Today I want you to come with me and Vidya to the goldsmith. Goldsmiths these days are very slow and three months pass in the winking of an eye,' Paro said.

'What did he say?' Khatri asked.

'Said he would jump in the lake.'

'The bastard!' Khatri laughed as he recalled what he had said when his parents announced the date of his marriage in Peshawar. He had said he would jump off a cliff, eat poison, put his neck to the rail and wait for the train. But one stolen glimpse of the young Paro had changed his mind.

Khatri had laughed for the first time in many days. He felt better.

'Can't you and Vidya go by yourselves? I am tired and want to lie down. Besides, I don't know anything about gold and silver.'

'Brother, you talk like an old man,' Vidya said.

'I am an old man,' Khatri said

'Am I really?' Khatri wondered when he was alone. 'I am only four times eleven years old. That is four years less than four dozen. That is not old.'

Then what was the trouble? Khatri rubbed his hands as he asked himself this question. Suddenly the answer came to him. His hands. He was not using them for what they were meant for.

Instead of lying down in the palang bed, Khatri came down to the restaurant.

'What do I want air-conditioners, telephones and all this paraphernalia for? It was only for him. And now that it is here I can get out of this silken garb too.'

Omi, standing a few yards away, had a feeling that his father was thinking of him. He walked up to him and stood by his side.

'Are you alright, Father?'

'Nothing wrong with me. Why do you mother and son keeping

asking me that? As if I was an old man.' Khatri smiled, showing a perfect row of small white teeth. 'I am only waiting for your exams . . .'

Omi realised in that instant that there was nothing that he could do to stop his marriage. He knew that he would never do anything to take that smile away from his father.

Upstairs, when his father was not around, Omi sulked. But downstairs in the restaurant, he worked hard. Money was flowing in. Omi found that his father was trusting him with it increasingly. It worried him. Suddenly he realised that he could do whatever he wanted with cash. No questions were asked. But he also realised that he had stopped misappropriating funds, small amounts which he needed for himself. Suddenly there was no need to do that. Suddenly all the money became his. It worried him even more. So, every morning when he took the last day's earnings to the State Bank, he deposited everything into his father's account.

Life carried on as usual on the surface. His friends, with the exception of Titli, still came and drank endless cups of coffee. He never told anyone, not even Arun, about the preparations for his marriage. He was sure they would laugh like mad. But as the exams got nearer, they came less and less. A month before the exams, they stopped completely, much to his relief.

'Bridegrooms should look happy, not miserable like you, Om,' Aunt Vidya said one day.

'Please, Aunt Vidya. You love your nephew, Omi, don't you?'

'Yes, a little bit.'

'Then do something for him. Stop this marriage.'

'You are a fool, Om. That's all I can say. The girl is so beautiful that you would faint if you saw her. You would want this marriage to take place tomorrow.'

His mother and aunt had been to Dhulkote recently to discuss some finer points of the final arrangements which are usually left to ladies.

'Ma, I am warning you. I am giving you notice now. I will run away on the very morning of this blasted wedding. Count me out of it.'

But Paro had no time to listen to his nonsense. She was simply too busy. With Vidya she was going here in the morning, there in the afternoon and somewhere else later on. Munni's saris had to be chosen, their embroidery supervised. Silk for Munni's blouses and materials for her other clothes had to be chosen and given to tailors. Gold and silver for Munni's jewellery had to be bought and its making supervised. Materials for Omi's suits, jackets, trousers and shirts had to be chosen and taken to tailors. Materials for her own clothes and those of her husband's had to be chosen and given to tailors. Beside all this there were at least one hundred and one other things she had to do. And Paro only had two hands. She had no time for her son's nonsense.

'You mind your own business and your business is your exam,' Paro said to her son whenever he tortured her a bit too much.

The exams came and went. In their wake came unheard-of uncles and aunts, cousins, nephews and nieces. The courtyard behind the restaurant looked as Sector 23 had on the day of the Hindu march. Khatri hired a bus. With all these people and friends from Chandigarh, they all went to Camp Baldev Nagar. There they stayed in rooms loaned by old friends, to go to the station from there for the wedding.

'Omi is getting married, Omi is getting married, Omi is gettng married,' said the whole of the Camp.

Bhajju came, Satish came, Harpal came, Bali came, Des came, Punnu came . . . all a foot taller with beards and moustaches. Banarsi and his wife came; Lallu, his mother and Ram Rakha too. In fact the whole Camp came.

'Don't forget to ask for your railway trolley, Omi son.' said Bali.

'Give us a ride in it some time, won't you?' said Harpal.

'And I'll tell Ram Rakha to keep his horse ready.' said Des.

'Once he gets his wife and trolley the bugger won't recognise us,' said Punnu, the umpire of tree-cricket fame.

Then the boys gave Omi his wedding present. An atlas

The earth around the railway quarters smelled of freshly sprinkled water. A huge shamiana sparkled with hundreds of little bulbs glowing with coloured lights — red, yellow, blue green and white. There was the WELCOME gate of banana trees and lines and lines of coloured flags of muslin-thin kite paper, which ruffled and fluttered in the wind coming from the Kasauli mountain. Scores of children, washed, oiled and dressed for Munni's wedding, ran to and fro, getting in the legs of the adults who hurried about with final arrangements and final touches. From the roof of Kandhari's house a loudspeaker blasted away pop hits, the best of the Binaca Geet Mala, the top ten of Hindi films. Gusts of wind carried them as far as the level crossing and even the first house of the Camp itself.

Suddenly somebody spotted the growing trail of the gas lights which illuminated the march of the barrat, the bridegroom's party, on its way to claim the bride. The gas lights grew larger and larger and soon the music of the band was heard heralding the groom, who was seated on a steed, hugged by the customary young nephew. The lights grew brighter, the band louder, clashing with the pop hits from the loudspeaker.

The barrat wedding party stopped at the WELCOME gate. The loudspeaker was switched off. The band played on. The children came and surrounded the barrat. Omi, a silver crown on his head and his face covered by streams of jasmine and roses, was surrounded by relatives. His horse, equally heavily adorned from head to tail in tinsel-bits of silver which shone and shimmered in the multicoloured lights, neighed uncomfortably. Khatri, elegant in his Nehru coat of pale raw silk, standing next to the horse, comforted it by patting it gently. Paro stood by his side, wearing a pale-blue silk sari embroidered in gold thread. Vidya, in a similar sari, stood behind her sister. The rest of the barrat stood around them, but on the outside of the banana gate.

On the inside of the gate stood Kandhari with garlands of flowers and rupee notes. His family stood behind him. Buried in the crowd of ladies and children behind Kandhari was the mass of scarlet silk, gold and silver lace and filigree — Munni, his Munni, the bride, the wife to be.

Then a tall man stood up on a table and the band stopped playing. A hush fell among the well-dressed men, women and children on both sides of the banana gate. The tall man unfolded a piece of paper, cleared his throat and, in a loud sonorous voice, sang the sehra marriage song.

When the song finished Kandhari walked up to the gate with garlands in his hands. Khatri walked to him simultaneously with garlands in his hands. Garlands and garlands as the fathers embraced each other. Then came the uncles. Garlands and embraces. After

251

them all came the ladies and the children, hugging the mass of scarlet, gold and silver.

Omi was helped down, given a garland and pushed forward. A lady cleared Munni's head of flowers and gold and silver and Omi placed his garland around it as he had his first look at his wife. He looked back at Aunt Vidya.

'Request permission to faint,' he whispered.

Aunt Vidya smiled and moved his silver crown back a little, parting the streams of jasmine and roses. Munni had her first look at her husband. Music started again and everybody started to talk at the same time. The ladies took over and took the couple away, into the house. Then followed the feast, not quite a maharajah's dinner, but a great feast all the same. After that came the marriage ceremony, the night-long sitting with the pandit around the holy fire fed with pure ghee and samagri.

Next day, after lunch, the marriage bus, bedecked with flowers, raced through the hot breath of the early Punjabi summer. Khatri sat next to Paro behind the driver, his ears still warm with the last of the weepy tunes the band had played as Kandhari carried his sobbing girl to be delivered to Khatri's bus. Munni and her mother and other ladies from their side had sobbed bitterly on each other's shoulders. Khatri had stood behind them all until the bus was loaded up with his party and Omi's dowry. Now, sitting with his wife, he looked out at the blond wheat fields and felt a strange lightness in his heart. The hole in his heart had gone. He placed his hand on Paro's hand and pressed it gently. The marriage bus came to the Jhajjar bridge, their bridge, and Khatri invited his wife to look out. A trickle of water was flowing under it, reflecting the blue Kasauli mountain. Then Khatri looked back and, catching Bhajjan's eye, beckoned him to come up to him.

'You work in the restaurant from tomorrow, Bhajjan. I'll be looking after the little shop from now on.'